SEWING RESISTANCE

Seamstress, spy, survivor?

J.H. Foster

So Simple Published Media

CONTENT WARNING:

Some scenes in this book, while historically accurate, may be distressing to some readers. For more information, please visit www.escapeintoatale.com/books/triggers

Copyright © 2025 by Jan Foster

Published by So Simple Published Media

First edition 2025

Cover Design – getcovers.com

Paperback ISBN – 978-1-917062-11-4

E-Book ISBN – 978-1-917062-12-1

Hardback ISBN - 978-1-917062-13-8

www. escapeintoatale.com

TRUTH BEHIND THE TAPESTRY

March 23rd 1937. Austria.

My foot pauses on the pedal when I hear the rumble of trucks pulling into the convent's courtyard below. I glance down at the beige shirt held by the needle of my trusty Kohler sewing machine, then through the small window next to me. Adjusting the shirt to fit the smaller chest for one of the orphans will have to wait, as two jeeps, a covered truck and a long-nosed black car fill the yard below.

Soldiers scramble out, guns cocked. A tall officer steps from the back seat of the car. His face is hidden to me as he pulls his cap low, then straightens his long, black SS coat. I draw away from sight, mouth dry, mind racing. With so many armed men accompanying a senior Nazi, this cannot be a cursory check. As if confirming my fears, the barked order echoes up: *"Überall suchen."*

Would they search everywhere? I doubt they will leave out my room. My gaze sweeps around the neat, narrow space. It was once a corridor, but now my bedroom-come-workroom has a chest for clothes and a bed. On the shelf near the machine, I store sewing supplies and fabric remnants. Superficially, it's just an ordinary room. But, in the middle of the long wall is a faded wall tapestry, which appears to be decoration. The hanging has another purpose - behind it is the locked entrance to the room that the corridor once provided proper access to.

If my bedroom, then the next, are searched, explaining away the printing press would be difficult. The scruffy-looking man who rested there for a few days departed last night, using the knotted rope hanging from the window tucked into the ivy which grows up the side of the building. I pray he left no evidence of his presence behind, but, hearing the hammer of boots marching across the flagstones, I've no time to check.

As I push my stool aside and stand, I catch sight of Freddie's holey socks on the bed - my next project. Where's my son? My stomach clenches as I dash across the room. Wasn't it today the children are supposed to be learning about tending to vegetables? I fling the tiny bedside window open and stick my head out, searching for our ever-growing group of orphans and Freddie in the gardens and vegetable patches. No small, capped heads are bent over the beds, no sound of chatter or laughter drifts on the breeze.

Under the shadow of the mountain, the grounds seem deserted, but then, I spot grey intruders stalking through the beans. The muzzles of their guns poke through the leaves like wolves' black noses, peering, searching for prey. What can they be looking for? This is a small convent, dedicated to taking care of orphaned children, although, for the last year, it's been hard to ignore the comings and goings of late night visitors, and whispered conversations which cease whenever I walk in.

The classroom - the children must still be there. I close my eyes briefly as I shut the window and cross myself, sending the Lord a prayer for us all. The simple action does little to calm me, but then, not born to this Catholic faith, it's the best I can offer. I have learned the hard way that appearances matter, and, with my sallow skin, dark hair and eyes, I'm accustomed to visibly demonstrating how not Jewish I am now. After being orphaned ten years ago, in this second decade of my life, I follow the religion of my childhood benefactor and current home, and have forgotten everything I was born to. In dark times, Catholicism is safer, or so Herr Franz Weisz said, when he begrudgingly undertook my parents' wishes and provided a roof over my head. Until, I disgraced myself and ended up here, sheltered by the nuns. I have no desire to take vows, nor could I, but in return for mine and Freddie's board, I sew, cook and clean.

A cursory, almost habitual, check reassures me there's nothing to suggest wrong-doing visible, unless you count an old, much-treasured copy of Harper's Bazaar nestled on top of my clothes in the chest. Satisfied, I rush through the corridors towards the schoolroom at the other end of the building. When I open the door, Sister Marta's eyes widen and her mouth tightens at the interruption. The children's fearful white faces swivel to see who's entered, so I imagine she must know our sanctuary swarms with Nazis and has warned her charges to behave. My gaze is drawn to the front table where Freddie usually sits.

He isn't there. My throat tightens.

"Can I help, Hannah?" Sister Marta's voice wavers slightly. How hard it must be to stay calm for the children when we both know what's at risk.

My speech sounds thick as I reply, "I just wanted to...."

To what? Check on my son, when all the other children here have no parents to care for them? My stomach knots with shame. I should be protecting them all, like the good Sister is.

"If you are looking for Freddie, he was helping Sister Luisa with his camera, cataloguing paintings in the Chapel. All other children are accounted for here, safe with me."

I throw her a grateful smile and close the door behind me.

As I look back up the corridor, a soldier stands outside my room. He's young and skinny, barely a man, and probably no older than I. His expression changes from bewilderment to decisive. "Halt!"

I freeze, my hand still on the classroom doorknob. "Can I help you?" I doubt it, but I must draw him away.

"What's in these rooms?" He grips the gun slung over his shoulder and waves the muzzle at the doors as he strides towards me.

I want to tell him it's none of his business, but Mother Superior's voice floats through my head. "Rebellious behaviour will only get you noticed. Know your place, speak only of what you know and all will be well, Hannah," was her wise advice upon my arrival here, six years ago and pregnant.

"Dormitories for the orphans," I say, my head low. "And this is their classroom. They aren't locked. You can go in them, if you like." They are kept spotless and I'm certain the worst he'll find in there is a contraband catapult toy. Go into these rooms, I pray, not mine.

His lips pinch together as I urge, "But please, lower your rifle if you enter the classroom. I'm sure there's no need to frighten the children."

He nods at me curtly, then flings open the door nearest him. I take the opportunity to dash downstairs. My steps slow as I cross the stone flags of the entrance hall and sneak towards the Mother Superior's office. Through the doorway, I glimpse the officer's leather coattails, flapping as he paces.

"Father Tomas only read what he was given," Mother Superior says, in a prim voice. Last weekend, the whole convent, including the children and myself, had attended the Mass in the larger Church in town, upon Mother Superior's instruction. We had all been shocked at the strong opinion - an abject condemnation of the Nazi regime, in '*Mit brennender Sorge*'. The edict, written by Pope Pius himself in German, was delivered from the pulpit to the congregations of all Catholic churches simultaneously on Palm

Sunday. I recall the sharp intakes of breath when Father Tomas paused after reading out, 'The experiences of these last years have fixed responsibilities and laid bare intrigues, which from the outset only aimed at a war of extermination.'

For those of us from the convent in the congregation, it echoed Mother Superior's daily caution - each Jewish child we house here must be protected. Their very lives depend on our conspiracy of silence about their origins.

She invokes the authority of the Papal office, saying primly, "A Papal Encyclical must be delivered to the public as soon as it is received."

"I know it must, I was brought up a Catholic myself," the officer says. "But it is one thing to have an opinion, but quite another to act upon it, as you have."

A shiver runs through me as I recognise the deep, clipped voice of Pieter Weisz, son of my benefactor. I have not seen him in years. He'd already moved into the accommodation provided for him by the state, when his cousin - and my only childhood friend - Katarina and I faced the consequences of our actions, back in 1932. Pieter would surely know of my dismissal from his family estate, perhaps even why. And, he knows I'm Jewish.

PAINTINGS AND PROOF

H ide, my instinct reacts, before Pieter can see me. Before I can be his undoing, for he would surely shoot me down rather than risk me telling anyone his father housed a Jew, let alone built the family fortune by taking over my parents' business upon their unfortunate demise.

Mother Superior sounds indignant. "Act upon what? I'm not sure what you mean."

In a chilling tone, Pieter says, "Don't you? Perhaps within these walls, you do more than pray."

"Of course. Aside from our work in the community, we have orphans to care for."

"If I should find any of them are Jewish, there would be consequences," Pieter says.

"All children are innocents. Surely you can agree, Oberführer?"

"Not all children are, and a Jew is a Jew."

This antisemitic stance is well known to me. He has clearly risen the SS ranks in my absence, as well as cast aside the teachings of compassion from his faith. His coveted position was the very reason Herr Weisz was so keen to remove me from his house. The

SS must be beyond reproach, generations of pure Aryan blood proven, with no hint of association with a Jew.

I should run - now - but my feet refuse to obey. My hands shake... I cannot leave without Freddie.

Inside the office, the paces cease. Pieter says, "I'm under orders to expose those who assisted in delivering the Encyclical, then deal with them appropriately."

Find Freddie and go, I decide, mentally repeating it over and over until my feet finally comply. As I creep past the doorway, Pieter's voice reminds me of the cold deliberation of his father. "You can imagine my surprise when last night, my men captured a known dissident on the road, close by to this very convent, with copies of the Encyclical on him. A man known for spreading disinformation, for resisting. A radical who seeks to disrupt order in this province."

Mother Superior gasps. "Whomever he is, whatever he's done, that's nothing to do with us. We are a simple religious order, seeking only to do God's work."

"After 'questioning', the traitor admitted he'd been housed at this very convent."

Just past the door, I freeze. Under torture, I imagine most people would say anything to make it stop. But, there was a man here, until last night...

Mother Superior says, "We have no men here, Oberführer. Apart from a few young male orphans, there are only women living here, of course."

"Then it is women, nuns even, who have produced this pamphlet preaching rubbish, which we also found on him?"

The implicit sneer in his voice makes my blood run cold. Whatever was printed, I can only assume the contents are critical of the regime we live under. Why else would it be of concern to the SS?

I clench my hands together to stop them trembling. How had I not seen what was right under my nose? But I know, deep inside, the answer to my own question. Fearful, I had suppressed my curious, rebellious nature. For Freddie's safety was why.

In the silence I imagine Mother Superior is wrestling her usual inclination to voice the truth with the need to protect us all.

But Pieter isn't done. "Not only are you harbouring criminals, but abetting their pathetic cause. Which makes me think, what else are you hiding here?" He snarls, "Shall we see? How about the chapel? Lots of hiding places there."

Urgency to find my son overrides my caution. As I dart down the passage towards the chapel, the office door creaks behind me.

"There's nothing there," Mother Superior squeals, unnaturally high pitched. Her voice and the shuffle of her shoes are too close for comfort, but I don't look back as I slip into the cool recesses of our sanctuary.

I scan the empty pews, chewing my lip. On one side of the chapel, a selection of paintings I've never seen before are propped against the wall by the confession booths. "Freddie?" My whisper grows urgent as I tiptoe towards the altar. "Freddie? Where are you?"

"Mama?" He calls from inside the limestone pulpit. As he then stands, his hair pokes above the stone rim, white-blond wisps caught in the sun streaming through the windows.

"I'm coming, stay there!"

Pieter's voice echoes down the hallway. "There's rarely nothing in my experience. Where there's one rat, there's a nest."

"Get down," I hiss as I run towards the pulpit and up the few steps to reach him. "Stay silent until it's all over."

He crouches, arms wrapped around his knees, white-knuckled fingers grasping his camera. Relief floods my body as I drop inside the stone booth and clutch him into me. Freddie's hands shake and I place my fingers over his on the camera in case it rattles. His most precious possession, his only one, is this old Zeiss Ikon Box-Baldur. The metal box was all the rage in Hitler Youth, and passed on to me as a hand-me-down by Katarina just before she left for finishing school. I suppose it might have been Pieter's once upon a time. Freddie formed an attachment to it from a young age, although we rarely have money for film or to have his photos developed. Of course, he knows nothing of its providence, just likes to take it apart and put it back together again, twiddling the knobs and pressing the trigger with a very satisfying click.

"Resist any more, and you'll learn the consequences," Pieter says, closer now.

I bury my head over my son and hold my breath.

There's an audible bump from by the doorway, then Mother Superior squeals.

"How dare you?" Sister Luisa calls out. She must have been hiding in a confession box, but as I turn my head to look through the pulpit's entrance, she steps directly into my eyeline. "This is a place of worship."

"It's alright, Sister," Mother Superior replies, but it sounds forced.

Pieter's shoes click across on the aisle tiles. "Looks like you do have something to confess, Sisters. A fine collection of paintings, I see. Not the usual sort of pictures one might expect in a chapel. These look far too modern. Being something of an enthusiast, I'm always on the look out for works for the Entartete Kunst. That's the 'degenerate art' exhibition, which will soon be held in Munich. Something of a hobby for our Führer, and he looks kindly upon those who support his vision. Let's see now..."

"See it or seize it?" Sister Luisa snaps back. The woman has no fear. "I've heard what you're doing, taking paintings from people, from Churches even."

"But it's so important to show the people the right kind of art, wouldn't you say? So they might see the truth within. And, you never know what kind of filth you'll find in unexpected places."

"I assure you," Mother Superior's voice wavers. "You'll find nothing of interest here."

"Then why, pray tell, are all these paintings - showing nothing to do with the glory of God - displayed here?"

There's a shuffle of feet as Sister Luisa disappears from my view, then she says, "I'm simply cataloguing them. They were donated to us, for safe-keeping."

"Ah, but who did they belong to before, I wonder?" His shoes tick-tick-tick as he crosses the flagstones, closer to our hiding place.

"Stop!" Sister Luisa says.

My arms tighten around Freddie.

Pieter's voice is low and dangerous, but utterly clear. "Therefore, I conclude these can only be stolen. Or maybe given in exchange for something. Harbouring Jewish children, perhaps, or fugitives. Either way, they don't belong here, do they, Sister?"

"They are ours," Mother Superior interjects. Her voice sounds feeble behind us, then she whimpers.

I crane my head around so I can see out of the pulpit better. Pieter faces Sister Luisa, who stands in front of the paintings like a guard dog. "Are you calling me a liar?"

"I would never..." Sister Luisa blusters.

"Oberführer, no!" Mother Superior calls.

"No-one cares what you say. It's what *I* say that matters."

My heart is in my mouth as Pieter's arm rises. Then I see what was obscured before - the black snub of a revolver blends seamlessly with his dark leather gloves.

"No!" Sister Luisa's exclamation is drowned out by the shot booming around the room. Before my eyes, she crumples to the ground. I register the click of Freddie's camera as Pieter swivels on his heel, arm still extended.

"This lawlessness is unacceptable - even for the Gestapo!" Mother Superior exclaims.

But he sweeps the gun past the pulpit and aims it towards the doorway at the back. I clap my hands over my mouth and clutch Freddie into my chest.

"Resisting arrest, Sister? What if there's no-one left to tell?"

Bang! The noise echoes briefly, replaced by the receding tap-tap of his shoes as he strides out.

Freddie whimpers in my arms, breaking my shocked silence. I've been clutching him so hard it must hurt, but for the life of me, I cannot release my boy. Framed by the pulpit's carved sides, I can only stare at Sister Luisa's body. Blood saturates her white wimple. Despite me silently willing her to get up, she is utterly still.

Freddie wriggles. "Shh," I whisper into his hair.

I am frozen in fear, until I hear a groan at the back of the chapel. Mother Superior! Her moans galvanise me - perhaps she still lives? "Stay here," I order Freddie as I uncurl myself from him. As I stand, he looks up at me. Watery blue eyes meet mine and his fingers tighten around his camera as if it can replace my warm body comforting him. I tear myself away from his gaze and dash to the doorway.

Mother Superior lies, leg twisted awkwardly, on the floor. She holds her hand to her chest, but blood seeps out between her fingers. "Oh no!" I drop to my knees and push my palm over her bloody hand.

Her eyelids flutter open. "Run Hannah!" She croaks out. "Never look back."

"Don't try to speak." I bear down in a vain effort to stem the bleeding.

A gurgling noise comes from her chest and she tries to cough.

Her other arm twitches, fingers reaching for me as if she is desperate to say something more. I bend closer, folding my other hand over her cold fingers. As I grip her, I remember these arms of hers held me as I birthed Freddie. Comforted me as I accepted I could never go back to the Weisz's and life as I knew it. I long to feel the strength of her embrace again, but, I fear all I can do now is hold her in her final moments. Despite my best efforts, her blood pools around my knees as I sense her heartbeat slow. "Please stay with me, Mother," I plead, "Lord, heal your servant, I beg you."

But my prayer falls on deaf ears. I cannot call out for help. Can do nothing but hold her hand and be with her.

Her last breath drifts silently from her lips, soft and shallow. Her head lolls, and I know she is gone.

Before I can do more than bow my head with sorrow, gunshots sound from the courtyard. They are the rat-a-tat-tat of machine guns, not the calculated aim of a pistol. I cannot imagine what is going on out there, and I don't want to find out. We must heed Mother Superior's warning, so I dash back to the pulpit.

Freddie hunches against the stone, shivering. There's no time to comfort him; I grab his arm and pull him out. He resists, shaking his head, but I've no choice. I scoop him up, into my chest, and, like a limpet clinging to the rock against the waves, his legs wrap around my waist. My bloody palm holds his face into my collarbone so he does not see the terrible cost of resisting. The camera slung around Freddie's neck bangs against us with every step as I run past Sister Luisa's body, then Mother Superior's, and into the empty hallway.

Mindful of the danger outside, I dash up to my bedroom. My heart thumps a warning, my breath fast and too shallow to calm me as I'm greeted by confirmation of my fears: the tapestry has been pulled down, and the door behind it kicked in.

Stunned, I stand motionless, listening to the wind whistle through from the chamber beyond. In the stillness, I sense we're alone. They have made their discoveries, passed judgement on us all and delivered the punishment, all in a matter of minutes.

Run, Mother Superior said, but, in a moment of clarity, I understand the intention behind her instruction - we can never return. Still clutching Freddie on my hip, I accept in an instant we'll never come home and make my peace with it. I've seen before how the Nazi propaganda machine covers up the truth, paints the picture they want us to see. Anyone who tries to prove otherwise disappears – like some of the parents of the orphans here.

One handed, for I'm not letting go of Freddie for anything, I sling my old school satchel over my shoulder. I rummage through my chest then stuff my papers into the front pocket. Not knowing what's ahead for us, I grab my mother's yellow scarf, Freddie's holey socks, and shove what few pieces of clothing will fit into the bag. I fix the straps with shaking fingers. Sliding everything we now own across my back, I glance out of the window to the courtyard. Freddie whimpers as I turn his head into my shoulder, but I do not want him to see what I fear I must witness.

Below, the flagstones are strewn with bodies, mown down as they tried to flee. Children, nuns. Innocents. Soldiers stand around the walls, lighting cigarettes as they survey their morning's work. Guessing what happened sickens me.

Then, Oberführer Pieter Weisz emerges from the front door and orders them to pile the corpses and douse them in petrol. The young soldier I met in the hallway approaches him and points towards my window. I pivot away - a mouse does not wait for a cat to pounce, and they will surely come for the printing press before long.

As I head through the smashed door, my eyes fall on the dog-eared Harpers Bazaar left on the bed in my haste to pack. Girlish dreams I have to leave behind now our mere survival is in question. I reach beyond the windowpane and drag out the knotted rope from the ivy. Then, I climb onto the windowsill, take a deep breath and swing us out. As I rappel down with Freddie on my back, step by careful step, my mind flashes to recall the pages of that magazine, fallen open on a report from Paris's Spring Collection. I know then where we have to go.

THE WASHROOM

Paris, October 1938

I don't recognise the reflection in the mirror: lank dark hair, wrinkles streaking across a dirty forehead, and almost purple half moons under the eyes. Our trials are written, scratched and stained, onto the skin of the woman staring back at me. I slump against the basin, unable to tear my eyes from the first sight of myself in years. Tears prick and a little sob squeaks in my throat. I'm only twenty-two, but the ghostly face looking at me has aged decades in the last eighteen months of travelling. If I cannot recognise myself, will anyone else?

When we disembarked and hurried along the track to join the trail of ordinary passengers, khaki-uniformed men stood on the platform, watching everyone. I'd wondered then if our tatty clothes would make us noticeable, and I'd avoided any questioning gazes by looking down while I searched for this restroom. The risk of being stopped by officials has been a constant concern, even here in France. The sheer number of soldiers milling around made my stomach clench. Freddie froze at the sight of them, and I'd had to pick him up to avoid a scene, whispering in his ear, "No Nazis here, my love. See, they wear the blue tips of France on their collars, not red swastika armbands. We're fine."

As I clutched my son on my hip, I hoped we looked like any other mother and child, journey-sick and desperate to go home and rest. Inside the high dome of Gare du Nord station hall, it echoed with passengers greeting loved ones or tearfully hugging them goodbye. I couldn't stop the tremors inside; my mouth was so dry with nerves I couldn't catch my breath. The throng of families gathered openly expressing their love and concern caught in my throat and I clutched my child close. My blond-haired boy deserves better, but nobody is here to welcome us to Paris. No-one knows we are even alive. But, I remind myself, hiding has facilitated our survival thus far, and we are not safe yet.

A little warm hand creeps over my fist. Freddie's fingers wriggle between mine, seeking to entwine and break my reverie.

My heart melts at my son's pitiful but justifiable whine of pain as he clutches his stomach. He is everything to me and worth every calculable risk to my own life if it will keep him alive. But still, I cannot drag my gaze away from the apparition in the rust-dotted glass. She looks haunted, yet I must be strong, for Freddie. I cannot be *her*. My jaw clenches when a train rumbles and clacks past, rattling the windows of the washroom like the snakes writing in my belly. Just a train. Just a crowd. What else would you expect in a city? I should feel safer, grateful even to have arrived in one piece, but our journey isn't over.

Incessant, as all children are, Freddie tugs on my fist.

I glance down at his blue eyes, like his father's, but rimmed with dust and sunken with a lack of water. "Yes, *liebchen*, we'll find some food soon. Go to the toilet now. Then we'll wash."

Then I catch myself - no more German. I repeat my instructions softly in near-forgotten schoolgirl French as I crouch down and tug his coat's too short sleeves down his arms. His gaze widens as he doesn't speak French, only understanding my tone and actions. "Listen, we are going to see Katarina, who I grew up with."

Optimistically, I add, "You can call her Kat. Now, we must be sure we are presentable."

It seems such a benign statement to make, as if appearances are the most important thing. I doubt Kat's view on such things has changed that much – and they always were important to her. Besides, it's what's inside that counts, but people will always judge you by what you wear. Your name. Then, by what religion you were born into. And, if you are a Nazi, that means what race you will always be.

Freddie's smile is brief, revealing yellowed, unbrushed teeth between cherubic lips. As I'm bent to his height, Freddie stretches over and smudges his fingers under my eyes, as if his care alone could wipe away the weeks of living rough. He shakes his head as the stain and strain of our escape remains, then rubs his fingertips on his sleeve. The brown mud streak merges invisibly with the rest of the dirt. I cannot help but feel my spirits lift; his gesture reminds me of simpler times.

"From now on, you should call me *Maman*, like the French do. We made it! To Paris!"

His lip trembles as the enormity of our new location sinks in for us both. He hasn't called me anything, or uttered a single word, in the year and a half, since we escaped the convent. I have to believe he will talk again once we're settled.

I kiss his little knuckles and reiterate the mantra I started saying to reassure us both when it became apparent our journey wasn't going to be simple, but involve hiking and hiding in ditches, barns, and to get into the country and its capital city, jumping onto train-pulled cattle trucks. Since we are still alone, reassure him in German. "We'll get a little home of our very own, where we'll eat dinner and laugh together. Just you and me. And when we get enough money, we'll start our own dress shop."

We exchange smiles; his is more hesitant. I'm not sure if I'm telling him this or myself, but I have to believe these dreams will come true or else I shall not be brave enough to take the next step forward.

"Maybe we can live near a park, so we can walk and listen to the birds singing, like they did at the convent. And we'll explore this great big city together. How would you like to stand under the famous Eiffel Tower and reach up to see if you'll ever be as tall?"

He launches his arms in the air, stretching them to the sky.

"No more worrying. This is the start of our new life. Smarten up, Freddie, and let's go!"

He touches the splash of jaunty mustard-coloured silk around his neck and cocks his head. His eyes grow round and solemn. I know, in his own way, he's trying to tell me that he loves me by reminding me that I gave him my mother's scarf. His camera is stowed in my satchel for safekeeping, so the soft, now dirty, fabric gives him comfort. I can't believe he is nearly six, for he has the empathy of someone far more advanced in years. An old soul in a child's body. "I love you too, sweetheart. Always remember, you're my heart." I tap my chest. "That's *tu est mon coeur*, in French."

After we wrinkle our noses at each other, my heartbeat calms and his face seems more relaxed. "Now, go to the toilet – *va aux toilettes.*"

He scuttles into a stall and I peer down at my shabby dress, muddied from travel. Arriving in France crouched between animals meant we'd avoided border checks, but in Paris, I hoped we'd be freer. Will the stench wash out, or does it only mask the smell of my shame? My mind wanders to consider whether anyone else noticed our odour.

Act as if we belong, I murmur to the face in the mirror - more to remind myself as well - and above all else, blend in. Mother Superior had drummed it into me: rebellious people get noticed. They had paid the ultimate price for resisting, and I can't bear to lose anyone else. Besides, Paris, or anywhere but the land of my birth, has got to be better than where we have lived these past years.

Breathe. I must breathe.

The sigh which escapes my lips as I push aside the past is long and deep, but does the job. I glance again at the mirror. In the woman's tired eyes, there's a flash of steel. A hint of determination to survive, I decide. If she is really me, then I can obviously do this next step, for I've already come this far. My jaw clenches, unintentionally highlighting the dirty hollows of my cheeks.

The very least I can manage is to splash my face before seeing Katarina again after so many years. All I can do about my clothes right now is brush off the straw. My shoe still has teeth marks in the scuffed leather from a pig thinking it was a meal, but at least the sole hasn't entirely fallen off. After scrubbing at my skin, I glance again at my reflection. The woman defiantly stares back at me. Act as if, and maybe it will be.

Then, I help Freddie wash his hands and face. Perhaps when he sees how different Paris is, he'll speak again.

Something Peculiar

With my face washed, skirt straightened, hair slicked down, my stride across the station hall and outside has fresh purpose, although out of habit my head remains low. As we follow the crowd outside, it seems like everyone else has their heads down, strolling or strutting away from me and not meeting my eye. For a minute, I'm bewildered by the unfamiliar street, then it occurs to me, what might a tourist do? By the kerb, I spot a gendarme. Just a policeman, I tell myself. Where's the harm? Recalling the address I wrote on so many unposted letters, I ask him, "Could you please give me directions to Bd de Beauséjour?"

I'm confident enough with my French with this simple sentence, but I have to concentrate hard to follow his answer. He gesticulates as he drawls, "It's quite far, but a pretty walk on a day like today. It's in the 16th Arrondissement, so follow the river until you reach the exhibition grounds at the Palais du Trocadero. Then, head for the Bois de Bolougne park and you should find it. The little lad..."

He reaches for Freddie as if to ruffle his hair, but my son shrieks.

Confused, the policeman shakes his head as Freddie clings to my thighs. "I will hail you a taxi."

"Non!" I can't help shouting as he steps off the kerb and holds out his hand. "We don't need one." Picking up the heavy satchel, I tug Freddie's hand off my leg and step away.

"But all that way? Madame…"

Walking away as quickly as I can, his call soon fades in the cacophony of traffic. In my head, I am certain the gendarme only meant well, why wouldn't he? But my urgency to leave is driven part by fear of being asked for my papers, and part economics. Taxis cost money and I only have a few *Reichspfennig* left from the odd jobs I have done as we travelled. It's unlikely to be enough for a taxi, and using them would betray my origins. I do not yet know how the French view Germans, but my instinct remains - hide what I am.

As we walk the streets, lined with tall windowed houses and cafés spilling onto the pavements, I can't quite believe I am finally in Paris. The city of art, music, literature, cinema, and, most importantly to my younger self, haute couture. Had it been any other day, any other life, I would relish exploring the city, especially where I read the fashion houses are located. I yearn to amble down Avenue Montaigne, Rue Francois-I, Rue Marbeuf and the Rue du Faubourg-Saint-Honoré without a care in the world and money burning a hole in my pocket.

Exploring and dreaming will have to wait. I have more important issues to solve, like a roof over our heads.

Having left the riverside, after passing the now defunct exhibition grounds as directed, the traffic builds. I keep Freddie close as we trudge along the pavement. He skips with excitement, thrilled by the brum brum and throb of long bonnets roaring past, then coughing as the black fumes hit our throats. We venture through thickets of chimneys, cobbled narrow streets and slanting rooftops that seem to look down on us. Houses soar six or seven stories high with ornate Juliette balconies like eyelashes. Exquisite carved doorways announce the wealth and prestige of the occupants. Passing the tangle of side streets and off-shooting alleys, I cannot shake my inclination to hide in their shadows. But, with our fresh start, I look ahead, walk with purpose and try to enjoy the wide avenues as they glow a creamy orange with the sun's last rays.

Finally, we reach the right boulevard and I search the house numbers. Katarina's house is in the middle of a row of imposing townhouses, opposite a lovely park. I pull Freddie closer to me on the step with a blue front door and gold-plated knocker. My stomach clenches as the metal clunks down with a deep thud. Freddie's hand is hot in mine and I wet my dry lips.

After a moment, the locks click and the door opens. A housemaid with a shrewish face underneath her lacy headpiece peers around. She raises a thin eyebrow. "*Oui?*"

"I am here to see Katarina... Devereaux." I attempt a tremulous smile to lift my tired features. "I'm an old friend."

"Your name?"

The disdain in her voice matches her expression as she sizes up my tatty attire and the grubby urchin clutching my hand.

"Please tell her it's Hannah."

A brief nod and the door slams shut. I glance down at Freddie, whose expectant face has fallen.

"Don't worry." I smooth down his flyaway hair, and try to keep my smile steady.

The door opens again. "Madame says she doesn't know a Hannah. Go begging at some other house."

My stomach drops. "But..."

The maid starts to close the door, so I ram my foot in the gap. She gasps.

"Tell her, please, that it's her Maus."

She frowns and turns as if to say something, when the door is wrenched from her grip.

"Maus?"

Katarina stands in the aperture like a deer in the headlights, and doesn't appear to have aged one bit. Her blonde hair is shorter, artfully curled around her high cheekbones, which lends her eyes a feline look. She's as tall as she always was though, all slim legs encased with sheer stockings in heels, a smart knee length suit. She looks as if she has just stepped from the pages of *Modenschau*, our favourite fashion magazine when we were younger.

I straighten, my grin finally reaching my eyes, but, it's premature.

Mascara'd eyelashes bat her cheeks as she narrows her gaze. On Freddie. In German, she mutters, "And a mini-Maus..."

I clutch his hand and draw him closer. "Frederick, meet Tante Katarina."

In the silence which follows, while Katarina and the maid gape at him, my sweet boy looks ahead for a moment, before performing a little bow. Then, before I can stop it, his arm shoots up, straight, in the salute which he has learned to mimic in the eventuality of meeting someone he doesn't know.

The maid gasps as I grab his arm and yank it back to his side. My cheeks flush as Katarina's hand flies to her glossy red lips. She snorts in horror. Her head ducks out of the doorway and she checks up and down the quiet street. "Get inside," she orders. "Quickly."

The maid shuffles backward, hands clutching her apron as if Freddie, the three foot Nazi, would launch himself at her. As we enter, she grunts and I can't work out if it is because we are traipsing dirt onto the immaculate, shiny black and white floor tiles, or because with one stupid action my son has exposed us.

THE ASK

- -

Katarina hustles us straight through the hallway, past a curved staircase which rises elegantly up and around, and into a small, femininely decorated salon to the rear of the house. Entering it is like walking into an intimate insight to my old friend, a statement laced with Parisienne elegance. Lilac wallpaper with faintly glinting gold highlights lines the brightly lit room. Double window-doors open to a patio are left ajar to allow the cooling evening air through. Soft Tiffany lamps in each corner throw pools of light up to the high ceiling and down to an inviting chaise. Almost an entire wall is books – from classic fiction to modern paperbacks, even a few school textbooks. While luxurious décor is a reflection of the Katarina I knew, the brightness and style rejects the heavy darkness of our Germanic heritage. I could understand her desire to appear as French as possible in these difficult times.

As Katarina closes the door behind us, I steal a glance at her. The suit she wears so effortlessly is a Chanel; with the austerity and precision of the cut, it could be nothing else. In black, because as Chanel said in the last Harpers Bazaar Katarina and I shared years ago, 'black wipes out everything else around.' Or was there more to it?

Through her marriage into high French society and her own privileged background, Katarina could always afford to wear the very clothes we dreamed of as girls. She now has the lifestyle we drooled over in the pages of our magazines, whereas I have nothing but the dress and coat I stand in. And a beloved, but bastard, son. Just for a moment, envy engulfs me, and then I notice the quietness. The absence of children's clutter. A stillness and sorrow which shrouds her expression as she glances at my son.

"*Sitzen*," she orders Freddie, and points to a high-backed chair nestled into a roll-top desk, then repeats it in French. "*Asseyez vous.*"

"I'm sorry," I say. My head drops as the weight of responsibility for his actions squeezes my chest.

"Who is he?" Kat snaps at me in French. "Some stray you have rescued?" Without pausing for breath, she strides over to the sofa. "How dare you bring it here?" She exhales loudly, flopping down onto the cushions.

"He's my son," I mumble. With my dark hair and sallow skin and Freddie the cute embodiment of Aryan blondness, I understood her confusion.

"Your what?"

My mouth dries and I cannot find the words to tell her. I shake my head, as if that will rid me of my shame. Of course, I love Freddie, but his very existence spoke too deeply of my past misjudgement for me to express right now.

Seeing my lips clamped shut, she huffs.

I hear Freddie whimper and turn to see him struggling to pull out the chair.

He feels so heavy as I help him clamber up but he cannot have gained any weight for months now. I am the weak one.

He groans and crumples with hunger pangs. I shoot Katarina a pleading look. "Could we have something to eat? He's so hungry, he's in pain."

She rolls her eyes. "Your son, for sure. We could never fill you up either."

"Until a year ago, I had never gone without food for a day, that's true, but now…" I draw in a deep breath and count. "Freddie and I haven't eaten for three." I don't mean to snap, but she's never skipped a meal unless it was to fit in a dress.

Instantly, her face falls at my chastisement. Her hand drops to a small bell on a table. "Whatever happened to you?"

"If we could have some bread or something, I'll tell you everything. I just…" My mind blanked as I struggled to remember the speech I had planned in my head. "We just need a safe roof over our heads."

She tinkles the bell, then says the words I dreaded hearing. "You can't stay here."

"Please, Kat, I've no-one else to ask. Nowhere else to go."

She presses her lips together, eyes darting anxiously between myself and Freddie. The maid slides into the room. Funny, I hadn't heard her footsteps on the tiles outside. I would probably have been listening at the door too, I realise, if two bedraggled strangers turned up just before dinnertime then one acts like a Nazi.

Without looking at her, Katarina requests supper in the salon, and to bring extra for her guests. I look on awkwardly while Freddie arranges himself at the desk as if it's a private dinner table. As soon as the maid leaves, Katarina pats the sofa and nods at me. While I cautiously arrange myself on the edge of the seat, conscious of my filth on her satin upholstery, she calls to Freddie in German, "Food will come now. Wait quietly."

She's completely ignoring the fact he hasn't said a word. She turns to me. "Tell me what you can, in French if you prefer."

My heart squeezes and I mouth like a fish, but still the words won't come out, in any language. How can I tell her who's to blame for our having to leave? It was risky to just turn up here; I shouldn't have. Her family connections, the lost years - why did I ever think this was a good idea? While I'm silently cursing my stupidity, she reaches her hand across and touches mine.

"Six years, Hannah, or seven? Not a word, call, or even a letter?" A petulant expression I know too well crosses her face. "It's like you disappeared. You couldn't be bothered to come back for my wedding, to see me in the dress you made for me. I got married without my best friend there, for goodness' sake! And then..." she pauses, retracts her hand and twists her wedding ring in her lap. She swallows, her face creasing in pain. Her big blue eyes slide around the room until they rest on a small silver photo frame. A handsome young man stares back at her with a haunted expression. "Widowed."

I reach across the cushions. "I didn't know. I'm so sorry."

She jerks her fingers away from mine. "Why would you? You were there on the estate one minute, gone the next. Uncle refused to tell me anything when I returned after finishing school to be wed. Where you went or what happened to make you go. "

Dropping my head, I blink. I'd never posted any of the letters I wrote from the convent, for I was too ashamed. I had let her down. Then, like now, I could not bring myself to tell her what a fool I was. How desperate I had been to feel like a grown up, at the age of sixteen, that I had fallen into the arms of the first man to pay attention to me, and my actions had cost me everything, including my friendship with Kat. A friendship I - we - now need to salvage.

I don't mean to belittle her anguish, but I have to focus on my priorities now. I slipped into speaking German, hoping to get my point across better in our native language. "Can't we leave the past behind us, Katarina? I came to Paris to build a new life."

"Well, you picked a fine time for it, didn't you? The city is overwhelmed with refugees already. Besides, you don't look prepared to build a cardboard house, let alone a life for you and your son." She snorted and for a moment I glimpsed the old Katarina. "There's hand-me-downs and then there's this…" Her elegant, manicured hand waved towards my threadbare skirt and she coughed as if it were disgusting.

"You don't know, you can't imagine, what we've been through to get here," I mumble, glancing at Freddie who stirred at the noise. "You know what I am, and surely, you know what it's like for people like me in Germany now. We had to hide in the animal wagon just to cross the border."

Her lips tighten and her nose twitches. "That explains it. Another reason you can't stay here." Kat brushes the sofa down as if our dirt has legs of its own.

"Like a little mouse, Kat, that's how we survived this far."

With a big sigh, she pinches the bridge of her nose. "So, you're illegal, undocumented, Jewish immigrants as well."

"But now, here, where we could be free, I need my big Kat's protection. Your help. Please." The lump in my throat from begging won't budge and it hurts to swallow.

She shakes her head. "I've done everything I can to fit in here. It cost my late Pascal so much money to help the French forget I'm a German."

"I can see that," I say, gesturing to the suit, the décor, the beautiful rug which Freddie has somehow left muddy footprints on. "Just like I can appreciate how hard it has been for you to lose Pascal after so brief a time together. But you were lucky to have had the romance. Not everyone can say that."

Her eyes narrow on me and it's as if she can see into my shame. All I knew of her romance was the whirlwind nature of it; Pascal Devereaux was the brother of her fancy finishing school friend, who my guardian, her Uncle, dismissed initially as a girlish fancy.

I only had this address because she had written telling me she was to visit him here before returning to Germany for the wedding, and begging me to make her a dress. Then, Herr Weisz forbade me any contact with the family, and my circumstances forced me into another life.

"We can stay hidden, believe me, Kat. We've grown used to it."

Before she can push for answers again, or I can ask for the details, the maid clatters in with a tray of bowls and a sour face. Silence falls as she sets them down on the coffee table in front of us. I catch her grimace at the sight of Freddie, with his owl-like eyes and mouth a-gape at the rich-smelling casserole. He's half out of his chair in a dash towards it when I stay him with a glare.

"Would Madame like any wine this evening?"

Katarina responds, "I think I will, yes. Bring me a bottle of Châteauneuf-du-Pape, please."

"That's the last bottle from the cellar, Madame. Just so you know."

Katarina glances at me, then dismisses her maid with, "You can go home then. I won't be needing any further assistance this evening. And, if you want to keep your job, say nothing, to anyone, about my guests here tonight. They won't be here long."

Kat to the Rescue

The maid scowls as if Katarina has scolded her, and I suspect this isn't the first caution about gossiping.

As soon as she's gone, Freddie lunges forward and begins shovelling the food into his hungry belly. I almost smile at him, but my mind jumps ahead to what's next and my stomach sinks. An autumn night on the streets, even with a full belly, is no place for a child. I pass Katarina a bowl. "Surely, in this big house, there's somewhere we can at least rest our heads for the night? In safety and warmth."

She draws in a deep breath then says, "You ask a lot, Maus." Her gaze flits to Freddie, busy scraping the bowl. "Although it's now more obvious why you left the Weisz's, only to appear on my doorstep and expect me to fix everything. It's too much."

"Katarina, I don't need you to fix anything. I can work! I'm not completely incapable. All I'm asking for is a few days, long enough for me to find a job and a room to rent."

"Pah! You really have no idea, do you? Thousands of people, just like you, have swamped the city. There are no rooms to be had. No jobs to work. Besides, you need the proper papers."

"I have a passport, but," I admit, "I read in a paper, all German Jewish passports were invalidated earlier this month. I... I didn't get a new one with a J on it because we were travelling." Being homeless has few advantages; hiding is - was - more important. Freddie has nothing to say who he is at all, not even a birth certificate.

"There's no getting around it, even here," she snaps. "You are still German, and an unpopular Jew. No-one wants you, don't you see?" Her eyebrows draw together. "People here place too much faith in men keeping to paper promises, like the Munich Agreement. The French still believe the Maginot Line could hold any advance back. When it falls..."

"If it falls," I interject. The knowledge of those concrete fortifications, guarded and defended and all that stand between the might of Hitler's army and France's borders, has given me courage through the entire, arduous journey here. I cannot contemplate its destruction.

"When it falls, I have even less faith in politicians finding any other solution than war." Her lips clamp together as the doorknob rattles again.

I sat for a moment, considering her words while her wine arrives. Katarina was likely right. In my heart, and with my head, I suspected invasion across the rest of Europe was Hitler's intent. In all the months we spent travelling, walking for miles and miles through a Germany swarming with troops being trained, to pretend he planned anything otherwise would be foolish. For all the peace it promised, the Munich Agreement hadn't stopped Hitler's preparations, or the factories being converted to make munitions, or the rights of those of us with my heritage being eroded day by day. I may have been raised a Catholic but what I am is like an inescapable mark that won't shift. I can say all the Hail Mary's in the world - for that is the only religion I really know - but all my adult life I've been told how different Jews are, and lately, how dirty and despicable.

"If I ever meant anything to you, Kat, please just help us now. You are my only hope. My only friend and family." I could not keep the pleading from my voice.

Freddie pushes the empty bowl deep into the desk and lays his head on his arms. Within moments, we hear the soft breath sounds of contented sleep. I cannot bear to leave this quiet, warm room, not after he has endured so much lately. My gaze lowers as in her silence, I fear I have lost any chance of a normal life for us and our long journey here has been wasted.

The image of the determined woman in the mirror swims before my eyes, renewing my resolve not to give up. While Kat stares stonily at her hands, I look around for inspiration. There has to be something I can say to make her relent.

On the table beside me lies a newspaper, and I push aside the torn out, completed crossword puzzle to see the headline. The article's words blur, letters wriggle as I try to read the text, but reading has always been tricky for me. It's something about an assassination in Germany, a diplomat killed by a Jewish teenager.

My eyes wander away and I study the framed photograph. Katarina and Pascal pose in front of the Weisz's mansion. Both Kat and I were orphaned at a young age and brought up under the watchful eye of our guardian. Being a blood relative afforded her privileges, and forgiveness for our escapades. Too often, I had borne the brunt of reprisals.

In the photo, she is resplendent, like a lily in bloom, dressed in the gown I designed and sewed for her before I had been forced to leave. Beside her, pale Pascal looks like a wilting weed in an ill-fitting suit which hangs off his sickly, gaunt frame.

I say quietly, "You owe me, Katarina. You wouldn't have had a wedding dress, wouldn't have had a marriage at all if I hadn't done something far worse to make Herr Weisz view your relationship as a salvation. Not after…" I raise my head, "What happened at the pogrom. You would still be in Germany, enduring what's happening there."

Her eyes flare as indecision plays across her face.

Although I hate to do it, I play the biggest card left in my hand and look her dead in the eye. "And you should know, Herr Weisz's cruelty was surpassed by his son. We wouldn't have had to leave the convent, our home, at all, if it wasn't for Pieter."

Sometimes it's better to be blunt delivering the truth. Her mouth drops open a little but I continue, because Freddie slumbers still. "Your cousin's actions are why my son doesn't talk any more."

The speed at which her head jerks away and hands clap over her ears astonishes me. "No! I won't believe it."

She can ignore what I say all she wants, but some day she will hear what he did. I glance at Freddie. "I won't speak of it, not yet." I'm not sure I can find the words either right now. The horror is too fresh. "But Pieter, and what he believes, is why you owe us, Katarina. It's your family and its allegiances which brought Freddie and I to this…. desperate situation, and there's only you to save us."

"I disowned the Weisz's when I moved here, especially Pieter, with his ambitions and obsession with Nazism." Her chin juts out. "I've heard nothing from them since the wedding. As soon as Herr Weisz's financial obligations to keep me shifted to Pascal as my husband, he couldn't wait to get rid of me. I'll never go back to being German again."

I hadn't realised how ostracised she had become from the Weisz's. In my imagination, she lived a life of luxury, supported by a close knit, wealthy family. "You are the closest I have to family, like a sister. Please, don't abandon me again, Katarina." Although we had never spoken about what happened after that fateful day in Bavaria years ago, when she'd left me during a riot, guilt was the only leverage I had left. "Not like you did before. Today, you can be my saviour. It's your choice. I'll - we'll - leave if you want us to. But please, Kat, if I ever meant anything to you, help us now."

She stares at me with pouted lips. My stomach turns over with relief as the ice queen finally thaws. With a 'Tsk' of disapproval, her eyes slide to the door. "The cellar has its own exit, out through to the back yard. You and the boy can stay there for a few nights."

I sag with relief. "Just until I can find work and a room for us, I promise."

She reclines into the cushions with her wine glass. A sightly smug smile plays on her lips. "In truth, I would welcome the company, as long as you promise you will only be visible when Francine isn't here, or when I have no other guests. As for a job, I think I can help there, too."

My heart clamours - not only at her change of heart. With a twinkle in her eyes, she glances down at her suit, her fingers straightening the hem across her knees. She grins. "I always did say you could sew for the best."

"You don't mean.... You know her?"

"I'm one of Chanel's favourite customers. I've had a front row seat at her collections for the last three years. Perhaps there's something she can do for me now. For you. If I say she should meet the most talented designer I ever knew, she will at least be intrigued. And I know your skill with a needle, which I assume the Nazi's or nuns haven't crushed out of you."

My spoon chinks in the bowl as I drop it, and I can hardly breathe.

"You have more in common with her than I think most people know." Katarina's lips stretch into a thin smile. "And then we can call ourselves even. The past is behind us."

I sincerely hope she is right. In this city of dreams, of fashion history and future, could mine possibly come true?

Rue Cambon

A week later, I stand alone in a room above Chanel's salon on Rue Cambon. The dying sunbeams warm the gold leaf wallpaper as the evening falls. The opulence of my surroundings reminds me of Herr Weisz's taste in decor, but the elegant showroom is a million miles away from the stuffy pomp of his estate. With my livelihood hanging by a thread it seems apt: drawing the parallel between the two people who, unknowingly, defined my life before and one who could shape my future. My mouth dries as I tweak my skirt so it hangs straight across my knees. The only thing newish on me are the gloves I wear, on loan from Katarina and hiding my fingernails. No matter how much I scrub, my hands still feel stained with grime. My fingers are thin from malnourishment. I glance down; my old shoes, scuffed and holey, but rubbed and buffed clean of mud, let my outfit down, but there is nothing more to be done about them. I have not a sou to spare on a new pair, and leather is expensive everywhere.

The door at the far end creaks as the handle turns and a slim fifty-ish brunette sashays in. Dark eyes appraise me up and down as she approaches. I recognise her face from the magazines I read all those years ago. My heartbeat thunders in my ears, but I jut my chin forward. The mouse Herr Weisz ignored has survived thus far. In clean, presentable clothes which I made myself, if I fail to squeak now, another cat would stalk past me. This lioness's den is where I'm meant to be.

"Mademoiselle Chanel," I say and bob.

Her generous lips part slightly and she cocks her head to the side, her face neutral. "You are the girl sent by Katarina Devereaux?"

I incline my head, cheeks flushing.

"She spoke highly of you. Did you fashion this?" Her hand drifts up and down my dress.

I nod. "The sisters at the convent I... lived at until recently, inspired me towards a simpler style. We had limited access to different fabrics, mostly cotton linen and heavier wool, but before then, I used to sew with finer material." Withdrawing a folded silk blouse I stitched for Katarina while she made this appointment, I offer it up for inspection. The nuns were meticulous in their checks, and I anticipate Chanel has the same exacting standards.

Chanel's eyes narrow. "Who taught you?" She runs the fabric through her fingers, holding it up to the light and examining the embroidered lapels.

"I learned the basics in school, but mostly I taught myself."

"Is this from a pattern? Or do you free cut?" She hands me back the blouse.

"I can do both." I long to tell her about my designs, but, cowed in the presence of my idol, I cannot find the words. The vacancy I'm here to apply for is a common workshop seamstress, although I covet so much more. "And I'm fast, Mademoiselle."

"Are you?" Her eyebrow arches and she reaches to examine the seam between sleeve and shoulder on my dress. She inhales deeply, then nods to herself. Mentally, I thank Katarina, who allowed me to bathe before coming. I scrubbed both myself and my dress with lye soap; the mild yet caustic scent still lingers about my person, reminding me of the nun's insistence that cleanliness went hand in hand with godliness. I could use all the Almighty's help now, any sign of a future brightening for Freddie and I would be welcome.

I stand in silence like a human mannequin while she tugs on the fabric, inverting the cuffs, the hem, and the seams of my garment, appraising. She stands back suddenly, little finger curling over her closed lips.

Then she nods. "The hours are eight in the morning until seven at night. One hour for lunch, which must be taken outside the workroom. My workshop manager will sort out your wages when we have assessed your speed and suitability at the end of the week. Prove yourself and you can stay. Fail and you leave immediately with no reference. You can start tomorrow. Bring your references and papers."

I wasn't expecting the hours to be so long, or to be so confined to the workroom an hour's walk away from Freddie. I gasp, surprised at the speed of her decision. Perhaps Katarina can write me a reference? "Thank you, I won't let you down."

She arches an eyebrow. "I have nothing against Germans, but these days…"

My guttural accent despite my reasonable fluency hadn't entirely concealed my identity, but there was a bigger problem and we both knew it. "I'm Austrian by birth," I sputter out. That I was Jewish I kept to myself. "But my parents died young and I… I was raised by a guardian in Germany, then the nuns back over the border near where I was born took me in."

She pauses, one hand toying with the string of pearls around her neck, then glances back at me. Her eyes glitter and she blinks away a shadow to her gaze. "I trust my terms are agreeable."

I swallow as she stares at me hard, as if she knows I haven't told her the whole truth. How can I tell her my only papers note I'm Jewish? But then, this isn't a Nazi state, surely it would be acceptable to admit it? But, before I can say anything else, she spins on her high heel and stalks towards the exit. My throat makes a little squeaky noise as I bite my tongue.

"Tomorrow then," she says as she pulls the door open. "Your family would have been proud of you, no?"

Torn between delight and terror, I think of my only remaining relative and the implications of starting tomorrow. "Mademoiselle!" I blurt. "I have to make some arrangements for my son."

"Your son?"

"A school, and someone to mind him while I am at work. I've only just arrived in Paris and..."

Her thin eyebrows draw together.

"A day or two, please. I can start on Monday?"

Her lips pinch, then she nods curtly. *"Ca va."*

And it's as simple and as complicated as that. I have a job! For Chanel!

New Day, New Life.

The stone cellar floor is unyielding but we've slept on worse. At least it's warmed by our bodies, huddled together under a thin blanket and our coats. Finally, weak sunshine brightens the gloom, hazy through the dusty panes of the slim door and I can stop pretending to sleep.

"Time for me to get up, little one," I murmur into Freddie's head, nestled into my shoulder. "Maman must go to work."

Just the thought of where I will be working adds a spring to my step as I hurtle around the cellar, pulling my knapsack out from its hiding place in the coal chute and stuffing my flannel night-shirt inside. I dress in the same semi-smart clothes I wore when I interviewed for the position, wishing I had any other choice of outfit. Kat's clothes, if she would deign to lend them to me, would swamp my slight figure. While I tidy away any remnants of our existence, poor Freddie sits on the blanket, sleepy-eyed but watching me with a baleful stare.

"Quickly, outside to wash your face, young man."

He winces at the prospect but follows me out into the crisp dawn air. We shiver as I have to break a thin film of ice from the small fountain in Katarina's courtyard, then splash our faces and rub them clean with a rag.

A noise from the kitchen startles us both, the rattle of blinds being drawn very obviously. I spot Kat's face, moonlike in the darkness of the room, peering out at us, and I wave. She unbolts the back door and beckons Freddie in. With a smile of gratitude to her, I give my boy the briefest of hugs, drop a kiss on top of his head and whisper, "Be good for Tante Katarina."

He whimpers, clinging to my threadbare coat. I blink away the tears which blur my focus; leaving him wrenches my heart, but I have no choice. Without money, we have no chance of a future, and not arriving for my dream job before I've even started is unthinkable. But... his expression...

"Sewing a future for you both, Maus. Remember that," Kat mutters under her breath. "Hurry, before Francine gets here. I will take good care of him, don't worry."

I push my lips together, surprised by her unexpected understanding of the situation, yet reassured.

Peeling his hands from the fabric, I kiss his knuckles and say in a choked voice, "Go and see what's for breakfast."

The mere mention of food, of course, persuades my son to switch allegiance.

"Good luck," she says, and I hasten to the little gate at the end of the courtyard. I dare not look back in case the sight of my boy, who I have never left for more than a few hours before, changes my mind.

The wide pavements with their cafes grind and splutter into life during my walk across the city. Quiet avenues fill with bicycles and berets as people wake up and head to work, some grabbing a meal on the way. I can't afford to be tempted into a quick stop for repast. Instead, I make do by inhaling the warming chicory smell of their coffee and freshly baked pastries as I pass, and imagine that one day, I too could savour such delights. I would forgo the newspaper as I sit, but revel in the chilly air wrapped in a warm coat, and fill my gaze with the street fashion parade. But today, I stride on.

As I pass several other couture houses en route, my anticipation grows with every step. I will never tire, I'm convinced, of this city; my joy at being amongst the great fashion houses of France fills me with energy. Arriving too early on Rue Cambon, I stamp my feet to stay warm as I examine the display of hats, dresses and suits Chanel has placed in the windows to entice her clientele. The frontage of number 31 is a white beacon; above it, the arched windows with their balconettes like inviting eyes. Except, it's closed.

I spin around on the narrow pavement, glancing up towards the red and yellow brick Ritz hotel, further up the road, then opposite, to a plainer, more austere building. My chest tightens as I read the carved letters above the doors, announcing it's a school for boys. I confess, all thoughts of Freddie left me while I marvelled at my surroundings and relative freedom. The windows have bars on, and I wonder if it is to keep the boys in, or protect them against the world? Will he stay quiet like I'd told him? Katarina's patience and her plans for Francine's cleaning the upstairs all day could only last for so long, and only until I find suitable education for him.

A gaggle of girls, with an older woman waddling ahead of them like a mother goose, titter and gossip as they walk down the street. They all wear hats, which makes me feel dowdy in my simple cotton headscarf and they don't give me a second look as I loiter outside number 29, at the door which says simply, Employees. The stout leader drops her cigarette butt by my shoes, then casts a beady eye up and down my clothes, much as Chanel did. Her black hat is a particularly fine felt, brushed and spotless with a wide swooping brim.

She barks, "New starter?"

"Hannah Edelstein." My name is what it is; I'll have to produce my papers anyway. I jut my chin out. "Seamstress, from Austria." Mitigate the pain somewhat, I hope, by eliciting some sympathy.

The woman's jaw clenches as she produces a key and proceeds to unlock the premises. "Madame Du Bois, deputy millinery work-shop manager. I work under Madame Manon, Chief Seamstress. I'll have to check if you are assigned to this workshop or one of the others."

As she pushes open the door, her brood file in. Their twitter is quickly deadened by the rolls of fabric hanging along the corridor and thick rugs embossed with the signature linked C's. I follow Madame Du Bois inside and copy her as she removes her hat and coat, storing them on a row of hooks. The windowless hall is heavy with the scent of smoke and perfume, but the floorboards gleam with polish underneath the mats.

More and more women arrive as we traipse upstairs. My heart pounds as I'm led through a series of halls and stairs, towards the rear of the building and into a workroom. The space is crammed with wide cutting tables, the walls lined with Singer sewing ma-chines. Massive fabric rolls are propped vertically against the wall at the back, bold stripes of colour kept as far away from the floor to ceiling windows as possible.

Madame Du Bois weaves her way through the tables and stools, tutting as she pushes them under the surfaces, closing open scissors and replacing them in wooden pots. My smile lifts in kinship with her sense of order. I cannot abide a messy work area myself; clutter distracts me from a design.

We reach a tiny office, bursting with filing cabinets and a small desk. There's barely room to hang a dress, but seems more spacious than it is because of the huge window overlooking the workroom. Women are already settling at their work stations, banging drawers and switching on machines. She closes the door behind us, narrows her eyes and folds her arms. "I suppose you're a refugee? Without the proper paperwork, there'll be no job, no matter who got you through the door."

Starting Work

To be labelled with refugee status would require me to register with the authorities, Katarina had already told me as much. If my papers are out of order, or I haven't any at all, I would be deported. I stare at my tatty shoes and swallow hard. "Not a refugee, as such. I have family here." Partly true.

"There should be no issue then." She lifts an enquiring eyebrow. "Permit to work? Passport?"

"I... I brought my passport with me, and my permit is... in the works. Bureaucracy, eh?" I shrug and flash what I hope appears a confident smile. I didn't want pity or her judgement, only the opportunity to prove myself and earn a living on merit.

Her lips tighten briefly and I'm not sure if she believes me. She reaches into a cupboard and pulls out a piece of paper, slapping it on the desk as if it's proof of my guilt. My stomach roils as she passes me a pencil. "They'd better be, or everyone here will know who's to blame when the authorities turn this place over for evidence of wrong doing."

It's not just the formality of stating who I am, and where I work now, which concerns me, when I have spent the last six years hiding, but it's also clear: she means for me to complete the form myself. If I sign stating I have a right to work here when I don't, Chanel herself will come under inspection for failing to check properly.

My thumping heartbeat matches the now active beat of mechanical needles, incessant and quick. But I take the pencil with trembling fingers and don't meet her eyes.

"Let's hope your hands are steadier with fabric in them. Fill in what you can, while I find out where you are supposed to work." She shuts the door behind herself, as if that will close out the thud-thud-thud of sewing machines or stop the alarm bells ringing in my head.

My hand steadies as I block print my name. The rows of letters jump around on the page, but I can understand the next issue: the line item after my name asks for my religion.

I write as clearly as I can, Catholic, for wasn't I educated by nuns? Even Chanel assumed, and I must allow one more little lie to trouble my conscience if it means survival. How bad can it get, anyway? This is France, a free land. A Catholic land.

The form is only half completed when Madame Du Bois returns with another lady, tall and thin with a stern face. "This is Madame Moreau. She'll take you to your workstation."

I smile, but all I receive in return is a stony, silent glare.

Madame Du Bois glances at my form, "Finish that in your own time. I've work to get on with."

Nodding meekly, I stand, roll the form up and follow Madame Moreau out. The workroom is noisy with seamstresses chatting as they lay out fabric and thread machines. As we walk through them, I catch their conversation.

"Terrible really, all those shops."

"They deserve it, leeches."

I wonder what they are talking about, but daren't stop to ask. Madame Moreau leads me through yet more corridors, downstairs and then more stairs until I'm sure we must have reached the basement of one of the buildings. I'm completely disorientated, but, when she opens the door to a tiny room and pulls on the light cord, my mind calms. The sewing machine at the end of a long table is all I need to prove my worth.

She bustles about the room with brisk efficiency, pulling out a pattern and some heavy tweed, and a tray with needles, scissors and pins in. "You have an hour. Lining fabrics are in the cupboard."

I meet her hard eyes and know I will move heaven and earth to pass her test. "Certainly. See you then."

As soon as she shuts me in, I pull out the wool, twisting it this way and that to get a feel for the weight of it, then I shake the pattern paper out so I can examine the components of the jacket. I make some adjustments, positioning the sections to cut so the fabric's subtle design will meet nicely, drape stylishly and compliment the wearer. As she hadn't specified which size to make, I choose my measurements, simply because I know my diminutive figure well enough to be able to cut confidently and fast. The light bulb makes a low humming noise as it warms up and I pick up the scissors.

Once I have pieces cut out, I neaten the table by sweeping the loose threads to the corner and think about the lining fabric. Deciding on a contrasting light colour to the dark tan-based tweed, I snip quickly, then pin the pieces together, ready to sew.

The cast iron sewing machine is older than the ones I saw in the workrooms, but in perfect working order. No need for instruction - my luck is in, as it's the same Kohler model as the one at the convent. Within minutes, my foot pounds the treadle and the straight seams whizz through. I lose all track of time, my fingers working furiously to complete as much of the garment as possible. There's no over-lock function or foot on this machine, and no specifications on the pattern for how to do the buttonholes, so to make them look neat, I fashion them into a feature using the lining material and hope.

I'm just pulling on the jacket to position the buttons around my chest and checking the sleeve length when Madame Moreau returns. She freezes in the doorway, her mouth falling slightly open.

"I'm sorry," I say, holding the lapels of the jacket. "I couldn't find any suitable buttons, but it won't take me long to sew some on, then I think it's about done."

She steps almost hesitantly into the room and gestures for me to remove the jacket. Her lips press together as systematically she tugs on every seam and inspects each join, mute and utterly focused. I'm desperate to win her respect so I stay silent while she yanks my hard work. Her expression gives away nothing. Then, holding the jacket's collar between slim fingertips as if it's a filthy rag she just picked off the floor, she says, "Follow me."

Another workroom, this time up in the attics. Madame points to a vacant workbench right in the middle. "Make it again," she orders me. "In the peach linen." Her head jerks towards a mannequin in the corner, which wears the design; behind it, a long roll of gorgeous soft fabric is propped against the wall. "Buttons and accessories are added by the artisans after."

As I go over to the roll, she strides across the floor to another seamstress and flings my jacket down on her table. The workroom falls silent. "This," she hisses, "is how it should be done. In an hour, too." She wheels about on a heel and announces, "This example shows all of you. It can be done and it should be."

My cheeks flush at her backhanded praise, and I quickly focus on the beautiful, embossed needle cover of the shiny Singer 201 in front of me. I can almost feel the baleful stares hit the back of my head like rocks, and my heart sinks. Although I haven't come here to make friends, it would have been nice to have made some. Now, I'm the ugly duckling who's shown them up.

The women don't stay silent for long. As soon as Madame Moreau's gone, their conversation resumes. I lift the bolt closer to the cutting table and listen in.

"Five times the rat shot Vom Rath, I read. Right on the steps of the German Embassy here," a brunette in her forties says.

With a jolt, I realise they are discussing the assassination I noticed in Louisa's newspaper, days ago.

Next to her, a younger bottle blonde simpers, "Just vile, how dare he! They should shoot him for it. I know the Jew was only a teenager, and a refugee, but still... too bold."

The lady sitting nearest me shoots me a conspiratorial glance before turning back to the room. "They should all just go back to where they came from."

The brunette sighs theatrically. "I suppose we should be grateful the German's didn't cross the border and smash up the Jewish shops here in retaliation." She gives a cold laugh. "That's what they do to Jews, isn't it?"

My heart races, pushing ice cold dread through my arms. I have witnessed such actions, a 'pogrom' they called it afterwards. The terror and violence of that day manifests in my almost instant flinch. And, they clearly have no idea how difficult it is to get into France. Thankfully.

Blonde girl pouts her lips, although the sympathy in her voice doesn't quite ring true. "I read they target schools and hospitals, though, across Germany, Austria and the Sudetenland. Where's the decency?" She shakes her head and tuts.

"Still, there'll be a lot less of *them* now," snide brunette says darkly, then sniggers as she stabs a needle into the sleeve she's sewing.

Suddenly, I'm fuming. I turn to the fabric and deliberately thud it down on the table. Everything in me wants to scream, "If you knew what it was like there, you wouldn't be so fast to judge," but I hold my tongue. I cannot afford for them to make any more assumptions about me.

Madame Moreau walks back in, clapping her hands, making us all jump a little. "I thought I made myself clear. Perhaps if your needles were as sharp and quick as your tongues, we'd fulfil today's quota."

I let out the breath I'd unconsciously been holding, watching as the seamstresses' heads bend to their work. My hands shake a little as I palm the scissors to begin cutting. Katarina was right, it seems the anti-Semitic views held by some French people are almost as bad as the Nazis. They can never know I'm Jewish, I vow. Not if I have a hope of keeping my job here.

Chanel and Churchill

▬▬▬▬▬▬▬▬▬▬▬▬▬▬▬▬▬▬▬▬▬▬▬▬▬▬▬▬▬▬▬▬▬▬▬▬▬▬

Eventually, as the cold winter thaws into the Spring of 1939, the workshop women forget I'm the foreign interloper in their desire to find out quite how I am so quick to sew. Willingly, I demonstrate the techniques I use, from a co-ordinated pause in power with a spin of the fabric around the needle, to how to examine the fabric before laying the pattern on it. I ache to be given free rein to share with them, or anyone, designs of my own, but, after the April show we swing straight into preparations for the August showcase. Tempers fray with the increasing heat. Chanel herself, when she is in Paris, drifts in and out of the workrooms several times a day, making sure her standards are being met. She barely gives me a second look. Although I bring in my sketches with every intention of showing her them, it never seems the right moment.

There's no-one here, aside from Kat, who I would call a friend, but gradually the seamstresses become less antagonistic. Everyone shares a greater fear, although we avoid talking about the shadow of Hitler-led threat, inching closer. To acknowledge it may cause us all to unravel, like pulling on a poorly knotted thread. My luck holds as the managers are too preoccupied to ask for my missing work permit.

Weeks turn into months, and, despite Kat's initial hesitation, our living situation remains stable. She was correct - there's hardly any affordable flats to rent on my paltry wage.

"I told you it wouldn't be easy," she sniffs, on an almost weekly basis. "I suppose another week here won't hurt. At least the cellar is cool on the hot, close summer nights."

I've come to realise people on the brink, fearful of change, betray their hidden anxiety for the future in the smallest details. What appears to matter most to the seamstresses are mundane preoccupations, like the ever-decreasing availability of imported foods, or who was seen wearing what at the latest party. Such concerns serve to avoid talking about what really matters, and are picked apart and deliberated upon for hours. Perhaps it is because we work in the world of fashion that every nuance is assigned a meaning, every thread or change of skirt shape can be tugged upon as if it will reveal something deeper. Paris is desperate to show it isn't affected by what's going on with neighbouring countries, with near constant parties and events throughout the spring and summer. Great for business, I suppose. Life continues much as it apparently usually did, meanwhile, we seamstresses escape what is going on 'out there' with fashion, frivolities and gossip.

As the spring turns to summer, I feel like I am several entirely separate people - by day and at work, I'm a quietly confident Austrian Catholic who doesn't gossip and out-performs even the most experienced seamstresses at Chanel.

My other persona exists in almost complete darkness. Lurking in the shadows and sleeping in a cellar, I'm the Jewish mouse-mother who lives in fear of someone asking for her family's papers. Freddie and I spend weekends and nights quietly in the cellar, pretending not to exist at all. I try my hardest to teach him writing and numbers, at nights and weekends, while Katarina has friends over for weekend wine. She diligently attends the local Catholic church, being sure to be noticed there, as if her prayers will ward off any unwelcome questions. She has become obsessive about the news and devours every newspaper she can buy, on the pretext of needing the daily challenge of the crossword. Our relationship revolves around arrangements for Freddie, and food. Keeping our presence in the house is a constant drain on her resources, although I give her most of my wages as rent. We remain a trial of her patience, a bind to her liberty.

Yet, my silent son has wormed his way into our hostesses heart, and, while I work, he's allowed to spend time with her whenever Francine, the housemaid, isn't there. Katarina cut down her hours, so she only comes to clean when he can be left alone downstairs napping, writing in the diary I gave him for his birthday or drawing with his crayons. I think she likes having someone to talk to, even if he doesn't talk back.

Each Monday, after my dawn scuttle across the city, inside the workroom walls whatever's happening in the wider world doesn't matter to me. During the working week, I can easily leave the house only to return, unseen through the back yard gate, for supper. Freddie and Kat have discovered a mutual passion for taking things apart and putting them back together - an extension of his obsession with his camera. The wireless, a rescued sewing machine for me, and several household appliances have provided him with a foundation in engineering. His ever-growing bond with Kat is built upon French, as she is an excellent interpreter. Everything he hears – be it the radio or conversations - is in French, so that when he does talk, we hope he'll have absorbed enough to make sense of it. She is amazing, truly a more inventive teacher than I could ever imagine being, endlessly making games of the most mundane of tasks with him. In return, I give her most of my wages for our shelter and board, but I'm saving a little each week for a train set for Freddie for his birthday. It breaks my heart that here, he has no toys or friends of his own age. He cannot attend a school without papers.

It is a blistering July day when, mid-morning, I'm ordered to fetch some lace from an artisan a few streets away. Despite my protestations, Madame Moreau insists, "It's your turn. I can't see why you wouldn't want a nice walk on such a fine day."

Usually, I spend as little time as possible outside. It's not unusual, in these suspicious times, for people to be randomly stopped in the street by the police and their identification documents requested. In my logical mind, I've nothing to fear. There's no reason I shouldn't be in Paris, but past habits are hard to shake. All I have to rely upon to avoid being asked is a false sense of security from being dressed in innocuous but serviceable clothing, nothing which would draw the eye to me in either admiration or pity, or suggest I am anything other than an ordinary Parisienne.

Blinking as I emerge on Rue Cambon in bright sunlight, I turn in the direction of the Ritz Hotel, where Mademoiselle Chanel keeps a suite, as well as her apartment above the shop. Most mornings, as I'm usually the first to arrive, I nod to the regular doorman manning the rear door while I wait for the workshop to open. He always smiles gently back at me and tips his hat. We've never spoken, but he's one of the few people who notice me at all and there's a friendly twinkle to his eye which I find oddly reassuring in a fatherly sort of way.

Several *flic* – a slang word the French call the police - chat with some other men in uniform on the steps of the back door. Blocking the narrow street are two enormous black cars, only half pulled up onto the pavement, their engines running and pumping out grey smoke.

As I approach, the policemen straighten, toss their cigarettes away, and look alert. My shoulders stiffen, for surely it cannot be me they have noticed? The old doorman opens the glazed doors and out steps Chanel herself, arm in arm with a slightly smaller man, rotund and balding. She looks immaculate, as if she has just stepped out of the pages of Vogue or Bazaar. The man wears a well cut grey suit with a waistcoat despite the heat, but his face is obscured by the rim of a trilby. A driver gets out of the front car and opens the rear door in readiness.

I can't catch what the stout man says to make Chanel laugh, yet she does - a loud and genuine guffaw. He pats her on the hand as they uncouple their arms, and she leans in to kiss both his cheeks.

As he turns to get into the back of the car, I catch sight of his face. A sorrowful expression creases his jowls, and although he looks familiar, I can't place who it is.

He pauses, half in and half out of the seat and looks up at the Ritz building with longing in his eyes. Chanel gives him a sad little nod, as if to say goodbye, then she steps onto the pavement and walks towards the shop.

The sense that they have parted, perhaps forever, lingers in the air, but, I cannot be caught gawking. Presumably a desire for privacy is why they left at the rear of the Ritz rather than the much more ostentatious front on the Place Vendôme. My heart pounds while I walk as normally as I can along the road, as if I've seen nothing, but the policemen stare at Chanel as she struts down the road. As we pass on the pavement, I notice her face is streaked with tears, but she looks right through me.

When I round the corner, onto Bd Capucines and away from the policemen, my breath comes easier and my heartbeat slows. Why wouldn't Chanel and that man see each other again, I wonder, before reason hit. Despite the Munich Agreement, the lack of young men on the streets tells a different story to what's reported in the society pages. Few people now believe Hitler will stop his quest for European dominion. Least of all me.

DO DREAMS MAKE A SOUND AS THEY CRASH?

September 3rd, 1939

Germany broke the Munich agreement and invaded Poland two days ago, and the French are holding their breath. I'm not alone in doing my best to pretend nothing has changed, but the cafes and roads are quiet today. Eerily so. The occasional truck rolls past, sandbags precariously balanced on the back but there's hardly any other traffic. Expecting imminent attack, the government ordered the evacuation of children from cities, so I expect the train stations are busier than usual, but otherwise, Paris's usual volume is muted. Of course, Freddie isn't on any list to be evacuated because he isn't 'here'.

When I arrive on Rue Cambon, I conclude maybe people think the safest place to be is inside? Perhaps I too, should have stayed in the darkness of the cellar, waited it out, but I cannot. One cannot hold your breath in anticipation for too long, and Freddie and I have travelled too far, endured too much to allow this threat to take away any more time and freedom from us. I have to believe I am safe and that life can continue as usual, despite evidence to the contrary.

The peace in the neighbourhood doesn't last long. As 8a.m. approaches, other seamstresses arrive, dawdling down the street, delayed by late-running buses. Fluttering hands express their nerves but we have all turned up, expectant of a normal day, for what's happening in another country, far away, cannot affect fashion, surely? But I have witnessed the preparations - an entire economy boosted by invasion plans and I stay silent, praying I'm wrong.

Some of the other couture houses close by - Schiaparelli and Gucci - open their shop doors but no-one knows why nobody arrives to unlock our workplace. Our sanctuary.

While we wait for a manager, within the crowd of hundreds of us, there's a ripple of excitement. Three of the seamstresses are engaged. Of course, they've no rings to show off, but the couples have already discussed how quickly a wedding could be arranged. I try to smile and offer congratulations, but we all silently understand getting married is more a practical measure than an expectation of permanent wedded bliss. I'm happy for them, but a relationship with anyone is out of the question for me.

We stand for ages, spilling into the narrow street. Taxis beep to move us out of the way, en route to collect people queuing up outside the Ritz with their suitcases and trunks.

Then, without warning, Chanel strides out from the Ritz and pushes through the crowd, a lioness stalking a path through a jungle. She's followed by a tail of workshop managers, their faces pale beneath their hats.

We naturally part to allow her through and she pauses at the doorway to the main shop. With her head tilted, Chanel looks around the crowd of employees. A hush falls. Her lips push so tight together all that remains is a thin gash of bright red. Her expression softens and for a moment, I think she might be about to impart some inspirational wisdom, to see us through these tense times.

One of her assistants rushes to unlock the door, and as if a bolt of energy lights her up, she pivots on her heels and pushes the shop open defiantly.

There's an audible breath of relief as the workshop managers unlock our employee entrance and we filter off to our various stations. My fears are absorbed like black velvet, anxiety softened by the comforting touch and routine of bringing out fabric and laying it out neatly on the table. Someone switches on the wireless in the corner, and I tune out the monotonous voice reading the news. No-one gossips or chatters, as if the intensity of the machines thudding will punch away our unease.

My reverie is broken when I take my pinned pieces to my Singer, and realise the belt which powers it isn't rotating. I glance up, and everyone's heads are bowed. Something has shifted in the room. My ears tune in, and we listen to the grave announcement about the formation of a British War Cabinet, now that the deadline has passed for Germany to retreat. It's mid morning, and, as I look around the pale faces, my heart sinks.

France will have no choice but to also declare war now.

Somehow, we quietly soldier through lunchtime to make up for the lost hours of this morning, or perhaps it's because we don't want to miss the moment of confirmation. Most of us hand stitch, finishing off garments. Some sombrely comfort those whose husbands, fathers or brothers are already mobilised, or about to be. When the wireless confirms France has also joined the war, I don't think I am the only one to feel numb. Maybe even a sense of relief that a decision has been made.

Just as I overhear Juliette telling Madame Moreau she needs to leave early, to sort out her children who are being evacuated later today, Madame Du Bois bustles in and claps her hands for attention.

"You're all to gather in the shop. Now. Mademoiselle Chanel wishes to address everyone."

My throat constricts as we file out in silence. We all heard the radio, there's no need for a formal announcement of the war.

While we wait for everyone to pack into the space, I glance at the rows of garments on hangers, the wall filled with boxes of her signature perfume, No. 5, and the hats in their own special room to the side. It is all I can do not to cry when Chanel descends the mirrored staircase and stops in the middle, just like she does during her shows. Her hands grip the banister, knuckles white. Silence falls, and she draws in a deep breath as she looks out over the sea of our heads.

"Now is no time for fashion," she says, without a quiver to her voice. "Go home. The business is closed."

While everyone around me gasps, my legs weaken as if they will crumple beneath me.

"You can't do this," the ballsy brunette in my workroom shouts - I now know her name is Alexis, and she's one of many Russian émigré's Chanel has employed since the revolution there. "Mademoiselle, please. We have mouths to feed."

Chanel says nothing. Her face freezes in an expression of desolation as she turns her back on us and retreats up the staircase.

The women round on their managers, a rising flurry of questions about when they will be paid, what they should do now, filling the air. I do nothing. I simply stare at the spot where Chanel stood, feeling my heart unravel, along with my dreams. My chance to shine before Chanel is gone, possibly forever. It hasn't even been a year of working for her. Now what am I to do?

Refusing to Budge

For several months, much to my surprise, little changed in Paris. But everything changed for me after that afternoon traipse home. Chanel closed all her workshops and, in doing so, many other smaller businesses ceased to trade also. I remember thinking how incongruous it was that flowers should still brightly bloom in their boxes, shop tills ring with trade, and people exchange pleasantries on street corners, when I mourned my collapsed dreams so keenly I could hardly see. For once, I didn't care if I was stopped. Perhaps being deported was what I deserved for having deceived Chanel in the first place.

My mood was not improved returning to Katarina's to tell her the news, although the loss of income was more of a surprise to her than the declaration of war. Freddie's joy at seeing me home early only made me weep into his blond hair as I hugged him. He's too young to realise the devastation which losing my job and the impending war means.

All I could think of was that he'd been safer - freer - in the convent. Perhaps we should have just waited it out there? Hidden in a cupboard. Someone would've come eventually to visit. Maybe the Church could have found us another home. He could've lived a different life if it wasn't for me.

How selfish I'd been to bring him all this way, to pursue my own dreams.

Maybe someone like me should never dare to dream; a mouse will always be small.

Katarina looked on at us, like some sort of mute guardian angel, wringing her hands together. Then she closeted herself in her salon. Freddie and I clutched each other, listening to her sobs echoing down to the cellar.

Our living-in-limbo began in earnest that day, and my lack of hope added to my exhaustion. I took to sleeping most of the day, and pacing the dark yard at night when the neighbours wouldn't see me. Apart from tutoring Freddie, the only activity which lifted my gloom was tending the few plants and vegetables we grew in boxes on the patio. I cursed the frosty autumn nights for they might harm our precious sustenance. Nothing seems to happen, day after day. Kat's papers, overflowing with dire warnings and survival guides, little affect our worsening poverty and dwindling food supplics. The grim reality of our situation crept up on us like a snowdrift.

Then, just before Christmas, Freddie caught a chill. Perhaps it was the damp, cold cellar we lived in, or the lack of proper nutrition. We had no medicine and he took ages to shake off the fever.

He was still weak and sickly by the end of January when I overhear Kat upstairs shouting at Francine, "Stop asking about the blankets – I gave them away. I told you."

"Just seems like an odd thing to do," Francine replies, "when you're not even lighting the fires to keep the house warm for yourself. And, I think we have rats or something. I keep hearing noises through the floorboards."

Kat snorted, knowing full well Freddie's coughs weren't rodents. "Don't be silly, it's the wind whistling. When it's warmer, I'll get the cellar door fixed so we can use it again."

As soon as she left, with a limp and sleepy boy in my arms, I climb the cellar stairs. "Please Kat, Freddie won't get any better living in the cold, damp cellar. Can't he sleep in one of the bedrooms instead?"

"But Francine," she argues. "She'd see him, or hear him." Kat shakes her head as I stare at her.

Freddie whimpers, his breathing shallow and rattling in his thin chest. I ignore her and walk into the salon to lie him on the sofa. Then, I hurry into the kitchen to boil some water. The house has been virtually stripped of adornment. The rooms are chilly and the kitchen store cupboard bare – evidence of the financial desperation I brought to Katarina's door. The only appliance left to sell is the old sewing machine in the attic, and I just cannot bear to lose that too.

Kat stands in the doorway, clutching her hands together and looking wretched.

"Kat," I turn to her. "I can do all the cleaning and cooking, then you'd save on Francine's wages." My eyes brim with tears. "I'm sorry we are such a burden to you, but at least, I can contribute somehow."

She purses her lips and relents. "She'll no doubt bad mouth me but, you're right. And, I simply can't afford to keep her on."

Relief sweeps over me and I grasp her hands. "I promise we'll still stay inside though, no-one will know we're here."

And thus, we move out of the cellar at last! Although our existence as shadow creatures doesn't stop entirely, the ability to see sunlight through the windows helps all of our recovery through the spring months.

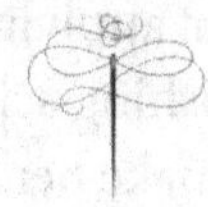

The last newspaper Kat bought was in May, with a big picture of Winston Churchill being elected Prime Minister of Britain on the cover. Seeing his face, recognising it from a year before, when Chanel had kissed him goodbye outside the Ritz, only reminds me of how quickly our circumstances had changed. How hopeful I had been, and how useless I am now. For all of our sakes, I resolved to make the best of our situation: one of us must find paid work, and soon. I learned quickly: resolve, by itself, isn't enough.

With the announcement of war, the French zeal for bureaucracy triples; above board businesses live in fear of spot inspections, heightening everyone's anxiety, especially mine. Although there are other couture houses which, according to Kat, haven't closed, touting myself for a job in them is impossible with an invalid passport and no work permit. The bureaucrats issuing the paperwork, which could certify me as a refugee and afford me some measure of protection, have virtually disappeared under their backlog. No work permit, no-one respectable would employ me. Even though

I offer, Kat refuses to ask her friends if there was any sewing they need doing, for fear of too many questions being asked.

In spite of ostensibly tightened border security, more and more refugees pour into the city from across Europe. Despite Kat's discreet enquiries, the black market costs of obtaining the correct permits, and thus be able to wander without fear of recrimination, remains extortionate and unreliable. Only she can leave the house in relative security. Her mood is always worse when she returns.

We don't speak about how Freddie and I simply don't 'exist'. Kat feeds three people with her coupon allowance for one, and prices soar weekly. She's never worked, believing she would always be looked after stopped her applying for any position. And, by her own admission, her finishing school education equipped her with few practical skills to make her a good candidate for manual labour. Completing crossword puzzles, throwing dinner parties and being well read are not talents in high demand, although she was always great at mending machines and anything electrical on the farm. More than a few of her society friends joined the '*Sections Sanitaires Automobiles*' to man ambulances, but, strangely, she never learned how to drive.

Since Kat isn't a war widow, her only income is a small stipend from her former father-in-law, who sends a monthly cheque from Switzerland. It doesn't stretch to black market goods. He wrote in February to say her brother-in-law, François, had been posted to defend the Maginot Line, which was evacuated after the Blitzkrieg on the border in May. He's not been heard from since. I feared the worst for François, even though I had never met the man.

The 'phoney war,' as the papers called it until then, ceased. France was officially invaded. The Nazi troops simply went around the fortifications and entered through Belgium and Luxembourg. Fighting happens hundreds of miles away, and we hear little about it.

3rd June, 1940

Katarina stops me at the bottom of the stairs, her cheeks are flushed as if she's been running. She took off her coat and began unpinning her hat. "The British have left, our neighbour with a radio just told me. Beaten back at Dunkirk. Abandoned us."

I stand there, motionless. Helpless. Shocked and yet also unsurprised.

She picks up a letter from the hall mat and stalks off to her salon. I find her in tears when I bring in our one daily cup of chicory coffee.

"What's wrong, Kat? Has someone died?"

She shakes her head. "Worse. I am to be evicted." She looks up at me, blue eyes rimmed red from crying. "Pascal's father never liked me, and now, he wants to sell the house."

"But it's your house? Didn't Pascal say so?"

"What he said and what the law dictates are entirely different. Women cannot own property. When Pascal died, his father claimed ownership as the nearest male relative. A drain on his resources, Monsieur Deveraux calls it. Calls me, really. And there's no cheque this month."

I place the cups down on the table beside her and sigh. "This situation cannot continue anyway. I don't care if the Nazis are coming." Which is a lie, of course. I glance around the room, working up the courage to speak plainly. One floor light and a small side table remain next to the sofa. The bureau, wall decorations, wireless, ornaments and trinkets - all sold. I've been eyeing up the curtains for weeks now in the hopes she can sell a dress I could make from them. Her own prized couture pieces have long since vanished.

I draw in a deep breath and spell out the harsh truth we've both been avoiding discussing. "Here and now, we've no money, no food, and there's nothing left to sell. I have to go and find work, no matter the risk. Any work." I pat her hand. "Maybe there's other seamstress jobs on the backstreets somewhere, where they won't ask too many questions."

"You can't." Her voice is flat. Hard. "It's too dangerous. You should leave Paris."

"So should you, according to your father-in-law."

She is silent for a moment, staring at the photograph of Pascal. "Well, I'm not going to. He'll have to come and physically throw me out."

I suppress my smile. "Good for you. But staying put doesn't solve all our problems. We're starving. We need money."

"No. There's no 'we'. Just take your son and leave."

"I won't. You need to survive, too. You housed us when we had nowhere to go. I'm not leaving you on your own now." I ignore her narrowed eyes and plough on. "I can't run any more, Kat. We're all staying in Paris, somehow." My heartbeat flutters; defying her is new territory to me, but we are no longer girls arguing about whether we should sneak out or play records any more.

She fans herself with the letter and glares at me, for the heat of the June day is rising as fast as our tempers.

I say firmly, "If my identity could be overlooked before, maybe it can again."

She snaps, "It's your identity which is the problem, and that's not going to change."

"Unless... it does."

BOMBS

A smile touches my lips before I say, "Katarina Devereaux, between us, we are perfectly employable."

Her eyebrows knit together. "Whatever do you mean?"

"Wait here," I say, dashing to the door, leaving her looking flabbergasted. I run upstairs, grab my passport, then into the hall to rummage through her handbag for her *Carte d'Identite*.

She's taking a sip from her cup when I return, nose wrinkling at the bitter taste of burned ground nuts.

"I don't know why I didn't think of it before." I open out the documents in front of her. "Look, all we have to do is swap."

"Swap what?"

My fingernail flicks up the edge of her photograph on the *Carte*. "If we cut out my photograph from my passport, glue it onto this card, then I become you. No-one can really check fingerprints in the street."

Kat takes the cardboard wallet and examines it. "The description under '*signalement*' won't match the photo. I'm taller than you, with blonde hair and blue eyes. You're small, have brown hair and eyes, and darker skin."

She shakes her head and hands it to me. "Put it back in my handbag. It should be me going out to work... only, I am so useless."

"You're not useless, only inexperienced." I'm not giving up this easily, and I have more experience with manual work. I swallow my innate fear of discovery and run my fingers through my dark mane. "You can cut it short and dye it blonde for me. I've barely seen the sun and my skin must be sallow enough to pass as 'light'. And, I'll wear massive sunglasses and say they made a mistake if they challenge me about the eyes. They won't, because my face will match the picture, only older."

"But you're still too short! Too young."

"That six looks very much like a zero," I say defiantly. "Or at least it will when I've curved the top over. Pass me a pen."

Kat splutters. "You're mad. Anyone living at this address wouldn't look so..."

As her eyes drift to the frayed hem on the better of my two outfits, I interject with, "Scruffy. I know. I'll make a dress which will look more befitting someone of this address. Stylish, to suit your name as well."

"You'll ruin what's left of your passport. You can't get another, you know. What about if you have to leave Paris? Jew or not, you still need something to prove who you are."

"It's useless anyway, if the Nazis catch me." I shrug. "You saw in 1933 how they treated us. It's only got worse, believe me. Nothing has changed. They invade a different country, but they'll impose the same opinion. Not that France is universally welcoming to Jews either. I might as well give my photo a second life and make it mean something."

"I don't see how you can be so blasé about this, Hannah!"

"There's no choice, don't you see?"

"And what am I supposed to do if I go out and someone asks me for my *Carte*?"

I snort. "Katarina, I have seen you flirt your way out of far too many situations to be concerned about that. Besides, the flic never check pretty ladies, stylishly dressed. Confidence is everything, and your ditzy memory is to blame, dear officer." I play at fawning like she used to with boys when we were silly girls. "How forgetful of me - bat those eyelashes - I just rushed out of the house without it."

Then I grin. "If they still insist you present yourself and our *Carte* at a police station, we swap back the photograph."

"You really are brazen, aren't you?" She smiles, because I'm telling the truth. Her beauty sways most men; it's mousy me who cannot help but look suspicious. "I thought the rebel in you had disappeared, along with your job."

I shake my head, a lump in my throat at the sudden sense of camaraderie which I worried had gone from our friendship of late, and stare at the curtains. "She's still there, I think, but now I have to disguise her differently."

Kat pops out to borrow some glue and bleach so we can 'adjust' the *Carte*, and me. An hour later, I'm in the attic and the cut up curtains are taking shape as a dress. A wail pierces my ears. It's followed by a distant boom. I sit bolt upright on the sewing stool, heart racing and palms instantly sweating. My foot freezes above the pedal of my machine as I listen to the unfamiliar sounds.

Freddie! Where is he? I'd left him drawing in the bedroom below, but just as I swivel around to run and find him, Kat calls up the stairs, "Hannah! Go to the cellar!"

"Where's Freddie?" I holler as I scramble down the ladder.

"We're going to the air raid shelter. Pompe Metro is the closest."

My mouth dries. I cannot go, and neither can Freddie. "He can't. No papers, remember?"

I hurry down the corridor, then clatter down the stairs. Freddie is holding Kat's hand, his little face bemused and pale like hers. Around his neck is the child's gas mask she got him, a Donald Duck she calls it. "What about the cellar here?"

Her eyes flash mine. "Not deep enough," Katarina blurts out. "The Metro isn't really either, but it's the best we have." She glances at Freddie. We both want the most protection for him. "I'll say he's my son."

She's a genius. Both are blonde haired and blue eyed, even if they aren't at all related by blood. "They won't check children, I'm sure. Most have left the city anyway."

The booms sound closer than they did, and the brief gap between them allows the brrr of planes to reach my ears. Freddie perks up at the noise, while I'm torn with indecision. He probably doesn't realise the rattling echo is the big guns which Katarina told me they had placed atop the higher buildings of the city, in readiness for a Luftwaffe attack.

"Go. Be safe," I urge. "I'll be fine here."

Flashing across dear Kat's face is a mixture of emotions - disbelief in what I say, sorrow at parting, and relief at being given permission to get to safety. She hastily looks at the tiles, her fingers shaking around the black case of our *Carte*.

Outside in the street, shouts to run for shelter reach our ears. I thrust the gas mask boxes at her. "Hurry!"

Then, the strangest thing happens as she opens the door. Carrying on the wind, children's voices lift in song.

Allons enfants de la Patrice

Le jour de gloire est arrivé!

It's the Marseillaise - the French National anthem! 'Arise, children of the Fatherland Our day of glory has arrived' - the words could not be a more perfect expression of their show of courage!

Kat pulls Freddie over the threshold, then glances back at me. His eyes are round, as if torn between leaving me, or the thrill of going outside, or perhaps he wants to see other children.

He hesitates but Kat starts to sing as well.

"*Contre nous de la tyrannies, l'étendard sanglant est leve...*" 'Against us the bloody flag of tyranny is raised; the bloody flag is raised.'

They don't look back as they march down the pavement. I close the door behind them, whispering the next lines to myself as I head to the cellar.

L'étendard sanglant est levé Entendez-vous dans les campagnes, mugir ces féroces soldats? Ils viennent jusque dans vos bras Égorger nos fils, nos compagnes!

'Do you hear, in the countryside, the roar of those ferocious soldiers? They're coming right into your arms To cut the throats of your sons, your comrades!'

A loud whine comes from overhead, prompting me to rush down to the cellar and curl up in the darkest corner, where Freddie and I used to sleep. By the time I stop shaking, the noise has disappeared.

Still, I wait, praying with my ears pricked for the klaxon to tell Paris the danger has passed.

But, the attack is not over, and within half an hour, the rattle of guns and droning pitch of propellers starts up again. The bombs drop closer this time, so close the glass panes on the cellar door shake. I hear the crash of chunks of walls hitting the ground. Unable to hold it back any longer and with the stubborn resistance of earlier dissipating, I let out a sob.

Freddie.

Katarina...

The tears spill hot from my eyes as my mind is consumed with worry for the only two people in my world who matter. Did they make it to safety in time? Perhaps they are dead on the street?

Despite the danger, I have to know what's happening out there. My legs ache with stiffness as I straighten, crawl from the covers and dare to peek through the glass door panes. Lifting my eyes to the sky, I offer up a prayer. All I can see is huge, swirling flocks of birds, but I smell the fires which must be raging somewhere through the cracks in the cellar door.

For a few minutes, I'm frozen by the dusty window. The June blue sky above, peppered by puffs of cloud, eventually calms my heartbeat, even though the booming, whirring, crashing sounds of invasion continues. The wind drives the noise away from where I'm standing. I cannot run now, and praying the relentless advance of war to cease has had no effect. From past experience of German efficiency, they will not stop until they have what they want.

As I breathe, accepting my fate because God has not answered my prayers, the sunlight catches a falling feather. The white purity of it stirs me, as it spins in the breeze then drifts up, destination unknown. This small symbol of peace will find safe harbour some-where, perhaps, and that gives me hope.

An urge to do something more than wait for my demise over-takes me and I clench my fists. If a bomb falls on me, on this house, at least my end will be swift. I hid before, when Pieter mowed down Sister Luisa and Mother Superior in front of our eyes. How quickly and irreverently death can be dispatched. I know, if it's your time, there's no warning that's going to make a difference. However much I hate the powerlessness of my position, I'm caught in the winds of change, just like everyone else. There's no point in trying to run. Instead, I must glide through this time, like the feather, until I - *we* - can rest somewhere safe.

So, I head upstairs, back to my machine and sew our best hope of avoiding a slow death by the hands of hunger.

EXODUS

Katarina returns from the Metro, jumpy with adrenaline and a delighted Freddie. For the first time in so long, he saw other children there. He still didn't speak, Kat told me, but his face has a flush of colour, missing since he'd been so ill at Christmas. I hope it isn't the thrill of danger which affected him so.

As a result of the enforced socialisation in the subterranean shelter, Kat informs me no-one's even thinking about hiring people. The war situation changes so swiftly, she begs me: wait it out. We'll muddle through some how as long as I stay inside.

The next time the air raid siren calls, while she and Freddie dart to the Metro for shelter, I ignore the drone of planes above and prepare for when I can emerge. I refuse to believe that life will not continue somehow. Someone will always pay for a maid, a servant, surely? Even a job in a factory would suffice.

In between finishing the curtain suit and rubbing bleach into my hair in readiness for a job hunt, my day is spent cleaning and tidying the house. After nearby streets were hit, ash from fires drifts in and covers every surface.

After three days, the intermittent droning of planes overhead, the clanging of fire trucks, and dashes to the Metro, stops. Hours after the last fly-past, Katarina spots notices, posted on municipal buildings, declaring Paris an 'Open City.'

We couldn't celebrate, our terror merely swapped from the fear of dying in our beds by a bomb hitting, to the unknown dread of what came next. Would the Nazis just walk into Paris? Would they go door to door and kill us all as enemies?

Katarina went out early the next morning, trying to buy some bread. She returns home quicker than usual, slamming the front door shut and calling up the stairs, "Close all the windows!"

Even at night, the temperature barely cools and closing the windows stops any through draft. Inside, the rooms fast become insufferable. "Why? It's boiling," I say.

"Just do it, Hannah."

We pelt around the house, but not before the whiff of gasoline catches in the back of my throat. Within minutes, we gather at the kitchen window, looking outside at the air, which has a visible black tinge as it billows over the yard walls.

"They set fire to all the oil and gasoline tanks," Katarina says, her voice thick with emotion. "So the Germans couldn't get their hands on it to feed their war."

My smile is one of pride - the defiant Parisian orchestrate a final, filthy shot at the advancing Nazis, despite our collective anxiety. Then, to our horror, a bird drops from the sky, then another, and another. I press Freddie's head into my stomach so he doesn't have to witness the smoke poisoning everything. But through the cracks, under the door, the toxic smoke also reminds me of the insidious nature of our new overlords. No closing of doors will be able to keep them away.

15th June 1940

The agony of indecision and fear is over-ridden by hunger. In the early hours of morning, while it's still dark enough for me to slip out of the yard unseen by any neighbours, I set out to find work. With Katarina's doctored *Carte* in my pocket, my bleached blonde hair hacked off into a gamine cut and the curtain dress rustling with respectability, I leave Hannah Edelstein behind. It's ironic that for all those childhood years of wishing I was more like Kat, neither of us could have foreseen me actually pretending to be her. I have whispered 'Madame Katarina Devereaux' over and over until it feels like a natural moniker to introduce myself as.

A quiet, alien world greets me. A few people walk about wearing their gas masks, as if that would counter the black smoke which lingers still, days later. Perhaps they wear them to hide behind, I wonder, as I drag in shallow breaths through Freddie's mustard silk scarf instead. My previous history, fear and anxiety, want me to hide too, but to pull the disguise of gentility off, I must be brazen. Before too many roadblocks could be set up, or whatever restrictions the invaders would put on us, I must find work. My family needs money. We need to eat.

As the morning brightens, a strange atmosphere develops on the boulevards. A preoccupation, as if we wait for the grey and black uniformed presence to appear. By midday, I notice people are leaving. There aren't many children because of the evacuation months ago, but adults, young and old, drag suitcases or heft rucksacks and cloth bags, as they close up their homes. Metro station's dark street mouths are crowded with travellers, hustling and jostling to escape The few cars left in the city are stuffed with treasured household items and furniture as they trundle along, hopeful of making it beyond the outskirts before they run out of petrol.

My feet ache from walking to couturier after couturier in Katarina's heels, and every artisan workshop and haberdasher I know of. All are closed for business or have no vacancies.

A painful knot of desperation and hunger grows in the pit of my stomach. Where are the brave optimists? Those who defiantly sang of rebellion? Life will go on. It has to. With each rejection, my concern increases and I, too, feel like abandoning my quest.

But I can't abandon Paris. Late afternoon, I find myself on Rue Cambon, as if my legs have borne me here of their own volition, to remind me of my crushed dreams. Chanel's shop sits in darkness, the mannequins in the window reaching white-gloved hands towards me in invitation. I cannot take their fingers in solidarity; the glass has black soot creeping from the corners. Before my mind can consider how long it would be before the display is entirely shrouded, I force my body to turn away.

Stiffly, I walk towards the Ritz. My favourite doorman has his back to me as he rubs the golden door handle. The windowpanes of his door sparkle, crystal clear. Inside, chandelier lights twinkle and make me smile. I pause, grateful for this moment of normality, when the doorman turns and catches sight of me.

He grins as his fingers drift up to his hat rim in the familiar gesture of acknowledgement which we exchanged every dawn for months. "Bit late, aren't you?" He chuckles and jerks his thumb towards the workshop entrance.

I look down. "Mademoiselle Chanel closed up shop."

"She's gone, you know," the doorman says. "Left a while ago. Must have known this was coming."

"All of Paris seems to be leaving."

"Including most of our staff," he chuckles. "We still have guests, but no-one to serve them."

My eyes flick to meet his. "I'm staying. I can work."

His expression softens as he looks me up and down. "That haircut of yours, your shoes... you look different now. As if you want to be someone else, if you don't mind me saying." His eyes narrow. "People only do that if they've something to hide, in my experience."

What he was really saying didn't escape me. "I'm trying to find a job, that's all. Any job which pays." I stare past him, through the door to the bright lights and I swallow. If I cannot sew, perhaps I can clean. "Do you know who I should ask for?"

"Monsieur or Madame Auzello run the day-to-day operations, or at least, they did until Monsieur got called up a few days ago. They left young Elmiger in charge. Being Swiss, he is suitably neutral for what may happen next."

He swings the door open and, with a sweep of his arm, invites me inside. I step into the cool, marbled corridor, then he touches my elbow. "This way to the management office, Mademoiselle...?"

His voice lifts in question.

"Madame Devereaux," I say, even though my mouth is dry with the lie. I must get used to it.

"If you say so," he responds. "I'll vouch for your reliability, but you'll need to explain what you can do. Convince Monsieur Elminger, not me."

The sides of his lips twitch up in that kindly fashion I remember.

"Thank you, Monsieur...?"

"Jaques, just Jaques," he replies.

Unwelcome Arrival

My interview is more of a confirmation of my immediate availability and willingness to do the dirty work of cleaning than the scrutiny and test required by Chanel. Monsieur Elminger tells me with a shake of his head, desperate times have hit the Ritz. He's down to only forty or so employees, from over four hundred, although, understandably, guest numbers are also diminished. "But, we must stay open. They will return, and my uncle, who owns the hotel, expects business as usual."

"I'm happy to do anything - cleaning, serving, sewing, whatever you need," I offer, and hope he doesn't ask about my previous work experience. "And I'm staying here in Paris, no matter what."

"But you are not, I think, originally from France. Why are you still here?" He looks at me with tired eyes.

"Those of us who were not born French," I meet his gaze as I take a calculated risk, "may find it hard to reach a safe harbour outside of Paris. I was Austrian," I admit, "many years ago. Then I married a Frenchman. I have chosen my side."

He nods, mind made up. "Speaking German will be an advantage. You can start tomorrow as a chambermaid, but you might have to double as a waitress until we find more staff," he replies, glancing at my proffered identity document. His stiff formality returns. "I'll submit the permit paperwork then, but with everything going on, who knows how long it will take? I need the position filled now. Thankfully, we don't need to wait for your husband's permission these days, Madame."

I twist together my naked fingers. One detail I hadn't worked out might trip me up, if he notices the absence of a wedding ring. I should have thought to ask Katarina for hers; thank goodness indeed the law had changed.

As if there's something peculiar about my delayed response, his eyebrow rises. "Your husband, is he serving?"

Better to keep as true to Katarina's life as possible. "I'm a widow," I mumble. "Since before all this."

He nods. "I hate to say it, but I think there will be many women in your situation soon. Report at six o'clock in the morning, for a double shift. Present yourself to the Housekeeper's office. I'll instruct one of the other chambermaids to have a set of uniforms ready."

"Thank you." Having a uniform also circumvents my lack of wardrobe choices, for which I am very grateful. "But a double shift? When will I finish?"

"Late," he admits, "but I'm sure there's a bed in one of the attic dormitories, if you would prefer to stay here. If you work after curfew, or do not wish to live alone," Monsieur says, somewhat stiffly and without meeting my eye. "You could reside here for a nominal rent which I will dock straight out of your wages. You need not fear, Madame, we have a strict approach to fraternisation with the ladies upstairs and the men - those still here at least - on a lower floor. Standards must be maintained, always."

"I'll report here tomorrow morning." I pocket Kat's *Carte* and stand. "Thank you for the opportunity."

As he holds the door open for me, his bright eyes run over my body, lingering on my hair, dress and shoes as I pass. It takes a conscious effort not to look back as I walk towards the exit, for fear I am again being judged.

During my brief visit to the Ritz, the streets of Paris have changed. It's almost imperceptible, but in the shifty looks between citizens, there's an edge of tension. Wrapping myself in a bubble of joy at finding employment, I ignore the people scurrying inside buildings and the distant rumble of engines, and hurry instead. The curfew will soon fall and anyone out on the streets will be stopped, although there are few policemen around to impose it.

The evening sunlight bathes the cream stone buildings with a comforting warmth. Unfortunately, it cannot ease the aching balls of my feet, unused to walking so far in heels! I'm so preoccupied with not visibly wincing with each step that I almost miss the warning signs until I glance along our boulevard. I stop short.

Outside Katarina's house, a black car is parked. On any other day, this might seem innocuous, but Paris has almost emptied of private vehicles; those I saw earlier were packed with people and luggage and heading out of the city. Our neighbours, diplomats according to Kat, left weeks ago.

This car is empty, and something about it seems alien.

My heart thumps with dread as I turn off the avenue and scuttle down the side alleyway, towards the back entrance to the yard. As I approach the gate, raised voices drift through the open salon windows.

"Unacceptable. Can't you go somewhere else?"

It's Katarina. Agitated and speaking in German.

A deep voice from our past sends tremors down my spine. "I thought you, of all people, would welcome us with open arms, dear cousin."

Pieter Weisz.

I freeze against the high wall, pressing my body into the bricks as if they will shield me. Of all the Nazis to arrive in Paris, why did it have to be him? Of course, he would come straight to his cousin's door, just like I had.

"How many?" Katarina asks.

"However many rooms you have. I'll requisition the entire house and oust you, if you object."

"That's what your plan is? Simply march in and take what you want?"

Pieter snorts. "That's what will happen, yes. So either you accommodate them willingly, feed and board men I can vouch for, or others - strangers - will take the rooms anyway. I'll take an official residence of my own, of course, but let me see the rooms now."

There's a pause and I let out the breath I'm holding. A pain stabs at my heart as I realise who's playing, perhaps sleeping, in those same bedrooms. Sweat dampens my palms. Would Freddie recognise the man who destroyed his childhood at the convent? Because he hasn't spoken since, I've not asked if he saw a face underneath the black-rimmed cap. How would I even have phrased the question?

Nevertheless, my son is in the same building as a killer!

My mind races as I plot how quickly I must run in, undiscovered, and rescue my poor boy, but Katarina jumps ahead of me. "I'll still need a bedroom for my son."

"Your son?"

"And, I lost our papers when we tried to leave."

Pieter snarls, "Like all the other rats on the road, you ran from us? Why? You are German and have nothing to fear."

There's a fraction of a pause before Kat says, "Do you think I want to be here? No. We got caught in the crowd at the station, and somehow, his papers and mine got dropped. Lost. It's the only reason we're back home now."

"You're proposing I fix your stupidity, I presume? Because of who I am."

"Yes. Pieter, you're a powerful man, and my cousin. If you can't help me, then I don't know who can."

My heart is in my mouth. Clever Kat. Flattery was always his weak point.

"My job isn't in administration, you know. These are not matters which the SS deal with."

"But you'll know someone who can help get us replacement papers quickly. You know me. You can certify who I am."

I close my eyes, picturing her charming her cousin into doing what she wants as she used to, back on the farm.

She cajoles him. "I can't take in German officers if I'm not legitimate, can I? That would get you in trouble for even suggesting it?"

Pieter growls, "If you had papers, would you try to leave again? I would make sure you didn't have a home to come back to."

"As long as you can vouch for the boarders, and they pay, why would my son and I need to leave?" She coos, "We are German, after all. Tell me, how is my uncle?"

"He'll be surprised to learn you bore a child without even telling us. I thought that half-dead, half Jewish wastrel husband of yours was incapable."

I hear her sharp intake of breath, then the sound of a slap. "My husband is dead, and he wasn't at all Jewish. That was his stepmother," she screeches. "There's no taint to my boy. None."

Then Katarina yelps in pain and I start. Violence and Pieter always went hand in hand. I should have expected nothing would have changed. My legs tense, ready to rush in and defend her, but then...

"How dare you!" Pieter says, in a cold, calculating voice. "You should be more grateful. Insolence won't be tolerated."

I wish I could see what's happening in her salon, but fear holds me still. He wouldn't shoot his own cousin, would he?

"Let go of my wrist, you insufferable bastard," Katarina says.

"Learn some respect then," Pieter snarls. "You have spare rooms, yes? I've already organised paying boarders. All good, respectable men, under my command. You should thank me for rescuing you from financial ruin."

I long to dart inside, to rescue Freddie and Katarina, but I'm torn. If Pieter sets eyes on me, then all our efforts to hide, to change who I am, will have been in vain. Freddie will no doubt give the game away by rushing into my arms if he sees me, and Kat has provided a plausible reason to keep him with her.

A bang on the front door echoes through the salon window and reaches my ears. My hands ball into shaking fists. Oh god, what now?

Pieter's voice is clipped and laced with sarcasm. "Your guests are here. Greet them, make up the beds then be a good *haus-frau*." He snorts. "I half expected to see that Jewess Hannah cowering here, but for once, I'm glad I'm wrong. There must be no stink of *Juden* what so ever. If I ever set eyes on her again..."

My stomach sinks, to him I will always be little Hannah Edelstein, Jew. I have grown up under his nose, but with his father Herr Weisz's protection. Above all else, Kat must keep my son safe and her house, even if it means living with the enemy. If I enter while Pieter remains, everything we've done to survive would be undone.

I cannot go inside. Cannot rescue them now. Perhaps not ever.

LEMONADE

The ache in my feet is nothing compared to the pain in my heart as I traipse away. Retracing my steps to the city centre, my cheeks streak with tears. Before I know it, I'm back at the Ritz.

Jaques' face is grey as he holds the door open for me. "Wipe your face and straighten up, young lady," he mutters, not even asking what has happened. His eyes absorb the slump of my shoulders and trembling bottom lip. He proffers a handkerchief. "Appearances are everything in this place."

In his words and tone, I hear echoes of my father, when I was a child running in with a grubby face after falling out of a tree I'd been warned not to climb. I long to fling myself into his arms, but dare not. I hardly know him after all. He pats my shoulder as I blow my nose in an unladylike fashion. "I'll see it's washed and returned to you," I whisper.

"Keep it," he says. "Ask Frank at the bar for how to find the women's dormitories."

I stiffen.

"No, no…" Jaques says with a chuckle. "Don't get the wrong idea about him. He's not… inclined, but he's a friend to… people like you."

I try my hardest not to frown, unsure about what he's inferring. "The homeless? Or the staff?"

"To those who need a fresh start." He pushes me gently through his door.

In the hallway, a woman draped in fur bursts into tears on Monsieur Elminger's shoulder. At her feet, chests and suitcases clutter the floor. He catches my eye and frowns as if I am witnessing something deeply personal.

"Some of the room allocations are being shuffled around," Jaques mutters, by way of explanation. "Not everyone understands why." He approaches the old lady, nudging me towards the bar. "Come, come, Madame Corrigan, I have a taxi on the way for you."

I know then who she is, and wonder where she will go. How strange it is to have something in common with someone so famous.

Jaques pats her hand as our manager shoots him a grateful look. "We'll see you again, in no time, I'm sure Madame," Elminger says before he slides away. In the absence of valets, Jaques has no choice but to pick up one of her suitcases as he leads her out.

"What'll it be this fine evening, Mademoiselle?" The barman's cheery voice greets me as I step over the threshold. The bar with its windows facing Rue Cambon is empty, and no doubt, in my stylish curtain dress, he's mistaken me for a much needed customer. "You look like you could use a little pick me up?"

Suppressing a smile, although the evicted old lady's face still haunts me, I say, "Perhaps when I've earned enough to pay you for it."

"Ah... well... let me see... I do have need of a guinea pig. A new cocktail I'm inventing, in readiness for our imminent arrivals. I still need a name for it... So what do you say?" He twirls a gleaming silver shaker then scoops some ice cubes in.

"I'm not much of a drinker," I reply. "The doorman, Jaques, told me someone called Frank could point me in the right direction for the staff quarters?"

"Indeed I can, absolutely. Famous Frank, some say. How about an old favourite? A Bee's Knees or Mimosa, both specialities of this fabulous hotel, and invented by yours truly." He presses his fingers to his chest and cocks his head, then he picks up a book from behind the bar and slaps it on the mahogany bar top.

'The Artistry of Mixing Drinks by Frank Meier' has been thumbed so many times the cover wrap is stained. The white edges are a smudged rainbow of grenadine and crème de menthe, speaking and smelling of more carefree days. Having never touched a drop of alcohol, and probably never would, I flick through the pages of recipes just to be polite.

It's been years since I'd even thought about cocktails, but the photographs and layout suggest the colourful concoctions would bring the party to any occasion. Herr Weisz used to employ master mixers at his lavish balls; I witnessed their effect on his guests by peering through the landing bannisters when I ought to have been in bed. In my head, I hear the strains of jazz music and laughter mingled with the divestment of sensibility, resulting in lewd behaviour the nuns definitely wouldn't have approved of. I glance around the empty bar, under the sparkling chandeliers I can almost see the ghosts of party-goers, sneaking glances at their own glamour in the mirrors. A world a mouse such as I would never be comfortable in.

Frank pours from various bottles into the mixer, puts the two halves together and shakes it like he's making music. He grins at my sad little smile, then sets the shaker down. "*Mais…*" he draws the 'but' out like a sigh. "A cocktail is not for everyone. Sometimes it feels too… celebratory?"

He peels the top half of the shaker open a crack and sniffs. Then coughs and blinks rapidly. "Perhaps I'll keep that one for later in the night. Of course, you seem too sensible for such silly concoctions. I can make you something else. On the house, this once. Just to keep my hands busy." His irrepressible cheeriness is contagious, even if his attempt to invite me to drown my sorrows falls short.

I glance down at my egg-shell blue dress; I'd felt so optimistic putting it on this morning, before my fragile existence fractured. Could I find the strength to hold myself together now?

"Well, anything to take away the dusty taste in my throat would be welcome. It's been a bit of a day." And I haven't eaten or drank at all.

"I have just the thing." He stretches behind him and pulls out a tall jug covered with a cloth. As he pours the cloudy liquid over a glass of ice, he says, "My own refresher," and winks. "Subverting the sour."

I sip it and immediately I'm transported to the sunny meadows of my childhood. It's lemonade, just like my mother used to press, both sweet and sour. My taste buds tingle despite the chill, so delicious I gulp it down like a greedy child until, distressingly, the glass is empty. The flush of both sugar and ice sends shivers down my arms, and he laughs as my lips pucker with the aftertaste.

"I'd say that's the lavender twist, but those were the last of the best lemons. The punch dies as they shrivel." He tilts his head and examines me. "I think you needed the sweetness most. More?"

My head spins as I nod. I cannot help but recall what my mother used to say, 'When life gives you lemons, make lemonade.' I repeat the phrase to him as best as I can translate it.

Frank's eyes twinkle as they meet mine. "Lemons and life, eh?" He slaps the bar. "Finish that, then, I'll show you upstairs."

New Residents

The moment I realise I've unwittingly jumped from frying pan into fire comes the very next morning. After a restless night in a strange bed, torn with pangs of regret for leaving Freddie with Katarina, I present myself at the Housekeeper's office as the sun streaks into the sky. With ruthless efficiency, a sturdy, stern-faced girl thrusts two sets of pressed uniform at me, then a list of rooms to clean. She doesn't meet my eyes as she mutters a warning about standards and room checks. My shift is twelve hours, during which I would usually be expected to service twelve or more rooms as a minimum, but there's so few of us, it's likely I'll have to clean more.

Minutes later, changed into a dark blue chambermaid's dress with a white collar and my hair hidden underneath a white lace cap, I feel both smart and innocuous. I load a trolley with sheets, towels and cleaning equipment. Happy to be useful and daydreaming about the food I can provide for my loved ones with the wages, I drag it down endless corridors while guests still slumber peacefully.

But, an hour later, before I've even finished one room, all staff - including chambermaids, servers, chefs, valets and even Jaques - are ordered into the canteen for an urgent meeting. Packed together, silence falls along with several tears as the radio informs us: Paris has officially fallen to the Reich.

Monsieur Elminger stands on a chair. He opens his statement with a joke: the Nazis who are about to arrive made reservations weeks ago, before they entered the city. Then, he lays out his plan for how the Ritz will now operate, and I realise he wasn't joking at all. The ornate palace side of the hotel, facing onto Place Vendôme, is now designated for senior Nazi officers only - by order of the Reich. Ordinary guests and residents, when they return, will be accommodated in the Rue Cambon side of the hotel. The staff - stretched as we are - must work wherever we are sent; no exceptions can be made for personal preference. Above all else, we shall host our 'guests' as the Ritz always has: with the utmost in professionalism, luxury, and with a personal touch. There'll be other changes in the near future, he acknowledges, to keep the Reich happy and the Ritz's reputation intact. The Imperial Suite, for example, the largest and most prestigious rooms we have, is to be re-fitted in readiness for Hermann Göring, with an extra large bath for his 'treatments'.

Elminger's face is carefully neutral as he reminds us, the few remaining staff, that the Ritz is a business, in private ownership. If we don't treat all of our guests, welcome or not, with the level of service expected of a luxury establishment, then our German overlords could simply requisition whatever they wanted. Some other hotels, he mutters darkly, closed their doors when the 'invasion' began, and suffered this fate. Le Hotel Meurice, he predicts, will never recover. As his final act, he turns the hands of the clock above the door to German time before wishing us *bon courage*. He doesn't look at our devastated faces as he hangs his head and leaves us to return to our duties.

Since there is no large central foyer for guests to be greeted in and Monsieur Elminger does not want to appear 'above' them on the Grand Staircase, with typical Swiss diplomacy he awaits their arrival on Place Vendôme. That afternoon, in the fourth floor bedroom I'm cleaning, I open the window a fraction. In the distance, orders in stilted French rasp through a megaphone, warning all of Paris to stay inside.

Below, on Place Vendôme, Elminger waits in front of the magnificent hotel façade. Long, black cars with little swastika flags on the bonnets sweep around the statue of Napoleon, into the square.

At that moment, I hate the General Manager. His calmness in allowing them into the hotel seems symbolic of the acceptance with which the French government had allowed them into Paris. I couldn't see much else once he and the officers moved inside. The noise of a pompous parade through the city gives me cause to sit on the bed and question if I can live, cheek by jowl, with the very men responsible for the madness. No matter how much their presence fills me with fear and a flicker of fiery anger, all a person like myself can do is watch.

I - we - have no choice, I come to understand, as I fiddle and faff with starchy bedsheets then give up. Monsieur Elminger's stoic message of that morning hits, and I crumple with sobs. For me, this 'take what you want' attitude is not a new tale. The only difference between here and what happened at the convent is whether blood would be spilled on these marbled floors. The artwork here is just as valuable, if not more so, but the attitude and ability to protect who and what we love are a world apart. Much as though I dislike the Ritz's plan, the logic of giving the invaders what they want before they take it seems a safer course of action. Would things have turned out differently if Sister Luisa hadn't resisted?

Looking out of the window again, Elminger greets officers with a handshake and an expressionless face. Paris, the authorities, even the staff here, have to paste acquiescence over their emotions and go back to work, however unjust.

That night, in a different uniform, I serve fillet of sole poached in German wine and asparagus with hollandaise sauce to a Nazi-packed dining room, without a whisper of rebellion or a spilled drink. A mouse's squeak cannot be heard over the drunken cheers of victory.

A week later, and my one comfort is that Pieter, who must have been part of the advance party, still isn't on the booking list at the reception desk. Perhaps he is not senior enough to warrant a room at the Ritz, but then, I've heard the officers due to reside here will mostly be Luftwaffe. Where the SS will go, I can only imagine, and it's a small relief it's not where I have to sleep. I can only assume he's gone to his assigned, official quarters,. As yet, I have not dared to return to Kat's to find out, nor have I had time.

My beloved family left behind on Bd de Beauséjour are constantly on my mind so, at the first chance I get, I write:

'Dearest Katarina and darling Freddie,

I hope you are both well? In the hopes that you are both keeping safe, please find enclosed a repayment for the curtains. I will earn more and send spare when I can, and write when I have more news. Miss you both so much. Remember, you are always in my heart.

Love, Maus'

I fold the Ritz letter-headed paper into quarters and pop it inside the plain envelope, together with my week's wages. As I scrawl Katarina's address on the envelope and pass it across the bar to Frank, he reads the name. Madame Devereaux. He slips it into his trouser pocket and asks, "A relative?"

"Sister in law," I say, explaining away our shared surname and looking down. Tears threaten behind my eyelids, but I swallow my pain. Should Pieter discover the note, I doubt he would even recall 'Kat and Maus' so my message is about as secret yet personal as I could get.

To fill the silence between us, I casually say, "Are you sure it's not too much trouble to have it dropped off?"

"I've a lad goes past there on an errand this evening. Now hurry along, I have to open the bar soon, my little edelweiss."

With so few members of staff, rumour about my Austrian heritage quickly reached him when someone heard me talking in German to an officer who was struggling with our French menu in the restaurant. Frank confessed to me a few days ago that we shared a common birthplace. It's a secret which bonds us, although now, his 'legal' name is as French as Kats – mine – and he has all but forgotten his homeland too. I dare not tell him the full truth, of course.

I hand over his black jacket. "All fixed, as promised."

He doesn't give the invisible stitching a second glance, just pulls it on and does up the buttons. "Thank you. Now, you'd best get on. Word is, the dragon lady is back, although she hasn't made her way in here yet to say hello. All this mess," he sighs, then overly dramatically brushes his sleeves and straightens his lapels in a mimic of Monsieur Elminger. "But, we can't have them complaining or I might find myself having to do my own patches next time, and then what would I look like?"

He shoo's me out with a little giggle, although his threat is no laughing matter. Of an evening, the bar has already become a cosmopolitan mix of reporters, ambassadors and out of uniform Germans. Frank does his best to keep it genial, but last night he tore his sleeve while tussling a drunken guest out. The combination of a well-stocked bar and the intoxication of their easy victory creates an avalanche of cleaning up for us all.

I scurry down the main corridor, the 'Hall of Dreams' which links the two halves of the hotel, feeling grateful for Frank's light-hearted approach to our new residents. It seems slightly rebellious, and that pleases me. A camaraderie builds among the staff as we are pushed to the limits in our desperate attempt to stay safely under the German's radar and avoid being singled out for attention. Frank is more blatant about mocking them when no-one else is watching, though.

The glamour of the Ritz stops beyond the public areas, a bit like Chanel's boutique with the workshops above her stylish and scented shop. Service corridors between kitchens and dining rooms, or winding through the older palace building part of the hotel, are grey and utilitarian, and smell of lye soap and stale food. My twin bedded dormitory in the attics is functional rather than homely, but spotless. I find the stark simplicity comforting, especially when I am drop dead tired from changing sheets, sweeping and scrubbing. The very lack of adornment soothes my soul as it separates me from the very opulence which our new masters revel in. The absence of children and their effects makes it easier for me to keep thoughts of Freddie at bay as well.

Reaching the discrete doorway to the servants' corridors of the Place de Vendôme side, it's instinctive to look over my shoulder before I pull open the door to slip unnoticed into the working hallways. My eye catches movement at the far end of the corridor, coming from the Rue Cambon half, and I freeze for a moment. Then I remember, I'm perfectly entitled to use this doorway - it's for the staff after all. We're supposed to be courteous to our guests as well as unobtrusive, so I bow my head in subservience, half in, half out of the door.

A man, dressed in a suit rather than a uniform, strides past me as if I'm invisible. As the sound of his heels retreats, I look up. I breathe a sigh of relief, before my heart skips a beat.

I catch his profile as he pauses to look through the window of one of the miniature shops in the Hall of Dreams. His tall, slim silhouette in the distance is someone I think I recognise. A man from my past, who knows who I am. And, if I'm right, his presence here inextricably binds him to my future safety.

A DRAGON AND A KAT

<hr>

It cannot be, surely. In, of all places, the Ritz? What on earth is the Baron – the man who took my virginity then left me pregnant – doing here? I do my best to steady myself with several deep breaths, but all the while, my instinct is to duck. To run.

I peer around the door and stare at his retreating back. If I am to be sure it is who I think it is, then I should run after him. Touch his arm and drag him around to acknowledge me: Hannah Edelstein. Make him face the consequences of his actions. Yet I dare not.

I cannot.

My feet bear me down the service corridor instead. I'm barely conscious of passing anyone else; the chatter and clatter of others fades into the background as I race up to my bedroom and throw myself onto my bed. Luckily, no-one else is there, so there is nobody to witness my collapse.

I curl into a ball, memories washing over me. The shame I felt. The degradation. A glimpse, possibly a mistaken one, of the man downstairs brings back every regret about the last time I rebelled against restrictions. The memory of his haughty profile - half in shadow, half lit by the modern bright lights of my sanctuary - releases a flood inside me which I have held in for years.

When I can no longer sob for myself, self pity turns to mourning and I cry for my Freddie, the beloved but unintended consequence of my interaction with that man. What am I to do now? Every which way I turn, there's danger. Everyone I love and everyone I fear are in the same city, the same place even, at the same time, and it's all just too much to bear.

On some level, I'm aware that shock has tipped me into a fugue, a sobbing and pitiful state. It takes the rattle of the doorknob to bring me to consciousness again. I glance through the skylight, to the sun high in the sky, beaming mercilessly down on me.

The door swings open and a voice I don't recognise says, "Lazing about when you should be working. What do you think this is, a hotel?"

I raise my head to see a middle-aged woman glaring at me. She's carrying a leather-bound notebook in one hand, the other fist placed firmly on her hip. Her nostrils flare as she huffs her annoyance, but bags under her eyes give away her strain.

"I'm sorry, I just...." I stutter out, floundering for a good excuse. "Needed a moment to gather myself. I'll get back to work now."

Honesty isn't usually the best policy in my experience, but I'm too distraught to think of anything better. A lone hiccup betrays my state somewhat.

Her lips purse. "It's understandable, if not acceptable, dear. These bastards are enough to get anyone down, but, there's no point in sitting up here snivelling. Life must go on, no matter how dark it seems right now." She smiles reassuringly. "I didn't mean to shock you. I just wasn't expecting anyone to be in here. You are?"

"Han... Katarina Devereaux. Chambermaid, waitress..." I sit upright and brush the wetness from my cheeks and hope she doesn't notice my slip.

Her nose twitches. "I'll have to have words with Elminger."

I nod, still not meeting her eyes as I stand, straighten my uniform and make for the door. "It won't happen again, Madame... I apologise, but I don't know who you are?"

"The co-Manager, dear. Madame Blanche Auzello. My husband - pray God he survives - and I manage the Ritz. I'm just reviewing what's changed in my absence... and what else needs to change."

My heart sinks as I realise this might be the dragon lady Frank referred to, although she seems... nice. Her French, albeit fluent and grammatically correct, suggests an American background. I bob a curtsy, then retract my step towards the door. "I'm sorry we met under these circumstances, Madame."

"I expect high standards from my employees." She sniffs and looks down her nose at me. "Especially new girls."

I glance at the small wardrobe and cross my fingers she won't turf me out immediately. Shirking my duties isn't in my character, even though hiding increasingly is.

"Well, what are you waiting for? Work! We don't pay you to sit around in the middle of the day. Of course, we can't pay you at all unless all your papers are in order."

Not every job provides a roof and meals; at all costs, I want to keep mine. "They will be - the war, you know." I swallow and head again for the door. "Delays everything."

She stares at me, hard. I'm reminded of Chanel's invasive examination of me, as if she needed to see into my soul and assess my worth, so I lift my head. Then I smile, because not only does the recollection of that day give me courage, but also, I recognise the couture suit Madame Auzello wears. "I used to work for Mademoiselle Chanel, as a seamstress," I say, pointing at her outfit and hoping to forge any kind of human connection. "And I always thought that skirt was one of her finest designs."

"Is that so? I shall bear you in mind, then, if I ever have need of someone to take in a dress. Being a chambermaid requires a different set of skills, timeliness and cleanliness, for example, as well as discretion." Madame Auzello's eyes narrow a fraction. "Best show me you have a talent for them as well."

I need no further encouragement.

As much as is possible, I keep to the service corridors of the hotel from then on. When in the public areas, my eyes dart around, searching in case that familiar figure reappears. While everyone else's nerves settle as the Nazis embed themselves, mine constantly jangle. My only solace and security is in the disguise of my uniform - no-one pays the servants a second glance. I wear it all waking hours to remain 'Maus' and top up my hair dye every few weeks.

As for what I might say if I see *him* again, I'm undecided. How on earth can I even begin to explain? Or should I even tell him?

I don't hear back from Kat or Freddie for weeks, and their welfare remains on my mind until, one afternoon, I'm working the Grill Room and spot Kat gliding in. My heart flutters. Her eyes sweep around as the Maître D' shows her to a table in the corner, a distance away from the other guests quietly sipping coffee. Most of the diners are off-duty officers, not in uniform, and a smattering of well-dressed older women. She isn't out of place in a stylish suit I have not seen before, but I can tell from the way she holds herself, she's on edge.

Unfortunately, she's not been seated in my section. "Swap tables with me," I ask an unfamiliar waiter, who holds his left arm somewhat awkwardly close to his chest. He's about my age, lanky with unruly dark curls which fall over his forehead. My tone is laced with panic, but I must make the most of the unexpected opportunity to talk to Kat.

"I'm supposed to..."

"Please. It's just... I know her," I argue before he can wriggle away and cause a fuss with management.

"She's in my area. My customer." He moves towards the table, so I stand in front of him. He jumps as if I've threatened him; the movement causes a white tea-towel draped over his arm to slip, revealing clenched fingers and a too-curled hand.

I say, "If she tips, I'll let you have it."

He tilts his head to one side, a startled look on his face as if I have said something offensive.

"Not because of your..." I gesture to his disability. Heat rises to my cheeks and I check myself. "I'm sure you're perfectly capable of serving... just for doing me the favour."

Our eyes meet for a second before he relents. "I suppose."

Before he can change his mind, I dash past, grabbing a menu on the way. Katarina glances up as I approach. "Good afternoon, Madame. Welcome to the Ritz."

She takes the folder and whispers, "Thank God you found me," as she pretends to peruse the menu.

A few officers in uniform enter, loudly guffawing at something. Her head jerks up. "I'm meeting someone." Her expression is hidden by the swooping brim of her hat, but her hands shake until she rests them on the table.

"Pieter?"

She shakes her head a fraction and I glimpse her lip curling. "No. One of my new house guests. We have arrangements to discuss."

"Is Freddie...."

"He's fine. Enrolled in a school. Pieter arranged it."

My mouth is dry. A school no doubt approved by the Germans. "Are you here for a meal or just a drink?" My voice lowers. "Can I see him?"

"Ah..."

"Please, I miss you both so much."

She looks at me beseechingly. "You don't understand. He's my son, now."

"I understand." My heart is breaking to even acknowledge the change in our circumstances, but I know it's a necessary cover for his safety. For mine. "I heard you arguing with Pieter, that day. I know you had to lodge Nazi officers in your house."

Katarina closes the menu with a snap, warning me of the proximity of the Maître D'. I pretend to straighten the tablecloth then clear away the superfluous settings. "Did you get new papers?"

She nods.

"So you're Madame....?"

"Weisz. Both Frederick and I."

I can't help it when the cutlery chinks loudly together in my hands. Her eyelids flare, warning me. "Pieter insisted."

"Does he live with you?" I fear my heart might thud out of my chest and land on the table.

"No, thank God. At a hotel befitting his rank."

"Well, he's not here," I say quickly. I would know. I check the guest list each dawn. "Freddie - he might recognise Pieter."

Her voice is so quiet I can barely hear it over the noise of the room. "He's not spoken, but just the sight of their uniforms.... He's a shadow, Maus."

The haunted look in her eyes tells me everything. I desperately want to reach over the table and grab her hand, tell her of my gratitude for providing for my son and protecting him as I cannot, but then, a handsome man with a blond moustache and a stiff bearing strides towards us.

Katarina pastes on a fake smile and raises her arm in a wave.

"There must be some way I can see you both," I insist, before our privacy is lost.

"We do love to visit the park - the Bois de Boulogne," she says lightly, as if she's recommending a holiday. Her white teeth flash as her smile broadens in greeting to the approaching man. "Especially on Sundays after church." She stands and offers him her cheeks. I step back to give them some room, my mind whirring.

"You are here already," he says in German as he pulls out a chair then beams at Katarina. "It's my pleasure to treat you after everything you have done for me."

She flushes.

White teeth flash and his eyes wrinkle at the corners. "Naughty girl. Have you ordered yet?"

"I was waiting until you arrived," she purrs back at him in German. "I've only been here a minute." She turns to me and says in French as if I have no idea about her flirtation. "We'll order in a moment. Bring us some water and a wine list for now, please."

It's as if I don't exist; her focus entirely switches back to the arrival. As I pivot away, my heart sings with hope. There's a chance I can see Freddie!

"I'll take it from here," the new waiter says when I collect a wine list. He snatches it from my hands. "I can't afford to get in trouble on my first day."

I glance at Kat, who's engrossed in conversation. She's steadfastly ignoring me and I recognise that single-minded focus of hers. Whatever she means to get from this man, an officer most likely, her message is clear. Stay away.

I lift an eyebrow. "Can't have that, now, can we...?"

"Marc."

I don't know him well enough to ask if he would eavesdrop on my behalf, but, since we share a desire to stay out of trouble, I'm somehow more at ease with him. For once, I'm not the lowest in the pecking order and it feels strange. "Katarina Devereaux."

"What a beautiful name," he says. His eyes meet mine, warm and a chocolate brown like mine, then he smiles shyly at me.

As I walk back to my area of the restaurant, it occurs to me that I've never had a male friend of similar age, or been around men much at all. The thought makes me slightly uncomfortable.

An all girls school, a convent, and then Chanel's workroom filled with seamstresses are the company I'm comfortable around. But, I remind myself as I clear some plates, the few men in my life have brought me nothing but heartache, with the exception of Frank and Jaques. As a sex, they are best avoided. This world is skewed enough in their favour, and I'll probably wreck what little stability I have if I go against what I know to be true.

DIVERSIONS

Time couldn't pass fast enough after seeing Katarina in the dining room. I went about my daily chores, uninterested in anything except marking off the hours until I could see Freddie. Thankfully, there's also been no sign of his father in the Ritz, so I tell myself I was mistaken, or that if I wasn't, he was just visiting. Why would he be here, anyway? He isn't - or wasn't - military. Perhaps I was mistaken.

Minutes scrubbing sinks drag into hours, and the days seemed twice as long as they ought to until finally, it's Sunday, and my half day off. Sunday, fun day. Freddie day.

But, before I can reach that happy moment when I will see my boy, further trials than time must be overcome. Practically dancing out of the door, I spot guards at one end of the street. My chest tightens as I hold my breath. Because I haven't left the Ritz in weeks, I was unaware of the checkpoints which seem to have sprung up. Even to leave Rue Cambon, I risk exposure. My fingers reach for Katarina's *Carte* in my pocket; I know I should test it out. It passed the Monsieur Elminger test, yet still, I hesitate on the hotel steps. My heart isn't yet brave enough, my mind ill-prepared for such a challenge.

But I cannot risk missing Freddie. I force my breath out and decide to go the other way, even though it's a diversion. The only bright side to my hour-long meander through the back streets is noticing the spotlights are back on in the windows of some of the haute couturiers, like Nina Ricci, Lelong and Balagencia. I daren't waste time gawking. Wherever I see a checkpoint ahead, I casually veer into a side street.

Wriggling through alleyways, I try to avoid the red and black swastikas hanging from windowsills, flag poles and roofs, but my route through to the 16th Arrondissement is littered with buildings the Nazis have claimed. There's no avoiding walking past the Gestapo Headquarters on Avenue Foch on my approach to the park. I understand then why Pieter was so keen on Katarina's perfectly situated house being used for his officers - proximity. It's a mercy the wide road is lined with leafy trees so I can walk on the other side in relative obscurity.

When I arrive at Bois de Boulogne, I'm drenched in sweat as the humidity rises with the sun. There's a huge task ahead of me too, because this is the second largest park in Paris, and I have no idea where to begin my search for Katarina and Freddie.

I lurk close to the entrance I know is nearest Katarina's boulevard. Two women on bicycles zoom past. I watch the street anxiously. Despite all my diversions to avoid checks, I'm still too early. Pacing, lingering, on the pavement, I notice hardly any men pass. It feels like the only Frenchmen left working are the elderly, the unwanted or disabled, like Marc, the waiter I inadvertently offended when I saw Kat. Her 'friend' hadn't left a good tip, and they haven't dined with us since. Then, I remember the spate of seamstresses getting married and wonder how many are widows already. The war, and any fighting, seems still so distant but I decide I'm too obvious waiting on the pavement. Slowly, I walk a loop around the quiet park, taking in the lower lake.

By my sixth lap of the gardens, I grumble to myself that Katarina could have given me a bit more of a clue. Name a feature, like the grottoes or waterfalls perhaps, to meet her by. In the absence of solid information about where to meet, I wander around for hours, entirely wasting my one morning off per fortnight in the hope of seeing my son. My shabby coat grows uncomfortably hot, but I daren't remove it. My Ritz-branded chambermaid uniform would mark me out as what I am now – a servant, far from her place of work and obviously lingering. I thought wearing it would save time as my shift starts straight after lunch and I didn't want to waste a minute with Freddie, but under the scorching sunlight, I regret my decision.

Have I missed them somehow? Could I have misunderstood the message?

The blistering humidity of late August clouds over just as the sun reaches its zenith, then dissolves into a monsoon. Blustering, spitting, the sudden downpour refuses to vacate the park. The church bells have long since stopped ringing, and anyone on the sodden pathways uses them only as a cut through to reach shelter, rather than for a pleasurable stroll. My mind darts to all manner of ominous conclusions about why they haven't appeared.

I keep dawdling along, hoping, but when my headscarf's edges are so wet they slap me around the cheeks like limp fish, I am forced to admit my presence here now borders on foolhardy. I should leave, I know, but that would mean acknowledging defeat.

Hearing the splash of footsteps behind me, I wheel around, heart pounding with expectation.

A pair of grey uniformed Nazis march purposefully towards me, puffing on cigarettes as the rain pours off the beaks of their caps. One looks at me with baleful, accusatory eyes as they approach and I freeze.

Breathe. Act as if you belong… the nun's advice runs through my mind like a mantra. Stand in their way and they will run you through.

Survive.

I force a small smile, step aside onto the sodden grass to allow them through, then nod politely. Acquiesce, even though my fists clench around Katarina's *Carte*.

One checks his watch, then strides past me as if I am roadkill, and I can breathe again.

My next thought is, What the hell am I doing? If I tarry here much longer, not only do I risk losing my job, but of course I'll be noticed. No-one in their right mind hangs around a park in this weather. I press my lips together and step in the opposite direction to the Nazis. I cannot give up on hope, but neither can I stay here all day.

I've half a mind to march to Katarina's house and demand to see Freddie, but, as I leave the gates, I reconsider. It's without a doubt a foolish idea. I've just dodged a confrontation, yet in my desperation to see my son, I'm considering entering into another one. One which puts him at risk.

I let out a sigh and trudge back towards the Ritz. Only thirteen days until the next Sunday.

A fortnight later, I try again. "Good morning," I say as I wave goodbye to Jaques, standing on the step outside the Rue Cambon entrance.

"Have a nice morning off," he replies, just as a car trundles to a stop. He hurries to open the door as I walk away. "Welcome back, Mademoiselle Chanel," he says, loudly.

My stride falters and I look over my shoulder to see my former employer's head, angled to peer up at the hotel. Jaques glances at me and flares his eyes.

Chanel snaps, "Those stupid soldiers sent me around here to enter! Imagine!" She huffs and peels herself out of the seat. "And then that blasted checkpoint. They didn't even know who I was!"

"I'm so sorry, Mademoiselle." Jaques helps her to stand. Chanel's slight frame looks almost brittle, with stick-thin arms poking from her three-quarter sleeves. In her late fifties, and although relatively unlined, her face appears more gaunt than my last sighting of her.

I hastily bend down and fiddle with my shoe strap so I can linger unobtrusively. Chanel was - is - an important, well known guest at the Ritz, as well as having her apartment above the shop. Perhaps she has returned to re-open, like the other couturiers? My heart skips a beat and a smile stretches across my cheeks. Can life return to normal? I wonder if I dare to re-introduce myself.

Her voice is shrill as she grumbles, "Is there anyone who can unload my luggage? This won't do you know, Jaques."

She sniffles as he opens the boot and starts to pull out suitcases. He stops, pulls out a handkerchief and hands it to her. She dabs at her cheeks and looks up towards the roof of the Ritz. "They said there might be a room in the gods. I suppose I'll manage, but really... I'll have to see if Blanche can put me in something better. Just until this rabble leave, then things can return to what they were."

A proud, famous woman, but now an ordinary, second class French citizen, like the rest of us. Perhaps it isn't the best time to ask for my job back.

"Well, everyone here will be delighted to have you safely home again. Familiar faces, especially with a name like yours, are always taken special care of here," Jaques says. He trots up and down the steps, piling her luggage close to the door.

My heart sinks as I twig the meaning of my friend's earlier eye-flaring caution. How did he know, or did he guess? The dear man must be the best secret keeper in Paris! If I want my dream job back, I've no choice but to address the name issue now and remind her of who I am, in the relative privacy of the quiet road.

"Mademoiselle Chanel," I say, turning around and injecting joy into my tone. "How wonderful to see you back in Paris!"

Her face creases with confusion, the hand clutching Jaques' handkerchief drops. Damp but alert eyes dart over me, as she searches for my name, my face, to place where she knows me from. "It's good to be back..."

I seize the opportunity to address my concern. "I'm Madame Devereaux now," I say, "I married into the family!"

Her smile shows her instant relief, and recognition.

I trill, "New name, new hair, new job," as if changing names happens all the time. To avoid looking at Jaques, whose smug expression screams 'I knew it,' I glance down as if I'm pained. "Sadly, my fortunes have not prospered since we last met at your workshop. I so miss sewing for you, but I'm grateful to have work at all, here at the Ritz. Do let me know if there is anything I can help you with during your stay. Repairs, errands..." I raise my head and meet her eyes. "Anything at all.... I know how you value loyalty, and you were so kind to me when I first arrived here from the convent. Those were simpler times..."

Her red painted lips curve up at my reminder of our shared heritage. "I will dear. I'm only stopping to see some old friends, but it's lovely to see you again." She turns to Jaques. "Save your back and send a youngster up with my luggage?"

There's a lightness in my step as I turn and walk towards the park. Chanel may not yet plan on opening her doors again, but when she does, I'll be ready.

Noose

....

Alternate Sundays, I wander the park, but Freddie and Katarina never arrive. Or, if they do, I miss them. No messages reach me, even though, using Frank's network of messenger boys, I send them the greater part of my weekly wages. I can only assume the money reaches them. I asked Marc to let me know if she dines if I'm not working, but neither Kat nor her officer friend have returned.

As the weeks turn into months, I learn to live with the near constant heartache of missing my son. It's a battle I have to keep to myself, but others, friends I have made here, suspect there is more to my sad eyes than the bitterness of having to serve our Nazi overlords with a dignified smile.

Every day, I distract myself by fulfilling my obligations and trying to stay unobtrusive. Gradually, enough staff return, or are recruited, for my hours as a waitress to reduce, and I take on more of the little sewing jobs which arise - fixing buttons and hems on our guests clothes, including officers uniforms. It's a far cry from what I love, and my hands shake as I stab at the military issue wool, but at least it's keep my fingers nimble and mind busy.

The war happens elsewhere, but for the small encroachments to our liberty chipping away at the new 'normal'. Cocooned, living and eating at the hotel protects us, to a degree, from the everyday realities of the Occupation, whilst we are simultaneously confronted by it - *them* - on a daily basis. For our guests on the Rue Cambon side of the hotel, ordinary people's experiences are cushioned by the luxuries they can afford, or the Germans buy favour by supplying their needs in return for company and entertainment, perhaps something more. Certainly, Frank is kept busy in the bar and with a growing clientele of French women eager to press themselves against a handsome, well-mannered Luftwaffe officer. Seeing them, drunk on bought-for-them cocktails and draped over the very men responsible for the unwelcome change in administration, sickens and shocks me. Not least because I worry for Katarina and about Freddie.

The noose which holds me at the Ritz tightens. Management 'takes care' of the administrative details for live-in staff, protecting us from having to worry about it all so we can continue to work efficiently. Monsieur Elminger's responsibilities have changed since the return of the Auzello's. Now, he controls our ration cards in exchange for three meals a day, but the soups are more watery than they were and meat is rarely on offer.

Towards the end of summer, food becomes a growing preoccupation for everyone. One day, I accuse Marc of stealing as I catch him cramming leftover bread from guest's plates into his pockets before he leaves for home. He's snappy as he explains what life is like outside of the hotel to me: every citizen not only had to register with local authorities, but then with their local butcher, baker and so on, to supply their ration quota. Each day, he points out, his elderly mother gets up early and scrambles to queue; specific items may only be bought on specific days and with the correct coupons. The Parisian must queue to collect their weekly stamps, and queue again to buy the goods at the right shop. Rations started with food and petrol, but soon extend to fabric, tobacco, coal, and even wine.

Prices, for the French, rocket, while the Reichsmark enjoys a buoyant rate of exchange. Despite this, the city is beginning to populate again; more people return home or, German tourists visit, believing Paris is safe and affluent. When all you hear on the radio or in the newspapers is German propaganda, it's easy to think everything is fine, but once you live here, when you take in your clothes so they fit your slimmer figure, or listen to a drunken German's boastful plans, it's a very different story.

By October, when the puppet French government in unoccupied Vichy introduced the '*Statut des Juifs*,' excluding Jews from working in the civil service, professional services, the military and the media, my fears France was to mirror the Germany I escaped came true. All Jews were ordered to present themselves at their local commissariat for a census. Then again, a few weeks later, to have 'Juif' stamped on their *Carte d'identité*.

"My mother and I wept all night afterwards," Marc admitted, the day after he'd had his card marked. We chat and help each other out when we are on the same shifts in the restaurant, but the insight he offers me is an intimacy which touches too close.

I hurried to serve a customer after that, my cheeks burning with shame, for living a lie. It is scant comfort to me that I still use Katarina's identity although, as time passes and who I was drifts further from my memory, it gets easier to pretend I am a Devereax.

In November, when all Jewish-owned businesses had to display a large poster screaming 'JÜDISCHES GESCHÄFT' or 'ENTREPRISE JUIVE' for all to see, Marc didn't turn up for days. I found out from one of the kitchen staff, he was demonstrating against the new restrictions. To help keep his job open for him, I covered his shifts and told the Auzellos he was too poorly to work. They were too preoccupied to question much further.

Marc returned, subdued and with a blackened eye and a gash above his eyebrow. "All I did was write on the posters how that family had served France in the Great War, how patriotic they were. Their livelihood shouldn't suffer because they also attend a synagogue on occasion. And now," he winces, "Monsieur Auzello has told me to stay in the kitchens, not wait tables anymore."

"You were lucky, this time," I say, as I press ice wrapped in a towel to his eye socket during a break. I want to tell him about the terror I felt when the SA smashed up Jewish-owned businesses years earlier, but I hold back. "It could have easily descended into a riot. You could have been arrested."

"I know. Mother doesn't want me to get involved."

"Mother's worry about their children, no matter their age."

He glances at me, dark-eyed through long black eyelashes. "Especially if they are an only child."

He refers to himself, I tell myself, for I've not mentioned anything about my Freddie. Fear clenches my chest thinking about my son - will he be scarred forever from growing up in the presence of those who hold bigoted views? Is he still too afraid to speak? I glance at Marc again, with growing respect. Who will speak for the silent, if not those who still have a voice?

As if he can read my mind, he mutters, "If we don't say something, who will?"

My heart is in my mouth, but I agree. "It's hardly the sort of thing we'd see in the newsreels at the cinema, is it? Unless it was showing the Nazis in a positive light." Little by little, as they did in Germany, the thin veneer of acceptable behaviour towards the Jewish race is polished with propaganda.

The scorn on his face suggests he has seen all too much of such shine. "This time last year, before the Occupation closed down the film industry here, I was apprenticed to a studio, you know. Now people like me can only dream of filming live action to show what's going on to the world." He blinks away tears.

The urge to do something brave, take a stand against these little oppressions as Marc does, stills my hand on the side of his face. I cannot reassure him that things will improve, for that would be a lie. I am - we are - powerless. Too small to stand up against the surging tide. And yet, if someone doesn't resist, the wave will drown us all.

"That cut should heal in a few days," I say, standing. "And maybe next time you go to the cinema, the film will provide some distraction, at least."

Two days before Christmas, I return some half finished bottles of wine to Frank's bar after another busy shift in the restaurant. Marc, unhappily demoted to a lowly pot-washer, balances a tray of cleaned cocktail glasses on his crooked arm as he follows me in.

Frank catches sight of us and growls, "Was that Emile Henniquin, Deputy Director of our fine Municipal Police in again tonight? He didn't dare show his face in here, I notice."

"Why?" I ask, trying to be neutral as Frank harrumphs and rubs at the bar top. A few weeks earlier, several students, some of whom ran 'messages' for Frank, had been detained after a peaceful demonstration on the anniversary of the end of the Great War. When chanting started, echoing de Gaulle's 'Vive La France' call, Nazi soldiers had charged them with bayonets and fired shots into the air before arresting over a hundred of them. Frank had seethed ever since, but I hoped with wallets loosened by Christmas cheer on the horizon, he might have calmed down. He shoves some bottles back into place then huffs.

"How about I finish up here?" Marc offers in a quiet voice.

"Yes," I add. "We can close up for you." I push the tray across the mahogany and glance around. A few customers are still talking quietly in the corner, their backs to us.

Frank's shoulders slump. "I'm nearly done. For tonight, at least. *Mais*…. I'll be glad to get past this day."

I swallow. A tingle of premonition runs down my spine as I recognise a bad news expression.

He continues in a low voice, "They executed a man earlier today, for resisting." His lips press together briefly as I lay my hand over his. "I knew him. Wouldn't have said boo to a goose before all this."

"I'm sorry. What was his name?"

"Jaques Bonsergent," Frank mutters. "An engineer he was. A whole life ahead of him."

Marc shifts beside me, his fingers fluttering up to the scar on his forehead. "The police have gone from failing to salute to working hand in hand with them. I thought they looked uncomfortable when the Gestapo ordered them to intervene with civil unrest, when I… but now, I fear you may be right, Frank."

The couple in the window seat laugh as they stand. As the gentleman turns towards the bar, I notice his profile. He pulls on his coat, showing me his full face and my stomach contracts. "Night Frank," he calls, in a jovial tone.

I'm trapped, processing that my glimpse before, shoved to one side as paranoia, was correct after all. The father of my child, the man who stole my innocence, is here again. My knees weaken as my friend the barman unwittingly confirms my memory.

"Until next time, Baron Von Dinklage." My stomach turns as I listen to his false bonhomie. "Always welcome in here."

In my desperation to avoid being spotted, I pivot about on my toes as if I could flee again. But - not accounting for a friend standing right next to me - I end up with my face buried in Marc's chest.

"There's always a next time with you, Spatz," Chanel's unmistakable laughter tinkles. "That's what I adore about you."

With my head pressing into Marc's apron, I freeze until the smell of detergent and cooking is overtaken by a waft of her perfume when she stalks past. My cheeks burn as Marc's arm snakes around my shoulders. I don't know why I feel betrayed, but somehow, I do, and the touch of Marc's warm skin is the only thing preventing me from lashing out.

Fabrication

As soon as Chanel leaves, I pull free of Marc's embrace and dash to my bedroom in the attics without explanation. All night, my emotions vacillate between anger, hurt and with what, by the light of dawn, I now consider a probably ridiculous sense of betrayal. I can do nothing about the apparent reality though: my idol, the epitome of French style and the woman who gave me a chance at a future is friends with not just a Nazi sympathiser, but the man who caused my shame and left me with my greatest love.

And yet, without that shame, Freddie and I would not be in Paris today. Despite everything we have gone through, if our encounter and my resulting pregnancy hadn't happened, I would still be in Germany, and God only knows what would have happened to someone like me there. Certainly, upon reaching maturity, Herr Weisz's protection would have ceased and I would be an ordinary Jew. Would I have had the motivation to come to France at all if not to protect my son and follow my dreams?

As if the Head Housekeeper, Claudette, knows my torment and wants to twist the knife, the very next morning, I drag myself out of bed to discover I've been assigned to clean Chanel's room. Usually,

I'm sent to the Place Vendôme side of the hotel, mostly because I don't complain as much as the other girls about servicing the Nazi suites.

I'd all but given up hope of an excuse to interact with her once more, so it's hard to keep the grin from my face. Finally, I might have the opportunity to speak to her again, be permitted entry into her world maybe, but, today, of all the days. Although Chanel has made no announcements about re-opening her couture business, the shop is open, selling only her famous perfume, I'm desperate to keep myself in her mind.

Claudette warns me Chanel's a late riser, so I distract myself with other rooms on my list before working my way up - literally and figuratively - to knocking on her door just after midday. I don't know whether to be relieved or not when there is no answer, so I let myself in.

Inside, I'm greeted by the sight of what has obviously been a continuation of a cosy evening. The air is thick with stale smoke so the first thing I do is throw open a window and empty the ashtrays. Only some of the stubs have her red lipstick on, and the breakfast tray was set for two. The bed's rumpled, twin indents on the pillows. I'm experienced enough at cleaning rooms by now to understand: their relationship has moved beyond a casual drink in the bar.

Anger simmers through as I scrub, snap sheets and straighten. The room, although decorated to be unique while still matching all the others, feels impersonal. My fury builds as I'm confronted with the intimate, innately human evidence of an ordinary life. In the closet hangs her dresses; her make-up is strewn about near the mirror. She - the famous, fabulous Coco Chanel - could be any guest here, and yet, to me, she isn't.

When there's no more upkeep to be done, I stand at the doorway and stare at my handiwork. I wanted her space to be different. More. Instead, there's not even a sketch of a design to sneak a peek at. A swatch of fabric or button to show who lives here. Tears prick behind my eyelids and my heart breaks all over again.

Once I have seen the evidence of Chanel and Hans together, I cannot help but spot them everywhere. Over the next few months, their romance spills into public spaces of the hotel like the spring blossoms adorning the avenues - beautiful, fragrant, and stylish even when strewn all over the floor.

Always dressed in a sharp suit, the Baron, or 'Spatz,' as he's informally known, mingles and lingers around the lounges and bars at all hours. Subtle questioning of Frank informs me he's a Press Attaché for the German Embassy, but work is clearly not his only reason for being here. Sometimes I notice his name assigned to a small room of his own, as if for appearances' sake.

If I happen past him in a corridor I duck my head. Like all guests, he looks right through me. I'm no-one, and that suits me even though his face makes me think of Freddie and my chest aches. My disguise of cropped, bleached hair and a servant's uniform builds my confidence that my former paramour won't look too closely at my features and remember the sordid night we shared, back in Germany, after a terrible, dangerous day. Long hours and little sunlight ensure my visage remains more haggard than the 16-year-old he seduced eight years ago.

But at night, desperation prompts me to wonder whether he, being Pieter's ally of old, could be a route to seeing Freddie and Katarina again. I'm trapped between longing and lurking, living and hiding, evermore sure it's only a matter of time until Pieter shows his face at the Ritz. My fortnightly visits to the park yield nothing, and, whenever I'm there, I battle a constant temptation to bang on Kat's door. Only fear keeps me in check - not for myself - but that my appearance will ruin everything for my only real friend and her child-saving disguise as his mother, and of course endanger Freddie. Just as I would rush to hold my boy in my arms again, I'm certain my son wouldn't be able to resist me, but then there's the threat of Pieter's presence, and that's enough to keep me stuck.

One day, I'm cleaning Chanel's room when I find evidence their affair has re-ignited her spark of creativity. It's subtle, but now I'm a regular intruder into her sanctuary, I notice it. Magazines which are usually tossed unopened on the coffee table lay open with scribbled notes about types of fabrics alongside some of the fashion plates. I perch on the chair arm, heartbeat racing as I study the tiny scratches, picturing in my head how her suggestions would change the designs in reality.

The door swings open and I drop the magazine back on the table and stand.

"I won't be a moment *chéri*, I know exactly where I left it," Chanel says. She frowns, eyes scanning the messy table.

My head lowers and I reach over to plump a cushion. She prowls across the room, stroking a massive fur collar hung around her neck. I can sense her gaze on me. "You.... Devereaux isn't it?"

I nod. "Yes, Mademoiselle." I'm mollified she remembers.

"I need you to find me some black silk velvet. Five yards or so should be enough. Put it on my tab." She grabs an address book from the bureau and flicks through the pages.

I wonder if she plans to add a cape or even recreate her iconic tomato red evening gown of a decade ago. I remember seeing the striking photograph with the structured, draped neckline and gloves in fashion magazines, inspiring numerous girlish sketches of my own.

Then reality rips through my fantasy. "Mademoiselle, the rations... that's way in excess of what I could possibly..."

Chanel pauses mid stride and looks at me. "Ah. Yes. Rations." She sighs. "How tiresome. All the fabric mills commandeered for the war effort. And English velvet is the best of course, but there's no chance of that. You'll have to be inventive then." She opens her clutch bag. "This situation, intolerable," she mutters under her breath as she rifles inside for a purse. "Here, this should smooth the way." She thrusts a fistful of Reichsmarks at me. "Keep it off the tab," she says with a wink.

My hand reaches to take the money, then wavers. If I agree, I'm complicit. The black market no-one speaks of in the hotel is one matter, but taking German money seems wrong. They are the ones who have created the need for such a dark economy in the first place! And, if I get caught...

But if I refuse, the expression on Chanel's face tells me I won't get another chance to prove my loyalty.

The notes rustle as I pocket them.

Black Market

A week passes and I'm still at a loss about where to get such expensive and specialist fabric from. I can hardly march into a haberdashery and say, ignore the restrictions, it's for Chanel. Other fashion houses are operating, however, they're limited in what garments they are allowed to produce and with how much cloth. Besides, she isn't asking as a business, but as an individual. The predicament puts me on edge. Even Marc notices when I bring him more dirty dishes and we accidentally collide.

"Be careful!" I snap.

"Whatever's eating at you can't be any worse than the staff's lunchtime soup."

He was right, the watery broth had been overly salted to disguise the lack of substance. By contrast, the menu for Germans in the restaurant remained as varied as it ever was, and only French guests had to submit their ration tickets, which were equally ignored depending on the company they kept.

Marc leans in. "Are you alright?"

I keep it as vague as I can. "I've just been asked by a guest to get something unusual. Something someone like me would never be able to purchase ordinarily, but they are most insistent. And now I have to seek alternative avenues to get it."

"Ask Frank," he advises. "Evading the restrictions is a national pastime. Everyone's doing it, or at least, everyone who can afford it," he finishes darkly, then glances at a suitcase full of vegetables by the back door. One of the chefs was counting out cash to a farmhand. "It's 'grey' if there's no receipt for it, or for feeding family, apparently."

I suspect the higher prices such arrangements provided by agricultural workers outweighed the risk involved. Such transactions once considered shameful are rapidly becoming not only a necessity, but it's almost an act of patriotism to use under the counter or 'directly from farmers' food. Housewives demonstrate in the streets, saying the very existence of the *marché grise* or *marché noir* proved shortages were artificial, caused by a diversion of supplies to Germany and enforced by the Vichy regime.

"Frank runs bets, not the black market. Besides, it's not food I'm after."

Marc snorts. "If anyone knows someone though, it would be him or Jaques, perhaps."

I cannot bear for Jaques to look at me with disappointment in his eyes.

In between servicing bedrooms the next day, I detour into the bar before it opens. Frank's slicing lemons but catches my eye in the mirror. "Edelweiss! Why the long face?"

I ask, "If one were to need something specific for a guest... something not readily available, who would you speak to?"

He peers over his shoulder at me. "You're not the first, and I doubt you'll be the last to enquire after such things. You understand the risks?"

I nod. Technically, it's a crime which will get me fired or worse, but, if everyone does it, why shouldn't I? I could name five staff members who siphon cigarettes, leaving the rest of the packet under pillows in ladies rooms, since they are now not allowed to buy their own. And this isn't for me, is it?

"*Mais*..... You have a contact already, I think?" His eyebrow rises. "In the 16th Arrondissement?"

I gasp. "You know something?"

"I hear things."

I pause, mouth dry as I attempt to rein in my hopes. "Is it a man or a woman?"

"A relative of yours, I believe. A woman with an 'enterprise'."

Kat! My lips stretch into a grin so wide my cheeks hurt. It pained me to think she was involved in what the French call '*collaboration horizontale*', which I had suspected from her flirtation with the officer before. Then my smile fades; although in some ways, being active in the overground trade of goods seems more legitimate, it is just as dangerous.

He gives a little shrug and looks at me from the sides of his eyes. "But, perhaps, if you do not wish to go in person and visit your 'sister-in-law', I could send a note?"

I decide it's more important to establish contact and arrange somewhere we can talk freely. Mind racing, I gesture for one of the pads he keeps on the bar, not that he ever needs reminding of what people have ordered. "How is it done? In person, or do I request what I want and wait for a delivery?"

"For a new relationship, a meet would usually be best to build trust. You then pay and they hand over the...."

I pass him Chanel's order. "Would you mind writing, so it's not coming from me? It's complicated, but there are people in her house which I'd rather steer clear of. "

He nods. "Naturally."

"Where should we meet?"

"I would say here, but... it will make your involvement more obvious." He frowns as he reads my request. "Won't be cheap.

How about the catacombs? Suitably macabre for your first foray into the underworld, or is it?"

Perhaps seeing disgust spread across my face, Frank tries to reassure me. "They used to hold concerts there, not so long ago. Deep in the tunnels, past the Ossuary itself." He leans over the bar. "And, where there's hundreds of kilometres running underneath the city, there's plenty of opportunity to be had." He stands upright again and reaches for my ready pencil. "Or, if you don't want to enter to make the exchange, then there is a cemetery close to walk around. Pay your respects to the fallen." His voice catches and he clears his throat. "I'll sort out the rest."

Although the idea of a creepy, bone filled attraction revolts me, at least he's given me an alternative and I trust him. And I cannot wait to see Kat again. "Frank, I cannot thank you enough."

"Then perhaps you can do something for me while you are there?"

"Anything."

His eyes moisten and, finishing the note for Kat, he scribbles a man's name down on another sheet. "Lay some flowers on his grave for me?"

"Of course I will."

His lips press together briefly before his expression returns to its usual bonhomie. He extracts his wallet and passes over some Reichsmark notes. "Get a decent bunch, please. I'll let you know when I hear anything back."

Snooping

May 15th 1941

Waiting for a reply from Katarina takes an age. Like a candle in a dark window, the hope of seeing her overtakes any qualms I harbour about the reason why, carrying me through the humdrum of my existence. Eventually, when Frank tells me to leave him alone with my pestering, I seek Marc out, in case he has any inside knowledge about how long such matters take. But, he's not in the kitchens each time I look. Again, no-one has seen him for days.

When Marc does turn up for work, the first I hear of it is the sound of breakages in the kitchen. He's ordered out and I find him slumped against the service corridor wall. Noticing his pale pallor, I rush over. "What's wrong? I was looking for you."

He shrugs my hand off his shoulder.

"Are you ill?"

We don't get paid if we miss work due to illness, and he and his mother rely on his mediocre wages to live on.

Marc's lips press together and he shakes his head. "It's probably nothing."

"What is?"

"My neighbour, the Pole with the young child, got orders to present himself at an examination centre yesterday. Then, this evening, the police banged again on his door, before asking at our house. They've disappeared. Didn't show."

"Why would he disobey?"

He looks at me as if I am stupid. "His father disappeared not long after Hitler invaded Poland. Then, my neighbour escaped to Paris, thinking it was safer. Perhaps instinct?"

I could identify with his friend. Hadn't I too fled Germany to protect my child?

"It's only going to keep happening," Marc says in a hollow voice. He cradles his withered arm. "And when will they come for me? I'm no use to anyone."

There's nothing I can say to ease his concerns. I pat his shoulder. "Perhaps it won't come to that. The Nazi's are still bombing Britain. Maybe that's their main focus now, or Russia. I saw some reports about that in one of the officer's rooms."

Marc's expression tightens. "Papers?"

I nod. "Some of the guests are so untidy."

"Well, let me know if you see anything about rounding up Jews again, will you?" He half jokes.

"Of course I can," I reply, not really imagining I would find much, but it appeases him. The notion hammers away in my mind as if I'm pressing my foot to a Singer pedal as I leave to clean the next room.

A few days later, I'm cleaning a visiting officer's suite, when I come across a crumpled scrap of paper in a waste bin. I flatten it, hoping for a titbit I can pass onto Marc, but it's only a scrawled list, in German, of uniform items and quantities to be bought.

The thought occurs to me that such information might be useful, to someone at least. Most of our Nazi occupants are high-ranking, sometimes holding meetings in their suite's lounge areas. I would imagine them to be more security conscious than those who boast of their achievements in Frank's bar, so I cannot immediately see that much of use could be discovered. I hardly think I'll stumble onto a handy piece of documentation outlining plans for global domination or mass genocide, but still…

Besides, to whom would I tell such mundane details, anyway?

'F. It would be an honour to pay homage to your friend with your contact. Black is such a suitable choice and I have obtained sufficient to meet requirements. This Sunday as proposed, 11am. KW.'

I stuff the note, passed to me last night by Frank, into my pocket and glance towards the black hut where you could buy tickets to visit the Ossuary catacombs. Opening hours are chalked on a board outside and already an orderly queue forms, mostly off-duty soldiers judging by their German chatter, stiff bearing and shorn hair. A few women hover beside them, my own discomfort reflected in their faces. As I amble along the line to the end, I can't spot Katarina. With Frank's flowers in the crook of my arm, I tweak my curtain dress so it hangs straight, then look around while I wait. It feels strange to wear normal clothes and stand here in the street; the silence of a Sunday is only broken by a low murmur of German chit-chat until a church bell tolls 11.

The admission window bangs open and we shuffle forward. My heart pounds, dread rolling off me in waves. "One please," I mutter, pushing change through the slit. How on earth will Kat find me inside? Underground, in the maze of sewers. With all the bones...

"You can't leave flowers in there. Read the rules," the elderly woman inside barks, gesturing to the corner of the screen separating us. In both German and French, stark warnings about behavioural standards are displayed; at the bottom, the typed capital letters order, 'No Jews'.

"They're for a friend, for after," I stammer, unable to take my eyes off the instruction. "I'm visiting someone. A friend. Later."

She hands me some change with a suspicious look. Shut up shut up, I tell myself. Too much talk.

KΛT-Λ-COMBS

"**M**e, she's meeting me, Sophia," a voice to my side cuts across my embarrassment. Katarina shoves a note through the hatch and I look up in time to see the old lady smile. "Keep the change, for your grandson," Kat says in a warm tone.

"Bless you dear." Sophia waves us on as Kat links her arm with mine.

Saying nothing in case my relief makes me gabble, I allow myself to be hauled towards the entrance. A photograph, pinned by the door, shows a stone carving: 'Stop! The Empire of Death lies here'. It does not help ease my disquiet, but Kat merely states, "Watch your step. It's a long way down."

Our eyes meet and she gives me an imperceptible nod. I notice then that she carries nothing but a large patent handbag on her arm. She's also wearing a pair of stylish new heels.

We traipse through a narrow passageway of rough bare stones to reach the stairs, lit with dimly flickering lights on a cable. At the bottom, an even narrower corridor. Goosebumps rise on my arms, partly because of the change in temperature, but also because

I cannot help but feel I'm being forced down a path I am fearful to tread.

Beside me, Kat grips my forearm. "Not much further." We snake through passages, following the crowd, going underneath the actual lintel pictured at the entrance. Entering the 'Empire of death' we soon arrive in a chamber filled with whispers of the past. This is the ossuary, where the overflow of corpses dug up from graveyards have been stylistically arranged. Inside, sound is curiously both deadened and amplified, voices blend together as if they are one. Dead and alive. Skulls and the ends of bones are arranged around the walls to form a picture of terror. In the middle, a bulging pillar of femurs and skulls looks as if it might burst. Above, a massive slab of limestone presses down, forming a low ceiling. I cannot breathe.

"Beautiful, isn't it?" Kat says. She's switched to French, as if she wants her voice to be all I can hear when all around us German tourists grow excited by the grisly display.

"Morbid," I reply, finally dragging in a breath of the stale air.

The group thins as they explore. Kat hovers by a stone cross as we gaze silently at the knobbly ends of joints and tops of skulls artfully arranged to make the chamber round. Once she has judged the crowd dispersed enough, I follow her as she heads along the predetermined route out of the ossuary. We weave through endless tunnels, sometimes passing through more chambers filled with the grey-white or browned skeletal remains stacked and displayed. On occasion, we pass a single lightbulb dangling over a barricaded-off pit to one side of a tunnel, filled with piles of disorganised bones as if they have been dropped there carelessly to fill up a hole. All those individuals had stories of their own, lives lived, and now they were just jumbled together, the sum of their parts making a whole, morose attraction for thrill seekers.

Without warning, Kat glances behind, then grabs my arm. She pulls me into a darkened recess and breathes, "Here," in my ear. Then, suddenly, she's almost my height, her heels in hand.

Through the darkness, she stoops and steps carefully but with purpose down another passage. We walk, heads low and blindly for a few minutes down a dusty, uneven path. Then she drops her grip and I sense her moving away.

"Wait," she orders, just as I feel panic rising in my throat. Enveloped in the absolute black, the clink of metal keys, then a click are as loud as my heartbeat, thudding in my ears. A squeak of un-oiled hinges. A wrench on my jacket pulls me forward.

"Kat! Where are we?"

"A place to keep things."

I stumble behind her, my fingers guiding me along a cold, brick wall. A trickle of water ahead suggests we head into the sewer system.

"The Romans built this part," Kat remarks, in a conversational tone as if she's some kind of tour guide. "The sewers, mining tunnels and catacombs link for hundreds of kilometres, like a city beneath the city."

"Can't we use a torch or something?"

The dust beneath our feet scrunches as she pauses. "Stay put." The air here tastes different - fresher but with a tinge of rank sourness I can't quite place.

She clicks a Zippo lighter, its bright spark then transforms the room into a warm glow as she bustles around lighting candles. I gasp as, when the flames flicker and lengthen, I see we're in a different kind of chamber, blessedly free of bones but built with bricks. Stacked crates and sacks form a neat wall of supplies - from liquor to cartons of cigarettes and cans.

Kat bends over in a corner, candle in hand, and retrieves a paper-wrapped bundle. As she shoves it in my hands, my lips tremble. While the fabric is my future, all I can think of is the past.

"Freddie?"

"He's fine. Safe." Her tone is soft, caring and reassuring. "Still doesn't speak, but we rub along well enough."

The lump in my throat almost prevents me from speaking. "I come to the park every other Sunday morning. Why haven't you met me?"

She looks at the crate wall. "Since we met in the restaurant, things moved quickly and I had to go along with it." Kat paces away from me, leaving me standing in the centre of her store-room. "I've no choice, you see. Comply and assist, or I get reported for black marketeering. That's the way it works."

Tearing open boxes of cigarettes, she begins stuffing the soft packets into her handbag until it's bursting at the seams. "The racket is co-ordinated by one of the Nazi officers bunking in my house. He siphons things away, deals with the paperwork side. Somewhere close to here – above I suppose – there's a manhole. They drop goods down by night then someone stacks them in here. I have to be the one to distribute them, like a common delivery boy, then take payment and, if I'm charming enough, another order. That's how I snuck in your request. I'm landlady, cleaner, chef and shopper, but only this officer knows what takes up the time when I'm supposed to be in church or queuing for food. Freddie and I..."

"You bring a small child down here!"

"It's the only way we avoid suspicion. He loves it."

Before I get too upset about my son enjoying the macabre, I control my voice to ask, "Then why didn't you bring him today?"

With a few strides, she returns to me. "Because..." Touching my arm, her eyes fill with sorrow as if the gesture will melt my stiffness. "This morning, his Uncle Pieter unexpectedly turned up and wanted to take him for ice cream. I could hardly say, 'Come with me instead. I'm meeting your mother,' or even, 'We have to make a dirty delivery which takes priority,' can I?"

She's left him in the care of evil incarnate! My lips mouth but I can't find the words. A keening sound echoes around the room.

"Hannah! Hannah! Stop making that awful racket. Someone might hear and think it's ghosts."

Her fingers tighten on my forearm, then I realise the noise came from me.

She pulls me into a hug, saying, "I came because I hoped it was you who needed the fabric, or at least, it was someone from the Ritz itself who could maybe pass you a message."

I let out a ragged breath and the echo subsides. My chest is still tight but I reply, "Does Pieter come often? Does Freddie... recognise him?"

I've never told her the details of what I witnessed her cousin doing, of the nightmares I still have about it. That night when we arrived in Paris, I had been careful with my explanation, to save her from knowing the full truth about her family.

She shakes her head and looks at me as if I'm peculiar. "He tolerates Pieter because he brings him sweets and cakes and kicks a football with him in the yard. And my cousin, for all his vileness, dotes on him, especially now he believes he's pure Aryan. I never know when he's going to arrive on my doorstep. His job has odd hours." Kat begins blowing out the candles.

I take a step towards the passage. "What does he do?"

Still holding the last candle, the room is in near darkness, save the contours of her sad face highlighted by the warm glow of the flame. "I think it's something to do with rounding up Jews. He was happy when he arrived today. Said something about progress. How well work was going."

My breath catches as Marc's desolation pops into my head. "How awful."

"I know." She goes ahead of me in the corridor, candlelight bathing the walls enough to see the mouldy green slime creeping up the bricks. "But, what can be done? You and I know it's just a policy the Nazis have."

My palms sweat as Marc's anguished face swims before my eyes as she holds the door open for me. Just a policy? Before we can enter the public area again, as she snaps the padlock shut, I blurt, "It's people's lives, Kat." My voice drops to a whisper. "If it weren't for your kindness, it could be me. Could be Freddie."

She's silent for a moment while she dusts off her feet and puts her shoes back on.

But being with her, sharing in her dangerous lifestyle, sparks something of the old me. I say, "What you should do is tell someone. Whatever you know. Whatever you can find out from Pieter. Or tell me, and I'll find a way to warn them."

"What good would it do?"

"I don't know. But if you knew something bad was about to happen, wouldn't you prefer to have a choice about what to do about it? Some notice to make a decision? If you'd known Pieter would appear at your door then dump loads of Nazis in your house, perhaps you might have moved elsewhere, rather than be stuck in this position of risking your life by working for them?"

She shrugs. "That would have left you and Freddie alone, and at least I can eat now, but I accept your point. You did at least give me the choice to turn you away." By the candlelight, I watch conflicting emotions flicker across her face. Regret. Determination. Fear. Her features, thankfully, settle on resolve. "You're right, Hannah. I would have wanted a choice. Preferred freedom."

"You're in such a unique position to help, as am I." As soon as I say it, I realise we both could overhear something. It's not enough to blindly hope for information left lying around. That helps no-one.

But she still hadn't agreed, and who would we tell?

"We can do this, together Kat. Ask the questions, get the answers, as only you can. I'll figure a way for us to make use of that information, I promise. We have an advantage few French do - we understand German."

I think of Marc's neighbour, and Marc himself. If he had the courage to stand up to the Nazis, so should I. "Your Uncle Franz knew this war was on the horizon you know. He said, when I left the estate, 'if you see an injustice in the world, you should always do whatever you can to protect the persecuted.' If you hate this situation as much as I do, we have to act to change it."

The way she sighs indicates that she's at least considering it.

"Remember when we used to sneak out under Herr Weisz's very nose? You're still sneaking, but I don't know who from. Pick a side Kat. It's us, or them."

She grins and I know she's chosen. "Rebel to the end, eh?"

"Rebel with reason," I reply and snuff out the candle. "Now please, get me out of this godforsaken place before I turn into a mole."

"Ha!" She giggles.

When we emerge into the sunlight, Kat glances at her watch. The queue has grown during our absence and eyes are on us. Standing awkwardly on the pavement, the time has come for us to part. It isn't seemly to embrace so I clutch my brown paper package and the flowers to my chest as if it were her I hugged.

"Oh!" Clapping my hand to my mouth, "Payment!" I reach into my bag for Chanel's money.

"Don't worry," Kat smiles. "Keep it for yourself, in case you need it. You've already paid enough."

We lean together, brushing cheeks for a customary farewell.

"Be careful. If you need me," she whispers into my ear. We swap heads, both smiling, then kiss the other cheek. "Now you know where and when."

"Give my love to Freddie."

She swallows. "He'd send his, if he could, I'm sure. See you soon?"

"In a fortnight. Maybe we can walk around the cemetery before you.... go down. Or, you can always write if you find something out. Care of Frank Meier at the Ritz."

"I don't trust anyone but you."

Without looking back, she stalks away.

ANGEL BENEATH

I rush back to the Ritz with mixed emotions. Chanel's maid, Domenger, opens the door and her smile quickly melts into disapproval. "Too early for turning down the room."

It's past lunch.

"Who is it?" Chanel's voice sounds weak and wavers. I hope the Baron isn't there as well, but, I've little option but to take the risk. I don't want to simply leave my parcel in her room, not after what I went through to obtain it.

"Housekeeping. The small blonde one."

She refuses to acknowledge the Ritz staff by name, and considers herself above us. "I have the item you requested, Mademoiselle," I call through, proffering the package to Domenger who shakes her head as if I'm handing her a bomb.

"Send her through."

Domenger stands to the side, glaring at me as I place the fabric on the coffee table. Chanel lies on the sofa, holding a compress to her forehead. Mercifully, no-one else is around.

"Are you well, Mademoiselle? Can I get you anything?"

She snaps, "I'm fine. Just a summer cold. Difficulty sleeping." Her skin looks wan and clammy but her cheeks are flushed. "I'm expecting some medicine to be delivered any moment." She wafts her fingers gracefully at the paper. "Let me see it."

After untying the string, I hold the fabric towards her. She pinches and rubs it, then nods. "Domenger, put this velvet in the wardrobe." Her eyes flick to mine. "Now I need you to find Blanche... sorry, Madame Auzello, and let her know I'm ready for the machine. Find her. Tell her only. Then forget the message, Devereaux."

Her emphasis isn't lost on me and I stop expecting a thank you or a compliment on a job well done. She clicks her fingers as if she's asking for the bill. "Hurry along now. The message is not to be written down and passed around, got it?"

Systematically, I search the hotel, tactfully enquiring if anyone has seen Madame Auzello. Her husband suggests she's likely doing the nightly checks on any empty rooms, in case we have late night or too-early arrivals. In the top corridor underneath the staff quarters, one moment, it looks empty, and the next, I hear her voice calling from behind me. "Where are you supposed to be?"

I'm sure it makes me look guilty to whirl around so fast, but how could I have missed her? She stares at me with unfocused eyes. There's a whiff of wine on her breath, and the sharp tang of medicinal alcohol about her. "Mademoiselle Chanel asked me to pass you a message - she's ready for 'the machine' now."

Her gaze darts down the corridor walls and she clears her throat loudly. "Right. Yes." She sighs, then rallies. "Follow me."

We use the service stairs, travelling all the way down to the cellars. I've no usual cause to come down here, and, brightly lit, they are nothing like the hellish descent I took earlier with Kat. Almost welcoming by comparison, but it's still a maze albeit pleasantly cool. We pass neatly labelled doors for the wine cellars, some of which are also labelled 'Shelter' with room numbers. These are, I presume, the supposedly luxurious bomb shelters prepared during the Phoney War – when war had been declared but nothing happened to us in France – to accommodate all the guests in the event of an air raid. Of course, Paris was only bombed for three days before capitulating entirely, so they can't have had much use. When we arrive at a door with signs suggesting it's both 'Storage 12' and 'Staff Shelter,' Madame pulls out her bunch of keys.

Inside, the domed chamber smells musty. Temporary camp beds are stacked neatly along one wall, shelves line the others with some cans and bedding folded in readiness for a lengthy stay. A quick calculation and I'm not sure there is enough floor space for all the beds, so I assume, should it come to it, we'd have to lie head to toe in the corridor.

Madame rummages her way to the far end of the room. "Damn it.... Ah... here." She beckons me closer. Wedged between crates is a tarpaulin covered table with an odd bump on the top. A lace of cobwebs disguises a grey box perched on one side of the table. She swipes through the web veil, then lifts off the filthy metal weight and passes it to me. "Find a place for this old thing, on a shelf or something."

Dusty wires trail like spider legs behind me as I cross the cellar to the shelves and look for a suitable new home for what I think, judging from a square section covered in mesh, is an ancient radio of some kind. I tuck it next to a battered suitcase, leaving a pair of unreadable dials to stare at me.

"Bugger, that's a weight," Madame says, as she tries to drag the now uncovered table across the cobbles. "Devereaux, you get that corner, and I'll..."

The radio's gaze is forgotten when I set my own eyes on what she's retrieved. I dash over, then my fingers trail across the cold metal of a sewing machine. "What a treasure."

She groans, but it truly is. An old cast iron Kohler fixed to a solid table top. The gold artistry on the plate above the needle dulled by time, but I can still make out the angel's features. With a massive pedal to power it underneath, I expect it's probably only capable of the most basic stitches. All the same, my heart thrills at the sight of the machine and what it means: Chanel is sewing again!

Between us, we can lift it, walk a few yards, before we have to put it down and flex our fingers. It takes an age to get it to the bottom of the steps. "I'll find some help," I offer.

She nods gratefully. "Someone who won't ask questions."

I rush to the kitchens and ask Marc if he can come. He's about to object but I flare my eyes in warning. "It's for the Dragon Lady."

He tucks his drying cloth into his waistband and follows me.

Marc's good arm is wiry enough to carry the bottom end while Madame and I take the table top corners. We lever the beast, as I now think of it, up the stairs, and along to a lift. While we wait for it to ascend, I rub the Kohler free of dust with Marc's dish towel. Once we reach Chanel's door, Madame dismisses Marc.

Mademoiselle Chanel herself lets us in, silent as we wrestle the beast into her room. She's alone, dressed for dinner already, and buzzing with such energy I wonder what sort of miracle medicine she's taken to enable such a swift recovery. She bosses us into a minor re-arrangement of furniture so we can place the Kohler in a well-lit corner of the room. "Of course, if I had my old suite, it wouldn't be so cluttered."

"If you had your old suite, Coco, I'd be questioning which side you were on," Madame Auzello snipes back.

When Chanel sits at the machine, I hear a small sigh, before she, too, traces her fingers over its elegant curves. She fiddles with the settings, testing the mechanisms, absolutely focused. It's on the tip of my tongue to ask to stay, anything to watch her at work, but Madame snaps at me, "Housekeeping should have needles that fit. It's their old mending machine. I'll have some sent up in the morning."

"Yes, yes. Black and light blue thread as well." Chanel replies. "I'll make a start then."

I say, "Do you need anything else, Mademoiselle? Scissors, chalk..."

"If I do," she responds, "I know who to ask." She flicks her eyes at Madame Auzello.

I bob a curtsey, firmly put back in my place. "If that's all then..."

No-one says a word as I leave.

Much Ado About Noting

Despite telling myself it's not my place to ask what scheme Chanel and my boss are stitching together, the possibilities give me a restless night. The next morning, I suspect Madame Auzello's hand in my room assignments when Claudette, informs me I'm to service Chanel's suite daily from now on. I'm over the moon about this for a second, then I remember - the more I'm there, the greater risk I'll run into her lover Spatz, or the Baron as I have to call him. I don't mind calling him by his title as it helps me to distance myself from Hans, as I knew him.

Making a start, I service two rooms close to each other on the second floor, then continue upstairs. I'm plumping cushions in an officer's suite when I come across a folded memo, slipped down the side of the chair, and written in German.

Following the success of the recent round up, date now confirmed for next operation, commencing 20 August.

Target - 11th Arr.

Ensure all preparations for the internment camps completed by this date. Gestapo and Prefectures will be briefed as discussed on logistics.

No arrest warrants to be issued prior to arrest.

S.S. Lt. Kronecker

For a moment, my head swims. Folding the paper, I can't help but glance over my shoulder as I slip it into my pocket. The round up - could that be referring to the recent spate of arrests which Marc's Jewish friend ran from? Did I read that right? I pull the memo out, read it again, slower and tracing my fingers under the words to be sure.

My heart pounds as pocket my stolen treasure again, then whirl around, straightening on autopilot while I think about what to do with it. As soon as the suite looks presentable, I lift the tray of dirty dishes and head down the hallway towards the service stairs. I want to show Marc what I've found. Maybe there's something he can do with the information?

As I round the corner, I nearly collide with the Baron!

It's all I can do to keep hold of the tray, but my abrupt stop loses a wine glass to the carpet.

"I'm so sorry, Monsieur," I mutter, dropping to a crouch and subtly turning my back to him as I place the tray down.

"Quite all right," he replies.

I reach for the glass, but he's already bent and retrieved it. As we stand, our eyes accidentally meet.

All I can think about is the note in my pocket and my cheeks burn. He frowns and I hold my breath.

"Hannah, isn't it?"

I swallow. Should I try to deny it? Pretend I'm someone else?

He wets his lips while his eyes roam my face. "You know Katarina, Pieter's cousin's friend, or something. Hannah.... *Wir haben uns schon mal getroffen.*"

We did more than meet before. The ache between my thighs lasted for days, my shame, for years. I reply, "*Es tut mir leid, dass ich dir im Weg stehe.*"

The sides of his eyes crinkle as he smiles, but my heart hammers as I realise - with my apology, I've confirmed what he's already remembered with my automatic response in German.

"Not at all. Think nothing of it." He stands, and continues in our language. "I like the brighter hair. Stylish. Suits you."

All of a sudden, I recall how charming he was. Is. His gentle understanding of the world. How seen he had made me feel, as a gauche teenager, as if being Jewish or youthful was less important than my intelligence and courage in the face of adversity.

Then, how much damage his lust had also caused rises over me like a tsunami. I grab the glass and slam it on the tray. The crockery rattles as I pick it up.

"Oh, don't be offended," he says, in a low voice. "I'm not your enemy, you know."

It takes everything in me not to say, Oh, but you are. Instead, I force a breath out and stand there awkwardly.

"Really," he touches my shoulder. "I'm happy to see you again." Hans glances up and down the corridor; all the doors are closed and we are alone. "But I didn't expect you to be here, in the lion's den itself."

Is he my enemy? He's certainly complicit, now he has progressed from simple journalism to Ambassadorial Press Attaché. His very job is to present what the Germans are doing here in such a way as to make it palatable.

The memo in my pocket crackles as I step back, and my ire rises. "You work for them. The Nazi Party."

Hans flinches.

When I look at him, I see his lips are pinched together. Then he says, ever so softly, "Not everything is black and white. My ex-wife Catsy was Jewish, like you."

"What's that got to do with anything? You're with Chanel now."

His eyes narrow. "Jealousy is not a good colour on you, Hannah."

"I'm not jealous!" At least, not in the way he presumes.

"That's good. Good."

"But you should understand, I'm assigned to clean her rooms now. It's likely we will run into each other again."

He offers me a half smile. "Perhaps you can keep an eye on the old girl when I'm not able to, then? Make sure she doesn't get herself into mischief."

I gape. "Why? Are you going somewhere?"

"No, no. I get called away on business sometimes, you know. Reporting to Berlin, occasionally. Being able to travel is a perk of the job. Not so easy for people like you, I suppose, and I wouldn't want to have to file anything bad about the staff here. Just, let me know if Coco's in trouble, will you?" He slips a business card from his top pocket and offers it to me. "My office will always know where I am."

"I'm sure I wouldn't even hear of anything." I gabble, nervous even to my own ears as I stare at his card. Announcing himself as Baron Hans von Dincklage, then in smaller letters: Press Attaché, German Embassy, Paris, and a telephone number. I'm guessing he has paid for the luxurious card himself, because there's no Nazi insignia, as if he is trying to present as neutral.

"You're a resourceful, observant and brave young lady, I remember that much. Listen, do this for me and in return, I'll forget I even know your name, Hannah Edelstein."

He's got me backed into a corner, but I'll be damned if I report on Chanel for his gratification. For myself, perhaps, but not for him. I palm his contact details, bob a curtsy, and lie while he can't see my eyes. "It's Devereaux now, and, as you wish."

"Good, good. Are you all right with that heavy tray? I could carry it down for you."

"Quite, thank you." The tray is perfectly steady in my hands as I head for the stairs.

RADIO

I shove my personal confusion to the back of my mind as I march into the kitchen. Given the Baron's proximity to Chanel, I suppose it was inevitable we'd cross paths, but processing my emotions must wait.

Marc shakes his head when I drag him into the storeroom to show him the memo. "I don't understand German. What am I supposed to do with this?"

I translate from memory in a whisper, but all he says is, "What if someone saw you?"

"They didn't."

"Or realises the note's missing?"

I grab his hand. "Marc, it's not as if we need evidence in a murder case. Isn't it enough there's a date and area, and they have a plan to do something then which involves round up's and internment camps? That's what this tells us."

He shrugs. "I don't know."

I feel like punching him. My feelings are all over the place after bumping into Hans, and I was hoping Marc would be excited as I am about what I've found. Clearly, he doesn't see my discovery that way. I sigh. "Look, if I copy the note down, translated word for word into French, then put the paper back so no-one knows it's gone, is there someone you can pass the information to? Warn people, perhaps, to expect trouble?"

"How am I meant to do that?"

"Ask around! Go to the synagogue and tell them. They can surely get the message out. Someone must have warned your Polish neighbour."

"An arrest warrant did that."

"Well, they're not doing that this time."

He slumps against the wall and hangs his head. "It's too dangerous." His long legs crumple and he slides down to a crouch. "Who would believe someone like me?"

I let out an exasperated sigh before considering what he's really saying. "I know. We're nobodies. People might think you're crazy, or a troublemaker." I slide down beside him against the wall. We sit in silence for a long minute.

Patting my knee, he says, "You tried. At least you tried."

"I don't think trying is enough. Information itself isn't enough, if you can't act on what you've found out."

Marc snorts. "People believe what they hear on something official like a radio, or see it in front of their eyes. If only we had a camera."

"What good would that do?"

He opens his fingers and thumb into a box shape, as if he was framing the shelves in front of us and hums the music at the start of a film, when they show the news before a feature. In a formal voice with clipped tones, he announces, "A top level meeting determines the outcome: the flics will pounce on the 11th Arrondissement on August the 20th, striking fear into the heart of every Jew there."

He pans his hands around and peers through them to my face. "Local correspondent Devereaux, responds with decisive action."

I giggle. "If only she could decide what that action is. Perhaps I should put on a show? Make a song and dance. Tap out a coded warning with my shoes."

His hands lower, leaving him staring at me.

"I'm joking. I can't dance and I'd never want to be in front of a camera."

"Tap." He frowns. "Perhaps that's it." He levers himself up, scratching his head. "A radio."

"A radio?"

"That's how troops relay messages to each other, with a code tapped over the airwaves. If we had one, someone might be listening. Someone with the power to do something with the information, stop it maybe?"

Sliding my back up the wall until I'm standing, I'm compelled to point out: "Anyone could be listening, though. The wrong kind of people."

But Marc is warming to his idea. "Then it would have to be in code, like the soldiers use."

"Which means whomever hears it has to be able to break the code to understand the message."

"Ah. Right. Just the warning then, plain and simple. Risk it but hope that more ears hear us. We need a radio unit."

The cellar, I'm sure I saw one there. Or rather, the pieces of one. A plan takes shape in my mind. "I think I can help with that."

"Great!"

"But it's not getting around the first problem of 'anyone bad might be listening'. Can't they track signals or something?" I've seen vans driving around with strange antennae on the top.

Marc shrugs. "All we can do is try, isn't it? Just... don't do anything stupid, will you?"

"Me?"

"Yes, you."

We exchange conspiratorial smiles. As he opens the storeroom door, he stage whispers, "I don't want to have to pat you down for hidden potatoes."

But something in his look tells me he's thought about it.

The next Sunday, I get up extra early and sneak down to the cellars. Wrapping the broken radio in some old uniforms I find in one of the crates, it fits snugly in the battered suitcase. For additional cushioning, I ram some towels around the sides then drape the whole lot with a few tatty black uniform skirts. If I get stopped, at least it will seem as if I've packed some clothes into the suitcase, to add to my cover story.

At this hour, the streets are relatively empty. I trudge along the grey Seine for a while, taking a circuitous route to the Catacombs. Freshly hung posters adorn the boards on the rails, advertising an exhibition called '*Le Juif et La France*' coming in September, which, with its caricature of a hook-nosed old man looming and grasping over a map of the world, is obviously designed to convince us of the harmful effects of Jews. Remnants of chalk paintings on the pavement are now unnervingly interspersed with more anti-Semitic pictures, so perhaps it's working. I pray for rain to wash them away as I wend through alleyways and avoid the checkpoints, but the day only heats up.

When I reach the cemetery where I laid flowers for Frank's friend, I linger reading the names on the gravestones and wondering about their lives, until I hear the church bells toll and I can join the Ossuary queue.

"No suitcases," Sophia, the Catacombs attendant, says when she spots me lugging it towards her window.

"It's for Madame Weisz though," I whisper. "Can I leave it with you for her to collect?"

She huffs and glances along the queue. "Depends how long she'll be."

I look over my shoulder as if she's pre-arranged to meet me. "She must be running late." There's a few people behind me, but no sign of Katarina.

"Probably that boy of hers," Sophia says. "Always wanting an ice cream before he comes in."

I chuckle. "Which will end up all over his face, no doubt." I've spent all morning trying not to get my hopes up about seeing Freddie, but now she mentions him, my eyes grow misty and a lump forms in my throat. "He's always been a messy eater."

"Go on then," she says in a gruff voice, taking pity on me. "I can't see you as the type to steal bones, anyway."

"Thank you." I pause at the entrance, re-reading the ominous warning above.

BONY BOY

The descent down the narrow steps is harder with the awkward, heavy suitcase. I wander through the bone-filled rooms, trying to replace my dread with a frisson of anticipation. The conversation among the crowd is muted, but enough for me to distinguish that, once again, I'm surrounded by Germans ghoulishly fascinated by the display. One of them makes a snide comment about how no-one would visit if they used the catacombs to dispose of dead Jews, which distresses me. Underneath, we're all the same skeletons.

The longer I wait, perched on the suitcase, the more I question if this was the right course of action. Someone, surely, will notice me. Ask why I'm staring so hard at the white cross.

Then, through the hubbub, I catch the welcome tone of Kat. "Come along, Freddie, no dawdling."

I stand, heart thumping, and search the chamber. In a burgundy hat and matching coat, Kat in heels stands at the entrance. I stick my hand in the air and wave, my breath coming in fast pants.

My darling boy, wearing the yellow scarf I gave him around his neck, spots me and tugs on her arm, pointing towards me with his other.

Leaving the suitcase, I push past a group and dash across, arms outstretched.

As Freddie flings himself into me, I bury my head in his soft hair and hide my tears.

He's grown, and stronger too. His arms squeeze my midriff but that's not what takes my breath away. Despite all the money I've sent, and Kat's enviable position, I can feel his ribs, and his arms are almost skeletal. My chest clamps and I never want to let him go again. "Freddie, Freddie. *Mon couer, mon couer*," is all I can whisper, over and over.

"What a delight to see you again," Kat snaps, the formal note to her voice reaching me.

I blink my eyes then raise my head. I have to swallow before I can respond. "An unexpected pleasure."

"Shall we walk together?"

I glance around the room, goosebumps springing to my arms as I search for the case. In the dim light, I can't see it. "I just have to get..." In my panic, I half drag Freddie, still clinging to my waist, across to where I last saw it. People turn to stare at us, but I paste a 'don't mess with me grimace' on my face and soldier past them.

To my relief, the suitcase is still there. It had toppled over in my haste to reach Freddie. I pick it up then adjust my son so he's more limpet on my side than in front of me. Kat's expression shows her disapproval and she offers her hand to Freddie. "Please behave, *liebchen*," she trills.

His head shakes, No.

"Let's go," I encourage, trying to move forward. But Freddie won't walk. He's like an anchor - if I take a step, he slides down my legs as if he can clamp me in place.

Kat tries again to rescue the situation, her cheeks flushing. "Come and see the next room, Freddie. You can show us your favourite skulls. I hate to say it, but he knows these tunnels like I know the back of my hand."

I know what he wants. He's such a big boy now, I'm not sure I can carry him for long. "Put your arms around my neck, darling," I whisper in his ear. "I won't let you fall. I'm not going anywhere without you."

He whimpers but complies. There's nothing like the feel of your child's warm limbs wrapped around you, especially with a sticky face pressed into your neck. I wouldn't change it for the world.

Kat picks up the case, shooting me a look as she assesses the weight of it. "Going somewhere nice?"

"It's a gift. For you," I mutter. "A project for you both to work on, perhaps? Like you used to. You know, taking electrics apart and putting them back together." I'm babbling now, as we walk. "I need it back, though, when it's fixed."

"So it's not a gift then," she laughs but it sounds forced.

All I want to do is sit and hold my son, but there's nowhere, no time, to stop for such luxuries.

She says nothing, just leads us through the route we took before, I think.

When we reach the narrow corridor, I have to wrestle Freddie off me, as we can't fit through with him on my hip. He protests until I take his hand. "I'm not letting go of you, remember?" I say, then, he pushes in front of me and leads me through the darkness. Somehow, he gives me courage and I'm not at all frightened of feeling my way through the cold passage.

While Kat lights the candles, I perch on a crate and pull him onto my lap for a proper snuggle. "I love you so much," tumbles out of my mouth before I can stop it. I'm compelled to tell him what I never had the chance to remind him of, before everything changed. "I love you, I love you, I love you. I can hardly believe I'm here, holding you."

He lets out a wail and dissolves into fresh tears. This wasn't my intention, but just shows the strain he must have been under. I can see he's been kept safe, but has he ever doubted my love for him? Guilt at leaving hits me in the stomach, and I wonder, have I made things worse by being here? I glance at Kat, seeking reassurance.

"Of course I told him you love and miss him." She says stiffly. "But he understands to be safe, he has to pretend I'm his Maman. But I'll never be you."

"Staying alive, secure, is all that matters. Really. You're saving both our lives - again, Kat." My voice cracks. "I can't thank you enough."

Her face softens, then her smile wobbles. She dashes over to throw her arms around us both. We huddle, warmed and fortified by each other. Her perfume blankets us with the scent of summer, and for a minute, we're safely cocooned in love.

She's first to pull away, when Freddie has relaxed into me and almost stopped sobbing into my neck. I watch her as she snaps the suitcase locks open. "Oh! A radio."

"Do you think it's salvageable?"

She holds up the wires and studies them, then prises off the outer case. "Possibly. Did you...." She mouths 'steal it' at me.

"Um... borrowed? I need to use it to send a message."

"It's not that kind of radio, silly."

My face falls. "What?"

"It's a receiver. You could listen to it, but I wouldn't have a clue how to make it into a transmitter. Well, I might... perhaps." She adjusts her hat and looks thoughtful.

"Please, Kat, it's really important. I need to warn people about... something that's happening. Give them a chance to get to safety."

She blinks. "People?"

I arch my eyebrow. "People like me. I found something out, at work."

"Don't say any more. If I don't know, I can't tell." She nods her head to herself. "I'll see what I can do. Now, I've got to get some supplies."

While she's packing her bag with contraband, I stroke Freddie's hair. "When we get out of here *mon coeur*, I need you to be a brave boy. Look after my big Kat for me, will you?"

His solemn blue eyes turn up to mine . He doesn't need to speak for me to understand the question in his expression.

"If I could be with you, I would. But, Kat will keep you safe, and that keeps me safe too. When this is all over, we can be together. Get a little house of our own, remember?"

A hint of a smile appears on his face and he unwraps his arms to stretch them up.

"And we'll see if you're as tall as the Eiffel Tower."

Satisfied, he snuggles back into me until Kat says she's ready to go.

Round Up

The summer months are humid and beset by storms, although it cools as August drags on. Try as I might to find out anything more, the officers' quarters I clean are frustratingly devoid of 'lost' or left behind paperwork. Chanel's fabric has disappeared and I've not seen any new clothes in her wardrobe. The machine is still in her room, untouched except by my hands to dust it. I hear she has gone to her estate in the south of France for a few weeks.

I've given names to the skulls in the ossuary now, having spent so much time down there hoping to see Kat and Freddie again, but they haven't returned. Sophia says she hasn't seen them since I gave Kat the suitcase. Without word from her, my worry about the position I have put her in eats at me.

With only a day to go before the date of the round up from the memo, I'm on edge as I hasten about my duties, bashing into furniture and tripping over my piles of sheets. By mid-morning, when I take a tray of half-eaten breakfast plates down to the kitchens, guilt and worry on my face draws stares.

"What's eating you today?" The pastry chef asks, nicking back the remaining crust from one of his croissants as I pass. There's no shame anymore, and no food goes wasted.

"Nothing," I reply.

When I unload the dirty dishes next to Marc's sink, I'm clearly not the only one bowed by the weight of failure. He hisses, "I thought you had a radio organised?"

"I've tried, but my contact has disappeared. Any luck just spreading the word?"

He glances over his shoulder. "I told a few people who have friends in the 11th Arrondissement they should leave, but no-one took me seriously. A radio announcement sounds so much more official."

"We can't give up yet." I touch his arm and our eyes meet. Lately, they've been meeting quite a lot, and his gaze usually makes my cheeks flush.

He studies me through long dark eyelashes. "I'd suggest 'that's easy for you to say,' but I don't think it is for you either." Then, he smiles at me. "Why's nothing ever simple?"

His tone and the way his eyes roamed my face tells me: he doesn't mean the radio, or what's happening with the Occupation. My heart thumps a little faster as I walk away. There's too much else going on for a romance, I tell myself, but I'm smiling anyway.

The next day, Marc doesn't arrive at work. I skip lunch and hurry towards the 11th Arrondissement, a nagging feeling tangling my guts. But, as I approach the Place de la Bastille, the area is blocked off. Crowds have gathered, jostling against each other as the Municipal Police and Gestapo patrol in front of roadblocks. Although

I search for Marc as I weave through, I can't spot him and my worry grows. No-one can get in or out; the whole area is closed and swarming with military and police. I pass the Opera House and try to duck up one of the side streets, but each road is blocked and guarded, or filled with trucks and cars with SS plates on.

A policeman stomps out from a house close to a roadblock, his short, dark blue cape flapping behind him like an irritated bird. He beckons forward a cattle truck that's parked on a kerb. While it's manoeuvring, other passers-by pause and stand with me, muttering between themselves.

More policemen troop into the street, handguns out and form a funnel between the doorway and the truck. I stand on my tiptoes, dread souring in my throat.

The soldier at the roadblock orders, "Show your *Carte* for checks." I step back, but then, shouts come from inside the building. No-one leaves; a hush falls - we're all frozen, staring at what's about to happen. Even the guard turns to look.

A few men, one still in his night-shirt, walk out, hands behind their heads. More and more people are pushed through the door until there's a group of about fifteen in various states of dress, awkwardly hemmed between the two lines of policemen. My view is obscured by the triangles of police capes, but Marc is tall, I reassure myself. I'd see his head at least.

The last to exit is an old man, wearing a three-piece suit. "My cane," he cries, turning on the doorstep to glance back. "Please, I must have my cane." Then he stumbles as an arm shoves him out.

"You won't need it anymore," an older, grey haired Gestapo officer snarls, emerging from inside. He stands on the threshold, brushes down his black greatcoat, lights a cigarette, then blows out a plume of smoke as if he's rewarding himself on a job well done. He barks, "Get them in the truck."

The tailgate bangs down, then a young, grey-uniformed soldier with a rifle around his neck jumps up to balance on it. He waves the weapon, training it on each individual as they clamber up and shuffle under the canvas covering.

Last in the queue again, struggling to make the jump, is the man in the suit. No-one helps him as he teeters, clinging to the wooden lip, trying to fling his leg up so he can roll into the truck.

Junior officers laugh and jeer, "Get on with it, Grandpa."

"We don't have all day," the SS officer says. He marches over. "Perhaps this will incentivise you." He jabs the lit cigarette end into his thigh, and the man screams.

"Just shut up!" A young-looking policeman says, breaking rank and stepping forward. Others in the defensive line exchange uncomfortable glances. The policeman's cheeks flush as he tries to lever the old man's leg up, but this only results in another screech of pain.

The SS officer responds by drawing out his gun and slamming it into the side of the captive's head.

The old man falls off the tailgate and lands on the tarmac.

From inside the truck, gasps and sobs. Outstretched hands seek to help, but they are warned back in by the gunman on the tailgate barking, "Stay."

As the officer steps forward and points his revolver at the man's head, his shadow looms over the shaking body on the pavement. Something in his stiff gait, the long legs and bearing, reminds me of Pieter. I step off the kerb. "Don't!" I cry out, terrified of history repeating itself.

The officer's head whips around and he glares straight at me. His eyes are shaded by the peak of his hat, but I sense their resolve in his stern expression.

It is not Pieter, but it might as well be. "Please, don't hurt him," I cry.

Another step closer; my hands stretch forward. "He's done nothing."

Curling his lip, the officer's arm straightens behind him.

BANG

Bang!

I flinch as he shoots the old man, all the while staring at me.

"Died in transit," the officer says, clicking to chamber another round.

I lurch forward, about to argue 'No he didn't' but his arm swings back, to point the gun. At me. "Unless anyone says otherwise."

Freezing, my mouth runs dry. The man only wanted his cane - Sister Luisa just wanted to protect us. My silence did not save the nuns then, my intervention could not save the old man now. I can't tear my gaze from the blood, darker than the shadow of his killer as it oozes through the waistcoat and over neatly pressed lapels.

How can they get away with cold-blooded murder, in front of so many witnesses?

What can a mouse do when she is too small to roar?

Fingers curl around my biceps, hauling me back onto the pavement.

"Don't give them a reason," Madame Auzello's voice hisses in my ear.

The SS officer's eyes narrow, on the American behind me. Quite deliberately, he shakes his head in a tut-tut-tut. Still holding onto my arm, Madame Auzello stiffens. By her side, I see her jaw jut forward. This obviously isn't the first time she and this man have met. A slight shift of his arm, and the gun is pointing at her!

She steps backward, her head lowered, and pulling me with her. The crowd shuffles, parting around us in silence, as she yanks me away.

"I should've done more," I cry, looking back.

"Hush. What can anyone do?" Still gripping my arm, she speed walks us past the checkpoints, the covered trucks rumbling away, and until the shouted orders which echoed through the streets are inaudible. We stop at the river's edge and she grips the railing.

"That was very stupid," she says, facing the grey water. I'm not sure if she's talking to me or the river, or perhaps herself. Then, she side-eyes me. "Why are you even here?"

"I came to look for Marc." Staring straight ahead as if I don't see her, I still don't dare tell my boss what we knew. The thought occurs to me, why is she here as well? "You?"

"Don't presume to monitor my movements, Devereaux." Her lips press together and she shakes her head.

"The less I know, the better, eh?" I say, echoing Kat's advice to me.

"Precisely."

We gaze across the calm waters for a minute, then I pluck up courage. "That Nazi knew you."

"We've met, under less congenial circumstances, shall we say." A wry smile pulls on her cheek. "Now, as he knows my face under these circumstances, I shall have to be more careful. As should you, and we'll both forget this conversation - this situation - ever happened."

"Yes, Madame." But I will never forget. How can I?

She turns and leans her back on the railings, still not meeting my eyes. "But, you have proven yourself to be useful, and brave. You just need to be smarter." Then her gaze swoops down to me and she switches into fluent German, "Before you take action."

Her tacit approval feels like permission. For a moment, I'm stood before the Mother Superior, showing her clothes I fashioned, re-purposed from stolen scraps, and seeking her approval, or judgement.

"I should have taken more action before all of this. We tried," I admit. "But it wasn't enough. Too many people stayed." I falter, desperate to tell her what I knew, but I cannot, so I hang my head. "We failed."

"You and Marc? You skirt too close to danger, child."

I nod. "And now he's missing. Maybe they took him too."

She touches my arm. "It is better to try something hopeful, however small, than stand by and do nothing. Nothing is certain in this world except hope and the sun rising. But - you must live to see the sun rise to have the hope. A body cannot do more than cast a deeper shadow over dark times."

My fingers grip the railing. "I need to find Marc." Please let him not be taken, or dead. My stomach knots at the mere thought.

"No, what you need to do is escort me back to the hotel. Frank's boys will find him." She tweaks my uniform straight. "Chin up, the sun will rise again tomorrow, but for now, you should stick to the shadows."

I gaze at her, straight in the eyes. "Shadows," I say, "can't hide the truth when you shine a light on them."

Butterfly Kisses

Madame Auzello didn't spare the francs to organise a search for Marc as soon as we returned. When my dinner shift in the Grill Room ends, I shoulder my way into Rue Cambon's packed bar to see if there's any update. Frank's throaty deep voice mimics Marlene Dietrich herself in a slurred rendition of her version of the song, Lilli Marlene, which appears to be being sung in both French and German - as if that will unite us. The curfew fell hours ago, so the crowd must all be residents.

I lurk at the edge of the bar, then mouth to Frank as soon as he catches my eye. "Have you heard anything?"

"He's been down at the *tôle*," Frank pauses to whisper across the bar top. The prison!

My look of alarm sends him rushing to put his arm around me. "Not in it. Demonstrating outside, my lad said. Near where he lives."

"They don't even need a reason to arrest?"

"I think the police have enough on their plate than to be worrying about a few people waving signs, eh? Cells all over the city are full, I hear, and he's miles away from the 11th."

Frank's only trying to reassure me but I explode. "All he had to do was..."

"Keep your voice down, Edelweiss." His eyes narrow. "For all our sakes."

My mouth clamps shut before I cause more of a scene in a bar full of celebrating Nazis.

Frank shoots a smile at the enquiring face a bit further down the mahogany. He jokes, "Women, eh? Always worrying over nothing." He says in a deliberately loud, calm and fatherly tone, "He'll come home, tail between his legs, soon enough." Winking at the drinker, he then pats my hand and joins in the refrain. "I'd hold you tight, we'd kiss goodnight. My Lilli of the Lamplight, my own Lilli Marlene...."

Frank's insinuation that Marc should come home to me, as a lover would a wife, doesn't irritate me as perhaps it used to. Maybe it's the relief of knowing he's not been taken to Drancy, or worse. I play along with a giggle as I turn to leave. Marc's alive, and still in Paris. I should be grateful. There's nothing more I can do now, except hope he hasn't been arrested for civil unrest or something. The curfew won't lift until five in the morning; I can go nowhere until then without ending up in the *tôle* myself.

As I wriggle through the crowd, I pass Hans entering. Alone. He gives me a tight-lipped nod of acknowledgement as he walks to the bar. At the door, I'm compelled to glance back over my shoulder. He's looking at me with a sympathetic expression. When our eyes meet, he looks down, twisting his finger as if there were a ring on it still.

Restless underneath my sweat-soaked sheets, I hear a gentle knock on my bedroom door. I open my eyes. Through the skylight, an orange dawn bathes the room in a peach glow. Another knock. I wonder if it's Madame Auzello with more news, or Claudette to tell me I've overslept, so I throw a blanket over my shoulders and open the door a crack.

Marc is standing there, dejection spread across his features. As he sees me, he slumps against the wall with relief. "Thank God."

"Thank goodness you're alright," I whisper, pulling the door shut behind me. My roommate is a deep sleeper, so as long as we keep our voices down, we should be fine.

"Hundreds." His voice is hoarse as he stares at the carpet. "They must have taken hundreds of Jews. All men. Why?"

I don't have an adequate answer. We're silent, contemplative as I touch his arm in solidarity. All I can think of is that I can't lose another person, it will break me. I swallow, looking up and down the empty hallway. This floor, where the female staff sleep, is nearly fully occupied now, but the one below...

"Move into the Ritz then," I say, knowing I'm being selfish. "I don't think this will be the end of it. I'll speak to Madame Auzello. I'm sure she can find space in the men's quarters."

He shakes his head. "I can't leave my mother. She needs me."

I grip his arm. "Your mother needs your wage, but I'm sure she'd rather know you were safe and alive. Send her money, but stay here, where we're protected. The Nazis aren't going to bang on the doors of the very roof they live under."

When he looks at me, the low light of the hallway does little to hide the hollows under his eyes.

"I didn't know where you were, Marc, so I went looking. I thought you had been taken."

"I couldn't even get into the 11th to bang on doors. It was all shut off. The Metro stations, everything. So I went home, sickened. Knowing what they were about to do. Then, I saw the trucks arrive at the police station. I just wanted to show them it isn't right, what they're doing to us."

"I watched a man murdered, Marc. Right in front of me."

His eyes flare and his hand reaches for mine. "You shouldn't have gone looking for me."

The strain of the day babbles out of me. "He pointed the gun at me, Marc, when I objected. And then I thought... you could have been arrested for disruption. You know how they feel about people who are... different."

He glances at his weaker arm. "I know. I'm sorry."

"You should have told me where you were going," I snap.

A lock of his dark hair falls over his forehead. I see the vulnerability and contrition in his haunted eyes yet I cannot stop. "I know I've no right to be worried, only, we're in this together, aren't we? I thought, since I found the note, we were."

"We can never be in this together, no matter how much I want that, because I'm not the same as you, am I?" Bitterness seeps into his tone. "No-one's hunting you down."

My words slip from my mouth like an unstoppable train of thought, powered by fear. "Not now they aren't. But they were. And, underneath all the paperwork lies and stamps differentiating us, I am the same race as you."

His mouth drops open a fraction and he frowns.

I must explain now or I might never get the chance again. "Or at least, once upon a time, I was designated Jewish. Taken in as a child when my parents died, and brought up a Catholic. Never quite allowed to forget what my parents were, even though I can't even remember what they did that's supposed to be so wrong. Katarina isn't even my real name. You see, without the help of friends, I would be..."

"In the same category as me. And, according to the Nazis, you either are or you aren't Jewish."

There's a relief in telling him, and, a risk. I nod and stare at the lump in his neck bobbing up and down as he swallows.

He says, "I don't blame you for hiding it. Plenty of others do. I'll never tell. I promise."

"I know you won't."

And I do. I'm not sure when it happened, but I trust him. "But, please, don't disappear again. I... I just need to know you are safe."

His face softens. "Does that mean you care? Because I snuck up here to see if you were safe, too."

I thump his good arm gently and he winces, but there's a smile playing on his lips. Then our eyes meet.

"Yes," I murmur, my hand rising to smudge away the dark circles. His eyes glance at my wrist, as if he is surprised by the contact, then, his head tips to meet my palm. His kisses the inside of my arm, on the pulse. "I care."

His hand reaches up to lay over mine. The touch of his curled finger, warm on mine, is gentle but firm, not quite what I'd expected it to feel like.

"That's good. Ever since you found that note, and wanted to tell me first so we could do something about it, I've worried about keeping you safe, away from all the trouble." His other, stronger arm snakes around my waist and he pulls me closer. There's a wiry strength in his hold as he guides my back against the wall.

While I'm adjusting to the unfamiliar, not altogether unwelcome, sensation of another's body pressed against mine, he whispers in my ear. "So, what's your real name?"

"Hannah."

His breath feels warm against my nape, sending a shiver through me.

"Pleased to meet you, Hannah." He kisses me on one cheek, raises his head, then gently, slowly grazes his lips on the other. His eyelashes feel like butterflies on my skin, then he pulls back and gazes at me. "Would it be alright if we are 'together'? As more than co-conspirators?"

"I think so," I mutter. My chest feels tight, uncomfortably so. His head lowers towards my lips - he's about to kiss me! The pulse at the base of my neck throbs, as if my heart wants to break free and spill out all of my secrets, and yet, the burning shame of my past experience traps me still. Quickly, I turn my head away.

"I know it's not exactly the perfect time," Marc says quietly, withdrawing from my embrace. "And I'm hardly the perfect man."

I grab his hand. "Perhaps there will never be a right time, and I've never known a man to be perfect. I don't even know many men, truth be told." I laugh softly, shaking my head free of the image of Hans. "And as you now know, I'm not perfection either."

"I think you are."

"Then you put me on too high a pedestal." I squeeze his fingers. "Perhaps, if you lived closer, we'd have time to get to know each other, properly." Maybe then I'll find the courage to tell him the rest.

He smiles. "That sounds wonderful. Ask Madame Auzello then, if you think she'll listen."

"I think she will," I reply, opening my bedroom door. "It's nearly time to get up anyway, so I'll speak to her this morning. I'm sure she'll help."

STOOD UP, TWICE

Business decisions and matters of the heart rarely mix, it seems. Madame Auzello doesn't agree, at first, and Marc continues to live with his mother an hour's walk away. September arrives and with it, a directive comes from Germany: all Jews over the age of 6 must purchase yellow cloth stars, and sew them onto their clothes.

Claude Auzello looks grave as he informs us of the new law in a staff meeting later that autumn. He's at great pains to avoid meeting our eyes, merely says of it, "Of course, our uniforms are sacrosanct. Integrity and pride are the backbone of our work, representing outstanding service. True patriots have nothing to be ashamed of here. If you can't stand by that, well, then there's no place for you at the Ritz."

I'm confused until we're dismissed and I can ask Marc what he meant.

"He's giving me, and the other Jewish staff here, reasons to ignore the directive. Patriotism. Uniform sanctity."

"So, he's not asking you to leave?"

Marc shakes his head. "I don't think so. He knew, when he put me to work back in the kitchens, that there would be a problem eventually with me serving Nazis. This directive," he says bitterly, "is another way of marking us out as different. The so-called apartments where they took the Jews to in Drancy ghetto are already emptying, I hear. Making room for more of us, no doubt. A bright yellow star - easier to spot, and not wearing it if your papers say you should, will be a good enough reason to arrest."

I look down at my dark blue uniform. Appearances are everything here. "So will you do it? Sew on a star to your ordinary clothes?"

He shrugs. "I don't want to get in trouble, and I can't avoid who I am."

"You just don't want it announced," I surmise.

"But there's a unity in it," he says, looking directly into my eyes. "We shouldn't be embarrassed. We have a proud heritage, and my people should stand together. I know my mother won't want us to risk being caught without if it's the law now." He snorts. "Mind you, she can't even thread a needle these days."

"If your mother's struggling to sew them on, bring them to me," I offer. "Wonky sewing won't do."

"She'd love to meet you," he says, shyly. We haven't spent any time together outside of work, our hours are so long, but clearly he's told his mother about me.

I'm still deciding how I feel about that when he offers, "How about it? I can collect you from here, a lovely brisk walk back home on Sunday morning? Your next day off, right?"

I study my shoes, guilt churning my insides. I cannot give up on my hope of seeing Freddie and Kat, even though the company and winter sunlight sounds vastly preferable to the dark catacombs. "I'm sorry, I have plans."

"Oh. Right." He reaches over me to put more plates in the sink and my stomach twists.

"It's not that I don't want to, just... I'm still trying to sort out that radio. Ready for next time."

He chews on his bottom lip for a moment. "Maybe another day."

I'm about to leave when Madame Auzello comes into the kitchen. She strides straight over to Marc. "Devereaux, don't you have rooms to service?"

"Yes Madame," I reply, but I walk away slowly, lingering behind the rack of plates instead.

In a low voice, I hear her say, "It's not often I agree with my husband these days, but, given the circumstances, we think it might be an idea to revisit you living in, after all."

He drops a plate into the water with a plop.

"But, you would need to 'fit in' if that were to be the case."

Marc nods. "It won't be an easy decision, Madame, but I'll give it some thought."

She glances through the plate rack, at me, as if she always intended for me to hear, then looks back at him. "I believe Frank might be able to source alternative paperwork to keep things all above board if you do decide to stay. Of course, there are certain behavioural expectations of live-in staff - no fraternisation, and no drawing attention to oneself, for example. No more demonstrations."

I hide the smile on my face as I leave the kitchen, heart glowing. It's a risky opportunity she's presenting, but, I don't want to influence Marc to act against his own beliefs, nor, as she is suggesting, dissuade him from expressing his opinions. I wonder if Frank can sort me out new papers though, perhaps when this is all over, and I might safely return to being Hannah Edelstein.

To my delight, it's worth standing Marc up. "No darkness today!" Kat grabs my arm and pulls me out of the Catacomb queue. Her face lights up at my relieved smile. As usual, she's dressed immaculately in another skirt and jacket combination I don't recognise. "Let's go for coffee instead."

Just the thought of it makes my mouth water. "Where? And where's Freddie?"

"With Pieter. Celebratory hot chocolates apparently. Sorry." She glances away, and I suddenly realise what Pieter might be celebrating. "Look, I don't have long, but there's someone I want you to meet. A client of mine."

We cross the road. I don't think I want confirmation of what Pieter has to be happy about, and I'm annoyed at him for taking my son away from seeing me. "Kat, the radio. Did you manage to fix it?"

"I needed some parts, and then this client mentioned they might be able to help."

"What, you just happened to mention it?"

"Don't get cross, Maus." She presses her lips together briefly. "It's not that easy to turn a receiver into a transmitter, you know."

"I'm sorry. I don't understand much about these things."

"I'm learning. Being trained up, you might say. Turns out I've an aptitude for… this kind of thing," she says, her eyes sliding towards mine in a shifty manner. "And, they also wondered if you might be in a position to find out other information."

They? I think of the note, my cheeks instantly burning. "Well, I don't know about that."

But I do. Last week I found the draft of an order for troop movements, the week before I glimpsed Goering's diary. Would 'they' be able to use such information? "I'm only a chambermaid. A waitress sometimes."

She stops mid pavement and tugs my arm like she's admonishing a child. "Hannah, I'm not stupid, and I'm putting myself at risk too. You're the one who urged me to do something about the situation, then you turn up with a radio asking to send a message."

Kat starts walking again, really fast, and I struggle to keep up with her long legs. "I'm trying to help, but you must understand how tricky things are for me. Bad enough I'm tangled up in the black market racket, and now this. One slip, or loose word and I'm exposed." She flings her fingers back towards the catacombs. "Christmas Eve is around the corner and my house guests are expecting a feast. A German one with bloody swastika-iced biscuits. And where the hell am I supposed to find fresh fish!"

I live alongside their presence too. At least the Ritz is planning a thoroughly French menu, for those who can afford to top up their rations, but we had to put swastika-embossed baubles on the Christmas tree.

"You're very brave," I offer when she slows her pace. I wonder what on earth she's got herself involved with, and how much it might impact Freddie, but I daren't risk a scene in public.

When we arrive at a café, she asks for a table at the back and we order what might pass for coffee, for three. It's deliciously warm inside, compared to the chill. We peel off our layers of coats and scarves. While we're waiting, she shifts around in her seat, touching up her perfect make up and bestowing subtle smiles at the other customers. I wonder if one of them is the client, but when I ask who we're expecting, she looks put out. "Don't you trust me?"

Our drinks arrive and she tells me all about how well Freddie is doing in school. The motherly pride in her voice reassures me, as well as making my chicory coffee harder to swallow. The morning flies past, us two women simply sharing refreshments as if there are no cares in the world but our own domestic troubles. Neither of us really relax though, even though we end up sharing the third cup. I can't help but notice how brittle Kat looks as she preens with every arrival through the door. It's as if she's putting on a polished front, but underneath the table, her leg jiggles.

No-one approaches us, and, as lunch orders start coming from the kitchen, Kat's face looks more and more resigned. Conversation peters out and she stops looking at the door.

"Please Kat, who is it you're expecting?"

Her lips twist as she considers how to respond. "An American journalist. Sort of."

My eyes narrow. "Sort of?"

"She's… resourceful and, not at all what she said she was really. She told me she was a regular here at this time, if I ever needed to contact her."

I hid my surprise. With the way she was behaving, I expected the client to be a man. Someone she wants to impress. There are plenty of journalists who hang out in Frank's bar, and I wonder if I've seen her client before. "Oh, an American. Do you think Roosevelt's re-election will bring them into the war finally?"

"I keep out of politics, and it doesn't seem to worry my house guests. I don't want to say too much, in case I'm wrong, but you'll like her, too. We all share a love of couture, and she has the best taste in hats! She's got this one with a huge pheasant's feather sticking out, as if it wants to tickle anyone taller than her into submission. She's… direct in how she asks for what she needs. She reminds me of you a little."

"How long should we wait?"

"She's not ordered from me, or offered to teach me anything in a while, and this is the only way I know to find her." She sighs. "I guess she's not coming."

Damn. No radio.

Kat pulls on her coat. "When she gets in touch again, I'll ask her to come to you instead. She wants to know any information which might help."

"What do you mean?"

A man with short, freshly clipped hair walks towards the bar, chinking money in his hand. He nods at Kat. "Madame."

She flashes the German a smile as he passes.

"Don't ask, eh?" I say.

"You don't want to know," she replies. Her neutral mask returns as she does up her buttons. "Safer that way."

THE LADY WITH THE PHEASANT FEATHER

A tall, thin-faced brunette stands by the Maître D's table, wearing a stylish hat with a long pheasant feather poking out of it. She wears a full skirt, thick tights and a well-cut jacket. Pierre is busy with other customers, so I approach instead. Her warm brown eyes run over me as I offer, "Can I show you to a table, Madame?"

Her lips part to reveal glossy, straight teeth and her accent reminds me of Madame Auzello's - perfect French with a hint of dollar about it. "I'm looking for Blanche Auzello. Is she here?"

She stares at me intently while I pretend to check the reservation list with a slightly shaking hand. "Madame Auzello is one of the managers, but I've not seen her today." My eyes double check her feather as I take a chance. "Perhaps you meant Madame Weisz? I do know that lady. I'm Devereaux. She might have mentioned me to you."

"Oh. Yes. She did." She looks me up and down, then a warm smile graces her face. "Perhaps you can show me to the bar then. The one on the other side of the hotel. We can talk on the way."

I glance across the room and catch Pierre's eye, holding up two fingers to indicate I'll be back soon. Luckily, the restaurant is half empty, so as long as I'm quick, my absence won't be remarkable.

As she walks with me towards the corridor linking the halves of the hotel, I notice she has an almost imperceptible limp, and one foot makes a strange sound across the marble tiles. When she shifts her weight from one leg to the other, her shoe slips a little, and I realise her skirt is actually split trousers - culottes. It's a bold fashion choice - most women coming here are keen to show off their feminine wardrobe and not risk defying the law against women wearing trousers.

"Oh, to wear pants again." She comments, catching me staring. "But, these are more practical for cycling."

"It's not that," I say. "Should we slow down, though? These tiles can be slippery."

"Not at all," she grins. "Most people don't notice, but then, I suspect you're not most people. I call the leg Cuthbert." She indicates her calf. "He's not so keen on polished surfaces, you're right. But, we persevere. So, you're the girl who made the request for a transmitter?"

"Yes. Did you manage to get the pieces for Madame Weisz?"

"One better - she's about to receive a fully working, portable model."

"Really?"

"Yes. There's just one snag. It's here."

"What?"

We pause and pretend to look in a shop window while she chews on her lip. "The courier had a bad landing. Broken leg, I'm told. And, he's holed up under the care of another contact of mine, someone very senior, somewhere here."

My heart thuds. Could it be Madame Auzello? I recalled the day she suddenly appeared in the empty corridor in the attics, smelling medicinal. At the time, I assumed she'd been day drinking! I glance behind me, a few officers amble along the corridor towards us. "Are you sure? This place is stuffed with Nazis."

She points to a pretty piece of jewellery, and from the side of her mouth says, "That's the point, and the problem."

The clip of their heels is like a hammer tapping closer. She gracefully turns and bestows a serene smile at the grey uniforms. They nod curtly in acknowledgement. Following her lead, I bob respectfully until the pair have passed us.

We start down the corridor again, her expression more stern than before. "My contact apparently got a man out before, just some cuts and scrapes on him."

"How did they do it before?"

"The gentleman simply walked out in a lovely new velvet dinner jacket one evening. Rather a dashing unofficial guest. Hate to think of where that one-off piece has ended up."

Then I remember why I'd gone looking for Madame Auzello - because I had Chanel's fabric and she needed a sewing machine. I drop my head so my smile is less obvious.

"This chap's trickier, because of his leg, as well as a lack of suitable clothing. Seems there's no-one who can help with that here now."

The image of Chanel, away again, prompts me. "I could help. I'm a seamstress. If you can help with supplies."

"Indeed. I'll bear that in mind. And, our mutual friend seemed to think you had something more to offer?"

I wet my lips then say, "In the course of my job here I might come across information."

"I see."

"I'm in and out of all the rooms here, I'm also a chambermaid. What's rubbish to one person is perhaps useful to another."

Her composed expression lifts. "I see. You're right. Anything would help. We've people who can piece things together from various sources."

"People?"

"It's not just me of course, or your friend. There's... a bigger operation behind us co-ordinating a response to information received." She waggles her eyebrows.

I realise then that this lady is juggling far more balls than I ever could. Kat was right, I do like her though. There's something in her earnest determination and straight-forwardness which inspires confidence.

"Anyway," she continues, slowing as we approach the bar door. "What I came for today is to leave instructions for this luggage, which needs removing. The equipment can't be operated from here. The signal would be too easily detected and the risk of a search in this place would uncover more than I'm happy to accept." She sizes me up. "The suitcase might be a little heavy."

Being a good foot taller than me, I'm suddenly made aware of my diminutive status. "I'm tougher than I look."

"I'm sure you are. So, if I left a message for my contact, suggesting where the equipment could be left, you could then deliver it." She pulls a notepad from her pocket and scribbles a missive.

I suggest, "How about your contact leaves the luggage with Jaques, the doorman? I can collect it from him, but where would I take it then?"

"To Madame Weisz's house."

My stomach flops over. Why couldn't it have been the catacombs? Funny, Kat's house was once a place of sanctuary, but me appearing there puts almost everyone I care about at risk. "But there's Germans there."

"I know. She's not too keen either, but we've no choice. The signal, you know. Needs to be clear."

"She's very clever," I say loyally, trying to push aside my terror.

She arches her eyebrow. "I know. She's a very quick study, picking it all up with surprising ease."

I thought of Kat's unusual ability with electrical and mechanical items, and her puzzle obsession. "She'll do the job admirably, I've no doubt."

The lady nods. "What's needed to make this all worth it, is any information you might come across."

I nod, distracted by wondering if I could instead hand over the radio at the catacombs.

"Anyway, must dash." She finishes the note and tears it out of her booklet. "Sorry it took so long to meet you. Anything you find out, send to Madame Weisz, but if you need me specifically, send a message via Greep using one of Frank's boys. Let's use a codename.... Mademoiselle..."

"Souris?" I suggest. Miss Mouse. It seems appropriate.

She flickers her eyes to Frank's bar and shifts around on one leg. "But don't trust his lads with anything of importance, ok? Deliver the luggage yourself to Madame Weisz, and use her as a conduit for information. I'll see she knows what to do with it."

"Good luck," she says, palming the the note with 'Madame Auzello' scribbled on it, before pushing open the doors. "Ah, Frank, do you have any of your wonderful lemonade? I'm parched."

I can do this, I think, returning to the Grill Room with a spring in my step. Only when Marc asks what's made me so chirpy do I realise - I don't even know the woman's name.

GOING TO GÖRING

C hanel is back, living in the hotel for the Christmas period, but her rooms are in disarray. Recently, she commandeered a bedroom directly above hers and paid for a staircase to be built linking the two, so she has more space for a salon downstairs. The hotel is so full with tourists and officers, keen to relax before Christmas, even if she wanted to stay in another room while they finish off decorating, I doubt there would be one available.

I do my best to clean, stepping around cans of paint as I head up the new, narrow staircase and into her bedroom. It's tiny, barely able to fit the bed and bedside tables in, and I suspect was probably allocated to an employee before. The massive wardrobe has remained below, and the sewing machine draped and in a corner as if she doesn't want the reminder of who she used to be. While I tug off the sheets, fragrant with No. 5 and 'Pour Un Homme de Caron', Han's cologne, from the bed, the painter returns. He whistles as he dabs the stairwell, pausing only to say "Non, non," when I try to descend. I have no choice but to lug the laundry out of the top bedroom and down the service stairs or risk getting paint on it.

Half hidden by the bundle of dirty sheets, I pass Madame Auzello in the corridor. She's tottering the other way, bowed to one side by a reddish brown leather suitcase. My heart sinks as I guess what's inside the luggage. I'll have to find someone to cover me if I'm to slip out and go to the Lion's Den at Kat's house before curfew.

"Can I get a porter to help you with that?" I say.

My offer of assistance is brushed off with a grimace and a shake of Madame's head. I glance along the hallway, trying to spot where she appeared from and failing, while she huffs and puffs towards the elevator. As she jabs at the button repeatedly, I hear her call, "Did you do the Imperial Suite yet?"

"I'm not assigned to Reichsmarshall Göring's rooms, Madame."

"They'll need help, and I need to know if there's damages to repair. A big party in there last night." Then she muttered under her breath, "*Die respektlose Kartoffel.*"

I'd heard Göring called potato before, and disrespectful as well, but never before by management. The most senior Nazi to keep quarters here, he has his own dedicated staff to serve him, but, this sounds like a direct instruction to represent the Ritz. Just the possibility of coming face to face with him makes my stomach knot. Plenty of other senior officers come and go, but I've yet to encounter the man they call the second most powerful man in Germany.

As I peer over the sheets, her face is the picture of innocence with a flashy smile of her own. "You never know what you might uncover or who you might overhear."

She knows very well I speak German, and once again, I sense she is inviting me to take action. "I'll finish up my assignments, Madame, then go and see if I'm needed."

"Good girl, Devereaux." The lift arrives. She steps in, then holds the doors open. "Oh, I meant to mention, Marc has decided to take up residence." She frowns. "I'm trusting you to make sure he doesn't get into any more trouble."

My heartbeat flutters. Marc and I have barely been able to speak, it's been so busy lately. My eyes fall on the suitcase as the lift doors close and a plan forms in my mind.

By the time I finish my previously assigned duties, it's after lunchtime before I can return to the first floor. The Imperial Suite is the largest in the hotel, with its own private dining room and kitchen, separate maid's quarters, two bedrooms and an enormous salon overlooking the splendour of Place Vendôme. In the hall-way outside, Colonel Speidel, the chief of staff for Paris's military commander, looks pallid as he quietly directs three young men in overalls to be careful. They hardly look old enough to be out of school. Speidel pays me no heed as I slip through the salon's half open doors with my box of cleaning equipment.

I stop short as soon as I'm inside - Hans and Chanel perch on one of the satin sofas. Opposite them, Göring lounges in a velvet bathrobe, flabby belly flesh half exposed. An unfamiliar man, wearing a sharp suit with massive hands and long legs, is perched next to him.

The room itself looks relatively tidy, although there are still boxes of empty bottles by the bar area, and glasses left haphazardly on the windowsills. All around the edges, standing on tables and easels, is a fine collection of artwork and sculptures. I am no art expert but I recognise some of the Old Master's styles from some of the coffee table books Katarina had in her salon.

My eyes meet Hans's but no-one else notices my entrance. He frowns, holding my gaze for a long moment before he looks back at the others in the room. My mouth runs dry as Chanel shares a cigarette with him.

The Reichsmarshall's eyes are bright and beady, his pudgy arms wafting around as his enthusiasm builds. "Ya, ya. We can hold it here, Bruno! Such an exhibition will be the talk of Paris."

The conversation is in German, which is probably why Chanel looks so bored. My heart thumps but I need to make myself look busy so I can glean as much information as possible. I traipse over to the corner of the living area and begin quietly clearing dirty glasses to a tray.

Göring leans forward and picks up a champagne flute from the table. "Depending on how well it goes in Russia, perhaps the Führer will come. Aren't you glad we rescued you from the winter there, before Operation Barbarossa began?" He cackles, patting the giant's knee, before he is overtaken with a smoker's cough.

Chanel's flash of concern is quickly replaced with a raised eyebrow as Hans translates about the exhibition for her. She fawns and switches the conversation to French. "All of Paris society must come to such an occasion. Do you think Breker would show some of his sculptures? Although," she waves the cigarette towards the side tables, crammed with ornaments and vases. "Herr Lohse here has done a fine job of securing these pieces for you, Hermann. So many admired them last night, it seems a shame to closet them away in one of your places."

Speidel enters, gesticulating for his workmen to begin packing up the paintings. I keep my head down and slowly wipe ring marks away from the windowsills.

Göring, still coughing, manages to say, "Plenty more where they came from. And Arno, yes, if we make his works the centrepieces of an exhibit. The E.R.R. will help select the display, ya?"

Lohse nods, watching closely as tarpaulins are unfolded and pictures placed on them. "I'm sure we can assist. Kurt will be delighted with the idea as well, Reichsmarshall." He growls, "Careful," as one of the workmen manhandles a vase.

Speidel rushes over. "That belongs here," he fusses, replacing the Ritz décor and reprimanding the teenager. "Only the ones I listed."

The boy looks bewildered, which I can empathise with, as the suite was already full of antiques before these additions were displayed.

"A public exhibition would be great publicity for all the work you're doing here reclaiming artwork for the Reich," Hans says. "But let's not get ahead of ourselves, presuming to know the Führer's movements. Spring. Perhaps May, do you think?" His eyes flick to Göring, who grunts and wipes the spittle off his chin.

The windowsills are clear, as Hans sips then turns to Chanel. In French, he says, "Art exhibition in spring, my dear."

Chanel stubs out her cigarette. "Paris is always at its best before the heat of summer." She twists on the cushions and lays a hand on Hans' arm. "Spatz, we should leave the Reichsmarshall to the rest of his day."

She stands, nods graciously to Göring, who dismisses her with a wave of his hand and a "Ya, ya. Thank you for stopping by, Coco."

The giant unfurls himself. "I won't take up any more of your time either. Lots to organise." He straightens his jacket before clicking his heels together and raising his arm. "Heil Hitler!"

Hans and Speidel follow suit, with perhaps slightly less enthusiasm, and then they all head for the door.

I pick up the tray of glasses and allow them to leave before me. Just then, an older lady, grey-haired and stout and in a black maid's uniform, comes through the bedroom door. I don't see her around the hotel much as a member of staff because she's assigned exclusively to Göring and this suite, but I know she lords it over the rest of us. She sees me and her mouth sets a downward turn. While I'm walking towards the door, she approaches.

"I could have done that," she hisses.

"Madame Auzello sent me to help with the clearing," I whisper back. Offering her a small, hopefully subservient smile, I take another pace.

"She should have checked with me first."

I freeze, mind blanking under her guard dog glare, before I realise she's just protecting her own interests. "I'm sure she meant no offence by it. You do so much already. Let me save your legs and take these down for you."

Her lips purse, then she stomps over to my cleaning box. "You can tell Madame," she grumbles, returning and shoving the box awkwardly under my arm. "Hilda needs no assistance with her duties."

Göring orders her to put on the wireless while he has his bath. Very carefully, so as not to chink the glasses together, I cross the suite, head down. He grunts getting up from the sofa. "The cleaning can wait."

She shoots me a final glare then waddles across to the unit in the corner. Goosebumps rise on my arms. Because of Hilda, I've been noticed. One mistake now, and I could lose my job.

The voice of Radio Paris, which is run by the German state, is ending a news broadcast. "Pearl Harbour remains in a state of emergency while President Roosevelt addressed Congress."

I stare straight ahead, processing implications while my feet automatically take tiny paces towards the open door. Between the heavy tray and the cleaning box digging into my ribs, it's no easy task. I'm nearly there when the radio announcer declares solemnly, "He has declared a state of war between the United States and the Japanese Empire."

I flinch at the smash of broken china behind me, followed by loud swearing from Göring. My heart hammers - with hope, rather than fear - as I escape.

LUGGAGE

The glasses clink together like warning bells in my head as I rush down the stairs. A tall man is hunched over the sink. It takes me a moment to realise my beau's hair has been cut short and he now wears glasses. His smarter appearance reminds me I need to re-bleach my roots.

Marc glances at the sparkle in my eye, the flush of my cheeks, then looks at the tray. His face falls. "It's never ending."

"But it might be." I beam. "I just heard on the radio, America has declared war on Japan."

"So?"

"So, that could mean they come to help us as well?"

He pulls the plug on the dirty dishwater and stares into the vortex. "Maybe."

His despondency concerns me. "Madame Auzello tells me you're moving here. That's good, isn't it?"

"They arrested my neighbours, then came for me while I was at work yesterday."

"Oh no! I'm sorry." Putting my hand on his shoulder, I turn his chest towards me, but his head hangs still. I can understand his change of look and sullen attitude. "But, I'm relieved you're safe. And," I lean closer even though he is stiff and unyielding. "Now you're here, I need your help with something. The equipment we need - I think it's time to deliver it."

The sides of his eyes flick to mine. "Really?"

I nod. "Better yet, I've found something else out. Something to tell. Come with me and I'll tell you all about it."

His lips lift on one side in a wry half smile. "I'm a wanted man now. I can't go out."

My shoulders drop. "Oh."

"But," he says, wiping his hand on a towel. "Only until I get new papers to go with my new look." Marc reaches to caress my cheek. "And then, I'm all yours. Properly all yours."

I search his eyes, then pull away. Although I have walked veiled in another's name myself, I don't have the heart yet to dash his hopes of our idyllic future by admitting my past. "I can't wait."

I'll have to go alone.

I head upstairs to change, grab my papers and shabby coat, conscious the curfew leaves me little time to get to the 16th Arrondissement and back. Jacques looks at me strangely when I ask him if anything has been left for a Mademoiselle Souris, but, he reaches into his cubbyhole closet and lugs out the same battered suitcase I saw Madame Auzello with earlier. Then, from his jacket, he extracts a small key which I pocket.

Although nothing is said, and every action deniable or unknown, confirmation of my suspicions places me as a small part of a larger network of people, actively doing something to help. My cheeks flush with victory - and confidence - as I cheerily bid him adieu.

Retrieving contraband is the easy part, staggering halfway across Paris, without raising suspicion, less so. My back aches from carrying the weight lopsided, especially with my usual winding circumvention of checkpoints. I head through the Jardin de Tuileries to reach the river.

The temperature plummets as dusk falls. I stop for a moment, shaking my cramping hands, fretting I won't make it to Kat's and return before the curfew. There's hardly any buses anymore, and I certainly can't afford a bicycle-taxi. I decide I can spare enough francs for the Metro to get me and my burden closer.

A group of off-duty Nazis led by their tour guide follow me down, then lurk at the bottom of the stairs. The platform at Concorde is packed, and for a minute, I'm taken back to that day when I arrived in Paris when the hustle and crowd overwhelmed a country girl like me, especially with her young son in tow. Now I have something equally precious in my charge.

The Germans are jovial, talking animatedly about their exploits the night before and how much of their wages they spent in having a good time. The elderly guide in charge of them turns a blind eye; either he doesn't understand what they are saying about women here or, like most Parisian, perhaps he chooses to ignore the city's growing reputation as the Reich's party capital in return for Reichsmarks and occasional handouts.

I push my way down the platform to get away. A choking smell of tobacco lingers, and diesel fug blankets the dim tunnels. It doesn't hide the presence of uniformed soldiers in the crowd or the homeless trying to sleep at the far end. People jostle together waiting, and, much as though it makes me anxious, in a crowd I'm less obvious.

When a train finally pulls onto the platform, all civility disappears as everyone bundles to get on. No room on the bench seats, the Nazis nab them. They can travel anywhere they want on the Metro, for free. My suitcase and I are sandwiched between some ladies clutching shopping bags filled with a haul of fabric and an old man, who whistles between his teeth incessantly as the carriage jolts and judders.

It's a relief to emerge at Pompe, where Freddie and Kat took shelter when Paris was bombed, and breathe fresh, chilly air again. But, my journey is far from over. The sun has dipped below the skyline, leaving an orange streak in the sky as I walk towards Katarina's house. I dare not hope to see Freddie, given what I'm carrying. He should still be at school.

As I stagger down the familiar boulevard, small differences strike me. In the slim juliette balconies, sacks sprout with vegetables. The sight of greenery, even in this cold winter, makes me smile. On some of the deeper ones, there's wooden rabbit hutches and bird cages with pigeons or chickens in. As meat is so expensive, I'm not surprised by Parisian resourcefulness. I'm so busy gawking at how the other half lives, I nearly forget what I'm here to do. The case knocks against my knees, jolting me to look ahead, and just in time. The officer Katarina dined with emerges from her house. Keep walking, keep walking, I pray, ducking my head.

And he does. An expensive smelling perfume trails behind him as he strides past me without a second glance.

I slowly release my sigh of relief. A few steps more and I pause to check he's gone when I reach Katarina's house. Someone's developed green fingers, because her once cream frontage is stained brown and her balconies are lined with sackcloth and topped with delicate carrots frills. Although there's no sign of life, no lights on, I decide it's better to try the front door rather than go around to the back yard, as it would be easier to explain my presence if Kat doesn't answer.

Luckily, she answers when I knock. "What are you doing here?" She bustles me in and slams the door closed. The hallway is cold, but warmer than outside. "Someone could see you."

"I brought this. It's... what we've been waiting for." I put the heavy case down on the tiles and hand her the key to unlock it.

Her eyebrow arches as she takes in the suitcase. "Bring it upstairs then, before Freddie gets home."

Although I'm disappointed, I'd already resigned myself to this likelihood. "Is he well? Enjoying school?"

Has he spoken? Does he miss me?

She starts climbing stairs, leaving me to lug the case after her. "He's fine. As well as he can be, under the circumstances. He's taken to wandering the catacomb tunnels while I'm packing orders."

"Is that safe?"

"He's a boy, no-one notices him at all," she snaps, as if I dare to criticise how she brings up my son. "He keeps finding new places for us to emerge. He's a little cataphile rat." She seems flustered as we rush up to the hallway beneath the attic. Clambering up the ladder, then flinging open the hatch, she pauses to catch her breath. "Hurry. Good thing no-one's home, you're as red as a berry, Hannah."

My arms feel weak as I heave the suitcase into her waiting hands before climbing up myself after her. "Did they tell you how to use it?"

Kat flips open the lid and starts untangling wires for the headset. I'm quiet as she studies the contraption as if mentally running a checklist. After a minute, she puts on the headset and plugs it in. "Pass me that notebook." Her voice is brisk and business-like as she points to a slim black book on my old sewing machine table.

As I hand it over, I say, "I have news to transmit, Kat. Big news."

She twists a dial, listens for a few seconds then her fingers brush over the tiny steel tapping button on the floor in front of her. She hesitates, then glances up at me. Her face is pale and tight, and I know she's putting on a brave voice for my benefit. "So soon?"

I nod.

"Once I do this, Maus, there's no going back. We're in the thick of it."

My heart thuds in my chest as I struggle to find appropriate words to reassure her - us both really - that this is the right thing to do. The risk of discovery is greater for her - I'm merely the messenger. I drop my hand on her shoulder and ruminate while she half-heartedly flicks through the pages of her notebook. All I can mutter is, "I know, but we have to," which seems utterly insufficient.

"I've got to sign in first." Her hesitation, finger hovering above the button then back to the notebook, again and again without tapping anything makes me think: will she go through with this? Am I asking too much of her?

"Is everything you need here?"

She nods her head as if she can read my mind.

"You could teach me," I say, with false bravado. "I'll do it."

Without a note of malice in her tone, she says, "It's bad enough you can barely read, imagine trying to transpose letters into a code." Her fingers reach up to touch mine. In a soft, choked voice, she asks, "What's the message?"

"Art exhibition, in Paris, probably May. Göring's involved, and Hitler might come to it."

Her hand retracts. "That's it?"

I should have thought it wasn't anything substantial. I have no date, or place, nothing certain. "Well, it's news, isn't it? Movement of senior officers, possibly the most senior, but simply informing them about when Göring's in town is too easy. It's common knowledge. Hitler's whereabouts aren't."

She shrugs and begins scribbling. The resulting letters are jumbled together - a cypher I would have struggled with, but for Kat it somehow all fits easily. All those crosswords and clues she used to do, it's no wonder she's picked up the subterfuge so quickly.

"I should go," I say, looking out of the small attic window and remembering the curfew.

Kat's reply is muffled by the pencil between her lips as her hands are busy with holding open the notebook. Her finger hover over the button. "Stay, just for a while." She spits out the impediment. "Please."

Looking at her, huddled over the suitcase, I realise that she doesn't want to take this step alone. I crouch next to her. "You're awfully clever, you know. I wouldn't have a clue what to do."

My praise seems to embolden her and she begins to tap with one finger, the other hand tracing the pencilled letters on the page. I've never seen anyone send a message before, but her strikes are firm and fast, which can only be a good thing, can't it?

When she's done, she smiles at me victoriously. Her headphones look like black bugs growing out of her ears and I grin back at her. Then, her eyes flare. She scrabbles on the floor to find the pencil and I freeze.

Her head bows as a message comes back, the scratch scratch of the lead like quiet slashes to my skin. Her jaw clenches and I hurry to her side. "A reply so soon?" I say when she pulls the headphones off.

Her breath quickens as she translates what she's written into legible words, then holds the pad up. I'm not certain I read it right, so I raise my eyebrow at her.

Kat whispers, "Find out when and where, then Hitler will die."

CONFIRMATION

"What?" I cannot keep the horror from my voice.

Kat looks at the page again, chewing her lip. "Yes. I've got that right."

We stare at each other, cogs turning as fast in her head as they are mine. "*Merde*," she says. "I didn't think..."

"This could change everything," I reply, tongue thick in my mouth. I can hardly believe I'm considering supporting their suggested course of action, but, such is my desperation. "We have to see it through."

She snorts. "If you imagine for one second it will be easy, you're madder than I thought. Even if Hitler comes to Paris for some silly art exhibition, he'll be surrounded by guards. They're mad, all mad, if they think they can get close to him."

"I never suggested taking action would be easy. It's an opportunity, though, and rare." My eyes flare, partly with vindication and partly because Kat should understand how 'not easy' it'll be. Equally, how worth the effort. "You only live with a few Nazis - I'm surrounded by them day and night. I know I can find out more, anything to help. I just have to poke a little harder." I shrug.

"Besides, it's not as if we have been issued kill orders ourselves." I gesture at the reply. "We aren't assassins, just messengers."

"It's pretty vague on the specifics." She sighs and gets up from the floor. As she tucks the suitcase into a dark recess, she says, "You'd better go. Freddie will be home soon."

"Since I'm here..."

"No," she says, firmly. "Too much of a risk. Sometimes Pieter walks him home."

I'm standing by the attic hatch as she approaches. Her fierce expression somehow reassures me that she will go to any lengths to protect my son. "You're right." However much it pains me. I clamber back down the ladder trying to hold myself together.

In the hallway, she relents. "I'll try to bring him to the park this weekend, if you can meet us there?"

"As long as it's not too cold for him. Keep him inside if it's frosty." We both remember the bitter winter in the Phoney War when he caught a chill and nearly died. At least, thanks to living with the Germans, the house is warmer. With her black market activities, she should be able to obtain medicine as well, should it be needed.

She swallows. "I will try." We embrace briefly, and I leave to ferret out what information I can.

Christmas passed in a whirlwind of cleaning up after parties and fruitless searching for information. Winter morphed into spring the fastest I can ever recall. Discovering the date from the vivants in Frank's bar was simple. Talk of the mid-May exhibition at the Musée de l'Orangerie in the Jardin des Tuileries, featuring Nazi-darling sculptor Arno Breker, made for hot gossip. But the war goes on, officers come and go and idle gossip alone isn't enough.

The Allies losses to the Japanese make for a bleak mood amongst the staff. All the other snippets I send to Kat, sometimes using Frank's messenger boys, are about troop movements. All we get back are repeated requests for intelligence about the Führer and his anticipated appearance.

I need hard evidence of Hitler's attendance. By the time Breker and his wife arrive at the Ritz in early May, I'm desperate.

Chanel attended a welcome cocktail party in his honour. The morning after, I somehow time servicing her room to perfection.

"Who is it?"

She lies abed in her tiny room above, judging from her feeble tone. "Good morning, Mademoiselle. It's Devereaux," I call up, then begin to clear away the dirty glasses. Her living space is littered with discarded clothing draped over the furniture. The old Singer still sits in the corner of the room, a pile of coats disguising it. My heart sinks. Not that she's ever the tidiest of people, but with all this clutter, how can she turn her mind to the simple, stylish creations she's known for? "Would you prefer me to service the rooms later?"

The Baron appears, casually walking down the slim stairs in a red plaid dressing gown. Our infrequent encounters have been cordial, and, because their relationship still raises eyebrows, he usually visits her when she's at her apartment above her shop. It occurs to me that he could help. He whispers conspiratorially, "She's a bit delicate this morning. Later might be better?"

"Would you like me to fetch anything?" I offer. "I know it's her maid's day off. Perhaps some coffee, or a doctor? Or is there anything I could get for you, Monsieur?"

He shakes his head.

"Some fresh clothes, maybe?"

His eyes question why I would go above and beyond my duties in such a way. "I'm fine, thank you."

I shrug. "It's not like Hitler is wandering the halls, or anything," I attempt to joke.

"I suppose not," he replies, meeting my eyes.

I chew the side of my lip then say carefully, "The Auzello's would surely give us some warning, if they knew of his arrival, of course."

His jaw clenches. I see then the resemblance to my son - when he's being stubborn his face has the same cast. The nose, the lips - as Freddie ages, the clearer his father's genes show.

I look away. "It would be such an honour for the Ritz to host the Führer. But someone such as yourself might know sooner, if he plans to come to France?" I glance at him and hold my tongue as his eyes narrow on me.

"I would."

For a long moment, he stares at me with his eyebrow raised.

My mouth is dry as I say, "It takes time to prepare rooms, especially for such a guest. Of course, we would welcome him here, show him our famous Ritz hospitality."

Imagine, Hitler and I under the same roof. The thought sends shivers down my spine, but the message, and the ones following, made it quite clear the importance of any opportunity to get to the architect of our misery.

His voice is cold. "I'm sure his staff will make adequate preparations for his arrival."

"We are the one of the closest hotels to the Jardin des Tuileries, after all, and the opening night party will be here." I'm babbling, thinking 'just say he's coming, just say it.'

"Indeed."

"Spatz..." Chanel's voice wavers down. "You could have let me know if the Führer's definitely coming. I need a new outfit."

His lips lift in the hint of a smile at me, briefly, as he calls back. "Arno only confirmed it to me last night. You have ten days to find just the thing." Then his eyes slid back to mine.

I feign a noncommittal expression.

"I wouldn't dream of buying someone else's designs," Chanel shrieks. "Devereaux? I want some satin, cream this time." The bed creaks as she gets out of it, then her face pokes around the staircase corner. She glares at the Baron. "If the theme is 'Strength through Joy,' I'll be damned if I won't show my strength and my joy with my own creations. Jean Cocteau will be there as well, and you know I want to work again with him. Devereaux, you can help, can't you?"

My cheeks flush. "It would be my honour, Mademoiselle."

"Drag that Singer out, and," she waggles a thin finger at the mantelpiece. "Spatz, give her some of the Reichsmarks, and, Devereaux, hurry. Six or seven yards should do it, and some lining." Then her skin pales. She groans and disappears upstairs again.

The Baron crosses the room and flips open the box. Even I can see it's almost empty. Tutting, he lifts up his dark green felt hat to find his trousers. He withdraws a wallet, looking at me with a curious expression. My heart thumps as he hands me a fistful of notes. "Buy whatever she needs."

I nod. As his hand closes over my fingers and the money, he stares into my eyes again. Something in his expression always makes me feel fully seen. Noticed. I remember what that sensation led to a decade ago. Now, it's unnerving.

He says quietly, "I'll let you know if he's staying overnight. Don't worry, he doesn't tend to pay much attention to the staff."

In a way, I'm flattered he shows concern for my well-being at all, but he is sorely mistaken if he thinks I am only concerned for myself. "Any timings would be most welcome."

He nods, then waves his hand around the messy room. "And come back to finish this later. I'll pull the machine out."

Confirmation of Hitler's attendance galvanises me, emboldens me. I plan to feign illness to miss the restaurant shift and go straight to Kat's. Marc frowns when I ask him to play along with my subterfuge. "What's so urgent?"

"I've got a message too important to trust one of Frank's boys with," I reply.

He studies my face. "You've found something."

I lean into his chest and mutter, "I've had confirmation *he* is coming, for the exhibition."

He drops his head as if he's nuzzling me. "Oh God. Do you think they'll go through with it?"

I shrug as I snuggle into his shoulder. It's comforting to share this all with someone, even if I cannot share everything about myself with him.

His breath is warm against my ear. "You won't actually be there, will you?"

And miss such a momentous occasion? Somehow, someway, I plan to attend. Pulling away from him, I say, "Has your new carte arrived yet?"

His lips tighten. "Even if it had, I wouldn't come. If the police caught me doing anything, I would become deportable." He's accepted not wearing the star, but, since he's already been arrested before, his photo is on file, along with his status. Everyone knows the flic conduct the round ups on behalf of the SS. I wish I could tell him to come, be a part of resisting, but I would not ask him to put himself in harm's way.

"You shouldn't go either," he says.

I say nothing back, just give him a brief hug and then leave. Increasingly, our roles are reversed - me becoming more brazen, and him more reticent. Perhaps if people I cared about were taken from me, I too would think twice about publicly objecting to our oppressors.

SMUGGLERS

Through the sunny streets, my brisk walk to Kat's dispels my concerns about Marc and I. We are just on different pages of our lives, I tell myself. Nothing to worry about. For now, I have to do whatever I can, for all those who have fallen already and to free us all. Once the war is over, Marc and I can think about a future.

I'm so distracted, by the time I notice the checkpoint barrier, it's too late. Turning back now would look too obvious. However, the confidence boost of Chanel asking me to help her, or possessing secret knowledge which could change the world, carries me through without a hitch. The soldier gives hardly a second glance at my ID and waves me through.

I'm still smiling as I stroll through the 16th Arrondissement, knock on Kat's door and wait. I know it's a school day, but I can't help harbour a faint hope of sneaking a cuddle with Freddie, as it's nearing mid-afternoon. Just to see him would fill my heart to bursting.

But, although her road-facing bedroom window is open to air the room, there's no answer to my knock. My stomach knots. An hour's walk and all for nothing.

Then, just as I make my way down the path, the handle rattles. I turn back with a grin on my face. Kat raises an eyebrow, then lets me in. As soon as the door shuts behind me, I whisper, "He's coming. The opening ceremony. It's on!" Then, "Is Freddie here?"

Her lips press together and she shakes her head. "Not yet, soon. And you shouldn't be here. Anyone could come."

"I know, but this is too important to wait until the weekend for." I can tell there's something amiss - her face is like stone. "What's wrong?"

"I've already had instructions for what to do if it is happening."

"Great!"

"You wouldn't say so if you knew what they were."

The expression on her face mirrors Marc's earlier. "What do you mean?"

"Observing is one thing. What they want me to do is more direct."

I stare at her, dread souring the back of my throat.

"Because it's such late notice, I'm the one who has to hide the... weapon."

My fists clench, but it's better than the first thought which entered my mind. Kat is many things, but I've never known her to shoot a gun. Not even on the estate we grew up on. "Where?"

She shrugs. "I don't know. Someone will deliver it to me - pray God it's a revolver - and I'm supposed to smuggle it into the exhibition somehow."

It is one thing to pass messages along, quite another to sneak the means to do the deed into a place which will no doubt be swarming with guards. Especially since Hitler will be there. I chew my lip. "A search might find it if you stashed it too far in advance. It'll be packed on the day. How are you supposed to find the contact and hand it over?"

"I see two options - risk hiding a package beforehand, which is easier and I can message where, but, if the weapon is discovered, whoever is supposed to pull the trigger won't have what they need. Opportunity lost. Or, I can take it on the day and secrete it somewhere before letting the contact know. I don't trust myself to do a direct handover, too much can go wrong. I'd rather be rid of it as soon as possible."

"We, Kat. You aren't going to be alone in this. I'll arrive early, find somewhere suitable and stand on guard, make sure it gets picked up."

Her gaze is steady but her mouth trembles a little. She clasps my hand. "Are you sure?"

"I'm sure. We'll be less obvious as a pair. Just some women, going to look at some art." I swallow. "With Hitler. And a gun."

We stare at each other as the enormity of the plan sinks in, wondering how we can possibly pull this off.

Kat says, "Maus, how am I going to get a bloody gun inside? They'll search every bag, so that's not an option."

"No-one will pat you down if you look the part. Even better if you're on the arm of an officer?" Inspiration strikes. "Let me look at your wardrobe. Perhaps I can alter something."

"Whatever do you mean?"

I start up the stairs. "Make a deep pocket maybe, to carry it in. We can fix this, Kat, don't worry."

She looks surprised for a moment, then frowns. "If I go with one of my boarders for cover, what's your excuse?"

While I'm thinking, Kat trots ahead of me and throws open her bedroom door. The bedsheets are rumpled still, as if she has been dallying. On the side of the bed, a newspaper. The answer hits me like I've been slapped with the solution to the crossword. "I know someone who might be able to sort me out with a press pass. "

I chew my lip as I mull through a plan. I might have to fabricate a hitherto unknown passion for art when I talk to the Baron. "I can meet there and help you hide it. Which reminds me, I need to order some cream satin from you, for Chanel. Seven yards, if you can."

Kat opens her wardrobe and rummages through the outfits. "Shouldn't be too hard to get hold of, now I know who to ask. It'll cost."

"She's making an outfit herself, with my help possibly, for the event." Somehow I'll also have to avoid being spotted by her too. Problems for another day, I decide as I reach for my bag and hand over the fistful of money the Baron gave me. "I hope this is enough."

She throws some dresses and skirts on the bed, then pockets the cash. "Any of these would be suitable for the occasion, so see what you can do."

I gawp at the pile of finery. Most of them are unmistakably couture.

"I didn't buy them," she snaps. Her gaze drifts to the bed and her face pinks. "Nor did I spread my legs for them. Pieter got them." She scowls. "For appearance's sake." After a sigh, she gestures for me to rummage through the heap. "I'm sure there's something suitable there. At least they'll have an outing."

Although I wonder who's sharing her sheets, a glance at my watch as I pick up the pieces reminds me we're short on time. "Plenty of choice here, to hide a bulge well enough. Why don't you go and set up the radio while the house is empty."

While she walks to the door, my fingers trace the hand stitched neckline of the one on top. I recognise a Ballagencia when I see it. Further down the pile, I spot a silky, embroidered Chanel. My mouth dries as I extract the dress from the heap and hold it up for closer examination. I notice the extra slim waist on the bias cut, the thinner than usual sleeves, stitched in neat needlework which is unmistakably mine. I sewed this creation for a Jewish client. "Where did Pieter get them from?"

Her fingers grip the door and she looks down. "I don't ask."

A wave of nausea brings bile to my throat. I'd never met the client, but I knew of her, and wondered where she was now or what dire straits had caused her to give up such a beautiful outfit. Or if she'd even had a choice in the matter. I swallow. "Go, send the message."

Setting the Chanel aside, it takes me a few minutes to select a suitable piece - a gorgeous culotte dress by Vionnet. A black net overskirt with lace applique falls over billowing pink chiffon, creating a voluminous skirt, underneath which I can fashion a slim pocket which won't pull with a weight. Worst case, a hand gun could be strapped to Kat's thigh and not be obvious as she walks. I could even freshen the 1930's design with some pale pink ribbon to the puffed sleeves.

As I fold the dress so I can bring it home, I hear the door knocker echo through from the hall. I glance out of her window to see two hats - one, a black-rimmed officer's, and the other a familiar-looking dark green felt. My fingers curl on the windowsill. Why is the Baron here?

CONFESSION

My mind races - Kat's with the radio in the attic, and Freddie is due home any moment. I should go - bolt out the back door and race to work before I'm missed. Kat - radio - attic... Freddie. Me. My heart pounds as I dither, not knowing which instinct to lean into.

Another bang on the door. Kat can't have heard it, she must have the headset on, or I'm sure she'd rush down. Voices from the doorstep drift up through the open window. I lean against the wall, behind the curtain. Frozen, processing the implications. The green hat... their voices. It could be Pieter in the black cap. With Hans. Freddie's father.

Then, my worst fears are realised.

"Freddie!" Pieter calls, in a jovial tone. "Home from school so soon? How's your new teacher, Madame Martin?"

Blood rushes in my ears as I wait, but of course, Freddie doesn't speak.

"This is my friend, Baron von Dinklage," Pieter says.

"Very pleased to meet you, young man," Hans says. There's something stilted in his tone I cannot place. He pauses, presumably waiting for Freddie to respond. I daren't peek down. Then he says, "My friends call me Spatz, like a sparrow, the bird, but my proper name is Hans."

The hairs on my arms stand as goosebumps slide up across my skin. Has anyone noticed their resemblance?

"Now where's your Maman, eh?" Pieter says, then the door knocker raps again.

Maman. I remember telling Freddie he had to call me that now, when we first arrived here. To hear Kat being called his mother tears at my soul, but I don't resent it as much as I used to, until now, with Pieter in his life. My stomach is churning and I hate his familiarity with my son with a passion which nearly makes me vomit.

I lurch away from the sanctuary of the wall and pound down the hallway. At the bottom of the attic stepladder I hiss, "Kat! Pieter's here!"

I can hear the tap-tap of her sending messages as I clamber up and stick my head through the hatch. "Kat!"

Her eye catches mine and she pauses, mid sequence. Exaggerating my lips, I repeat, "Pieter is here, with... someone else, and Freddie!"

Her mouth forms an O then she frantically resumes tapping. My heartbeat races almost in time with her little dots and dashes, then she waves her hand at me to come up, then points to the corner. I nod and climb the last few steps on the ladder as she unplugs the equipment. I shoo her downstairs and finish packing the radio away.

The hatch closes with a quiet thud and I hear the stepladder squeak as she folds it to put away. Then I sit, curled up, knees to my chin, perching on the suitcase in the darkest corner of the attic. Downstairs, I vaguely hear voices, muffled and raised. I can't make out what they are saying. Then, little feet thump along the hallway and a door squeaks then slams. I hold my breath, hoping, praying.

Be safe, Freddie, I beg. Stay away. My heart is in my mouth - only this morning did it strike me how father and son now resembled each other.

The minutes tick by, and I consciously force the stale attic air in and out, slow and deep to calm my stomach. I think I have never been so close to vomiting in my life, I'm shivering with the effort not to void the thin lunchtime soup.

Eventually, my breathing works and, although I cannot move or go anywhere, the nausea passes. Whatever Kat is doing downstairs, they aren't coming up here, and for that I'm grateful. I just have to sit it out. Stay quiet like Maus. Pieter can't hang around here forever, can he?

A cramp seizes my calf and, as I try to stretch it out, I hear Kat calling for Freddie to come down. Her voice trembles, as if she has been crying. I crawl over to the hatch, wincing through the pain in my leg, and press my ear to the wood.

His bedroom door squeaks open. Kat must be practically underneath me as I hear her say, "Uncle Pieter has gone now, but he'll be back for dinner soon. Let's go and sit in my salon. You can bring down your games, or draw your maps again, if you would like, while I prepare the food."

She's letting me know the coast is clear for now. My heartbeat slows as they pad away. I'm desperate to see Freddie, to hold him and whisper for him not to worry in his ear, then I really must head back to the Ritz. I hope Marc has explained away my prolonged absence for me.

After a few minutes, I open the hatch and poke my head down to check the landing is clear. Then, after limbering my legs a few times, I risk it. Kat's left the ladder propped against the wall where it usually is. I've no choice but to wriggle and back myself out as much as I can then drop down. The open hatch, well, she'll have to fix that when she puts Freddie to bed.

I land with a thud which I hope Kat can explain away, and dash into her bedroom. Listening for a moment behind her door, my shoulders brush something cold. It's Freddie's camera, dangling by its strap on a hook. My fingers trace the black metal box, and I wonder if he's still interested in it these days. He didn't play with it at all after we arrived in Paris, just always wanted to have it in sight. I imagine he must have grown out of the phase, for why else would it be hung in Kat's bedroom?

The thought crosses my mind that I could, if I had a working camera, take photos of any plans I come across. I've seen photographs occasionally, targets for the Luftwaffe who occupy the majority of the rooms at the Ritz. What I'd do with them I don't know yet, but still, maybe they'd be useful. Also, if I'm to be a reporter at the exhibition, having a camera adds authenticity to my disguise.

After stuffing the camera and Vionnet into my bag, I creep along the landing, down the stairs and sneak past the ajar salon door. I catch a glimpse of Freddie, sat cross legged on the rug next to Kat's shoes. On the floor in front of him is an old map of Paris, covered with coloured pencil scribbles.

"Why doesn't he talk?"

Hans's voice jolts me - I thought he would have gone with Pieter, but no, he's still here.

"I don't know," Kat replies. "He just stopped. When the war began, you know."

"Is he... well, otherwise?"

"Perfectly." Her skirt rustles as she stands. "I must go and get the dinner on, for the boarders."

Quick and quiet, I scamper past the doorway and into the kitchen. Kat isn't far behind me, but starts as she spots me lurking by the back door. She swiftly shuts the door to the hallway and whispers, "What are you still doing here?"

"I waited to see Freddie." Why do I feel as though I've done something wrong by wanting to see my son?

"Now's really not a good time."

I do my best to keep my voice casual. "Why's the Baron still here?"

She huffs. "Pieter's only nipped out to buy cigarettes, having invited himself and Hans for dinner." She takes down a saucepan from the shelf above the sink, then turns to me. The powder on her face is streaked with dried tears. "You should go, now."

I hand her a towel. "Kat, what's upset you?"

Her face is so thin, lines form on her cheeks as purses her lips.

"Please tell me Kat. Whatever it is, a burden shared is a burden halved."

She blinks, distracting me by smoothing down her skirt. "Pieter. He's going to move in here. I told him there's no spare rooms, so he wants my bedroom and I'm to sleep with Freddie. That's all."

"Why? Doesn't he have accommodation already? I thought he was getting a prime allocation?" Half the hotels in Paris are full of Germans - either lodging there semi-permanently or using the city as a holiday destination.

Kat shakes her head. "Says he's going to be travelling a lot more now, from here to the camps, then back here, and wants the certainty of home comforts here, waiting for him, whenever."

"He wants to be able to come and go as he chooses then?"

Her voice catches. "The paperwork's filed, to requisition my home as his own."

I touch her arm. "Can he do that? When you don't technically own the house anyway?"

A shrug of her shoulders. "They do whatever they like, don't they?" Her jaw clamps together, but there's no point voicing the anger. Yanking open the cupboard door, she stares into the half empty recess.

Then, in a low, dangerous tone, she says, "The Baron - Hans - suspects, you know. About Freddie."

My stomach drops and my mouth dries. Kat was there, that fateful night when we ran into Pieter and Hans, when we all got caught up in the pogrom rioting. While she was injured and driven home by Pieter, Hans led me into womanhood, and shame. In a hollow voice, I say, "Suspects what?"

Kat turns back to the kitchen having gathered soft, sprouting potatoes in her arms. "He remembers me from Germany. And you, no doubt. We both know we've never slept together, yet the resemblance Freddie has to him is fairly clear when you see them together. It's obvious Freddie isn't my son. I'm not stupid, and I can count, Hannah. So, I'm going to ask you for the full truth now, just so we can work out what to do next."

My heartbeat pounds, dread crawling across my skin. She sighs as she drops the food onto the table then her eyes meet mine. "Is Hans his father?"

Mute, I nod and blink away the sudden swell of tears.

"Does he know?"

I shake my head, no.

"Freddie? Have you told him who his father is?"

Another shake. We used to play this guessing questions all the time as girls, yes - no answers only, until one of us spilled the secret. Her lips tweak and I sense her anger at Pieter relenting as she draws close to uncovering my truth.

"Was what happened why you left for the convent?"

I nod.

Her expression softens. "Were you... did Hans force you?"

Slowly, my head shakes.

Her shoulders relax with relief. "I'm guessing it was only the once, though? After the pogrom?"

My cheeks flush as I nod.

Her eyes meet mine and her lips press together sympathetically. "That was unfortunate. Oh, Hannah..."

"I was young, and stupid. Naïve. I wanted to be an adult, like you." The truth blurts out as I lower my face and mumble, "The way Hans had made me feel seen, just for a few hours, that was my downfall. But, Pieter, knowing his friend well, knew what was likely to happen and told his father. Herr Weisz sent me away as a result."

She picks up a potato and paring knife. "I suppose I did think I was a grown up too, although I really was stupid and naïve as well. What's done is done." With a sure movement, the vegetable is halved. "Did you even know the Baron was in Paris?"

My mouth fills with saliva now the worst of my shameful secret is out. "Yes."

"Does he know you're in Paris?"

"Yes." Having finally found my voice, I have to show her I'm not utterly useless. "He's sleeping with Chanel. More than a simple reporter now, he's well connected with the party. Although he's been... helpful before, and might be again."

Kat looks thoughtful for a second, quick to join the dots. "Press pass, yes?"

"Despite his job, I'm not sure which side he's really on. His ex wife was Jewish, he told me, and he's sort of aware I'm not just a chambermaid."

She puts a finger to her lips. "Don't want to know." Her eyes shift from side to side as if she's heard something which I missed. "Do you trust him?"

I shrug. "I've no reason not to, yet."

Her voice is stern. "Then pray he doesn't say anything about Freddie, or you either, to Pieter. The last thing I need is for him to ask my dreadful cousin about him, or how old he really is. If Pieter finds out he's not my son and instead half Jewish... it will point to you being in Paris too."

She looks at me with wide eyes, and my mouth dries again. Then she points to the back door.

I need no more encouragement. "Sorry to leave you with all this. You'll need to pull the hatch closed. Please, tell Freddie... only that I love him."

"When I can, I will."

CAMERA

My confession to Kat and the threat of discovery heightens my awareness of danger, as I slip out of the yard and wend my way home to the Ritz. It's after curfew, I'm already late and risking my job, so I am in no mood to be challenged at checkpoints. Hurrying through the shadows, hours later, I arrive at my bedroom and spot light filtering through the crack at the bottom.

When I push open the door, the first thing I see is Madame Auzello, perched on my bed. "About time."

Marc stands beside her, looking miserable. "Where have you been?"

"I... I had to go and see someone, urgently. My sister-in-law..." The words dry on my lips. Which is worse to admit? The lie about being ill or my illicit activities? Then, I remember what might be an acceptable excuse. "Mademoiselle Chanel asked me to get her some fabric again, for the exhibition and the opening night party here. I had to ask my source."

"Your sister-in-law is the black marketeer?" Madame Auzello says.

Too late, I realise I've dropped Kat in it. I meet Marc's unreadable eyes, no hint of what he's told her already. My cheeks burn, and I squirm under their gaze. "Yes."

Madame's fingers rub together and her chin juts out. "Ignoring the obvious falsehoods you've both told, it's unacceptable to take time out of work for personal errands." Standing up, she glares at us. "In these troubled times, we do care about the safety of our staff. If I weren't so short staffed, I'd fire both of you."

"Yes, Madame. I'm sorry."

Marc echoes, "Sorry. It won't happen again."

"It had better not. Consider this your final warning, Devereaux. I cannot have you risking our reputation by wandering the streets all hours of night, consorting with criminals. I will not bail you out of prison."

She stalks to the door, I bow my head and stand aside. Her parting shot is: "No fraternisation in the staff quarters, either. Say your goodbyes, lovebirds."

Marc bends to kiss my cheek. He's stiff, formal, as if he's bestowing a dutiful peck on a disliked relative.

I do not sleep well that night.

The next week is a blur. Madame keeps me busy, too busy, and she's everywhere I turn. It's as if she suspects trouble on the horizon, or perhaps it's just my nerves? Maybe, on top of a celebrity-packed party here, Hitler will be staying. We are not friends or allies enough for me to ask Madame Auzello directly, and such news would not leave a paper trail.

Knowing if I put a foot wrong, any chance I have to help the cause compels me to act, as if her warning about firing me ignites my rebellious streak. Every spare minute I have, I hunt for information; no Nazi rooms are safe, as long as I can dodge Madame Auzello and Claudette. With my increased efforts, I'm able to discover several letters ordering an increase in usage of airborne poison gas, which I diligently copy down and send to Kat via Frank's boys. Nothing though, about where Hitler's movements in May.

Marc's mood vacillates: one moment he's sneaking mournful glances at me across the kitchen, the next he's actively avoiding being alone with me. Whenever I try to talk to him about what happened that night, he's got somewhere to be, or he feigns camaraderie with whomever else is around. I'm confused, and I wish we could just go back to how we were. However, after Madame Auzello's caution, it's clear he's a terrible liar. Any details about the secret mission might be too much for him. To keep him safe, ignorance is bliss, no matter how much I long to confide in him.

I meet Kat and Freddie at the Catacombs on Sunday and she hands over the fabric for Chanel. "I heard back," she whispers. "The package arrives tomorrow, and a description of who to pass it to. Tickets and companion for cover are all sorted."

The altered Vionnet I pass her in return is wrapped in brown paper. "I made the adjustments, a deep, secret pocket on the right." Tucking the packet of satin under my arm, I grasp her hand. "I can do the transfer if you want. I can."

"Have you organised your entry yet?" She snaps.

"No," I admit. Hans has been conspicuously absent, and Chanel is extremely grumpy about it. I can only hope that when she gets creating again, she'll be happier.

"Well, you'd better hurry up."

To avoid snapping back at her, I take my son's hand and ask him about school as we walk down a skull-lined corridor. His little fabric shoulder bag bashes against my calves, the cold metal of the torch he keeps inside will cause a bruise. I say, "Shall I guess which is your favourite subject?"

He peers up at me and shakes his head. In the dim, his little pale face with a tiny beak of a nose looks like an owl - white with a mop of blond hair like ruffled feathers sticking out from under his cap. "Don't you like Madame Martin anymore?"

Freddie stops, pulling down on my hand so I'll pause too. Using his fingers, he forms a square, holding it up to his face, squinting an eye while his finger clicks where a camera button would be.

"Your camera?"

Instantly, my guilt colours my cheeks. It's still in my bag, I'd clean forgotten about it, nor have I had a chance to see if it's working. Even if it did, I don't have any film, but that is a problem for another day. Maybe I won't need it, I hope.

Then his lips turn down and he holds his hands up and shrugs to say, I don't know.

"Oh Freddie, I'm sorry. I thought you might have grown out of it, so I borrowed it."

My confession does not have the effect I anticipated. Instead, he looks at me earnestly, blinking slowly.

"Do you need it back?"

His head shakes furiously, but there's still that curious, fearful expression on his face. He studies my eyes as if I should be able to read his mind. As he chews on his lip, I realise there's something he's holding back. What is he trying to tell me? I glance at Kat, who's watching our interaction. "Do you know what's the problem with his camera?"

"He was really protective of it when you left, then, when the boarders came, he put it in my room. He checks it's there from time to time." Her eyebrow rises. "He's been acting strangely ever since Pieter moved in. I caught him in my room that day. Maybe he was searching for it."

"I took it when I came over the other day, thinking I could... use it."

Freddie tugs on my arm, his lips and eyebrows pressed together. I crouch to ask, "If it still works, could I use it, please?"

He frowns, hard, then makes the sign of the cross. His finger mime clicking again, then puts his hands over his ears and curls up in a crouch.

My mouth drops open as I remember the last time he used it. The last time he spoke.

I whisper, "Did you have a film in it, Freddie? In the convent chapel?"

His bottom lip trembles as he nods.

My breath leaves me, and the wall of skulls blurs.

"Hannah?" Kat's voice sounds far away as I struggle to process. "Maus? Maus!"

I stare at Freddie, horror hitting me afresh. What my poor boy witnessed. What he did. The little click which recorded the precise moment when our world turned upside down. No wonder he hasn't spoken of it, or anything, since. His lips mouth, 'Mama, mama.'

Falling to my knees, I reach for his hand and grip it. He meets my eyes and I manage a nod. "I'll make it right," I mutter. "I promise."

Because I'm not sure how to deal with the camera, or what to do with any incriminating images on there, I try to push the issue to one side of my mind. Each time, though, I feel my connection to Freddie wither more. The promises I made him - to keep him safe, to make a home for us, to take him to the Eiffel Tower even - I haven't kept any of them. I cannot cope with the feelings of failure such thoughts lead me towards. If I let them consume me, I will surely die of shame.

All I know is that, if circumstances could only be different, maybe I can make it up to him. Be a mother he can be proud of. Make good on all those promises. More than ever, I must act to stop this war, so we can be together again.

Everything rests on the exhibition plans. And so, I take a bold step the next morning, find the card Hans gave me and, to avoid suspicion, pick up the telephone in Chanel's room while she is out.

Affecting Chanel's deeper tone, I say, "I need to speak to Baron von Dinklage, at the German Embassy."

Alice, the switchboard operator downstairs, says, "I'll place the call for you now, Mademoiselle." Holding the receiver, my hand shakes while the clicks and whirrs. There's silence on the line for what seems like an eternity, then, Hans' voice comes through. "Von Dinklage."

"Baron?" Perhaps I could be less formal, but it occurs to me suddenly that anyone could be listening in. "I'm sorry to trouble you at work. I'm calling from Mademoiselle Chanel's suite." I assume he will recognise my voice by these hints, and it works.

"Is she alright?"

"Quite. It's about something else. The item for Mademoiselle you ordered, I have it here, but the cost was a little more than anticipated."

There's a pause, while crackles disturb the line. I can just make out, "I thought what I paid would more than cover it."

"The difference could be forgotten, in return for a small favour." My mouth is dry, but I plough on with my ruse. "The supplier is an art fanatic, and covets an all-access Press pass to the opening of the Breker 'Strength through Joy' exhibition for their... friend."

I can hear him drawing in a breath then exhaling. "I see."

"So, can you help?"

"I'll see what I can do."

I ring off with a "Thank You" and collapse into the sofa cushions.

Strength Through Joy

I am a bundle of nerves - both joyous and anxious - as I walk along the river towards the Jardin des Tuileries. I scouted the Musée during a lunch break a few days ago, and found a suitably large potted lemon tree in which a gun could be dropped. The artworks were still being installed then, and first on my task list today is confirmation the pot's still there, as Kat has already passed on the message. Ever since then, the preparations for the day, both for myself, our mission, and for the Ritz, have fallen into place as if the mission is destined to succeed.

Even this rare day off has been granted without too much trouble, courtesy of the Baron putting pressure on a distracted Madame Auzello that Chanel needs my personal assistance today. She agreed, on the condition that I work at this evening's party. Of course, should our plan be a success, the party will no doubt be cancelled... what happens after that, I do not yet allow myself to dream about. One step at a time.

Hugging my secret and my handbag with Freddie's camera close to my chest, I remind myself there are many things which could go wrong, but the spring morning feels bright with possibilities and I cannot help but smile. Strange to feel absolutely no guilt at all about the plan. Hitler is a face on a poster, a name who inspires fear to most of us, and the architect of so much suffering over so many years. This isn't vengeance, it's putting a monster out of our misery. I do not consider him a person at all – it's almost like he is an idea, which can be snuffed out.

The only shadow dampening my mood is, with the influx of esteemed figures from the political and cultural scenes in attendance, military and police presence is high. So many uniforms patrolling the flowerbeds would, on any other day, make me jittery, yet given who I know will also be attending, it's hardly surprising.

With freshly bleached hair, camera around my neck and dressed in a smart skirt and a jacket I borrowed from another chambermaid, I feign a confidence I don't usually achieve. My disguise and I breeze towards the columned Musée de l'Orangerie entrance. As I flash my Press pass at the guards, my heart pounds. But, after a cursory bag search, I'm waved inside.

I'm early, but that was the plan. Lemon tree, still in situ. I use the wide ceramic lip to balance my bag while I rummage inside for a notepad and pen. It won't be long until the public are allowed in, and the official proceedings start. Until Kat gets here, all I need to do is wander around the airy rooms, pretending to make notes like a reporter. The exhibits - massive marble statues, bold, colourful paintings and reliefs hung on the walls - are almost secondary to the mounting tension in the connected rooms.

Photographers set up in well-lit corners for portraits, and there's even a film crew in the main exhibition area where the speeches will happen. Chunky, bulbous cine-cameras on their sturdy tripods perch atop wide wooden boxes, poised to record the crowd and capture the occasion for the news. It makes me wonder when the deed itself will be done, if Hitler addresses everyone perhaps, or as he's walking around?

I stop in front of a huge bronze relief of Apollo and Daphne, watching the camera crew's preparations and think of Marc. Of how he could probably tell me what they are doing and why. Of how much he would appreciate the sun on his face, the fresh air and scented gardens on the walk here. Of how much I wish he could be here to witness...

"Move aside!" A man with a red, round face and a long moustache glares at me. He's dragging a pole with a light fastened onto it. "Women," he grumbles to himself, as if I can't hear him, "always underfoot." Then, "Move along, Madame, I need that apple box."

I have no idea what he's talking about, but I step aside as he lugs the pole onto one of the sturdy crates and unfolds the flaps around the light.

There's no announcement of the opening of the exhibition, only a gradual increase of well-dressed socialites drifting in. With deliberately thoughtful faces, they gaze at the artworks, casting only the occasional glance at ever-increasing numbers of uniformed Nazis. As if I'm one of them, I hover at the edges of small groups, vigilant for Kat's arrival, and wary of Chanel's. Her dress is finished, and looks more appropriate for evening wear. As she loves to make an entrance, my instinct tells me she'll wait until later in the day to appear. I pray it is after Hitler does, but there's no guarantees. The Baron might, after all, want to milk the opportunity to be seen with her in front of his leader.

The morning wears on, with the sun beating through the glasshouse. Just as refreshments circulate, I spot Kat, on the arm of the same officer she was with at the Ritz. I have to admit, in his black uniform, he's quite handsome, but already looks bored with the proceedings. The altered dress, however, looks perfect on her - and you can't spot the bulge of a gun at all. Kat's shoulders hunch and her laughter is a little too brittle as she searches the room and fans herself with the exhibition programme. I train my gaze on her until she catches my eye, then I jerk my head towards the conveniences. When she's made her excuses, I follow.

As planned, she goes into a cubicle first, leaving the pistol behind the toilet bowl. The scent of her heavy lily perfume cloys in my throat as we pass, sharing a conspiratorial glance. I want to catch her fingers, tell her it's going to be fine, but neither of us can know that for sure. That we are here together has to be enough.

She's wrapped the weapon in Freddie's dark yellow silk scarf, and I tumble the cold metal into my bag. Hidden in the folds, a small photograph flips out and drifts to the floor - a man with a bushy beard, who must be the contact I should look out for. I catch it, memorise the face then palm it.

"Madame," I say, after flushing the toilet and rushing out to where she washes her hands. "You must have dropped this." I hand her the photo and tuck Freddie's scarf on top of my bag, leaving the corner flopped out.

"Thank you so much." She smiles, genuine because her part in this is now complete, and slips the photo into her pocket. My heart thumps, as mine is beginning. We return to the fray and go our separate ways.

I circulate the rooms, with my notebook and Freddie's camera for cover. The gun weighs heavily in my bag. I want nothing more than to get rid, but, standing by the lemon tree, lurk a pair of Nazis, sipping champagne. Casually, I walk away, searching for the man in the photograph instead. When the officers move away, I amble back, perch on the edge of the ceramic pot and surreptitiously slip the pistol down the side of the deep rim. I sit, unnoticed as I ostensibly make notes, but really guarding the gun while scanning the faces of the guests.

My stomach knots as, after what seems like hours, I still cannot spot the contact. A ripple of whispers warns me something is about to happen and I stand, going onto my tiptoes to look over the crowd. Under my breath, I curse my shortness - the hats and heels make my task almost impossible. What if Hitler arrives and no-one claims the weapon? Sweat breaks out on my brow, and, as the volume of the whispers rises to fever pitch, I know I must act to find the contact.

I catch sight of a cameraman, clambering up the wooden 'apple box' then turning on his camera. Chewing my lip, I saunter towards it, thinking the extra height might give me an advantage, even if it exposes me. En route, I brush past an old waiter. "So sorry," I apologise automatically as the empty glasses on his tray clink together.

He stops, rearranges the glasses so they are better spaced out and secure, and I notice his beard. It's bushy, just like the man in the photo! Smiling to myself, for who notices the staff, I suggest, "There's some more to collect," I say, searching his face to be sure before touching the fabric draped over my bag. "In the lemon tree pot over there." He meets my eyes, then glances down at the yellow scarf and nods.

"*Merci*," he grunts, then shuffles off. I want to follow him, make sure he finds what he needs, but daren't. Instead, I push through the crowd, who have clustered to face a small podium in front of Apollo and Daphne. Then, I step up, onto the apple box. The cameraman glares at me, but he's already rolling so he has no choice but to let me watch next to him. I pull out Freddie's camera, which draws a withering glance, quickly replaced by a pity-laden expression of superiority as he turns back to his job.

Applause swells, and Breker and his glamourous wife walk onto the platform. My heart is in my mouth, eyes darting over the tops of the hats, to the door, the windows, anywhere that Hitler might make his entrance while Breker drones on. Shaded by lemon tree leaves, the waiter stands, his tray balanced on both his forearms as he focuses on the podium. Underneath the silverware, I spot the tiny black snub of the gun.

ASSASSIN

Whatever Breker's saying must be witty, because laughter and claps punctuate the air. I become aware that I'm clenching my fists so tight they ache. Then, Jean Cocteau steps forward, and takes over. His gushing, poetic praise washes over me - there's no sight of Hitler. The ball in my stomach feels like it might drop, taking me with it.

Finally, raising his hand to acknowledge the applause, Breker and Cocteau leave the platform. While a few guests rush forward, waving their cream-covered exhibition guides to ask for autographs, the majority of the crowd disperses. Formalities seemingly over, many of the Nazis head for the door, including Kat and her escort.

"Is that it?" I mutter.

"What were you expecting?" The cameraman says.

"Just... something more."

He shrugs. "Plans change, I guess."

Indeed they do, I think. I glance at the lemon tree, where the bushy bearded assassin stands. He's staring straight at me, scowling, and lips pursed. His cheeks redden and he suddenly marches off, tray and the gun underneath held out in front of him as if that will clear his path.

I feel my cheeks flush. Stuffing the camera back in my bag, I jump down. For some reason, his anger makes me want to justify everything, to explain, even though I have no real explanation myself for what's not happened. In pursuit, he doesn't notice me as he stalks ahead and straight out of the Musée. He slides the silver drinks tray onto a step, pockets the gun, then weaves through people. He's walking so fast I have to run to keep him in sight.

Ahead, I see Kat, clutching her officer's arm, chatting casually as they amble around the Bassin Octagonal pond. They pause by a group of men. Kat's escort greets one in German loudly and with familiarity. His attention commands a loud Heil Hitler salute from them all. They must be tourists, judging from their casual attire and the tour guide, gesturing at the landmarks without noticing he's lost his audience. Then, one of the group repeats the salute, ending it with a rude finger gesture towards a statue. Others laugh, but Kat frowns at the disrespect.

The assassin halts a few feet away while the group are still chortling. To my horror, he whips out the pistol. Three rapid shots echo across the concourse. Ducks take to the air, squawking. Kat wheels around, hand flying to her mouth as she crouches to avoid being hit by the assassin or panicking poultry.

With barely a whisper, three Nazis drop to the ground.

Screams erupt. People start running everywhere, confused as to where the shots came from. Kat's officer drops to his knees as she stands there, mouth open but silent, face pale. I hurtle towards the group, and her. The killer shouts something I can't catch, then sprints away, heading for the busy Place de la Concorde. One of the remaining Nazis rushes off after him, shouting for the police.

It's pandemonium - a blur of colour and screams as the area clears of citizens. Reaching Kat, I grab her arm and pull her aside. "Madame! Go!" I shout in her face, as if we don't know each other.

She's too shocked to register what I'm saying, just gapes at the dead men, their blood pooling around the bodies. Her officer is pre-occupied, ordering people to help him stem the flowing blood, fetch help, find the assassin.

I tug Kat away, making for the gardens, the opposite way to the shooter. Her heels clip-clop as I half drag her across the stones. The Jardin, a distance from the street, is eerily silent, then police whistles sound. I glance back to see if anyone is following us, but no-one has noticed us flee - yet. Through the windows of the Musée, art-lovers mingle and whitter, as if nothing is going on.

Kat stumbles, yanking down on my arm as she falls. On her knees, she pants, then slams her fist into the gravel and swears.

"Get up. Hurry," I urge, helping her up. Any moment now, the Gendarme will arrive. I spot tiny flecks of blood, drying fast on the fabric. "If we're caught, we'll be questioned."

She looks at me defiantly, slapping the dirt from her skirt. "I know. I'm prepared."

"What do you mean?" I tug her along, but, something in her has changed.

She shakes her head furiously, then paces ahead of me. I stop, confused. She turns her head, as if I'm the dawdling child now. "They sent me tablets. In case of the worst."

My mouth dries. "Tablets?"

She nods, then continues ambling by my side like we have nothing to fear except a turn in the weather. "A kill pill they call it." After a moment, she offers, "Do you want one?"

"No." My fingers curl around my bag; I have too much to live for. I thought she did too.

We reach the end of the Jardin and stop by the Grand Bassin Rond. She rips up the photograph of the assassin, drops the pieces in the fountain pool then turns to me. "You should probably get back to work."

I glance down the pathway leading out to the road, towards the Ritz. I'm flabbergasted by how composed she is, when my insides still jumble around and my mind whirs. "How can I?"

For a minute, we watch the shreds of paper whirl and the world go on, silent between us while police sirens echo in the distance.

"You just do, Hannah," Kat says, then glances at her watch. "I should go. Freddie will be.... waiting for me." She grips my arms. "We just got to plod forward then. Keep doing what we're doing, for as long as we can. Until we can't. That's how."

The After

··

When Hitler didn't appear in Paris at all, I turn up to work at the exhibition opening day reception at the Ritz. Marc, knowing little of the plan, simply hugged me, without asking questions.

So for almost ten months, I follow Kat's advice. I keep doing what I was doing. The numbness after our failure faded, although her frank words about plodding on stays with me like a mantra. Notes, overheard conversations, paperwork, anything I found, I pass on in scrawled letters slipped into her hands or sent via one of Frank's boys directly to her house.

The mood in Paris darkens after the exhibition though, and retribution for the murder of the officers is swift. Anyone who was already suspected of resisting, and most especially, any troublesome Jews, are rounded up.

I keep my head down, only learning news of the city from whispered exchanges between staff. I carry on snooping and spying, ignoring the crushing sensation that my opportunity to make a real difference could never be repeated. Officers come and go, the war rumbles on in distant lands.

In the absence of other news, and with all radios in the bed-rooms and staff areas tuned only to propaganda stations, all fighting seems abstract. Africa, Russia – aside from occasional maps and aerial photographs from Luftwaffe officers, the countries where battles are fought are so far from my immediate, daily and horrible experience, I hardly consider the plight of the millions affected.

But for all Jewish people in Paris, living conditions get even worse. Jews are banned from all main streets, parks, restaurants and, if they dared to use public transport, they have to sit in the last carriage or at the back.

For my film-loving beau, the order that Jews could not visit cinemas strikes him the hardest, even though, with his new, fake *Carte*, he would pass unnoticed. He swears he wouldn't go until everyone was free to watch whatever they wanted. I don't have the heart to tell him only Nazi approved films are shown anyway, which are hardly the *avant garde* cinematic experience he longs for.

Days after Bastille Day, in the heat of midsummer, Jews from across the city are pulled from their homes by the police, and bussed to the Velodrome d'Hiver. When Marc hears of the raids, he asks me to accompany him across the city, to where he had lived, to check his mother is safe and meet her.

Sadly, she isn't there, and her neighbours shut their doors in our faces when we ask after hei. We began to fear the worst.

My snooping yields nothing about the operation which officers in Rue Cambon bar call 'Spring Wind'. No lists of names, no hint of what would happen to them or why they were kept in the old bicycle stadium, close to the Eiffel Tower.

One evening, we try to visit, only to be turned away at the barbed wire perimeter. All around the nearby streets, the air is thick with the smell of waste and the constant buzz of flies. Audible through the walls, we listen to children's pitiful cries for help, water, or their parents. My stomach churns – it could so easily be Freddie or I in there.

There is nothing we can do to ease the suffering. When the gates open, cattle trucks crammed with law abiding, star-wearing Jews of all ages drive out. Our glimpse inside exposes a horrific truth: thousands more people, too many to count, were packed together, without shelter from the sun.

We leave, tears streaming down our faces, and unable to discover if Marc's elderly mother was there.

A few days later, we try again, but by then, the stadium was largely empty. Quieter but no less smelly. Soldiers and policemen on the gate refuse to talk to us about who, if anyone, remains, or where everyone had gone. Later, through gossip, we find they have been moved to 'work camps' or Drancy, a ghetto now under the command of the SS.

The stench from the Vel d'Hiv lingers for weeks afterwards, spoiling the ordinary citizen's air yet somehow never quite tainting the continuous parties at the Ritz. Not even a new quota rationing couture houses can stop the spending splurge of the wealthy. French society and wealthy German tourists drink and purchase their blindness to what was happening.

Then, as if those of us who had secrets aren't edgy enough that summer, the Nazis erect a huge bonfire outside of the Jeu de Palme, near the site where I had witnessed the murders. I watch the plume of sparks and smoke from my bedroom window - a vivid orange-red glow against the black night. They could scorch away the blood which had been spilled, but the bitter taste of bonfire only cements my resolve to rebel.

I feel less alone when Frank tells me, the next day, they'd burned so-called degenerate art, made by Bolsheviks and renegade modern artists. Then he sneers, "A literal incineration of these ideas won't stop people resisting, even if it means the death of them."

I nod my agreement but say nothing. I'd seen the resolve in the eyes of the assassin, and in Kat's consideration of the kill pills. I too, would rather die than stop trying to do something to prevent the spread of Hitler's horrific ideology, and not just for myself and my family.

"I went back home," Marc tells me as August ends. "Everything was gone. All the furniture, books, everything. I don't have any other home now except the Ritz."

He doesn't share my resolution, caught up somewhere between anger and mourning. Not knowing what had happened to his mother keeps him in a state of despondency, preventing him from proper grief and acceptance.

Late summer, I meet Kat alone in the cool catacombs, and ask her if she knew of a way to find out who had gone where from the Vel d'Hiv.

She shies away from my gaze. "Pieter might know," she whispers, her voice catching. "But then, they're all just cattle to him. I doubt he even reads the names, just signs the transport orders. Using the police to do their bidding proves Vichy are puppets. Pétain has forgotten us all."

"Has Pieter moved in now?" I've not seen Freddie in months.

A despondent nod. "Just before the exhibition." She glances at the messages I wrote down for her to radio on. "I can't send all those."

"You have to," I said, "Whenever you can. It might make a difference, to someone."

"It does." Her eyes flick to mine." The Allies know what's going on with the annihilation of Jews. There's talk on the radio, they're putting out a statement. They have the evidence. We can't stop what we are doing, no matter how hopeless it seems."

"No," I say. "Whatever it takes. Something has to change. We might never know what gives the Allies the edge."

She nods, takes the notes, then tells me something shocking. "Freddie listens in to Pieter and the boarders conversations too, and writes me little notes like this to send."

I grip her hand, saying nothing. I'm scared for him. Proud of him, but scared of what horrors he might hear about.

"They don't know he understands of course, so they talk freely when I'm not there."

The thought of my boy, alone in a room full of Nazi's terrifies me, but what can I do? "He's a brave boy. A rebel."

"Wonder where he gets that from. Actually, I think his teacher, Madam Martin, is also influencing the children. He's almost two people now – Freddie with you and I, but Frederick in front of Pieter or the others."

The next time we meet, she pockets the messages silently. We don't talk about what she does with them, but I keep searching regardless.

I notice another subtle shift in the spring of 1943, nearly a year after the exhibition fiasco. Kat tells me, while Freddie runs ahead of us in Bois de Boulogne, her radio set has been collected by her contact, the woman with the false leg and pheasant feathered hat. "One of the other radio operators was captured by the Gestapo, and hasn't been seen since. For safety, my set has been moved so other operatives can also use it. If I say 'flat tyre' it means I'm being watched and can't do much."

She glances at me. "I can't send messages as often now, because the suitcase doesn't stay in one place all the time. Moves around if there's a risk of it being discovered."

"How do you know where it is, then?" I ask.

"There's a 'dead letter' box location, to say where it is, or leave each other messages. But, at least I can leave the house when the boarders are there without worrying about what they might snoop and discover." She shoots me a side-glance. "You won't believe it, but, I bought a bike to get me around." She shakes her wide legged culottes. "All the nippier, now, and stylish, even if the Germans still disapprove."

I joke, "Better watch out Freddie doesn't borrow your ride."

He's shot up since I last saw him, three months ago before Christmas, and although he's very much a boy, his white legs look like wheat stalks poking from his shorts - all knobbly knees and no muscle tone.

"He won't - Pieter's promised to get him a bicycle for Christmas," she replies. "Says he can get one easily enough, like the artworks he had delivered the other day from the Levitan furniture store. All confiscated from Jews. 'Aryanised' he calls it, but still, the house does feel more bearable, I suppose."

My heart sinks, but she carries on. "At least he's not around much at the moment."

"Something to be grateful for."

"There isn't a lot else," she agrees. "Ever since the Musee..." Her voice tails off and she wrings her hands together.

I squeeze her arm. "That was just one opportunity."

We stop to let Freddie chase the pigeons around the edge of the lake. Few have bread to spare for them these days, so they lose interest in him quickly and return to pecking for worms.

I tell her, "We're not so alone in this, Kat. Maybe others will act, or we'll get another chance. The war is still happening, after all, just, mercifully, not here."

I sit on a bench and check no-one else is in proximity. She joins me, and I tell her about the newspapers and leaflets which I found in a Gestapo officer's room last week, denouncing the Nazi rule. Défense de la France, Libération, Liberté, Libre France - I imagine they had caught someone with them, which made me sad at first, but then my heart clamoured with the realisation: dissenting voices were being shared! Many of them. In one issue, from February, the headline talked about the many resistance groups, urging them to act together, and condemning the repression of French liberties.

Although we have spent years now, passing information in the vague hope of it being useful to someone, this was the first time I truly felt a part of something bigger than my immediate circle of confidantes. We - Kat and I - are not alone in our fight - acts of rebellion were being encouraged across the country.

For myself, with my usual struggles with letters, reading the newspapers had taken me too long, costing me a lunch break as I was supposed to be servicing the room. "I wish you could have read them," I tell her. "The people writing them are awfully brave. Some had photographs in, which you know is forbidden these days."

"Foolish, more like," she says. "A printing press is a huge thing to hide."

I know this from first-hand experience at the convent. "How else will word spread? So few have a radio. A leaflet might encourage, at very least, raise a question, or give people hope. Then, the more who rally to help the cause, the better."

She stares straight ahead. "One of my boarders told me about men who try to avoid the STO – the mandatory work orders - and hide in the countryside, sabotaging railways and fighting the soldiers directly. Maquisards, he called them. Living a life on the land, lawless almost. Free."

The note of admiration in her voice makes me think she wants to join them, but then she turns her face away and mutters. "The

Gestapo only bother to torture some of them to give up their comrades. As for the rest..." She points two fingers, curling the others into a gun shape and jerks her hand. "No trial, no questions. Leave them where they fall, he said."

PROOF

The blazing warmth of summer turns cool, then cold, then absolutely freezing as we hunker down for winter. The atmosphere at the Ritz changes - everyone is preoccupied with what to eat, rather than the usual pre-Christmas socialising. Even Kat's black market contacts cannot supply the luxuries which our guests rely upon, and our staff rations are so tiny we shuffle, constantly exhausted, about our chores. A coal shortage, as well as intermittent power cuts, means people congregate in the warmer public rooms, more to keep warm than because there's much to talk about. We've stopped noticing how badly we all smell now soap is scarce. Half the rooms are vacant, the Luftwaffe required elsewhere, which leaves me with meagre pickings for information.

One morning, while I'm servicing the room opposite Chanel's, the Baron finds me. His pallor is grey and he looks unsteady on his feet, as if he's been drinking all night. He shoves a sheet of paper into my hand. "Do something with this. Please, for God's sake, just... do something."

I scan the sheet. It looks like an invoice, the kind I have seen before in the Auzello's office, but it's not. I stare at the letters, wishing they would stop moving around so much so I could understand better. It's so much easier to read and copy words down when I'm alone in my bedroom and can use a ruler.

He jabs at what I think is a tally. Classifications of people - Jews, homosexuals, Romanies, with numbers in their hundreds next to each line. At the bottom, adjacent to Pieter's signature, it says:

TRANSPORT DESTINATION #62: Auschwitz. November 20th 1943

I ask, "What is this?"

His voice is hollow, shaky even. "It's a list of those he's sending away from Drancy."

"Why? What's at Auschwitz?"

"It's a death camp. No-one leaves alive. They burn."

Nausea sweeps over me, even though I have only a scrap of bread in my stomach.

Hans sinks onto the unmade bed and drops his head into his hands. "I can't. I just can't. Catsy..."

I crouch next to him, my heart thudding as I remember him telling me his former wife was Jewish. My mouth is dry as I ask, "How did you get this, Baron?"

"Captain Momm," he says. "Katarina re-introduced us a while ago at some soiree. We knew each other in the army, before. Turns out, he supervises textile production for the Reich, here in Paris now." He sighs. "And Chanel thought he could help free Andre, Coco's nephew."

"I see." Over the years, I've seen many letters in her room, begging various people to pardon him, release him from his internment. Having served with the French army, he'd been captured right at the start of the war and put in a labour camp. Some said she adopted Andre's cause because he was really her own bastard son.

"We got to talking about a plan, a crazy plan. Momm wants us to talk to Schellenberg. He's in... intelligence, shall we say. Momm think's if he knew the extent, the numbers, he might... Never mind. Anyway, Momm gave me this to convince me, and Schellenberg, that something needs to change. He got it from some administrator whose boyfriend guards Drancy." He snorts. "Funny thing is, Momm's more concerned that his free labour might be taken away, that's what it comes down to. He wants a slow down of the eradication, so he can keep to his production quotas." He looks at me, and I can almost see his mind whirring, wondering whether to trust me. His eyes narrow.

I touch his knee. "It's alright." I think of Kat's refusal to hear details unless it directly affects her. Although I'd rather know, being of the belief that any knowledge can be useful. I try to reassure him. "Sometimes the less said, the better."

"You misunderstand. Whatever the plan is, or will be, I wouldn't tell you."

"Then why bring this to me?"

He pinches the bridge of his nose. "I just... I mean, I knew what the policy was. Knew Pieter was involved, but this... the scale of it?" His blond hair falls over his forehead as he shakes his head.

"What do you mean?" Ice runs through my veins.

"This is just one day, don't you see? One city, out of how many the Reich rules?" He frowns at me, as if I'm stupid. "Where will it stop? There are millions of Jews. Dissidents. Disabled people even. Anyone who opposes them." Then, bitterly, "Us." He clenches his fist.

I sit back on my heels, more shaken than I let on. We'd all seen it coming, this swell of antisemitism, leading to them being rounded up, but, until now, I hadn't realised the true aim was eradication. My fingers grip the paper and I scan the numbers again.

#62. Did that mean 62 transports had already left? I sum up the columns - 1200, on that one transport. Already, if my maths was correct, that meant over 74 thousand people, most likely more, had been deported to their deaths from Paris alone. I recalled the children crying at the Vel d'Hiv. Whole families had been rounded up.

My stomach tightens.

Marc's mother. Was she one of them?

I stand and pace away from Hans so he doesn't see my tears.

"One slip and it'll be you," he says.

I wheel around. "Me?"

"And Freddie." He's staring at me, blue eyes piercing into my face.

I gape like a fish, but then, his accusatory tone softens. "You're both Jews. All it takes is for Pieter to see you, and he'll figure it out."

I squeak, "Freddie?"

"I'm not blind."

"D... does Pieter know?"

"Katarina made a joke about how much I looked like her husband, which, having never met him, Pieter bought. But, he looks just like me when I was that age." He falls silent for a moment while I chew my lip and stare at the carpet. "You should have told me, Hannah."

I don't know what kind of acknowledgement of paternity I expected, but it wasn't this. And not under these circumstances.

He stands, runs his fingers through his hair, leaving his hand on his forehead. "I admit, I wasn't completely sure, until you just reacted."

Suppressing the urge to run, taking my guilt with me, I shrug. "He's my son. I cannot keep him with me, not now." The more I talk, the more defiant I feel. "I did what was best for him, and he's better off in a safe home, until we can be together again."

"And Katarina is doing a wonderful job of protecting him." He approaches and puts his hands on my shoulders. Sarcastically, he says, "But, kind Uncle Pieter is bringing him up as if he's his son. As a Nazi."

My head spins. The bike, the ice creams... how easy it is to impress a child. "Freddie doesn't know what Pieter's done." But I'm wrong. As my belly writhes, I remember the camera and my stomach lurches. Bile in the back of my throat as I chastise myself - if I'd only got the film developed. My head lifts and I meet his eyes, knowing horror must be written all over my face. "He is safe, isn't he?"

"As much as a Jew can be hiding in plain sight, surrounded by Nazis. All of which," he says, gravely, "I cannot agree with."

A flicker of hope stirs. "Cannot?"

"Will not." He glances at the paper in my hand. "Which is why you have to do something with that."

And, I must prove to Freddie just how evil his Uncle Pieter is.

New Year Bombshell

I t was the darkest, bleakest Christmas I've ever known. Paris is broken, and, with everything I have learned, it's as much as I can achieve to dress, do my work and half-heartedly snoop for titbits. Some news reaches my ears via whispered conversations of overheard bulletins – Hitler's war, in far-flung countries, is faltering. In our daily drudge to survive, it doesn't really make much difference.

Hans and Chanel disappear from the Ritz; Kat and Freddie are unreachable and don't turn up for our scheduled meetings. Their house, when I walk past it, is dark and seemingly empty. I dare not knock on the door, for fear Pieter will answer.

And then the war comes back to Paris. On New Year's eve, just before lunchtime, air raid sirens sound. An attack feels out of the blue, and puts everyone on edge. The staff pack like a can of sardines into three of the cellar chambers, while guests are shown to the more spacious subterranean quarters. Apart from one officer who demands his lunch be served promptly, irrespective of location, our evacuation is all very civilised and orderly.

The subterranean store rooms are bare. Anything wooden and broken has been burned for heat. Spare blankets and sheets, torn up for clothes. Shelves which once stockpiled cans and bottles gather dust.

I shiver, leaning into Marc's equally scrawny chest in the darkness. With his withered arm around my shoulders, we listen in the dark, silent chambers of the cellar, wondering if the Allies bombs will fall on our deceitful walls. We can't hear them, not even the drone of the engines, and I pray Freddie and Kat are safe. My shoulders ache from hunching, and all I can think about is the last time I had to shelter during an air raid. A different cellar, but closer to my boy. The fear for his safety hasn't lessened - in fact, now Pieter lives with him, it's worse.

Against my lower back is a soft bundle, which, when I reach around, my seamstress fingertips identify as silk. I trace neat seams bound with strong, quite coarse thread, and wide sturdy straps with dirt on buckles. It takes a moment of wondering what it can be before I twig - a muddy parachute! Lately, I've picked up several camouflage-patterned pants, discarded on bedroom floors. Maybe, I can distract myself by calculating how many pairs of knickers or blouses just one silky sheet would make. I wipe away a tear, not knowing if I will ever sew again.

Marc's arm tightens around me. "It'll be over soon."

I sniff, my voice tight and strained. "I'm not so sure it ever will be. Agony never-ending. Until it does and we're all dead."

In the silence, I sense what I said was heard by everyone. Bodies shuffle, others judder in sobs.

He strokes my hair and mutters in my ear, "I shall pray harder. Hard enough for us all."

Praying will do nothing. I've prayed before and things keep getting worse. How can he be so strong when he can't know what will happen? We're trapped underground, packed together like cattle in a truck. It makes me think of those carts we saw at the Vel d'Hiv. And before, when the Nazi killed that old man, right on the street.

My fists ball. I watched those atrocities happen, and said nothing. Did nothing. And now I'm going to die here, a no-one. I'm powerless, and all my weak voice does is make things worse. I said what we are all thinking, maybe. But I'm a fraud. A liar. Why would anyone listen to me?

The atmosphere in the cellar touches me, suffocates me, and it's my fault everyone in here now also fears the worst. My vision clouds as my lungs gasp for breath, but there is none to be had. I've lost years of my life, when I could have been with my son, for this? Their judgement, when they are all just as silent?

From a corner, a match rasps, and a candle flickers to life. I blink as its glow dances across the curved brick ceiling. My stomach cramps and I groan, collapsing into Marc. He catches me as my knees give way. "Let her fall down," someone says, as he lowers me to the cold floor.

As soon as I'm on solid ground, I curl up into a ball. Finally, I can draw in stale air, and my head stops spinning. All I can see are people's cork or wood-soled shoes and iodine painted legs, then I close my eyes. Marc crouches beside me, stroking my hair and shielding me from all the stares. And I'm so tired. So very tired of it all.

I drift in and out of sleep, uncertain of time, before the all clear sounds. When everyone else has shuffled out, back to work, Marc helps me to my feet. "You gave me quite a scare."

My head is low as I apologise. His arm stays around my waist as we climb the stairs, emerging into a sunnier space. But my heart still feels heavy.

He squeezes my hand. "Do you want to tell me what happened?"

I look at him, and I do. If we're all going to die, be buried under the Ritz or carted off to be burned, I want him to know all of me. "I was overwhelmed, that's all."

His gaze is wary, suspicious I'll hold back, again. "Seemed like it was more than that."

"I don't want you to think less of me, for what I went through before we met. But, my past weighs on me. The people involved. I can't bear for you to judge me for my mistakes."

"I won't," he says, and the conviction in his voice reassures me a little. "Tell me when you can, and I'll listen without judgement."

I nod and step away, back to the dirty sheets and scrubbing. He doesn't let go of my hand though. "We all have a past, you know," he says. "Things we'd rather forget we did. It's the future that matters."

Shooting him a small smile, I say, "I'm not the same person as I was. None of us can be."

Confession is Good for the Soul

That night, I couldn't sleep, and I've no heart to see in 1944 even though we survived being bombed. This time. In the early hours, I wander downstairs and help Frank clear the glasses in the bar. I need his cheer, and he delivers. Despite the punishing day we've all had, he's buoyant, on a survivor and cocktail high. When the last few revellers are politely bundled out the door, he laughs and says, "Ball-bearing factories! Of all things. Bloody ball bearings."

"What?"

"That's what the Brits hit. Never even came close to us." He leans across the mahogany bar, wiping it with his cloth, then taps the side of his nose. "But they'll come, don't you worry, Edelweiss."

"When?" I sag onto a stool. "And will they raze Paris to the ground on their way?"

He stands up, and his moustache twitches as his mouth tugs into a smile on one side. With twinkling eyes, he says, "It won't come to that."

I sit up. "What do you mean?"

Then he taps the side of his nose again, then points his finger to the ceiling. "There's what's happening here, and what's happening out there." He jabs to the window. "Something's going to change this year. You'll see."

But I don't.

My bleak mood doesn't lift. Temperatures plummet again and snow clogs everything. Chanel returns in February, equally bleak after having been in Madrid for weeks. She lounges around her room, racking up room service charges and refusing to see anyone or allow me to clean properly. The 'medicine' she uses is in even shorter supply than soap, and the lack of it makes her cranky. I overhear her arguing with Madame Auzello one morning, while I'm cleaning the room across the corridor. Then, Madame barges through the door.

"Insufferable! That sheet's not straight. You'd think after all this time, you could make a bloody bed right, Devereaux." She stomps to the bed, wrenches off the quilt with a grunt then dumps it on the floor.

I blink.

With a force at odds with her slim frame, she digs her talons into the sheet, tearing it as she drags it off the mattress. "Make it again," she screeches at me.

"As you wish, Madame."

My meek response inflames her. "Speak up, goddammit." Sheet still in her hands, she rips it again. Her cheeks flush red as she spends her fury.

As she chucks the shreds at me, we glare at each other for a moment.

"I'll speak when I'm properly spoken to," I say. "In this instance, saying nothing is probably better."

She sinks onto the bed and hangs her head. I pick up the quilt and shake it out.

"She's just so…"

"I know."

We share a conspiratorial glance. Then, she stands, takes a sheet from my trolley then helps me make the bed again in silence. As she runs her hand over the fold of the cotton, she says, "You know, unlike me, who says the first thing that comes into her mouth, your very quietness is your strength." Her eyes flick to mine. "Not everyone needs to be loud to have an effect. I know you do speak out, when you see an injustice, and then people listen. You might sneak around, quiet as a mouse, and when you're quiet, you're watching. Remembering the details." She shrugs. "And perhaps, that's what will be a greater legacy."

I don't know what to say to that, so I simply acknowledge her calmer words with, "Thank you."

"Can you fix that?" She points to the ripped sheet, then laughs. "Of course you can. You can mend anything."

Frank finds me in the laundry, trying to work out if I can, in fact, rescue the sheet and make a night gown, or if it should be ripped into smaller shreds and used as cloths. "One of my boys brought this. It's for you." His expression is grim as he shoves a note with 'Mme. Devereaux, Ritz Hotel' scrawled on the outside, towards me.

M. F is ill and I've not been able to get any medicine. Same as before. P is here. Stay safe and I'll be in touch if there's news.

My heartbeat stutters and for a second, I cannot breathe. Freddie, already weak from the cold and a lack of nutrition, must be terribly ill for her to send a message. I sink into a bundle of clothes and remember holding my boy as he wrestled with a temperature, unable to properly draw breath. His eyes, pleading with mine for a release from the pain in his chest. I didn't know what to do then, and I don't now.

And worse, because Pieter is there, I cannot go to him. Tell him how much I love him, how I would gladly take his pain if it would only relieve his. My chest constricts and my eyes swim with tears.

"Is there anything I can do?" Frank says.

I shake my head. "Not unless you can magic up a miracle cure."

He stands, hands shoved in pockets, looking wistfully at me. "I've lemons, kept aside for a rainy day. Let me know if you need a lemonade."

Only if you can send them across town, I think, shaking my head again because I cannot speak. The lemonade will be sour without sugar, and the lemons so old and withered, I doubt they have much goodness in them anyway. I appreciate he's trying to be kind, but my one thought is Freddie.

The next time I raise my head, he's gone, but then, Marc pokes his head around the door. He takes one look at me, curled upon the laundry sacks and comes over. "What's happened, love?"

My lips press together. In my fists, the note shakes.

"Tell me, please," he says, crouching and tenderly stroking my hands.

I look into his warm brown eyes and think, I almost don't care if he does judge. At least he said he'd listen. "It's... my son. He's very ill."

"Your son?"

But, instead of pulling back as I'd half expected him to, with his good arm, he bundles me into his thin chest. "Oh my love, you must be so worried."

I nod into his shoulder, then the sobs come. Heaving, unladylike, and ugly. He holds me through the worst, until I draw away from him. After a hiccup or two, I organise my thoughts. "I'm sorry. I've wanted to tell you for the longest time, but it never seemed like the right moment. And now, he's so ill, and I can't tell him how much I care because... well, I just want someone else to know he exists."

He gazes at me steadily. "Tell me about him."

I struggle at first, partly because Freddie's changed so much and I've missed years of his childhood, I don't feel qualified to speak as his mother. "He likes to chase pigeons. He's got the longest legs now, and I'm sure, if he gets through this, he'll be taller than me when he's grown. And, he's so clever - always able to take things apart then put them back together."

Marc smiles. "A fixer then, like his mother."

I nod. "And he's great at drawing, and remembering. He's got hair that's so blond in the sunshine you'd think it white, so not really like me at all." I half laugh. "Not naturally, anyway. That's the Aryan in him."

He blinks and I look away. I mutter, "His father, you know." I shrug. "I was young, and naïve. It could have been worse."

I swallow. Hans. Should I tell him his son is ill? He's never even acknowledged him, not really. But still. While I'm ruminating on the problem, Marc says, "You aren't the first to be in such a position, and you won't be the last. I'm the son of a woman who brought me up on her own. Never knew my father. Apparently, he died in the Great War."

"Freddie's the only blood relative I have. My parents both died when I was very young, and I have no siblings. For years, it was just us. And then, when we had to leave the convent we lived in, we came together to Paris. But then, Paris let the Nazis in and I had to leave him."

His sympathetic expression tells me he understands. "So, where is he now? Who's looking after him?"

"Katarina. The real one. My supposed 'sister-in-law,' who I grew up with. My one true friend, she took us in when we arrived here. He lives with her, across Paris."

"Ah."

"And that's why I can't see him. Her cousin, Pieter, is a Nazi officer, the SS, and lives there too." I draw in a deep breath and tell him the missing part, why I'm so secretive about where I go on my days off. "She's the one I meet every second Sunday on my day off. Freddie too, if he can make it without it being obvious. We all have to pretend he's Kat's son, to keep him safe. Because, he's half Jewish."

He frowns. "Doesn't Pieter know?"

"He thinks Freddie's a Catholic, like she is. And French, because of his father, Katarina's late husband. Besides, Freddie doesn't talk. He can, he used to before. He just doesn't now. Not since we left Germany. In that regard, he's also the perfect cover for her other activities." I look at him with clear eyes, hoping he'll fill in the blanks.

"The black market?"

I nod. "And, he's observant. Curious....Nosy. Rebellious, like me. Except, he can't, or won't tell. The perfect, silent spy."

He takes my hand. "He sounds like a lovely, and very brave boy. Like his mother. And, maybe, like her, he'll find his voice again, when it's the right time."

"I think it's the shock of what we saw." Talking about Freddie's lack of speech reminds me of my vow to him. "Until I can fix something, right a wrong…" I hiccup instead of saying what I really hope, but it doesn't matter.

"What 'wrong' do you need to fix?"

I sit up. "He had a camera, which I have here. I think, if I can find out what's on the film in it, it might help."

Marc smiles. "I'm pretty good with cameras. Want me to take a look?"

"Would you? I used to take the film to a shop to get the prints made, that was the only way to see if they were any good or not. It was terribly expensive, even then."

"Getting hold of photographic paper is the bigger problem, these days." He confirms my biggest worry. "But, if we can afford it, I know someone at Le Printemps, the department store, who can help. He used to work there anyway." He shrugs. "I can only ask."

My smile is soft. "Anything you can do, I'll appreciate." My soul already feels lighter from burdening.

He stands, then offers me a hand to help me up. "I think I'm ready now."

"For what?"

His eyes are hooded as he looks at me. "To do more. It's bad enough they took my mother. My home. Then, all this has broken your spirit too." He straightens to his full height. "I want to get more involved. Take action."

"It's too dangerous, especially for…"

He shakes his head. "I'm a new person now, because they made me have to be. And I want no more mothers separated from their sons. Protesting isn't enough. Nothing will change until we, the French, act to oust them. I'm sure, even with this," he waves his weaker arm and flares his eyelids at me, "I can be of use. Like you are, except I want to fight."

"The kind of people Kat and I know aren't... military-minded."

"But I know someone who might be. One of Frank's delivery boys - he joined the Marquis, rather than be sent to a labour camp. "

"The Maquis hide in the countryside, I thought?"

As we walk towards the door, he grins. "There'll be others, in the cities. I'm sure someone will know who to speak to."

I think of all the Resistance newspapers I've read, although few named themselves. "I know there are. We just have to ask the right person."

FÉVRIER

Of course, it's Frank, who knows everyone and everything. It's him who tells me Chanel was supposed to meet Winston Churchill in Madrid, except she didn't.

And it's Frank who holds me in a fatherly way as I sob with relief when word arrives, via his boys, that Freddie has recovered.

Kat herself writes a few weeks later:

P home. Business ceased – flat tyre! F all clear and back at school. Will write when I have news.

Frank warns me the Gestapo are tightening their grip on anyone who might be collaborating against the regime, even if it's to feed people. I suspect it's only Pieter's presence which keeps her out of the prison at Fresnes. Flat tyre – she's being watched.

I'm in a bind. Without Kat to pass messages to, where can I send the snippets I find? I've even tried waiting around in the café where Kat said the lady with the pheasant feathered hat frequented, but she didn't show up. I worry the whole network which we were a part of has collapsed.

My desperation and frustration spills out in a tricky, veiled conversation with Frank – the 'someone who knows someone'.

"More manpower might be required to tackle the mouse problem," I say, trusting he'll understand our jargon for the grey Nazi uniforms. "Marc and I... we want to... no, *need* to do more."

He suggests we find a man, probably a Communist, who drinks at a small café-bar, near to Montparnasse station. On a chilly Sunday lunchtime, armed with only a scant description, we don hats, gloves and coats. Even if it weren't a bitter February, the very absence of such clothing would draw attention to us.

"Where are you pair off to this fine day?" Jaques asks as we head out into the weak sunshine.

I'm not sure how he is still standing, the war has aged him so. "To see Paris in the spring," I say.

Jaques snorts, his breath billowing. "Some spring. Where really?"

Marc tucks my arm through his. "To find freedom," he says jauntily, as I smile at my old friend shyly.

"Bon courage," Jaques replies. "This winter is evil, and I'll be glad to see it gone."

Won't we all, I think. None of us mean the season.

Although I paste on a cheerful face, I suppress a shudder passing the Jardin des Tuileries. My heart lifts when we cross over the green river water and head south. We find the bar and lurk, nursing a terrible ersatz coffee between us. It makes for a strange first date, but, since we haven't ever managed to be out as a couple in public before – save our ill-fated trips to the Vel d'Hiv – I'm buoyed by the chance to be with him without all the Ritz staff staring at us. While we chat about inconsequential things like, how long the awful weather will last and make the vaguest of plans to visit the countryside one day, we keep grinning at each other.

Eventually, someone meeting Frank's description wanders in and takes a seat. He hands over a tatty coupon and a few coins and makes his order for coffee. From the rich smell, he's given the real stuff, instead of the ground acorn muck we were served. Somewhat brazenly, he withdraws a single sheet of a newspaper, headed *Defense de la France*, and studies it while the waiter prepares his drink. Recognising the title, I nudge Marc and flick my eyes towards the customer.

As we approach, intelligent eyes examine us through dark-rimmed glasses. Like almost everyone French, the man's face is drawn and thin. Slack skin from his chin nudges over his tight shirt collar as he lowers his read. From his attire, I guess he's in his fifties, but he looks older. For a long, silent minute, he takes in our shabby clothes and Marc's clenched arm as it spasms. *"Oui?"*

"We'd like to help," I say, wondering if I should have asked Frank for a code word or something. Too late now.

"With what?"

I point at the Resistance newspaper title and raise my eyebrow.

"We'll do anything," Marc says, taking my hand. "When the time comes to fix the mouse problem for good."

The man's moustache twitches as he stares at the paper on the table. "We need fighters, not lovers who think the fight is all terribly romantic. Aren't you scared of ending up in Fresnes?"

"Whatever it takes. We don't care," I lie, terrified of the possibility. Almost all the staff know someone who's been taken for 'questioning' in the Gestapo prison at Fresnes to the south of Paris. Not everyone returns.

The man grunts, picks up the newspaper and his eyes drop as if he's reading.

Taking a deep breath and straightening my shoulders, I say with a confidence I don't really feel, "You need quick thinking people, calm under pressure, who have good reason to resist."

He looks at me, surprised. "Maybe."

"And we're used to being surrounded by 'them'. We live at the Ritz," I offer, to which the man raises an eyebrow. "We work there," I clarify.

He grunts. "A den of iniquity and spies." He puts down the paper and stands, not noticing I am studying the floor. "Too many watch that place already."

After downing his coffee, the man tips his hat at the waiter and heads to the door. "If you are serious about helping, and willing to take the risk, come with me."

Marc and I exchange smiles and follow him out. Once on the street, the man pulls out a battered soft pack of cigarettes and offers Marc one. Marc shakes his head. Our new friend taps out a half-smoked stick and lights it. "Got to puff now. Once we're down, it's too dangerous."

I wonder what on earth he can mean, but then, we round a corner and he stops outside an ordinary painted wooden door on Rue Boulard. No markings to hint at what's inside. Puffing away, he glances up and down the quiet street before rapping out what must be a code and waits. Once he's down to the stub, he grinds it out and pulls out a key. He holds the door open for us, and we enter a dim hallway. "Walk three paces forward, then stop," he warns.

Once the door closed behind us, it's pitch black. A click of his lighter, the scratch of flint, and the dark walls are bathed in a flickering yellow glow. Another door, painted with Do Not Enter, becomes visible a little further down. An old man leans against it. He lifts a rifle, aiming at us. My heart thumps. Our friend pushes past Marc and I, and whispers in the guard's ear.

The muzzle lowers and the old man draws back bolts to the door. He watches on, still suspicious, as we pick our way down uneven stairs. Down and down we go with only the soft flame ahead to guide us. There's a faint whiff of sewer, but underfoot it's dry.

We emerge in a grey painted corridor and our friend flicks a switch and shuts the Zippo lid. Overhead, light bulbs buzz to life, strung on hooks from the ceiling, all the way down what seems like an endless tunnel. 'No smoking' is sprayed at intervals along the walls and, as we walk along, I notice ladders leading up to black shafts. "Manholes," I whisper. "I wonder where we are?"

The man ahead of us snorts. "Welcome to hell," he says. "Stick with me and learn this route. Stray and you'll end up in one of the Nazi bunkers. It's a maze."

We pass an arched aperture in the wall and I peer through. It's sufficiently dark to send a shiver through me, yet light enough to see piles of skulls inside, like I've seen many times in the catacombs. I pause for a moment, wondering how far away we are from Kat's cavern store. I've lost count of how many corridors we've twisted and turned through.

Marc squeezes my hand reassuringly. He points up to a stone street sign recessed in the wall - Rue Daguerre. "We're not completely lost. Above is the road named after the father of photography."

The man checks on us. "Catacombs, sewers. We sleep next to death and shit with the shit." He glares at me. "Begging your pardon, Mademoiselle, but you'd better get used to frank speech. We speak plainly down here."

Minutes later, we stop outside another iron door. "Centre of operations is further up. You'll do some basic training here. Get familiar with... equipment." He drags the door open and gestures us inside.

The room stinks of cordite and grease - no escaping the mechanics of war here. Around the walls, long wooden crates are propped open to show their contents. Row upon row of weapons, shelves groaning with boxes of bullets and ominous looking shapes under tarpaulins. I recognise the outline of the larger machine guns, because they installed them on the roof of the Ritz hotel when the Nazis invaded Russia.

He leads us past the first chamber and into a second. Piled in the middle of the cavern are a few German sub-machine guns, a couple of old-fashioned rifles and a separate heap of pistols next to a bunch of spare parts. A few men and one tired-looking woman perch on barrels, cleaning guns. Seeing our escort, they offer a salute with a flat hand to their foreheads.

"Lily," our friend says to the woman.

"Fevrier," she replies, nodding at him.

"Two to train. Ever held a weapon?" He turns to us with a raised eyebrow as Lily jumps off her barrel, snaps a mechanism on the black revolver she was wiping, then puts it down. The click echoes and I stare at the gun, thinking about the last times I saw such weapons un-holstered. Pointing at Sister Luisa. Pointing at an innocent old man, then me.

I know I should be used to seeing guns. All the officers wear them with their uniform, but, seeing so many just haphazardly propped around, I recoil. "I don't think I can," I whisper to Marc.

He glances at me. "That's fine," he says in a quiet voice. "I can."

"There's plenty else needs doing," Fevrier says. "What can you do?"

My housekeeping skills are hardly needed down here. Nor is my ability to snoop. His stern expression warns me, I must speak now or I'll never be welcomed back down here. "I can speak German. I've good eyesight."

His eyebrow raises and I can tell he isn't impressed. There has to be something I can do, if I can't pick up a gun. "Ah... I cook... and sew. I can sew really well."

"Follow me."

Relieved, I squeeze Marc's hand briefly then drop it, and we leave. The corridor widens, with posters pinned to the walls, which lends a sense of organisation even though they are mostly slogans

for the FFI and its Communist values. I'm escorted through a series of panelled rooms with office equipment. Two men, one with
a military bearing and fatigues, and another who looks decidedly
more casual, pour over a map.

"Colonel," Fevrier says. He receives a nod, then the Colonel
returns to his work.

"We need some alterations," Fevrier says, showing me to a tall
grey metal box.

"To what, and to fit who?"

Fevrier throws open the cabinet's doors then stands back,
watching my expression. Crammed inside are German army uniforms - black, grey, green, trousers, jackets, shirts. Various caps and
boots are piled at the bottom. Shiny skulls from SS lapels twinkle
up at me from the heap. "To fit slimmer people. French people.
Disguised, it's easier to gain access to certain places. Then we leave
behind a nasty surprise. Booooom!" His hands mime an explosion
and I smile. "Can you measure up some fighters who'll wear them,
and assemble some appropriate outfits?"

At last, something I can do. And I've repaired many a uniform at
the Ritz by now. Any revulsion at handling them has long passed.
I face him, unfazed. "No problem."

And, it isn't.

RIOT

S pring whistles past and ends with the news of the Allies landing on the shores of Normandy. Updates reach us via an illegal radio set which kitchen staff at the Ritz monitor day and night. They listen to the BBC's Radio Londres when possible, as the Free French transmit in French and English, then pass on the soundbites of hope in the canteen.

Days after the landings, while celebrating at Maxims, the Gestapo arrested Madame Auzello. Again, apparently, except this time she fails to return. Poor Claude, her husband and co-Manager, has been beside himself in her absence. He is also pulled in for questioning, but is released a few days later with no information on his wife's whereabouts. Despite their many public spats, it's obvious he's worried. With the hotel half empty, as the Luftwaffe try to stop the Allies' progress through France, he takes on her Dragon Lady persona. We, the staff, walk on eggshells around him.

All of which only makes me more jittery about Kat's predicament. I have not heard from her in weeks and Frank's boys report there's no lights on and no answer at her house, but there are signs of of people still living there. I'm desperate to see for myself, but every day off I have, I'm asked to alter uniforms for special missions for the Resistance.

It's Bastille day, which, officially, the French are no longer allowed to celebrate. When the BBC informs us there's a parade in London with de Gaulle, it sparks a rebellion. News spreads that some staff members are going out to the streets anyway, and I rush downstairs to find Marc in the kitchens. Ever since we've been frequenting the FFI, or FiFi, bunker, he's grown in confidence, and now, he stands at his sink, venting his frustration by banging pots about in the bubbles.

The Sous Chef de Cuisine begs the Head Chef, "We should be allowed to go. It's our country, our day to show them our right to liberty. *Vive La France!*" He sticks his arm in the air, and many join him.

Shaking his head, the Head Chef shouts over the staff. "*Non, non, non.* You cannot abandon us here, not now. We have jobs to do, and they will put you down like the dogs they think we are. I forbid it."

Marc catches my eye, his cheeks flushed. "It's a day of revolution," he says quietly when I reach him. "Maybe, after everything, you can understand how we feel."

"You have to do what you think is right." I touch his arm and look around. No-one is close. "There's a bigger plan, though, isn't there?" We've both remarked upon the increasing activity, down with the Fifi's.

He shrugs. "It's not happening today, is it? They want to go and protest."

"The Allies are still miles from Paris," I reply. "I heard Fevrier talking about it. They won't move until back up is closer. We just have to wait. Be ready for the call."

Marc explodes. "I'm tired of waiting." He points to the group of chefs, stripping off their white jackets and pulling on coats. "They aren't hanging around are they?"

My eyelids flare. "Then go if you want to." I'd never stop him, he knows that. Being French is all he has left to cling to. He's not prayed since we allied ourselves with the Communists.

"I'm sorry, but I am going."

My face must be paling because he softens. "I'll be fine. And... I didn't have the chance to tell you before, but through some friends I made below, I managed to get the film developed. I collected the prints yesterday."

"I didn't know you'd even removed the film!" My heartbeat raced. "Have you looked through them?"

"Only the first few, all paintings."

My face falls.

"Isn't that what you expected?"

I shake my head. "No. Yes... Can I see them?"

He dries his hands. "They're yours. I did it for you."

In his gentle smile, I realise how much it means to him to provide me with what he thinks will be comfort. He must have spent his own money on them, when I thought we were going to share the cost once he'd confirmed the availability of photographic paper.

Marc leans down and brushes his lips over mine. "They're in my bedroom, second drawer, under my jumper."

"Please, if you go out, be careful," I urge, before dashing up to his dormitory.

It's not only running up five floors which makes my pulse race. Nestled in the drawer, next to Freddie's camera, is a brown envelope.

Rifling through the prints, there's some nicely framed shots of paintings, some showing the confessional in the background. I can't catch my breath when I see the last photo: sharply focused, Pieter's face in a three-quarter profile. He's holding the gun, wisps of smoke hover from the snout. On the floor, Sister Luisa. Dead with a black hole in her forehead.

I sink to my knees, keening. Freddie, huddled in my arms at the time, clicked the button, captured the moment, and unwittingly caught the killer. I hold the photo up to the light, marvelling in some twisted way, how perfectly framed it is. I doubt anyone could take such a shot again if they tried.

The image of evil spurs me into action. My son still lives with that monster! I managed to shield his eyes from seeing Pieter at the time, but now I have proof, I must show him. They were, I believe, what he was concerned about in the catacombs. Maybe it will ease him to see the evidence. And, perhaps, by forcing him to recall the night when he last spoke, not only will he talk again, but he'll see Pieter for what he is. I leave the developed film strips in the envelope and replace it in Marc's drawer then dash up to my room. Work be damned, my son is more important, and there's no Madame Auzello to throw me out for disappearing, again. I'll make up for it later, I decide, and clean all night if I have to.

After stuffing the prints, camera and my *Carte* into my bag, I hasten downstairs. As I rush onto on Rue Cambon, Jaques calls out my name. I glance at him, impatient to get across town. "Can't stop!"

He frowns. "Don't go," he says. "There'll only be trouble."

"I'm not going to a parade, or a protest, or whatever they are planning."

My attempt to reassure him seems to work, as he touches his hat with two fingers and bids me, "Stay clear of the main roads, then."

As I reach the Place de la Concorde, I understand his concern. A seething mass of people shout 'Bread! Bread' as they march around the base of the obelisk, waving the *tricoleur* flag of France. Hundreds, maybe thousands of people, from all walks of life, are gathered - and the tone of their chants is defiant. It's the biggest protest I have seen or heard about in Paris since our Occupation. And it's not just here – although I cannot see them, in the pauses between chants, yells echo through the streets. I hope Marc's isn't one of the voices, but I suspect he probably is.

As I skirt the perimeter, a stream of black Gestapo Citroëns pull into the cobbled square and my stomach clenches. Where are the police? Civil unrest is usually their remit, but the blue of their uniforms is conspicuously absent. Gestapo will shoot first, ask questions later.

The protesters, inflamed by the arrival of our overlords, break formation and swarm towards the cars. I can only watch in horror, but the crowd stops short of attacking and converges in a line. Linking arms as if that will protect those behind them, they chant for bread again.

Trucks arrive and armed Nazi soldiers jump out. Yet more vehicles pull into the square, shooting from the back before their boots even hit the ground.

As the rat-a-tat-tat of shots pumps across the square, I dive behind one of the big stone lamp post bases. Screams of fury and pain fill the air. I hold my breath and pray. The guns cease, then the guttural bark of shouted orders - disperse or be rounded up. My heart pounds. I cannot get caught up in this now.

The crowd roars their disapproval of the orders, while I hot foot it towards the Seine. Once out of immediate danger, and separated from the Place de la Concorde by the wide sunny walkway, I pause for a moment to gather myself. Leaning against a tree trunk next to the bridge, I briefly close my eyes and focus on the burble of the river, rather than the shouts of riot a few hundred yards away. Breathe in, breathe out. In. Out. I tell myself, if they are occupied with this upset, then maybe, checkpoints will be unguarded and I can reach Kat's by a more direct route. In. Out. Go...

Centred, I push myself away from the smooth, comforting bark and glance again at the Place. A van zooms past.

Marc's face is pressed, pale, against the back window.

BRANDY

I race after the truck, waving, calling, but it's no use. The transport accelerates away, across the Seine. By the end of the bridge, I'm out of breath, my heart pounds too much, and I stagger to a halt. My last sight of his dear face is as the vehicle rounds the corner and down Bd Saint Germain, heading south.

Bent over, panting with my hands on my knees, fear takes a hold. I bite my lips together to stop myself from crying out, heaving air in and out of my nostrils. In the distance, more gunshots, but their noise is deafened by the thunder of blood rushing in my ears. I've no hope of catching the truck, and no way to know where he's been taken.

Or do I? I straighten, too suddenly and my vision swims. Yet my mind clarifies. With a determined step, I walk quickly down the riverbank, then cross back over to make my way to Bd de Beausejour.

En route, I am not distracted at all by the protests, or the swarms of black and grey uniforms shoving people into vans and trucks. No-one pays me any attention as I scuttle down the alleys and boulevards quiet and unnoticed, like a mouse once again. The more SS on the streets, the greater chance I have of talking to Freddie without Pieter's oppressive presence.

A horrible thought occurs to me as I storm down Kat's road – to find out where Marc has been taken, I may have no choice but to find the courage to speak to Pieter or one of his minions.

No cars park outside her house, so I assume she and Freddie will be alone. I stride up to the door and rap the knocker loudly. "Kat! Kat!"

After a few minutes, the door swings open. Pieter's tall frame fills the space and I quickly duck my head. While he looks down at me, I study the doorstep, thoughts racing, heart thumping.

"*Ya?*"

My mouth is dry as I mutter in French, "Is Madame Weisz here?" I keep my chin pressed to my breastbone, hoping against hope he thinks my subservience is due to his position. "Please." I know I should ask, and ask now, but at the unexpected sight of him makes me shake inside.

"Speak up."

I repeat my request, slightly louder, then wait. I can almost feel his eyes, crawling all over me. Then his voice is ominously dark. "Is it Madame Weisz, or Katarina you want?" A hand reaches down and tips up my chin. His pale blue gaze turns to frost.

Terror swells in my throat. I can only squeak, '*Oui*'. But as I hear my pathetic noise, I'm filled with fury at myself. I must roar! If not now, then when?

As if he senses my growing rebellion, his hand slides down to squeeze my neck. "Hannah Edelstein."

His grasp tightens. He steps backward, pulling me into the house with him. "I'd know that pathetic mew anywhere." He spins me in the hallway, fingers dragging my skin as he pushes me forward. I gasp for breath when his grip shifts to pinch the back of my neck like a vice, holding my head down. The smell of his pomaded hair turns my stomach as my eyes dance across the black and white tiles. Paintings are propped against the walls, a chest with a suit-case next to it. He's running, I think, like the other officers at the Ritz who've loaded their treasures into trucks and disappeared.

Kat's feet, stockinged and wearing heels, appear at the bottom of the stairs. His fingers on my nape force my skull up. She stands, hand on the banister, poised in a neat suit as if she is posing for a photo. Her eyes widen. "Let go of Hannah, Pieter."

With a wrench, he shoves me forwards so I'll fall.

Instead, I stumble a few steps across the tiles, arms out, and keep my balance. I will not crumble before him. My fingers catch one of the spindles and I use it to steady me as I turn. My chin tilts up, defiance flooding through me and I stand, abreast with Kat and glare at him.

"So, little Jew," he says. His lips form into a cruel line briefly, before he spits, "I thought you might have been disposed of long ago."

We stare at each other. I have not properly seen him for nearly a decade, but his hard, beak-like features are the same. But now, in the light streaming through the open door, I see he has grown fat about the cheeks and neck. He's dressed in ordinary clothes - a shirt and trousers which strain around his stomach. Fire rolls in my belly, and I'm glad he's not in uniform. To fight against everything he stands for will take an army, but one man can be taken down.

"Pieter was just leaving," Kat says in a cold, dead voice. "Fleeing while Paris is distracted."

A flash of shame crosses his face, before it's quickly replaced by a frown. "I can easily dispense with any problems which turn up before I go."

Marc's face flashes before my eyes. "Where will you send the people captured today?" I ask.

His lip curls. "Troublemakers? Why should I tell you?" He strides forward, grabbing my arm. "Time to drop you off as well."

As he tugs me towards the front door, my bag slides off my shoulder and spills as it lands near Kat's feet. I try to dig my heels in, but he's too strong.

"She's done nothing!" Kat hisses.

"She's a Jew!" Pieter spits. "I personally can vouch for that. Why even bother to deny it?"

My temper flares. "What does it matter if I am?" I jerk my arm free. "At least I'm not a murderer, like you."

Pieter snorts. "Everything I've done in the course of my work has been for the glory of the Reich."

Staring at his thickened waistline, my ire mounts. Paris has starved. Hundreds of thousands have died under his orders, by his hand. "Glory? Is that how you justify it? Do you think yourself untouchable when the reckoning comes, after the war is lost."

"We won't lose, you fool."

Katarina bends down and picks up my bag. "You will," she says quietly. "That's why you're running now, before the Allies hold you to account." She's about to shuffle the contents back in when she freezes, hand hovering over the photograph, half in and half out of my bag.

Pieter blusters. "There's nothing to account for."

"Except there is," I say. Kat has picked up the photo and is staring at it. Her gaze flicks to mine, as if to ask, can this really be him? I nod. "You can hide behind orders, burn all the records of those people you sent to the camps. Auschwitz and however many others there are. War has different rules, I know. But I witnessed what you did for purely personal glorification."

His eyes narrow. "What rot are you talking about?"

"Cold blooded murder, at a convent in Austria. Six years ago," I say. "Innocent nuns. Children. And for what? A few paintings to impress the Führer with?"

Kat's tone is like ice. "Children?"

"No-one cares!" He spits back, then laughs. "Do you think the Reich would regret me putting down traitors?" His arm slashes down. "No! They were traitors, printing lies about the regime. Worse, they were sheltering Jews, which makes them no better than animals themselves. Traitors."

"A child took that photo." I glance at her, and she knows who I mean.

Her fists ball. Then, as if a switch flicks inside, she spins on her heel and pivots past me, down the hall. "Pieter... you cannot leave without saying goodbye to Freddie. Lord knows when you'll see each other again."

My stomach clenches - she cannot be serious! She's abandoning me, with him?

"Freddie!" She calls, going into her salon.

Pieter huffs through his nostrils, looking at me suspiciously. I can hardly breathe, but he slams the front door, then stomps past me. "Stay there," he orders, expecting my compliance.

But, I have no intention of doing what he says, ever again, so I follow him. Goosebumps prickle up my arms as I stop in the salon doorway. Kat holds out a tumbler with a shot of tawny liquid in. Pieter takes it automatically, staring at my son, sitting on the floor cross-legged. The tableau looks as if it has been played out a hundred times before: a caring wife hands her hard-working husband a refreshment after a long day's work, their obedient child on the cosy rug.

My mouth drops open. Is this what Kat's life has come to? Playing make-believe with Pieter?

Freddie's eyes roll up, taking in Pieter, then, he looks beyond to meet my gaze. For some reason, his expression seems guilty, as if we have caught him doing something he shouldn't.

Flaring my eyelids, I try to warn him not to react, but it's too late. Freddie's lips open as if he wants to say something, terror draining his face as his gaze shifts between me and his so-called 'Uncle'.

Pieter notices. His head tilts to one side, fingers tightening on the glass as he calculates. Dates. Deceptions.

"Santé!" Kat trills, holding up her own glass. "To Uncle Pieter's safe travels."

Pieter's head snaps back to her. "You...."

"Drink up." All sweetness and light, she raises the crystal to her smiling lips.

As if on autopilot because his thoughts are confused by maths and memories, Pieter downs his shot, winces as if it's stronger than he expected, then slams the tumbler on the side table. He crouches in front of Freddie. "Your Maman has been a very naughty girl, hasn't she?"

Freddie looks at him, wide eyed. Mute. Kat puts down her glass without taking a sip.

"She's lied to me, and probably to you, too." He sneers at Freddie. "But maybe you know that already?" He shoves him backwards, then, like a panther, pounces to bend over his thin frame.

Freddie tries to shuffle away, but Pieter grabs his collar. It happens so fast, I don't have time to react. Pieter's mouth froths as he says, "Did she tell you, you're a Jew?"

I can hold back no longer, and it's clear Kat's lost her mind. Her laughter tinkles as if this is some kind of cocktail hour.

I roar as I rush inside, bag swinging, and clock Pieter around the head. The camera inside isn't heavy, but, with the force of my swing, it's surprisingly sufficient to knock him off balance.

He doesn't release Freddie as he collapses. Dragging in a breath, his eyes flare and he jerks his body into his chest, arms tightening like they are spasming. Freddie yelps as I reach for him, trying to pull him free.

Pieter's arms tense around my son, and he sounds almost wistful. "A rat like her, eh?" He moves his tongue about his lips, froth and betrayal confusing him.

I glance at Kat as Pieter sags back on the rug, fingers still gripping Freddie. Pieter groans, while she stands there with a victorious look on her face. "But this home now belongs to a Kat," she says. "And I can house whomever I want in it."

While Pieter stares vacantly at her, I bend down and grab my son. One tug and Pieter's grip loosens. "Rat..." he gurgles out. "You raaa..." The syllable turns into a cough, spitting out like phlegm.

"Maus," I say, pulling Freddie free and into my embrace. I hide his head, because no child should see death. Whatever poisons Pieter closes in. I shut my eyes as the hiss of Pieter's last breath bubbles out of him. My arms tighten around my boy. "It's alright, it's all going to be alright." I stroke his hair, blink away my tears to check over his shoulder to be sure the bastard is dead.

"What have you done Kat," I whisper, although I can guess what happened to the kill pill she'd once offered me.

"Served him some justice," she replies. She picks up Pieter's glass and the bottle of brandy. "A bad batch, no doubt. In his own crystal, too."

MAP

My mouth moves but no words come out. Kat's heels click across the wooden floor as she stalks out. I listen, stroking Freddie's hair still, as taps record her moving from chequered hallway tiles into the kitchen. I can't take my eyes off Pieter's body.

Should I run? Take my son and flee before…. Before what? She won't kill us, will she? I frown.

This is different to our plans for the exhibition. She doesn't know about the memo Hans gave me either, proving his responsibility for the death of hundreds. Killing him felt more… personal. We both knew Pieter. He was a person we grew up with, however awful he'd always been. What Kat did was calculated. Deliberate. The kill pills she'd been given - I was certain she used them in the brandy. While they served their deadly purpose, if she's caught or exposed now, she's no way out. Perhaps she doesn't care any longer.

The way she'd done it too – she was almost calm. Hysterical at times, but determined. Inside, my bowels churn with rage, and fear. Had she always been this cold? This capable? The ease with which she'd poisoned him terrifies me. But then, I've no idea what happened in this house, and they were cut from the same Weisz cloth. Would she turn on us too? Has she gone mad?

Freddie's still shaking in my arms while I muddle through my dilemmas when Kat returns, a folded towel and bed sheet in her hands. She doesn't even glance at the body as she drops them on the couch then crouches next to us. Her finger sweeps the unruly lock of Freddie's hair away from his forehead.

In a too ordinary tone, she says, "I know it must seem quite wrong, Hannah, what's happened. I was in two minds anyway, when he said he was leaving."

"I don't understand. He was going."

"Yes, but this house, you see, our home, would have stayed in his name as long as he was alive. He could have returned any time he liked, hidden here even, or ousted me. We'd never feel safe. Now he's seen you, even if he didn't deal with you today, then he'd come back, believe me, and take you to a camp, or worse. He has no qualms at all where Jews are concerned."

Kat sighs and strokes Freddie's hair again. Our fingers touch briefly as we both try and provide comfort to him. Sorrow stains her voice, "I realised if I couldn't leave, then neither could, or should, that monster." Her eyes flick to mine as she drags in a deep breath. "There's so many to face justice when the Allies arrive, but Pieter," she shakes her head, "he always wriggles free of recriminations. Always. I was happy to take my punishment when I'd done something wrong, but not him. This was the only way."

"But..." I didn't like to voice 'You Killed Him' in front of Freddie, but as our eyes meet over the top of his head, she knows I'm thinking it.

"Official justice, when it comes, would simply take too long anyway," she argues, standing up. "I protected us all. My home, your and Freddie's lives." She steps over Pieter's body towards the mantelpiece and picks up the photographic evidence. In a matter-of-fact tone, "Are you going to show our boy the truth about his Uncle Pieter, or shall I?"

At the mention of his name, Freddie lifts his head and wriggles against me. I look into his cornflower-blue eyes and remember why I came here in the first place.

Kat says, "Better to do it now so he doesn't waste time mourning."

I chew my lip, holding back a sob as I whisper, "I said I would make it right, son, and I nearly have. We nearly have." He blinks at me, and I pull my bag towards us. As I extract the camera, I say very carefully, "Aunt Katarina and I need to talk to you about what you saw, back when we were in the convent."

With a solemn face, he takes the Zeiss and holds with both hands. His whole body seems to relax now it's been returned. "A friend got the film developed," I say, pain shooting through my heart as I think of Marc. God knows where he is, and now finding out will be all the harder.

Before regret can consume me, Kat drops to her knees, her body blocking Freddie's view of Pieter's bloated face. She passes him the photograph. "Did you see this, Freddie?"

He tenses, doesn't take the print, but stares at it, blood draining from his cheeks. Pieter might have been thinner, but his face is easily recognisable. I'm sure Freddie would also have seen him in his SS uniform many times.

"Did you see it happen?" I ask. At the time, I was so sure he hadn't, as I'd pressed him into my chest. Still, he'd heard the exchange from inside the pulpit. The gunfire. He might have glimpsed the bodies as we ran away.

After a minute, he shakes his head slowly.

"But you know who it is in the picture?" I say.

He glances at me, then nods. His eyes widen, shifting to Pieter's body and back to me.

"Yes. Pieter was a bad man. He was responsible for killing our friends, Sister Luisa, Mother Superior, and, I'm sorry, but he's the one who also ordered all of your friends shot as well."

His lip trembles.

"But he's gone now," Kat says.

"He can't hurt anyone again," I confirm. He taps the photo then himself. I make a guess. "You were worried this whole time, weren't you? That the man at the convent would come for you? "

He nods, and my heart sinks.

"Because of what your camera saw."

Pulling away from me, he stares at the body as if checking for himself there's no movement.

I say, "He's dead, Freddie. Really gone."

With a look of relief, he points at his throat, then towards Pieter.

I say, "You recognised his voice?"

He jerks his head once, then taps his earlobe, then his mouth. His expression pleads for me to understand.

"Your voice?" My breath catches as immediately my son's face confirms my guess. He thought Pieter heard Freddie talking to me. Calling me Mama when I'd gone looking for him in the church. It doesn't matter whether he did or didn't - we'll never know, but maybe that's why my son hasn't spoken since.

And I left him here, under constant threat of discovery, when he knew all along Pieter was the man who killed his friends. "My brave boy," I say, aghast. "And you played along all this time?"

"Oh my god," Kat says, paling.

He just looks at me with his owl eyes and a shy smile spreads into his cheeks. Putting down the camera on the floorboards, his fingers creep across the floor and feel under the chaise. He slides out a large, folded sheet of paper.

"What is it, Freddie?" I ask as he opens the sheet out. Marked on the roads are tiny crosses. Coloured pencil lines run along roads, or straight across entire swathes of neighbourhoods. He points to the main entrance to the catacombs, where we were first reunited after I'd been forced to leave him, walking his fingers down the lines until he reaches a yellow outlined box. He mimes eating with a huge smile on his face, then hugs himself with an expression of pure satisfaction.

When he lays his head on my shoulder, I study the map, recalling the tunnels we went down, all marked, and the yellow box of Kat's black market storeroom. Square boxes indicate chambers, manholes are red dots, and stairs are tiny striped circles. My skin crawls. He's even indicated what I presume are the Nazi occupied bunkers with miniature crossed bones. "Did you draw all of this?"

He nods, and I understand then how much he wanted to record the escape routes. His happiness at being underground made sense, such is the fear he's been living with. Over half his life, he's hidden, watching silently over his shoulder for the bad man to take him, and only felt safe underground when Pieter came to Paris. Suddenly, the whole day, the whole war, sweeps over me and I sob. My arms bundle my son back into my chest, and Kat leans in, wrapping her arms around us too. Our ribcages shudder as the strain pours out of us.

DISPOSAL

"Hello... Brigadeführer Weisz?"

The voice in the hallway halts our sob session. Kat pulls away from us, her teeth gritting together so hard, her jaw twitches. "It's Pieter's driver. He gave him my house keys. I'll deal with him."

"Please," I hiss, "find out where they took the people they arrested today?"

"I'll try. Get rid of..." She jerks her head towards the body, then gets up from the floor, straightens her suit skirt and pastes a look of dismay over her features. In German, she calls out, "Oh Franz, is that you?" She closes the door behind her but I catch her saying, "I'm terribly sorry. Herr Weisz walked to fetch some papers from the office."

I help Freddie stand up but he still clings to my legs. In my quietest voice, I tell him to bring me the sheet and towel so I can make everything safer. While he carefully steps around the body, shooting it nervous looks, I pocket the incriminating photograph then open the patio door in readiness. After laying the sheet down, I swaddle the head in the towel so the caustic ooze from his lips doesn't wet through the cotton. As I pull off Pieter's shoes so they don't make a noise on the wood, I'm half tempted to strip him, for his fine clothes would be very welcome to others, but frankly, it's too grotesque and noisy to accomplish when there's a Nazi officer just yards away. I settle for rolling his corpse onto the linen and knotting the sides together.

Freddie watches on, holding Pieter's brogues, as I drag the body across the wood and out, onto the patio. The sun blazes down and I sweat as I lug my load, inch by heavy inch, past the kitchen window to the cellar steps. I'd rather put my boot onto Pieter and shove him down, but then his bulk would slam into the door. Can't risk a thud, so with great effort, I tumble him slowly down the cellar steps. The irony of him blocking the door I used every morning before he arrived isn't lost on me. I decide to leave him there. Getting rid entirely, hiding the evidence of Kat's crime, will take more consideration than I can muster right now. A bundle in the stairwell, looking like laundry waiting to be washed, will have to do for now.

As I tuck an errant elbow back under the linen, I gesture for Freddie to go back to the salon, and he disappears. After a final check, I climb, each foot I place on the worn stone bringing me closer to a freedom I have not felt in a decade. Sunlight blinds me as I emerge and bathes me with peace.

But, it's not over. Kat enters just as I close the patio door behind me. "I've bought us a little time," she says. "Pieter's driver has gone to look for him at the office, then, I expect he'll check Fresnes, in case he's got a lift there."

"Is that where they'll take the protesters rounded up today?"

She nods. "Almost certainly. It's where they hide all dissidents. Why?"

My tummy cramps. Marc. Imprisoned. I collapse onto the chaise. To stop my tears, I press my tongue to the roof of my mouth and swallow. "A young man, a good friend, I saw him being taken on my way here. Kat, you can't imagine what it's like out there. He was only protesting, like the others. But..." my eyes flick to meet her sympathetic gaze.

We both know there's no escaping the Gestapo prison of Fresnes. Anyone who comes back has friends in very high places. I wonder if Madame Auzello is there, and if anyone would vouch for Marc? Pain stabs my heart again when I think of what they might do to him, especially when they discover his false ID, or if he admits who he is, or what he knows. "He was a part of something bigger, more organised. Preparing for when the time comes."

Perhaps our friends in the FiFi bunker can help.

Her fingers fiddle together and she chews her lower lip. "When the time comes..."

I nod. "It can't be long now."

"Let's hope you're right. But, help might not come quickly enough." She glances around the salon then raises an eyebrow at me.

"I left him by the cellar door."

She frowns. "In this heat?"

She's right. We can't leave him outside. He'll get to stinking, or pop in a matter of days. Half dreading the answer, I ask, "Do you know anyone who can help with... disposal?"

Kat shakes her head. "I used to, maybe. For the last few months I've had to be... quiet. Pieter kept me on a leash, you might say."

"How about via the 'letter box?' You could ask."

Her shoulders shrug but she looks thoughtful. "I can do what I want now," she says, with a touch of wistful.

"At the very least, we should move him into the cellar," I say. "Where it's cooler."

"Only until we can figure something out. Until then, it's got to be business as usual," she decides. "Freddie, can you take Pieter's shoes and suitcases back upstairs? When Franz returns, as he will,

I'll say he's missed his master again, and made his own way out of the city."

I can't find a flaw in her logic.

She looks at me. "I'm sorry. Much as though I'd love to suggest you stay here, it'll look odd if you aren't back at work. They're sure to send more SS over to grill us, and you're more use learning whatever you can at the Ritz." She squeezes my shoulder. "Proper business as usual, eh? Give me a hand shifting him inside, then you'd better leave before curfew."

Freddie rushes over to me, throws his arms around my chest and squeezes me tight. I drop a kiss on his head. "I'll be able to see you soon though," I say, and pray I'm right. "Always remember, you're my heart. When this is all over, we'll make better plans."

He pulls away, grinning. It's as if the years have fallen from his face. He stretches both his arms up and I remember what I promised him when we first arrived here. "Yes, we'll see if you're as big as the Eiffel Tower, too."

Satisfied, but still not speaking, he trots off to the hallway. I turn to Kat. "Will you be alright? It's a pretty grim thought, sleeping under the same roof as..."

"What - sleeping with a body in the cellar?" Her snort is most unladylike. "Believe me, a dead Nazi is far preferable to live ones, any day." She grins.

I might have been fired up by our little victory, but for the lack of information about Marc. The next day, I ask Fevrier in the catacomb bunker if there's any way to find out for certain where the demonstrators were taken. He grumbles about the thousands of other resistance members held in prisons across the city, or worse, then walks off. I couldn't find the words to ask for help with disposing of a Nazi corpse.

My uniform alterations are finished. Everyone is preoccupied and on edge, and no-one seems to notice me. For hours, I sit in the corner of the command centre offices, waiting to be given another job to do, but Fevrier continues to ignore me. Instead, I listen to him talking to some men in flamboyant suits about cameras, of all things! My failure to kill Hitler at the exhibition haunts me, and all the talk of filming just makes me think of how much Marc would love to be involved.

I return to the Ritz, despondent.

A tense week follows. Frank is equally distracted. One of his bar staff went to protest and hasn't returned, but, there's a probability he simply went to join the Marquis. I tell him my worries about Marc, about where he could be, and my concerns that he might talk under pressure.

He offers no words of advice or help, only pats my hand in a sympathetic manner. From his tense shoulders and lack of usual bonhomie, there's something else wrong. He jerks his head at some Nazi officers, out of uniform. They're hunched over, jiggling their knees, and checking watches. "Make yourself scarce, Edelweiss," Frank says.

I've seen the officers faces in here before, having late night discussions. "Why?"

Frank flares his eyelids. "Tense times and we need privacy."

We? Was Frank working for the Nazis now?

He says, "Come back later – things might look different then." He shoos me out the door before I can ask.

The clients have gone when I return at closing time. Frank sits at the end of the bar, nursing a fine cognac.

"No cocktails to finish?" I ask, as he tops up his glass and stares moodily out onto the street.

"There'll be no victory party tonight." He sips. "So I might as well take advantage of what's in front of me before I'm taken."

"Why would anyone take you, Frank?" He's the heart and soul of this place, beloved by everyone, no matter which side of the fence they sat. "Maybe you need some lemonade, instead of the hard stuff."

He shrugs. "Ah Edelweiss, I wish I could still have the optimism of youth." He swills the ice in his glass. "I thought it was all over, and for a few hours, it seemed it was." He glances sideways at me through his eyelashes, with dull eyes.

"What's happened?" I ask. "Or can't you tell me?"

"It'll be all over the news soon enough. I've told you before, what happens in here is just a part of it. But, the man's impossible to kill." He gives a half-hearted laugh. "Not even when a bomb is detonated right at his feet."

"Not..." I raise my index finger and put it under my nostrils in a mock impersonation of the Führer. The irony if he was the target.

Frank's lips twitch and I'm confident I'm right.

Only, yet again, a failure. He taps the side of his nose while staring at me, then drags in a deep breath. "So those Yanks and Brits a few hundred miles away will be needed after all. Except, they'll take their time. Once they have liberated us, they'll have to feed us."

I think of the Fifi's preparations underground, and tap my own nose. "We'll see."

BLANCHE

The assassination attempt and coup against Hitler – by his own commanders – means anyone, German or French, falls under suspicion of treason. At first, only the elite SS were rounded up, but Paris quickly becomes a Gestapo state. Officers are everywhere on the streets. Any pretence of liberty has vanished. Simply looking sideways at someone, or any odd behaviour, could get you hauled off the pavement and taken. At the Ritz, while we're all suspicious of each other, we're also all stuck together.

Some staff are questioned in the Auzello's office, as the Gestapo hunt down anyone who might have had contact with the plot ringleaders. This includes Frank, but mercifully, somehow no-one from the Ritz is taken away. Perhaps their prisons are full, or maybe they realise if they remove all the domestics, bar staff and chefs, there'll be no-one left to feed and house them in the manner to which they have grown accustomed. Ritz neutrality is held up as 'normal' and affords us some protection in unsettled times.

It's far from normal though; one by one, the suites on the Place Vendôme side of the hotel are cleared of their paintings and ornaments. Monsieur Elminger is pulled into arguments on a near daily basis with over zealous packing boys, about which pieces of art were original to the Ritz and which have been 'added' during our Occupation.

In an all-staff meeting during the second week of August, Monsieur Elminger cautions the chefs: supplies are going to be 'tight' because the railroad workers are striking. The news is met by a chorus of groans. We're starving already, and no food coming in from the countryside by official or unofficial methods, means even the few remaining guests will have a reduced menu. Staff are down to one meal a day. Given Elminger is the one in control of our ration cards, he's lucky not to have a mutiny on his hands. "The police have been disarmed," he warns, with a grim expression. "For your own safety, do not leave the hotel. Or you might not be allowed back in."

Everyone understands. This is also a threat.

At the end of the meeting, he pulls me to one side. "Devereaux, I need you to do something for me."

"Of course, what can I help you with, Monsieur?"

His prim head bends to my ear. "Switchboard had a strange phone call this morning, from the Meurice Hotel. A woman, acting strangely, turned up there, claiming to be Madame Auzello."

I jerk away from him. "Madame? Really?"

He nods. "But, before we get anyone's hopes up, I want you to go and see for yourself. The new German military commander for Paris has just arrived to speak to his staff at the Meurice, and, well, it's best if there's no trouble." His moustache wriggles as he admits, "He's taken a suite here to live in. I'm to greet him shortly."

"So I'm only to find out if it's really Madame Auzello or not?" The fact that he instructed us all no-one should leave, and now asks me to put myself in danger - right next to the military headquarters, no less - isn't lost on me. If only I could still pass on information to Kat...

"Yes. Take Jaques, as it was the Meurice doorman who took the woman to Café Angelina, next door. Could be it's a crank." Elminger glances around the room to see if anyone's watching.

"Why me?"

"You seem to have a knack for going about unnoticed and she always spoke fondly about you."

On the off chance it is Madame Auzello, to whom I owe a great deal, I agree.

A quarter of an hour later, Jaques and I approach the arched façade of the Meurice, which was requisitioned when the Nazis first arrived and is still draped in swastikas. The doorman there is busy directing a series of luggage-laden cars in the Ritz's direction under the watchful eyes of soldiers. He catches sign of Jaques and tips his head with a wink. We walk straight past and into the elegant tea-house a bit further down the street.

A waitress rushes over when she spots the Ritz insignia on Jaques' coat. "Oh, thank goodness. She's through here." She shoots anxious glances at the customers as she rustles past. "We didn't know what to believe, and she was making quite the fuss."

We follow her into the kitchens where an elderly woman slumps on a stool in a corner. She's probably thirty pounds lighter than the Madame Auzello I remember, a stick-figure wearing nothing but a grubby shift with bare feet. I approach her slowly, for this poor lady looks nothing like our Dragon Lady. Long, straggly hair hides her downcast face. On her ankles, red manacle marks ooze with pus, and deep bloody scratch marks scale her calves as if she's scraped her legs with claws. She twitches, her hands suddenly tearing at her forearms with broken nails.

"Madame?" I say. "Madame Auzello?"

The woman shakes her bird's nest of a head violently, thin fingers swatting her face as if trying to dislodge an irritating wasp.

"Blanche!"

Finally she notices me. Her eyelids blink rapidly then her finger pokes my cheek. "Devereaux," she rasps. "Get me home." Her chin comes up and I see then that it is indeed Madame Auzello. Alive, if not truly well. Her eyes are wild as they dart around. "They... they... I told them everything, of course. But they didn't believe me."

"Calm yourself, Madame," Jaques steps forward.

Her face softens. "Oh dear Jaques. You'll help me, won't you? They don't believe it's me. No-one does."

He offers her an arm, which draws a gracious incline of her head, but she struggles to stand.

I rush to the other side of her. "Madame, lean on me." I hook my arm underneath her shoulder and help her up. She wavers as she stands. The shift she's wearing barely covers the marks on her legs and I realise she looks like what she possibly is: a prison escapee. We can't take her out onto the street like this, let alone into the Ritz.

I glance at Jaques. "One moment, keep her steady." I pull off my coat and thread her scrawny arms into it, doing up the buttons so she's slightly more respectable. She's lost so much weight, my slim size fits her now. From my pocket, I pull out my scarf and tie it around her hair. As I have my uniform on and I'm with Jaques, hopefully with her covered up, we'll not draw too much attention to her state as we help her past Hotel Meurice and home.

As we walk out of the kitchen, she cries out. I look at her bare feet and think, there's no way we can make it down the rough streets. She'd object to being carried. I'd give her my own shoes, but they're far too small. While she whimpers softly, we cast around the kitchen for ideas. Footwear is a precious commodity.

Jaques leaves me holding her up and goes over to a baker, who's trying his hardest not to be noticed as he pounds dough. A few quiet words later, some notes slide into the baker's apron, and he returns with a pair of clogs. I 'borrow' a kitchen towel and crouch down. She leans on Jaques as I wrap each chapped foot in the rough cotton and wedge it into the wood.

With her in-between us and held up by our linked arms, we all shuffle and clop through the tea-room. Chatter stops.

Blanche, showing some of her usual spirit, throws her head up. "What y'all staring at, eh?" She bares her brown teeth at them, and seems ignorant of the fact she has spoken in American-English. Bewildered, the customers purse their lips and look pointedly away. She glares at them, and their plates of food, wasting her remaining strength leaning forward on our arms, as if she's ready to take them on just for staring at her.

Before she can say anything more to cement the picture of a mad woman in their minds, Jaques opens the door and we drag her through it. Once the fresh air hits her though, she seems to fall in line.

As we totter past the Meurice, she turns to me. "Devereaux, do you see what they have done? Do you see it?"

"I do, Madame."

Linked through my arm, her hand waggles and she points to the swastika's hanging from the buildings. "No-one will see, though, when they're finished, will they? No-one will know what we've done to get rid of the vermin." Her fingers form a fist as we round the corner and head across Place Vendôme. It's as if the wide open space releases someone else inside her, as she stops for a moment, her head wobbling on her neck as she stares at the Ritz across the square. She shouts, "*Le Bosche est fini!*"

But, before she causes further upset, Jaques clamps his hand over her mouth. "Madame," he says, in a steady, authoritative voice. "We are bringing you home. But you must keep these thoughts to yourself."

Her eyes turn to meet his and she nods her agreement. As soon as she seems to calm, he removes his hand and we walk slowly over the cobbles.

"I was in Fresnes," she says, in a far more reasonable tone, almost her usual, lucid self. "I spoke only when asked, for weeks. I lost track. Then, when they started to…" She winces, wets her lips and carries on. "I told them almost everything they wanted to know, eventually. And then I shouted it. Over and over, expecting they would simply shoot me once they knew everything and I'd be done with it all. They'd have the last word on Blanche." She swallows. "I didn't expect they would simply let me out."

I say, "It's remarkable they did, Madame. You are very lucky. I don't suppose… I heard Marc was there, too."

Her voice catches. "Men and women were kept separate. I'm sorry, I never saw him. We were kept in our cells and had to stay silent. At first they took us outside, for exercise occasionally, until the prison got too full, then they used the yard for executions instead." Her head hangs. "I don't know. We heard there were trains, day and night, taking prisoners away. When they shoved me out the door, I thought I was supposed to get on one too, but instead, they dumped me out on the street. In the middle of nowhere."

"No sight of Marc at all?" The lump in my throat makes it hard for me to swallow.

She says, "There was hardly anyone left in the men's blocks."

And now the railways are clear, I think with a shudder. Someone else must be signing the transport orders now Pieter is…

With a spurt of energy, she says, "But we should SHOUT! If we don't, then how will people hear us? How will they know?"

"Shouting won't change the situation, Madame," I say.

"Then show them, goddammit." She frowns at me. "Somehow. This terror will be forgotten if we don't. Our resistance, the fight we put up, everything we did to show the Nazis not all of Paris capitulated willingly. Subjugation, that's what it is. If we don't shout about our part in forcing them out, then we'll just be a city which was liberated by the army." Her eyes narrow. "And that's not the truth of it, is it, Devereaux? We've resisted their rule all along."

I smile at her. "We have."

The sparkle in her eyes heartens me, and she grips my arm with bony fingers. "That's my girl. I know you can fix anything." Then, she looks ahead, to the Ritz. "Maybe even me."

Crew Member

With the return of Madame Auzello, it seems everything, everywhere, unravels. A few days later, the power goes out, and stays out. There's no gas either, so we couldn't cook, even if we had food. We are operating blind, and largely vacant except for the few remaining journalists and artists who can't seem to stay away. Effectively, the Ritz grinds to a halt. Occasionally, through the open windows, we catch the quick ratatat of machine guns but, with no electricity to power the wireless, we have no news other than gossip gleaned from Frank's few remaining boys, the only people who dare venture out. In no uncertain terms it's made clear: if we leave the hotel, we can't return. Either ride out the unrest within these walls - safe, possibly starving but at least neutral - or we're on the outside, alone.

It's a surprisingly easy choice between stay or go, because I'm not by myself in the fight for freedom. Although I have witnessed some awful behaviour, the person I feared running into the most is defeated. Dead.

I find some ripped trousers and a boy's cap at the bottom of the near empty lost property box, then slip away. Show people how we resisted, Madame Auzello said, and, in honour of my still missing beau, I think I know how to.

The streets are littered with tanks; soldiers huddle behind sandbagged artillery on corners. All the Metro stations are closed. There's hardly any civilians in the wide avenues and it's as eerily quiet as when the Nazis first arrived. I'm able to dodge in and out of doorways whenever the occasional vehicle sputters past. On the walls and lampposts, fly posters have been glued up by the city administration, calling for general mobilisation of the citizens of Paris.

In the tunnel outside the FFI command centre offices, it's dark, crowded and the air is thick with tension. A generator rattles, powering dim, flickering lights in the offices and contributing to the toxic atmosphere. Despite the no smoking signs, a fug of cigarette smoke makes me cough. Many of the men - some are only boys a little older than Freddie - and a few women, wear casual clothes. A couple carry guns. I hear raised voices and wriggle past them, stopping close to the office doorway.

Colonel Rol, the energetic leader of the Communists who have all but taken over this bunker, insists, "We go, now!" In his thirties, his charisma and drive commands the respect of someone far older. "The FFI insists upon action. We should occupy the main buildings of the city. Hound them out before they can burn everything to the ground on their way out."

Another voice, one I don't recognise, blusters objections about waiting for the Allies, who are only a hundred miles west of Paris. He's shouted down. I glance at the fighters next to me, counting again how few guns they hold. Willingness is one thing, but the Germans have tanks and far more weapons. I push aside the wave of hopelessness which sweeps through me as Rol-Tanguy says, "The people are ready for change. We take back our streets, one by one."

He strides towards the doorway, pokes his head out and everyone flattens to the sides of the halls. "You know which areas you've been assigned. Trust that the people of Paris will join you. We start with the north and east of the city. Spread the word. Move out!"

It's the order they have been expecting, and within minutes, the passages and offices clear. Heart in mouth, I linger, hoping to catch sight of the film men I saw before. Fevrier ignores me, as do the other commanders as they troop out. Finally, I recognise a film-maker, lugging a bulky looking briefcase as he heads down the tunnel.

I run after him. "Please! Wait!"

He turns his head, confusion crossing his face as his gaze lands on me, racing towards him in the near darkness. He's clean shaven and wears a frustrated expression behind his round rimmed glasses.

I say, "I want to help, with the film."

He sizes me up and down. "And have you any experience filming under fire?"

I shake my head. "But I'm a fast learner, and I want - I *need* - to show what's happening. What the people did to retake Paris."

"It's too dangerous." He turns away, and I reach out and tug on his sleeve.

To most, I probably appear to be any other street urchin, but the desperation in my voice must convince him I'm serious. "Monsieur...?"

"Monsieur Zwoboda."

"With respect, Monsieur Zwoboda, you don't know what I'm capable of."

He lets out a gentle snort of laughter. "In my industry, I'm more aware than most of deceptive appearances, girl. But still, filming equipment is heavy and expensive, and takes time to set up. There will be a lot of waiting around, not knowing if we are in the right place even."

His fist tightens around the briefcase handle. "Pah! They gave me a radio to listen in with, some basic instructions on how to tap messages, but setting up cameras to get the shot? No-one can tell me where the action will be." He rolls his eyes. "And they expect me to record the liberation for posterity."

"That sounds an *almost* impossible task," I say, a plan forming in my mind. "I guess soldiers don't think like creative people do."

He grunts. "When real bullets are pelting, anyone who doesn't know what they are doing would be at risk." He leans closer to me and I hear his barely veiled fear, "Have you seen a man die right before your eyes?"

"Yes. A Nazi officer as well." I stare at him, nose to nose. "And I could have held a camera straight then too."

He straightens. "I don't need people to point the cameras, I've plenty of those. Go away, little girl. This is no time for games, it's war."

My frustration boils over. I'm so tired of men telling me what I should and shouldn't do. "Then what *do* you need?"

At my raised voice, he lifts an eyebrow. "Advance knowledge. Time. Foresight. Hardly an easy thing to come by."

It's the moment for the mouse to roar. "Monsieur Zwoboda, I can give you that. I speak German, and I've been working for the Resistance – the Allies as well - under Nazi noses for the last four years. If anyone can tell you what their plans are, where they'll go, it's me."

His eyes widen, but I'm not done. "I know of a radio operator, with equipment. If you would only listen, I can send a message to you. Tell you where they'll be fighting, where the troops are building up, then you can be ready with the cameras."

For a moment, I think he'll walk away, but then he snaps, "Deal." From his jacket, he withdraws a scrap of paper and scribbles down a frequency. Then he shakes his head. "But, one person cannot be all over the city at once."

"Let me worry about that." I take the note and shove it in my pocket. "Just listen for the call sign - Mouse."

The man straightens his hat and huffs again as he walks off. It's clear he doesn't believe I'll provide anything of value, but he is wrong.

Cheeks burning from running, I slip into Kat's back yard and rap on her patio door. She and Freddie jump at the noise but rush over to let me in as soon as they see me waving like a mad person. "Kat, did you use the dead letter box? Do you know where the radio is?" Words tumble out as I clasp Freddie in a tight hug.

"Hello to you too," she snaps. "And yes to both."

"Is it... he...?" I jab down at the floorboards.

"Gone. I buried him, and I am never using the cellar again."

A slight smile rises to my lips. "Then we have work to do." I crouch down to Freddie's height. "Do you still have your map of the tunnels, my heart?"

His eyes gleam as he nods.

"Then go and get it, and a torch, please."

He scampers out and Kat frowns. "What's all this about?"

I look her square in the eye. "It's happening. The liberation. We have to show the world how we did it. And, for that to happen, we need the radio."

I've just finished explaining my idea to her when Freddie dashes back in, map in hand and tunnel bag slung around his neck. I ruffle his hair. "And I have a very important job for you, too."

My son grins up at me. Kat says, "Let's go then."

Although I'm relieved she's wearing soft, sensible culottes, rather than her usual sharp suits, I point to her shoes. "Some flats might be more appropriate."

She rolls her eyes. I flare mine and remind her, "Remember when we had to run, during the Pogrom?" When she broke a heel and twisted her ankle. "And we aren't necessarily going to be on the streets."

"I suppose it can get wet underground, even with this dry spell."

We follow Kat's lead to rescue the radio and head towards the Seine, then, rather than walking along it, she takes us through silent side streets. She tells us to keep watch while she slips through a gate, into the garden of a house set back from the road. My gaze wanders up, and I wave at faces pressed against the windows of the building opposite. A woman grins, or perhaps it's a grimace, then pulls her children away from the glass.

Kat returns, a familiar suitcase in hand and a grin on her face. "Freddie," I say, as we cross the bridge in front of the Eiffel Tower, "keep following where we go on the map, and let us know when there's an entrance into the tunnels nearby. We're going to play sewer rats."

One glance at Kat and she understands. Above all else, Freddie must be safe, and that means underground.

Over and Under

- -

There's an air of anticipation as we cross the river and head towards the city centre, but that might be only we three. Freddie shoots me a cheeky sideways smile as we pass the Eiffel Tower. The lift cables were cut by the French when we were occupied and still haven't been mended, which is a shame, as it would have provided us with a panoramic view over the city. A small, grey toned swastika still flaps halfway up, a larger one blew away hours after Nazis scaled the outside to display it. I tell him, "Soon. We'll go soon, I promise."

Freddie's map shows us that the majority of the catacombs, mines and other tunnels are on the south side of the Seine, and I want to be sure that whatever we report, wherever we are, we have an escape route planned out. We approach the area of Montparnasse, close to the entrance for the FiFi bunker is. The streets seem relatively quiet, deserted and still, as if the whole of Paris holds its breath.

A Nazi tank disrupts the silence as it rattles and chugs, spluttering up the empty road. Kat shoves the map into her trouser pocket. From the corner of my eye, I watch as two flic, loitering on a corner, laugh. This pair are the first we have seen, and still wear uniforms, half unbuttoned, as if they haven't yet been bothered to change after the end of their shift. Their gun holsters are empty and, from the way their bodies lurch in an uncoordinated way, that can only be a good thing. Yet, there's something furtive about their laughter at the tank.

"Wait here," I say to Kat. She grabs Freddie's hand, pretending to look a the menu in a café-bar window.

Head down, I saunter closer to the policemen. "It won't take long, not at all," one of them says to the other. From a few feet away, I can smell the wine on his breath when I pause to 'tie my shoelace'.

"Not after tomorrow," his colleague replies. "Will you be there?"

"I might."

"No-one will order us to the Prefecture, but... it's a show of solidarity, isn't it? I know we're on strike, but Monsieur Bayet himself told me what was going on."

The first flic huffs. "I'll be there, ready to fight. About time we showed them whose city this is."

"Bright and early," the second one says, then claps his colleague on the upper arm. "*À demain!*"

I stand as the two officers part, and check where I left Kat and Freddie, a hundred yards down the street. She's having a discussion with him, gesturing to the window and bringing out her purse and shaking her head.

The horizon glows a dusky orange, and it's still hot and sticky. There's a rattle of gunfire in the distance, and a truck filled with Nazi soldiers in tears around the corner. I glance longingly in the direction of the Ritz. By disappearing, I've deserted my job and home to do this. Nor is it safe there. If this insurrection fails, the Gestapo will only intensify their searches. Without any measure of certainty about Paris's fate, I can't bear to leave Freddie and Kat again.

A troop of Nazi soldiers, guns cocked all around them like spikes on a conker, march down the road towards us, and all pretence this is a quiet suburb is shattered. It cannot be a co-incidence the rise in the number of troops moving. Pivoting on my heel, the suitcase bangs against my calf as I quick-walk back to my family – too exposed on the boulevard. A trickle of sweat runs down my forehead, not only a result of carrying the heavy radio. When I reach them, one glance inside at the empty counter shelves tells me the horrible truth of why Kat's not gone in, even though they must be as hungry as I.

"Kat, quickly go in," I say, and Freddie beams at me. "Maybe they have a toilet as well?" I raise my eyebrow at her and lean in. "This frequency," I whisper, as I hand her the note with the settings on it Zwoboda gave me. "Say, Mouse says Prefecture of Police, dawn, tomorrow. No code, send it straight and fast."

Her lips press together as her eyes scan the street. My throat dries as the footfall of the soldiers approach us. She gives me a tight little nod and says, "Even with everything that's happening, they'll probably still be out searching for transmissions. We need to get off the main roads. If we get caught with the suitcase then..." Her gaze flicks down to Freddie then back me me, indicating I should explain to him what the plan was.

Kat takes the case, strides into the café, while I bend and talk to my son. "Freddie, its time for your important mission to begin." I pull out the catacomb map he drew and unfold it.

He takes it as I say, "It's mine and Kat's job to help make a film about the French people driving the Nazis out of Paris. To record what happens. It'll be a film, shown in the cinema."

I hope this final claim comes true, but I suppose it all depends on the outcome of all of our efforts. I paste a brave smile across my face as the troop marches past us. "But, we can't just walk around Paris with tanks and soldiers and gunfire all around us." I point at his map. "Can you find the closest entrance to the catacombs?"

He grins and immediately points to a tiny round circle. I can barely read his writing labelling where it is, but, I trust him. "Good boy," I say, "and from there, can you get to Kat's storeroom?"

Freddie studies the map for a moment then locks eyes with me and smiles again. My heart swells with pride, as the café door tinkles open.

Kat presents us with dusty bottle of the Germans' favourite soda - a tepid, cheese-tasting concoction called Fanta. Freddie takes a sip, frowns, hands it back to me, then sets off down the road.

"We need to eat," Kat replies. "There may be some canned food in my store, but I've not been in ages. There's nothing at home, anyway, only rutabaga."

Freddie's nose wrinkles, and I guess that's all they have been eating for a while, like the rest of us. His step is confident, eyes shining as he leads us along the road towards the Montparnasse Cemetery.

It seems macabre to be surrounded by graves, old and freshly dug, when deeper underground, even more bones rest. The sun dips beyond the skyline as Freddie trots ahead of us, down the tree-lined pathways between the gravestones. A few turns later, he stops and points at his feet, planted on the middle of a large manhole.

After checking no-one is around, I crouch down to figure out how to open it. On either side of the hatch are recessed handles. Kat and I turn the heavy iron disc before lifting it.

Freddie produces his torch and shines it down the shaft. He looks at us triumphantly, performs a funny little bow and sweeps his arm in invitation. I'm sure I'll never again be so graciously invited to descend slippery rungs into black tunnels, so I grin at him and clamber down. At the bottom, the temperature drops and it's honestly a relief. Down here, the sounds of a city at war are muffled, and I can relax. I call up for Kat to lower the case down to me, which she does, using her coat belt. Then, I wait in the gloom, listening to the clunk of their shoes on metal bars and whispering encouragement, until they are both with me, and the cover replaced.

My son guides us through cool tunnels, the antithesis of the humid evening air we left above. Some have high, vaulted ceilings with brickwork arches and cobbled floors; others are low, hardly more than plank-sided troughs where puddles fester and mould greens the walls. He stops occasionally, checking his map, then ploughs on, Kat and I following. At one point, I'm sure we go around in a circle, and the thought occurs to me that without Freddie's map, I'd be utterly lost in the darkness. My heartbeat flutters as we seem to descend, and I contemplate the collapse of a tunnel... our separation... never seeing daylight again...

Ahead, his blond hair flops about as he picks up his pace. Then, he ducks into a slim opening. We follow, feet treading a familiar, uneven muddy floor with walls which seem to close in on us. I sigh with relief as he barrels into the chamber storeroom where we have met many times before. He spins around with his arms stretched wide.

"You clever boy!" I sweep him into a hug.

Kat dumps the suitcase, whips the torch from his fingers and stands, hands on her hips, surveying the chamber. "Damn."

I lift my head from Freddie's shoulder.

The yellow ring of light lands on bare brick walls, formerly hidden by boxes of goods. Only then do I realise that the usually locked storeroom door was open. Someone else had been in our sanctuary. Kat heads to a distant corner and flips up a mouldy tarpaulin. "Thank God. Not quite the disaster I feared!"

She hastens back to us, juggling some battered cans in her arms and a broad smile splitting her cheeks. "I think one might be beef."

"And some sardines," I say, spotting an oblong can. My mouth waters at the very prospect. "But..."

Kat passes me the torch and reaches into her pocket. She extracts a flick-blade. "They learn a lot in Hitler Youth, including how to stay prepared."

As I take the knife from her hands, we exchange a look. "Not him." A shadow darkens her eyes, a wistfulness reaching her brows. "The one who ran this operation. Richter. But, he's disappeared too. Left me when I couldn't pay him for the goods. The customers couldn't pay either, but they were starving."

The memory of her rumpled sheets returns to me and the handsome officer who accompanied her to the Ritz and that fateful exhibition. I reach out and touch her shoulder. "Nothing is ever really black or white, is it?"

After we feast on the cans, Freddie falls asleep on my lap. In the dark, I hold Kat's hand and we talk of our lost loved ones, our fears for them and of them, and of the times when we dared to hope.

PREFECTURE

----

1 **9th August 1944**

When we awake, none of us have any idea of what time it is. The only way to know is to stick our heads outside. Freddie, refreshed after a sound sleep and a breakfast of cold, canned soup, bounds ahead of us and we have to call for him to wait while we catch up. He brings us out somewhere near Luxembourg Park, close to the river. This time, the exit is a spiral staircase with a door which is only loosely closed by a latch, at the north end of the gardens.

The dawn sun breaks over Notre-Dame, casting a hazy orange glow over the twin square spires. A picture perfect scene which re-ignites my desire to record the events which will bring about our freedom. On the same island in the middle of the Seine sits the stately Prefecture of Police building.

I want to know if our message got through to the film men. As it's so early in the day, and seems quiet, we can all travel above ground, for a while at least. I notice the fly-posters look different - strips reading 'We warn you! Think of the fate of Paris!' appear to be pasted over the general mobilisation call, but, when I trace my fingers over the paper, I discover the entire notice itself has been printed that way. We slip past the empty checkpoint gatehouse and across the bridge to the island.

As we walk past sandbag barricades in the centre of the vast space in front of the Cathedral, I second guess having Kat and Freddie with me. We're terribly exposed here because there's hardly anyone around. And no sign of a film crew setting up as we amble towards the Prefecture building.

A crowd of perhaps twenty men gather underneath a window. Above, a man sticks his head out, hair rumpled as if he's been woken from sleep. "What's going on?"

From inside the throng, someone shouts up: "In the name of the Republic and Charles de Gaulle, I take possession of the Prefecture of Police."

Half hanging out the window, the sleepy man's hands grip the sill and his face falls. Then he retreats and slams the window shut.

A group of three men, one wearing a dark checked suit and two others in police uniform, separate and march into the main entrance. The rest of the crowd disperse, heads down and striding away as if they have somewhere else to be. It all feels strangely anti-climactic. Easy. Maybe Col Rol was right, the people will support their action.

"Well, perhaps it's a good thing the cameras aren't here." My tone expresses my regret at sending the message yesterday, there is nothing to see here.

Kat gazes around the square, then suddenly yanks Freddie and I close. Hoards of uniformed policemen pour out of the main doors!

"Move away," one calls as we gape at the hundreds of men taking up defensive positions. Some rush over to the sandbags in the middle and form a chain to pass them into a pile in front of their building.

We shuffle to the edge of the cobbles and watch as, within minutes, the flics construct a barricade of their own. Then, from around the back of the Prefecture, trotting right past us, yet more policemen arrive, bearing machine guns to take sentry positions behind the barricades.

"We should go," Kat says, tugging on my arm.

"I'll stay for a few more minutes," I reply. Tactically, whomever has control of the police force could alter the balance of power across the city. "Can you radio again, though? Maybe there's still time for the cameras to get here. Go back underground, though, to send it."

She takes Freddie's hand, carrying the suitcase with the other. "Find us at the bottom of the stairs." Her eyes dart anxiously around the activity. "Maus, don't get into anything, will you? If it gets dangerous, run."

"I just want to discover what's happening, then I can tell you. I won't be long."

Lingering on the edge of the square, I watch as the police organise themselves. Faces appear at the windows, along with gun muzzles. The ornate, cream stone building becomes a fortress. I have to know why the flic, so long the instrument of the Nazi regime, appear to have switched sides, so I sidle close to a young-looking officer at the corner of the Prefecture.

"What's going on?" I ask.

"The Prefecture is now under the command of Monsieur Bayet." He speaks from the side of his mouth. "On behalf of De Gaulle," he says, proudly.

Col Roy won't be happy, I think. "Is the General close?"

The policeman shrugs. "Who knows."

We are both distracted by the rumble of a Tiger tank over the bridge behind us. "It's the Nazis," he says. "We didn't expect it to be easy." His fingers tighten around his machine gun and he pales.

My heart leaps into my mouth. *"Bon courage,"* I say, hastening away. But, my exit route back to Freddie and Kat is blocked by the tank, and the soldiers who are likely in its wake.

Head down, stomach churning, I walk as fast as is possible around the building, and cross over by the other bridge, heading north. I don't want to be trapped on the wrong side of the Seine, so I head down river, towards the Hotel de Ville. I wince, hearing short bursts of gunfire from the island, but keep walking, hoping to find another way to cross back.

However, morning has fully dawned, and each crossing I come to has a Nazi manned checkpoint. Anyone trying to get through is turned away. No longer the simple check I used to be more confident passing, the barriers have become a means of preventing free movement around the city. As church bells mark midday, to avoid barriers I end up heading down river. Much further and I'll end up miles away from where I know, to the east of Paris.

Frustrated, I double back on myself. Troops of Nazis brandish their guns at anyone walking along the river while they march along the quayside. I'm forced to divert away from the bank to avoid them. As I hurry through parallel streets, I'm encouraged by the sight of tricoleur flags, which appear in ever-greater number, draped from people's windows. But the swastikas remain.

My feet ache by the time Notre-Dame's spires are back in my sights and I edge closer. To my relief, the barricade on the bridge to the island now has a tricoleur flag – amended with the Cross of Lorraine in the centre of the white stripe, draped over it. It's become a symbol of the Free French – fragmented resistance groups, from the Communist FFI to the French fighting under De Gaulle with the Allies, to the Marquis, and several other organisations in between.

When I ask the policeman on the barrier who's in control of the police building, the FiFi's or De Gaulle, he shakes his head and shrugs. "De Gaulle isn't here. We are. Street by street, the French will take their capital back." His rifle stays trained on the bridge as he waves me through.

What awaits as I round the corner of the Prefecture is a scene of devastation. The tank has retreated, leaving in its wake soldiers and policemen, lying dead or groaning, on the cobbles. A fire rages close to the building. The front gates have been blown in, leaving the wood planks jutting out and black.

My notion of what a battleground looks like used to resemble some far off country field, where armies would valiantly clash on charging horses, but the reality strikes me so hard I sway into the corner. I reach my fingers down, in the hope the solid stones will centre me, but all I feel are blackened pock marks.

The policeman I talked to only hours earlier lies crumpled against the wall. Dead.

CeaseFire

After closing my eyes and sending a brief prayer for the young man sky-ward, I take a deep breath and look again. No-one is shooting now. The opposition has retreated. My mind cannot help but remember the last time I saw bodies on a much smaller, cobbled square, only this time, there are survivors. A pair of nuns tend to the wounded.

I rush past the inert body of a Nazi soldier to help the Sisters. Someone has already removed the weapons. "Where are the wounded going?" I ask as I roll a policeman, clutching his bloodied leg, onto a stretcher. He swears and passes out.

"We're setting up a field hospital at Hôtel-Dieu, around the corner," the Sister replies, lifting the stretcher with another nun. "Keep pressure on that leg, won't you? He'll bleed out otherwise."

I walk alongside them, holding my hands over the wound. Warm blood spills between my fingers, no matter how hard I bear down. We bring him into the hotel lobby, where I'm given a dishtowel to press on the bullet hole. I stay with the inert policeman as he's put down in a corridor. Staff, other policemen, and hotel residents rush past us, trying to work out who needs their attention the most. It's hard to hear what they decide as the hallway and adjacent dining room noisy are a cacophony of groans and screams.

My unconscious man's face is white against his dark blue uniform collar, except where blood has sprayed onto his cheeks. Red, white and blue, I think, and a surge of pride fills me as I press down. "Don't give up," I tell him, although he cannot hear.

When a nurse finally relieves me with a tourniquet to stem the blood flow, I wipe my hands on my trousers and head back outside. Only bloodstains remain, baking into the cobbles, watched over by policemen behind their barricades.

At the far side of the square, in the shallow shadows of Notre-Dame, I spot Fevrier, striding purposefully towards the Prefecture. He holds a revolver close to his chest. Trailing behind him, a group of other men dressed in fatigues or ordinary shirts, trousers and FFI armbands, clutch a variety of grenades and old rifles. Finally, dawdling at the rear, a man lugs a tripod with a camera screwed on top.

"Monsieur," I call out to Fevrier.

He tosses me a glance, frowns and continues. "Can't stop. Under orders."

"From de Gaulle?"

He freezes mid stride. "De Gaulle?"

"The Prefecture was taken in his name, earlier this morning. The police have chosen a side."

Fevrier looks around, eyes widening at the blood on the square. "I was expecting to walk into a battle, I admit. Colonel Roy sent me to claim the building in his name."

"Casualties on both sides, but the fight is over for now."

He grunts, "Not quite," and says over his shoulder to his men, "The Hôtel de Ville, then." They all, including the cameraman, set off towards the river.

For a few seconds, I watch his retreating back and wonder, who really has control of the city?

Kat and Freddie are at the bottom of the Montparnasse Cemetery stairwell. After sitting for so long, they're stiff and cold. "I was about to give up and head home," Kat chides.

"Home? Kat, I don't even know where home is anymore. The road leading to your house will no doubt be blocked because it's so close to the Gestapo headquarters, and we can only go so far underground."

"Fine. Back to the storeroom?"

I shrug. "I don't think we can do much else. Before we go, can you send a message saying 'Fevrier going to the Hôtel de Ville, from Mouse.'"

While she sets up her radio and taps it out, I catch my breath and think of my bed at the Ritz. Uncertainty returns. Having seen the number of troops patrolling Rue Rivoli, and knowing Fevrier intends to do something at the Hôtel de Ville, I can only imagine how difficult it will be to get back to the place I've called home for the last four years.

When she's finished, I say, "A camera did turn up, to the Prefecture. After the battle." I grimace. "Which I'm glad we all missed."

"Good." She holds a finger up and she listens to her headset. Freddie tugs on my hand, no doubt bored and anxious to get some food from our dwindling stock. "Hang on," Kat says, then groans. "Ceasefire proposed." She tears the headset off and tosses it into the case. "I don't believe it."

My heart sinks. A ceasefire is not freedom. Nor is it negotiation which might lead to liberty. A temporary pause in shooting at each other is all. Nothing in my exchange with Fevrier, or Colonel Roy's earlier impassioned speeches or orders leads me to think such an agreement would hold.

Besides, why would anyone trust the Nazis to stick to it? Wouldn't a ceasefire just afford them the chance to regroup and re-enforce?

Underground Encounter

I f there is an official ceasefire in place, no-one told the Parisian. For two days, I continue to make brief forays above, into the city, emerging in various places south of the river. I run on adrenaline, skirting corners and ducking as members of the Resistance, or untrained citizens, take pot shots at any Nazi soldiers. From open windows, or hidden behind statues or lampposts, gunfire can erupt from anywhere and it's terrifying. As Zwoboda worried, the fight for liberty is impossible to keep track of or anticipate.

But, where I do spot a build up of troops, I return to Kat and Freddie, and we duly send a message. For safety's sake, we don't linger to see if it's received or acted upon, but scamper off to another place. Freddie's map is invaluable; I merely have to suggest an area to try and he somehow guides us to close by. Kat and I are mere moles, blindly following our young leader.

On the third morning, new posters are plastered to walls: the FiFi's order all residents, in Arrondissement, to build barricades. The wording rings with authority, effectively acknowledging the all out war on the streets. It's clear the supposed ceasefire has collapsed. From what I saw, it was never taken seriously anyway.

When I descend into the dark to tell Kat, she's silent for a moment. Freddie's owlish eyes dart between us, but I don't know where to suggest we go next.

Finally, Kat says, "The Allies aren't coming, are they?"

I reply, "I don't even know where the battle lines are. It's chaos."

She flicks on her torch. "Come on..." Another click. Click, click, click. Nothing. In the darkness, I hear her knees creak as she crouches. Like it's an afterthought, she adds, "Is now a bad time to tell you the radio battery is also dead?"

Letting out a sigh, I lean against the manhole shaft and I close my eyes to better consider the problem. Where we are stinks; the air down here must be close to where the sewers run. What should be a simple thing to overcome, purchasing batteries, feels insurmountable. Paris has virtually shut down, no businesses are open, and there's no food to be had. I've not seen a lightbulb lit in over a week, above or below ground, and we've used up the last candle in the store. Our last message simply suggested the Hôtel de Ville was where I thought things might happen again. I had no proof, but, by now, I understood the warning signs of trouble.

"There's nothing for it," Kat says. "Mission over."

"This isn't fair," I wail.

"I know, but we don't have a choice. We'll all have to go up," Kat said. "We can go back to my house and hide in the cellar. Wait for the Allies to come."

No light, no tunnels. At least we can see above ground, and we can't stay here. "Come on, Freddie," I say, climbing back onto the rungs.

I look back to see him shaking his torch. It sputters, then gives off a faint glow. Then, he slides out the battery, holds it up and points at his map of the tunnels.

I frown at him. "Your battery might last a little longer, but the others don't work. We're effectively blind."

He replaces the battery, steps into the dark tunnel and again, gestures to his map.

Kat shrugs. "What have we got to lose, Hannah? It's trust our boy, or go up into the danger above."

We move in single file, Freddie leading, then me, with Kat taking up the rear with the suitcase. It's slow. Freddie's torch flickers maddeningly, and Kat stumbles behind me on loose stones. I have absolutely no idea where we are.

Finally, we reach a spiral staircase and Freddie pulls out a ball of string. As he ties it to the railing, a shiver runs through me. Is this a part of the tunnels he doesn't know?

I whisper, "Where are we, Freddie?"

He doesn't answer. Just looks at the map, folds it, and starts unspooling the twine.

Kat says, "Trust him, Hannah."

I do. I want to. But I also know something he perhaps doesn't: the Nazis use these tunnels. I overheard the FiFis whispering about it.

Up until now, wherever I left them, they had an escape hatch or door, should anyone approach. Now, Freddie wants to take us into further the depths of darkness, or worse. "Of course I trust Freddie," I say, and prepare myself for a backlash. "But, there are Nazis down here too."

Kat scoffs. "Aside from your Communists, who else would have batteries? You think Col Roy had any? Or the Ritz, perhaps?"

I fall silent. It's a fair point.

Leaving the suitcase radio at the bottom of the spiral steps, we walk faster. The string gives us something to follow in the darkness. Old quarry tunnels twist and turn, and then, Freddie's twine runs out. We've reached a metal door which he presses his ear to. He passes me the end of the string, tapping the doorway in a suggestion we stay here before he disappears inside.

Kat hisses, "Wait!"

But it's too late. He's gone.

After a moment, Kat whispers, "Stay here. I'll get him." Before I can argue, she squeezes past the heavy door and disappears as well. I can't follow or we'll lose the string end and have no way back.

My heart hammers as I wait, peering through the crack. From the dim glow of his torch, I can make out their figures, creeping down a corridor. Shelves line both sides, stuffed with crates and supplies.

Freddie's torch gives up and we're all in the dark. Seconds, minutes, pass as I listen to the soft sounds of them rummaging through boxes. Please hurry, I pray, my fingers twiddling the end of the string. As long as I don't drop it, we can get back.

A sliver of light flashes against the walls.

Footsteps. A man's voice, speaking in German. "Halt!"

My stomach contracts. Kat and Freddie are frozen in the beam of a powerful torch.

Kat whimpers, "Kurt? Herr Richter?"

It's her officer, the one who accompanied her to the Exhibition. He broke her heart, demanding money from the black market sales which she didn't have, then finishing with her.

"Katarina?" He sneers. "What are you doing down here? Stealing?"

He's drunk. I can hear it in his slur.

Under the flash of his moving torchlight, I spot Freddie clutching a metal box about the size of a car battery. My heart leaps. It might work, if only we can escape.

But Richter steps closer to them, his accusations escalating – spying, stealing, owing him. "Haven't you already taken enough?"

Kat plants her feet, shielding my boy with her body. "I owe you nothing."

My heart leaps into my throat when he asks Freddie where Pieter is.

"Gone," Kat answers for him. Defiant. Defensive.

He snarls, "Then why are you down here? Looking for another sucker to support you, eh? I told you, it's over between us. Our business is done." Herr Richter spits on the floor. "How did you find me?"

Kat's body stiffens, her finger jabbing at a box on a shelf near Freddie. Luckily, the Nazi doesn't seem to notice as he blunders on. "Or are you working for the Communists now? Spying. Is that it? You're with the Resistance and you're losing."

I notice Freddie slide a metal box into his tunnel bag. Stolen right under the Nazis eyes.

"Ha!" Kat says. "We both know who's on the losing side. You should have scurried away while you had the chance."

I'm not convinced by her tone. Panic rises in my throat as I hear what sounds like a nail landing on the concrete floor. Quickly, I tie the end of the string to the door handle, prepared to rush in and grab them both.

"So long, Kurt," Kat laughs. Her arm rises, tossing something through the air. She turns, crouching and pushing Freddie to the ground.

"Noooooo," Richter screams.

BOOOOOM.

The explosive force slams the door into my calf. A flash of bright light blinds me. My ears ring. Dust clouds the air. I hold onto the tied string, hands shaking, waiting for them. Praying. I can see nothing. Hear nothing.

PURSUIT

<hr>

I blink, eyes to the door crack again. A smoke-shrouded figure uncoils, emerging at the far end of the corridor like a creature in a horror film. The cloud seems to part as the entity rushes towards two bulges on the floor. My throat tightens – if he can survive, have they? Herr Richter towers over the smaller bundle, covering him in darkness as his bulk looms in front of the faint glow of his torchlight.

How is Richter still alive?

He shouts, "I know what you did," then spits on the floor, close to where Freddie and Kat lie. "Such a good boy, helping your dear Maman with her deliveries and chopping the vegetables. But you did more than that. I found Katarina's notebook. All those lines of letters, I knew she must be a spy. And so were you."

Richter bends, gun outstretched, aimed at Freddie's head. He speaks quietly, in a deadly, almost conversational tone. "To think, all those times you sat quickly in the corner, playing with your toys, when you were actually listening to our conversations and passing important information on. Such a smart boy. I bet you can talk, too. Am I right?"

Freddie scrabbles on the ground, to my relief. Faintly illuminated now by Richter's torch, he doesn't appear hurt. Next to him, Kat stirs.

I push myself through the doorway. My only advantage is that he doesn't know I'm here, and it's completely black at this end of the corridor. My only weapon... well, I have none. My hand drifts down to my bag. Unless...

"I quite like it down here," Richter says, letting out a small chuckle as he straightens. "The darkness. The silence. The coldness and the emptiness. Buried under the earth. Nobody to hear the sound of a gunshot, or the scream of a kid."

I creep closer. As luck would have it, my entry is further disguised by rocks crashing down at Richter's end of the corridor. While the walls collapse, I don't hesitate to seize the opportunity and break into a blind run, towards the falling masonry and my family.

Richter's head turns to see the destruction behind him, just as my bag, heavy with Freddie's camera, flies from my fingers like I'm bowling. My legs don't stop pumping while the metal Zeiss smashes into the back of Herr Richter's head. He staggers forward as the blow comes out of nowhere, then trips over to a sprawl on the floor.

As I pelt towards them all, I cry out, "Freddie, run!"

Freddie leaps to his feet, but something pins him down. He can't stand upright! He tries to yank his bag strap, hooked around something, as hard as he can, but it won't budge and he's trapped.

Behind him, I spot movement on the ground, followed by a groan. Herr Richter's getting up!

My heart pounds twice as fast. Reaching Freddie's side, I say, "It's only a bag, but there is only one Freddie," while yanking the strap hard. He stumbles backwards as his bag frees.

Kat sits on her knees and looks around, bewildered. I lean down, grasp her wrist and haul her upright. She remarks, "You never cease to amaze me, Freddie." She pushes her hair back from her face and glances at me. "And your Mama has a good aim."

"All mothers have good aim when their son has a gun pointed at their head! Now, let's get out of here, and quick."

I grab their hands and we run, blind in the darkness and away from the feeble torchlight, back down the corridor towards the door.

Heavy boots slap behind us. Richter's voice is even more slurred as he calls out, "Stop, or I'll sh... shoot!"

Freddie flings the door open and dives through. As Kat and I stumble through the doorway after him, Kat pauses and looks back. She pivots on her toes, reaching for the nearest shelving unit, grunting as she tips it over. A clatter of boxes, bottles, bits and bobs crashes to the floor, making a truly satisfying noise and an even more satisfying mess.

I find the string on the door handle and exclaim, "Got the string! Now hurry!" I grab Freddie's wrist then close his fingers over the waist of my trousers. Kat pulls the door closed behind us and grasps his other arm.

What little light there was disappears. We shuffle forward, and I wrap the twine around my wrist, inching us through the complete darkness as if I'm winding a bobbin.

A shot thuds, then another, bangs deadened by the rocks enclosing us and the iron between us. Richter swears so loudly, we all hear it even though the words are muffled.

Step, step, step, we creep away.

After a minute, when we've rounded a bend in the tunnel, I ask, "Is anyone hurt?"

Kat replies, "No. The grenade I found must have missed, then he missed."

"Sounded like he shot the door too."

Her reply is a snide, "I said he was good looking, not clever."

He's persistent and determined, I'll give him that. "Freddie? Are you alright?"

He doesn't let go of my waistband, but he pushes me onward to show he's fine.

Through the tunnels, Richter's voice echoes, sending a shiver down my arms.

"Where are yooooou? Katarina... come on." Staggered footsteps slap as he treads, alerting us to how closely he pursues us. "We're equal now - I won't shoot if you stop trying to blow me up. Where are you?"

I hesitate for only a second, then begin to furiously wind the string. Any attempt to sneak quietly away is ruined by my haste to trot us through the twisting tunnels.

Richter's footfall and the occasional flash of his torch give him away as he chases us, but we turn and then turn again, racing through black quarried shafts. Like a little trail of mice holding onto one another's backs, we scamper with certainty because of Freddie's foresight with the twine.

No-one speaks, until eventually, the sound of footfall from behind falters, then disappears.

"Here!" I exclaim as we reach the spiral staircase. The suitcase's handle creaks as I pick it up. Freddie drops his grip on me and runs, sure-footed, up the metal stairs and shoves open the door to the street.

Together we race up and out, towards whatever comes next.

The Spaniard

━━

A soon as we are all through the doorway at the top of the stairs, Freddie slams the door shut. Tucked away in an dim alleyway around the corner, off the main street, we pant like we've just finished a marathon, and I feel just as exhausted. It takes ages to catch our breath, leaning against the cool brick wall. I can only hope Herr Richter is lost, that he never finds his way to the spiral staircase.

Freddie drags himself over to Kat and I, extracting the metal box from his bag. Her eyes light up as he passes it to her. "Clever boy," she says, and smiles. "A car battery, and 6-volt one too. That should work."

I cannot help but hug him, delight at his survival coupled with relief that our escape had, against all odds, succeeded. I tried not to think of Herr Richter, lurching around the tunnels, hopefully lost for good.

Kat flips open the radio suitcase against a shadowed wall and rummages for wires in the spares cubbyhole. She hooks up the battery to test the radio. I hold my breath as she stares at the dials.

A battery is only any good if it has charge. Kat shakes her head, then removes the wires and examines the bolts on the top.

"Perhaps it's just dirty?" I suggest, crouching as Kat turns the battery box over in her hands to examine it. I wipe the metal bolts with the hem of my blouse. "No...it's not just grime."

Kat then grins up at my son. "It's sticky".

Freddie's hand flies to his mouth as she peels a blob of something off the battery, then hands it to him. "What a waste," she laughs.

While I scrub the remnants of the sweet from the radio connections, he picks hairs and fluff off the treasure! Kat reconnects the wires. "That's it," she says, triumphant while putting on her bug headset. "We're back in business." She listens for a moment then smiles. "And just in time - tanks seen on the Rue Rivioli!"

The staircase door around the corner bursts open, the bang of metal on concrete a muffled warning. I freeze.

Herr Richter's head pokes around the corner. A lump bulges on his forehead and half his face is streaked with blood. With wild eyes, he catches sight of his prey.

Us. Caught doing exactly what he accused us of. I grab Freddie, shielding him with my body as Kat slams the suitcase lid down.

He storms towards us in the alley, gun in front of him, yelling, "You thought you could escape, but no one escapes from us."

"It's me you want, Kurt," Kat says, with a wobble in her voice and wrenching the headset from her ears. "I'm the one who betrayed you. Let them go and you take me. Please."

"It's too late for that, Katerina." The madman starts to chuckle to himself, but it is laboured and ends in a cough.

We can only gape at him in horror as he lurches towards us, his pistol waving in all directions. We're pinned – the alley has one way in and out, and he's blocking it.

Every step closer he makes causes more blood to seep from his wounds. He's weak and vulnerable.

If we timed it right, we could rush past him, to freedom.

"It's over," he splutters, blood oozing from his lips. "I win. You lose, traitors." He holds his beaten head with one hand and stretches out the revolver. It shakes slightly as he struggles to keep it pointing at us.

I catch Kat's eye, about to mouth 'Run' when...

BANG! BANG BANG BANG.

A distant volley of shots echoes around the alleyway. But not from Herr Richter's gun. We all look beyond him, towards the mouth of the alley as another ripple of gunfire sounds. The low rumble of a tank.

My stomach clenches; I fear it must be the Germans taking the fight back to the Resistance. I glance up - black smoke plumes rise against a deep red sky.

"Reinforcements," Richter smiles as he stumbles against the wall to stop himself from falling. "Perfect time, wouldn't you agree?"

I shout, "Nothing will stop us from driving you out. The people can't be silenced. And we helped record it on film." I pull Freddie and Kat close, ready to whisper Run in their ears.

Kat says, "We all did," but there's an edge to her tone.

"Oy! You! Put down your weapon."

Our mouths drop open as a soldier appears in the alleyway entrance, holding his rifle steadily pointed at Richter. In unfamiliar fatigues, he's not French, or a Nazi. "I said drop it. Now!"

Herr Richter leers at Kat, then allows his weapon to fall. He slumps to his knees and makes a half-hearted attempt to raise his hands in the air.

My shoulders sag with relief as the soldier kicks the gun away, then turns his rifle around and rams it into Richter's stomach.

We stare as the soldier drags Richter to his feet, groaning with his mouth pouring blood. As he tugs him out into the street, Freddie runs up to him and offers the soldier his grotty sweet.

The soldier grins. "For me?" Then, he shakes his head, gently pushing Freddie's hand back. For a moment, my son's face falls, but the soldier says in Spanish-accented French, "You're too kind, but let me give you something in return – for all the hard work you did holding these guys off. You're very brave you know."

He reaches into his pocket, pulls out a whole bar of chocolate and presses it into his sticky fingers!

Kat and I glance at each other and laugh. Freddie scampers back to us, eyes wide and mouth agape. Very gallantly, he breaks off a piece for both of us before consuming the rest in seconds. We're so busy enjoying this rare taste of joy, we don't even notice the lone soldier and Richter disappear.

Our Spanish saviour is the only soldier we see as we walk towards the town centre. The streets are strangely empty but, an immense crowd has gathered outside the Hôtel de Ville. They have come because of a rumour – food and aid could be found here. But, no-one is leaving laden with supplies and disappointment lingers in the air.

As we push through, I overhear the whispers circulating: no guns or ammunition to spare, but people could put their name down to patrol the Metro for advancing troops. A fire at the Grand Palais, a Resistance base, can't be put out after the Germans sent in two remotely controlled Goliaths packed with explosives. The circus who were there have lost everything; no-one knows how many died, but it's a sign Paris will burn before the Nazis give it up.

Then, poking above the crowd, I catch sight of a film camera on an apple-box. Zwoboda balances on the base of a nearby lamppost, arm hooked around the metal, and the bulky briefcase radio dangling from his fingers. He gestures towards the town hall and tells the camera man on the box to aim the lens there. He doesn't see me until I leave Kat and Freddie for a moment, telling them to stay there for a minute, then I push through the throng to get closer.

"Monsieur Zwoboda!" I shout. "I saw a Spanish soldier!" But I don't think he heard me.

He looks down, his face creasing in a broad grin. "Mouse! Keep it up!" He's possibly the only person smiling in the whole square. "Couldn't have been here, there, or anywhere important without you. De Gaulle will soon arrive, but our triumph is already captured!" His attention snaps back to the task at hand, and he issues rapid-fire instructions to the cameraman.

And that's it. The only acknowledgement I think we'll ever get for all our efforts. Whatever the outcome, someone is telling our story. I ought to feel elated, but images of the blood spilled on cobbles flash before my eyes, and the cries of fallen men echo in my ears. My stomach contracts, and in an instant, any self pity or desire for accolades dissipates.

I worry Zwoboda speaks too soon, because aside from the Spaniard, we've not seen any foreign troops. My heart is heavy, or perhaps it's just hunger and dissipating adrenaline as I re-join Kat and Freddie by the lamp-post where I left them. "No food here," I tell them, and they nod, wearily accepting.

We plod down a boulevard, towards the only place where I hope we might be able to scrounge a meal.

But then, I almost jump out of my skin as the bells of Notre-Dame clang! It's a noise I've not heard for four years and can only mean one thing.

MARSEILLAISE

Our faces light up with hope, and I say, "The Allies must be here! The Nazis have gone!"

We stop walking, frozen as dozens more church bells, hundreds perhaps, ring out announcing our liberty.

Citizens pour outside onto the roads and look around at each other, hardly daring to believe. A hushed awe falls over us when, as if a Christmas fairy has sprinkled dust over the capital, all at once the lights which have been off for so long blink to life! Through windows and with the flicker of streetlights, the dusk of night is held at bay.

Realising the electricity must be back on, some people dash back into their homes, throw open the windows, and hold radios out of them so we can all hear the news.

A reporter's voice talks excitedly, his words confirming what we all hope is true: "For several hours, here in the centre of Paris, in the Cité, we have been living unforgettable moments. ...These soldiers of the Leclerc Division and their comrades of the FFI at the Place de Hôtel de Ville... machine guns over their shoulders, automatic weapons in their arms, revolvers in their hands, renewing an old acquaintance, seem to me to symbolise the resurrection of France! The union of the fighting external armies and those of the Interior who have been hunting the Hun for the last five days, and who have already liberated the public buildings, and taken the main strategic points of the city."

I think of the film-makers and that they were, after all, in the right place to record the moment, and I feel a surge of pride as I meet Kat and Freddie's eyes. A radio announcement is fleeting, heard and then gone, but a picture lasts to show new generations what we did.

I grab Freddie's hand, and Kat's in my other and we turn around and follow the crowd, down towards the river. The last words we hear on the radios runs around my head as we walk: "The vanguard of the Allied army of liberation tells us that, in a few hours, the bulk of the British, American and French troops will be at this place, the Hôtel de Ville, right in the middle of Paris, and that we will able to hail them, and the last Huns will have been chased from the capital!"

I want to witness the Allies arrival – and from Kat and Freddie's buoyant looks, so do they. Our tiredness forgotten as we hustle back the way we came.

More and more people surge into the avenues, their voices raised in song. The Marseillaise sweeps through the city, the national anthem's words bringing even the darkest corners of Paris to life. Ahead, across the water, lights blaze through the windows of the cathedral. Barricades are still manned, but, chugging down the avenues are army trucks, tanks and motorcycles with sidecars, all draped with different flags. Men in unfamiliar army fatigues grin at us, tossing out sweets and accepting shouted thanks in all manner of languages.

As we pass the bridge and approach the Hôtel de Ville again, caught up in the midst of the crowd I forget the danger. All around us are smiling faces, and I hope that the film crew are still in place to capture this moment. We can't get close to the square now because it's filled with too many people and tanks I don't recognise, and open topped jeeps, and soldiers in green uniforms... the noise is both deafening and glorious!

"Let's go home," Kat shouts over Freddie's head.

After so many nights sleeping rough, the prospect of an actual bed appeals more than I can express. And, it will be quieter there. We switch course and head for the 16th Arrondissement being to the west of the Seine.

But suddenly, over the sound of singing and cheering, the rattle of gunshots.

A ripple of panic spreads. The crowd scrambles to get away, off the central streets.

A Return to Rue Cambon

We're pushed, jostled about, and the soldiers are instantly on their alert once again. Freddie stumbles, crying out in pain as his ankle twists. I drag him up, onto my hip and stagger away as fast as I can. Because Kat's house is across town, we rush north, to the nearest - the only - possibly safe place to go. Panting, aching, I carry my son all the way until we reach Rue Cambon.

Outside Chanel's shop, I have to put him down. My arms ache too much and I'm out of breath, and it seems quiet enough here that he could walk. Under the lights outside the shop, he sees the tears forming in my eyes and tugs on my arm with a question on his face. My voice is thick as I tell him, "It used to be my dream to work there. And I did. Now I just dream of living another day."

Kat says, "Maybe you will work there again, Hannah."

I've gone through too much to repeat history. "I think it's time to stitch together my own future."

We walk past someone hunched in the dark staff doorway, wrapped in a blood-splattered coat, legs curled to their chest. Their shaved head is down on their knees, as if they cannot face the world. With Freddie's hand in mine, Kat by my side, I pity them. Somehow, we emerged the other side of this Occupation not only still alive, but also, together. Not alone. But, we've nothing to offer, so we leave them to sleep. Perhaps by the light of day things will look brighter, for all of us.

To my dismay, when we reach the Ritz entrance, Jaques isn't at his usual post. The doors are locked. "Wait here," I say to Freddie, then shuffle down the road to peer in through the windows of Frank's bar. Inside, the lights are blazing, and a party is in full swing. I spot the familiar faces of some of the correspondents swigging what remains of the hotel's stock of wine. They are so carried away, no-one seems to notice my face pressed against the window.

I return to Kat and Freddie and collapse on the stone steps next to them. Although I suppose I could walk around to the front and try my luck, I'm overwhelmed with the highs and the lows of the day. Of the war. I pull my family into a hug. For a minute, we huddle with our heads touching together.

"Hannah?"

My head jerks away from Kat's shoulder and I look around.

A man, the one from the doorway, leans against the wall. I squint through the dim, heart clamouring. One arm is twisted up, so tight his curled fingers graze his stubbled chin.

"Hannah?" He calls again.

"Marc?" I stand, not able to believe it can be him.

He lifts his head and drops his tatty bag to the pavement. Under the streetlight, I see his dear, kind eyes gazing at me. He runs towards me and swoops his strong arm around my waist.

"How... What happened?" I ask, laughing with relief.

His lips lift. "I don't really know. One moment, I was bundled onto a train, but it went nowhere. The next, there was a fight going on all around us." He shakes his head, curls falling over his forehead. "Then, the soldiers, Spanish I think, opened the doors. They gave us food, and water, and then, I followed them into the city."

I take his hand and press it to my heart. "And you found your way here." My gaze drops, regret surging through me. "But I wasn't."

He looks sheepish. "I'm a patient man. I knew you'd come home if you could. When you could. I didn't have to wait too long."

His head bows to my shoulder and he hugs me close. "I'm so glad you're alive," I whisper. It still doesn't feel real. The rattle of his breath in his chest as he drags in air worries me, but, pressed into his bony ribcage, I can hear his heart beating strong and true.

"Who is this?" Kat calls over.

Our heads lift and we gaze into each other's eyes and beam. Only then does it sink in. "Marc," I say. "Would you like to meet my son and the real Katarina Devereaux?"

He nods and we walk over to the steps. Freddie's examining us both with a curious expression on his face. "Freddie, this is my friend Marc. He's the one who got the photos printed from your camera."

While Kat smiles knowingly, for we have spoken about him many times, my son stands. He sticks out his little hand towards Marc. "*M.. mm...merci, Monsieur Marc.*"

I gasp, but Marc takes his hand and shakes it formally. With a huge grin, he replies, "It's a pleasure to meet you."

Not one, but two people returned! "You spoke! In French!"

"In Paris, I must call you *Maman*," he says, repeating what I told him when we arrived at the station. "*Tu est mon coeur.*"

"And you are my heart, always." I tap my chest.

He looks at me slyly, through his long eyelashes. "And he has your heart as well." Then his eyes flick to Marc.

"Yes," I reply, glancing at my family. "You're all in my heart."

The sound of scraping in a lock makes us all turn to the door. There, wrestling with the key, is Blanche. She leans on the handle as if she needs its support and pushes the door open. "What are y'all doing out here in the night?"

Her voice is slurred, the American twang to her French made more obvious by the wine I smell on her breath. "Madame Auzello," I say.

"Well, come in then! Don'cha know it's gonna be alright now?" She props herself upright and holds the door open for us. "My boys will be coming into the city soon, and then it'll be over." She tilts towards me as I pass her. "There's none of *them* left in here, don't worry. What are you wearing?"

I can't help but make the vague effort to straighten my stained top and boy's trousers. "What about the Baron, and Mademoiselle Chanel? Are they still here?"

"She's packing for Switzerland," she slurs, as we troop into the hallway. "No idea where that double crossing, two faced Nazi-Baron toad is though. Good riddance."

"I'll lock up, if you like Madame?" Marc offers.

"Thank you, dear. Welcome back. No need to ask where you've been." She hands him the bunch of keys, then her eyes fall on Freddie. "Frank's deserted us."

She's mistaken my son for one of the messenger boys, but before I can correct her, she says, "I'm sure we can find you some breakfast though." Blanche turns to me, suddenly sober and shrewd. "You know where to go. I'm sure there's enough beds in your room for you all. You can start back at work tomorrow."

"Afternoon?" I negotiate.

She sighs then yawns. "Deal. It's been a long night, and we're all so very tired."

"Thank you Madame," I say, catching my reflection in the mirrors lining the hall. I hold my chin up, recognising myself. The woman staring at me may look bedraggled, but she is a survivor.

She is loved and will be heard. I vow, "Just until we all get back on our feet. I have a dress shop to save up for."

Authors Note

Thank you for reading 'Sewing Resistance', I hope you enjoyed it. You can also discover Freddie's story in a 'parallel read' – the middle-grade, illustrated novel, 'Boy, Resisting'.

A review would mean the world to me – it only takes a few minutes and lets other readers know if this is their kind of book. Please follow the link to be taken to your favourite bookish website: www.books2read.com/sewingresistance

It would take another day for Allied troops to liberate Paris fully. Only after another battle at the Arc de Triomphe would De Gaulle walk into the city to give his now famous speech. There was a lot of confusion at the time, as he expected to enter as the conquering hero, but actually, was forced to admit that the loose coalition of Resistance fighters had already driven out most of the Nazis. Worse, a largely Spanish detachment, led by Captain Dronne with his 9th Company, had entered a full day earlier! Dronne had been ordered to carry straight on into the centre of Paris after a battle, near Fresnes in the suburbs, earlier that day. Their progress was delayed by grateful crowds somewhat blocking their way, rather than Nazi opposition. The 9th Company entered from the south and made for the Hôtel de Ville, which had been captured and held days earlier by the Communist led FFI (FiFi's). Dronne's troops are the many language'd Allied liberators which are celebrated at the end of this novel.

Madame Auzello actually escaped the prison at Frenes when the Gestapo fled Paris a few days earlier - they simply opened the doors, leaving anyone left alive there to find their own way out. Sadly, the majority of the prisoners were trained out to Auschwitz before that liberation occurred, and only a few were left behind, locked in a train going nowhere, awaiting their presumed fate. This is the imagined ending to Marc's imprisonment.

Within days of the Liberation, the half hour long film, **'La Libération de Paris,'** directed by Zwoboda, along with other members of the Resistance, was released across France and then to the world. As the Allies moved into Paris they also filmed, but nothing better shows those moments which, for me, defines Parisian resistance, as they took back their city, street by street, shot by shot, in their ordinary clothes. Hannah, Freddie and Kat's role in helping them to find out where to go is imaginary, although Zwoboda did find out where to send his cameras by radio...

Real Stories

Portraying real people in historical fiction

Although the storyline and many of the characters in this book are a work of fiction, they were inspired by true heroes (and villains). Where possible, I have tried to use real names/positions when referring to actual events. The main characters (Hannah, Kat, Freddie, Marc and Pieter) are entirely fictional, but you may recognise other names in this novel - Coco Chanel, Winston Churchill, Hermann Göring are all familiar figures in wartime history. Lesser known are the staff of the Ritz - Claude and Blanche Auzello, Frank Meier the barman, Jaques the doorman, all of whom actively worked for the Resistance movement. Hans Von Dinklage was harder to research, but appeared to me to be quite morally grey, from what I could ascertain about the truth of his dealings during the Occupation.

Where possible, I have drawn upon first hand or official accounts of these real people's activities, to make your reading experience as authentic as possible, but for story purposes, their characteristics and conversations I applied some imagination. I beg the forgiveness of any surviving friends or family of these people if I have unwittingly portrayed them in an unfair light; any mistakes in this portrayal are entirely my own interpretation. Because history is often layered with opinion, it's hard for me to say precisely what is true and what isn't in a story where real people are featured, and I hope to set the record straight below.

The unnamed woman who provides the radio and other orders to Hannah is modelled on **Virginia Hall**, one of the bravest and most inspirational of SOE agents. She has been a heroine of mine for many years, and I am so pleased to have finally been able to weave a little bit of her extraordinary activities into this story. That said, the actual Virginia Hall (and her wooden leg, Cuthbert!) was only in Paris infrequently when she ran her network of resistance cells. It is estimated about 1,500 people worked under her, and she trained approximately 500 in disguise, subterfuge and stealthy activity. I have read absolutely no evidence of her ever having been involved with staff at the Ritz - any and all suggestion of it, please consider fiction.

Much has been told before about **Chanel** and her Nazi lover, **Baron Hans Von Dinklage** (Spatz) - and it's certainly a sensational story. Chanel had been watched by the Nazis for some time before the Occupation; whether she knew this or not when the Allies briefly questioned her after Paris was liberated may explain her actions during the war. Her name was also found on Resistance papers, without details of her involvement. She was, however, the linchpin for Operation Modellhut – an ill-fated trip to Spain to see Winston Churchill, who she was great friends with, to convince him to enter talks with rebel Nazis and thus end the war. This mission suggests she and Hans were not the diehard Nazis which made for such sensational reading in bibliographical books and TV shows. Sadly, it is also true that she was a heavy user of morphine throughout the war (her 'medicine'), and unable to sleep without it. Her initial connection during the interview with

Hannah is based upon Chanel's experiences as a child, growing up virtually orphaned in a convent.

The Baron/Spatz/Hans himself appears to me to be a political player without being a politician. His Jewish ex wife, who he remained close to despite divorcing her before the war when her race became a liability, worked for the Resistance movement as well. Evidence suggests he worked for the Abwher (German intelligence), as well as his offical job promoting/defending the Nazi cause as a Press Attaché. His loyalties shifted continuously, suggesting to me that he was a double agent playing both sides of the war.

At the Ritz, at least **Blanche and Claude Auzello**, and probably **Frank**, ran entirely separate subterfuge operations. There were likely many others, but given the secretive, undocumented nature of resistance work it is hard to know. Certainly, their activities suggest they were deeply embedded with a network of brave people seeking to affect the war. We do know, Claude worked with the Swiss to send messages about troop movements to the Allies (coded as vegetable and wine orders). Blanche harboured fallen Allied airmen in secret rooms, constructed between bedrooms and helping them to get to a safe pick up point disguised in evening wear. Her arrest and imprisonment at Fresnes is on record, as well as her confusion and turning up at the wrong hotel upon her release.

Frank Meier was an Austrian Jew who ran the Ritz bars, with connections to ID forgers (including one known as Greep) and a team of message boy runners. He also ran a gambling ring. As barman, he must have overheard many a conversation, with some evidence that the failed plot to assassinate Hitler (known as Operation Valkyrie) was discussed in his presence. The news of the plot's failure was relayed to the conspirators remaining in Paris at the Ritz.

Frank possessed forged identity documents himself, as did Jewish Blanche 'Rubenstein' Auzello, who converted to Christianity to circumvent the Ritz's quota for Jewish employees in the 1920s. He disappeared after the liberation, leaving his underground betting network missing/owing substantial sums of money. There is no record of his sexual orientation; any inference behind his mourning when Jaques Bonsergent, one of the first to be killed for resisting, died, should be read as fictional. His cocktail book is still in print, however.

The character **Fevrier** is the code name used by Marcel Flouret, one of the several leaders of the loose coalition of the Communist dominated resistance. **Lily,** who 'trains' Marc and celebrates the D-day landings with Blanche, is loosely based on Lily Kharmayeff, who also worked for the French underground and was great friends with Blanche Auzello as well.

Twisting the Truth – Fact and Fiction

As much as possible, I have tried to use real events as my inspiration for this story. The course of the war and specifically, the events which happened in Paris, are as true as I can make them, but to keep the story flowing, sometimes it's necessary to tweak what happened. Here's my confession about where/when I deviated, and why.

I can't find evidence that Virginia Hall interacted with people at the Ritz, but it seems feasible to me that in building her massive networks of underground fighters, saboteurs, and spies, she could have recruited someone like Hannah or Kat. References in this book to a mysterious woman who co-ordinated resistance activities in Paris are an amalgamation of her and other female SOE agents.

There is no suggestion at all that Hans fathered an illegitimate child or was present at the pograms of 1932/33 in Germany – these ideas are entirely my own (fiction) and I apologise unreservedly for any offense given to his surviving family for my improvisation for the storyline.

There is also no suggestion that Hitler was likely to attend the Spring 1942 Arno Breker exhibition, but there were many similar attempts on his life throughout his rule. Hitler was such a fan of Breker, he declared him "the best sculptor of our time" and commissioned many pieces of art from him. Breker himself was a card-carrying member of the Nazi party for years. The exhibition itself was a glittering occasion and hugely popular – over 120,000 French citizens visited during the ten weeks it ran. It was also a propaganda triumph for the Nazis, with supporting parties and receptions for visiting celebrities, spurring anti-Semitic sentiment.

The events on the occasion's opening night, however, cast a longer shadow. Several German officers (tourists) were killed on the streets of a suburb (which, for story purposes, I placed in the Jardin de Tuileres instead). These murders almost certainly resulted in the step up in reprisals against the Resistance and Jews, including the Vel d'Hiver / 'Spring Wind' operations, although you could argue this was just a part of the increased pressure to eradicate the Jewish Population. Certainly, there was increased pressure on the police to assist with the round ups and the Gestapo to hit their targets of Jews to be taken to camps.

The destruction of degenerate art in a bonfire, outside where stolen Jewish-owned artworks were kept in the Jeu de Paume, occurred in July 1942, shortly after the exhibition and murders. Thousands of priceless works of art were burned.

For story purposes, I blurred the distinction in laws about identification as a Jew, although the gradual imposition of their restrictions and the deportations is correct. As an occupied country under the Reich, the order to wear a star on your clothing if you were a Jew over the age of 6 was in effect from September 1941. In France specifically, it became a criminal offence to not have one sewn to your clothing if you had, as ordered, registered yourself as a Jew from the end of May/early June 1942.

Tech gear.

For those who love the detail, the following items are the equipment used in this story:

- Freddie's camera - Zeiss Ikon Box-Baldur (1936 model)
- Portable radio receiver/transmitter as used by Katarina - A Type 3 Mark II suitcase as developed by the SOE.

The Liberation of Paris.

Approximately 2,000 Parisian civilians were killed in the liberation of their capital, along with about 800 Resistance fighters from the FFI and policemen, and over 100 soldiers from the Free France and U.S. forces. Given the Resistance had far fewer guns (mostly old handheld revolvers or ancient rifles from WW1 as well!) than the estimated 20,000 Nazi soldiers left in Paris, with their tanks, artillery and machine guns at the time of liberation, these numbers are astonishing.

My understanding of what happened during the 19th - 25th August (when de Gaulle entered Paris) has been greatly assisted by a number of literary sources, and most especially, the maps and infographics created by Akhil Kadidal / Achilles the Heel, without which I would have struggled to visualise what happened, where. Check them out at https://achillestheheel.com/tag/paris-1944/

Book Credits

Researching for a fiction novel is not quite the same as for a thesis or non-fiction. To get a sense of the era, I read and watched a lot of stories set in the time period and didn't always take note of them, but, here are some of the resources - literary and online - which I referred to time and time again to try and ensure accuracy in the portrayal of Hannah and Freddie's (fictional) story. Below, a short list of the most thumbed or clicked pages I used when writing 'Sewing Resistance' and 'Boy, Resisting'.

Books:

Sleeping with the enemy - Hal Vaughan

A Woman of No Importance (about Virginia Hall, the SOE agent)

Les Parisiennes by Anna Sebba

Suite Francais by Irene Nemerovsky

Coco Chanel by Justine Pericardia

The Hotel on Place Vendôme by Tilar J. Mazzeo

Online resources:

• An interesting Phd thesis on Radio by Denis

Courts - Talking to France: Radio Propaganda from 1940-1942 https://wrap.warwick.ac.uk/id/eprint/8954 9/1/WRAP_Theses_Courtois_2016.pdf

- The Parisian Police and the Holocaust: Control, Round-ups, Hunt (1940-44) Laurent Joly, Benn E Williams. Journal of Contemporary History, 2020, ff10 .1177/0022009419839774ff. ffhal-03091688f

- An inspiring story about hundreds of illicit photos taken by Raoul Minot (referenced as the contact at Le Printemps who could get photos printed by Marc) https://www.npr.org/2024/10/28/nx-s1-5157701/france-wwii-war-photos-mystery

- I have loved reading the various papers produced by the Resistance - the sheer audaciousness, and certainty, that they will not give up their liberties without a fight shines through in each. You can see scans of them here: https://gallica.bnf.fr/ark:/12148/bpt6k1479844/f1.item

- A brilliant set of 47,000 human experiences of World War 2, collated by the BBC can be found here: https://www.bbc.co.uk/history/ww2peopleswar/categories/

- Liberation of Paris - maps, articles and infographics created by Akhil Kadidal https://achillestheheel.com

The Catacombs

The Catacombs have been challenging to research, however, I have been lucky to find a treasure trove of online, visual and cartographic resources to help bring the maze of tunnels to life. An amazing resource can be found here, including a stunning detailed map compiled from a number of different resources h

ttp://exploration.urban.free.fr/catacombes/indexus.htmand here
http://exploration.urban.free.fr/catacombes/indexus.htm

Film

If you would like to watch the actual film made in the final few chapters of the novel - La Liberation de Paris - it's publicly available to watch at: https://archive.org/details/LaLiberationdeParis1944

The US Army also had a film unit with them, shooting in colour, from when they entered the city. You can see it here: https://www.youtube.com/watch?v=cNtEt-J9Ib4

ABOUT THE AUTHOR

Jan Foster (also writing historical fiction as J.H. Foster) writes in between being a mum and a small business consultant. Before COVID, she volunteered reading with children in her local school, helping them find the joy and escapism in books. Before that, she ran several businesses herself and she continues to passionately support small-medium sized enterprises. She loves history and folklore, which has fed into her 'Naturae' historical fantasy series of novels. Real life heroines and heroes always inspire her (in that order), which is why she offers readers a blend of fiction laced with reality. Only slightly obsessed with Vikings and Tudors, Jan thoroughly enjoys research trips and burying her head in books to flesh out the details of these time periods in her novels. That's her excuse and she is sticking to it!

Jan is based in the North West of England and tries to drag her family and dogs out into the wilds or into windswept castles as much as possible - when it's not raining! Passionate about getting kids active, she writes the Mitch and Mooch series to support children with not only reading and comprehension, but also encouraging them to try out new activities.

You can follow what Jan is up to on social media @janfoster-author or check out her website for more details on publications and other articles or short stories written by her www.escapeinto atale.com

Have you read the prequel? You can sign up to Jan's Rebels Newsletter and, as a thank you, read 'The Rebellious Maus and the Pogrom' for free! You'l also receive a bonus epilogue and deleted scenes! Subscribe here: www.escapeintoatale.com/rebels

Rebellion comes with a price

As the Nazis rise to power in 1932, Hannah, a teenage Jewish orphan living under the care of her Catholic guardian, longs for freedom from the increasingly oppressive regime at home. Her only friend, well-intentioned and wealthy Katarina, persuades her into one last jaunt together before they return to their respective schools.

But their escape takes a dangerous turn when they become caught up in a violent pogrom, facing life-changing personal and political repercussions.

Fans of historical fiction and gripping drama will be captivated by this short, fast-paced tale of courage and consequences.

Other Books by the Author

The Naturae Series by Jan Foster

Risking Destiny

Discover a villain's creation in this Viking Age tragic romance Prequel.
www.books2read.com/riskingdestiny

Destiny Awaiting

The enemies to lovers Prequel. Escape to Agincourt, wherein averting a war between their races and their countries, Aioffe and Tarl's battles of the heart are destined to fight with faith and hope itself.

www.books2read.com/destinyawaiting

Disrupting Destiny

Book 1 –Tudor reformation tears a country and fae lovers apart. Can a secret destiny bring them together?
www.books2read.com/disruptingdestiny

Anarchic Destiny

Book 2 – A forgotten heir, a queendom in crisis… chaos will reign as Bloody Mary makes her move for power.
www.books2read.com/anarchicdestiny

Destiny Arising

Book 3 – Five crowns will fall in a deadly prediction. Can Aioffe catch the killer of queens before she's next to die?
www.books2read.com/destinyarising

Fables from Naturae

Historical Fantasy short stories featuring characters you love from the Naturae Series in pacy adventures in a magical past.
Myth, Mist and Madness
www.books2read.com/mythmistmadness
Blind Bill
www.books2read.com/blindbill
A Rose in Midwinter
www.books2read.com/arim
As Above, So Below
wwww.books2read.com/asabove

<u>Rebels and Resistance Series by J.H. Foster</u>

Gripping WW2 historical suspense novels – parallel stories to share

<u>**The Rebellious Maus and the Pogrom**</u> – A YA Prequel Novella to Sewing Resistance set in 1930's Germany

A young Hannah and Kat decide to ignore their guardian's advice and go shopping. Can they escape danger when a Pogrom leads to a riot and will Hannah risk everything to impress a handsome saviour?

BUY NOW www.books2read.com/rmatp

or **READ FOR FREE by subscribing to my mailing list with a historical focus – www.escapeintoatale.com/rebels**

<u>**Sewing Resistance**</u> – Seamstress. Spy. Survivor?

As Nazi forces tighten their grip on Paris, two women are drawn into the heart of the Resistance. Bound by friendship, a silent son, and driven by survival, they risk everything in a dangerous fight for freedom. *Sewing Resistance* is an unforgettable tale of love, loyalty, and courage under fire.

BUY NOW www.books2read.com/sewingresistance

<u>**Boy, Resisting**</u> – Silenced. Steadfast. Saviour?

A middle-grade, illustrated novel **co-authored with James Warwood**

Silence was supposed to keep me — and my secrets — safe. So I accidentally became a spy...

BUY NOW www.books2read.com/boyresisting

Find out more about works authored by Jan Foster/J.H. Foster at **www.escapeintoatale.com/books**

Join the Escape Into A Tale Newsletter and receive a free gift of a book and much more!
www.escapeintoatale.com/subscribe

Boy, Resisting - Chapter 1

- -

My name is Frederick and I have a secret. Want to know what it is? Of course you do IF YOU'RE SNOOPING AND READING THIS!

My Mama gave me this book for my birthday. "So you can keep a record," she said. "It's important to remember who you are, and what happened to you. Write in it. Doodle. Whatever you want."

I think she meant write about the Nazis, because they're why we came to Paris. Because they were after us.

That's the secret... not really!

You see, I'm a nobody. Insignificant. Just a boy. If you knew me at all, then you'd also understand, I'm not so stupid. If I did know anything dangerous, I wouldn't write it down. There's nothing important, no secrets you'd be interested in here.

Unless, I am the secret... got you again! Or have I...

Mama's not so good at reading and writing. She says the words all jumble together, so I'll write what happened here, for us both.

I'll practise my drawing too, because sometimes a picture can show better than words. And, I like drawing.

I doubt could ever forget what happened, because I'm good at remembering, but maybe Mama will. Someday we might read this notebook together and remember. Maybe she'll disappear, because that happens to people too, and then what happened to us won't matter. Except to us.

Or, maybe I'll die and she can use this book to remember me by, like a story.

Not to shock you, and I hope you're not as unlucky as me, but... I've seen dead bodies before. I wish I hadn't. It's only fair to warn you, IF YOU'RE READING THIS, I might talk about them. THAT'S NOT THE SECRET, but how I saw them and why could be.

I was born in a convent in Germany, well, Austria, which was a part of Germany then. I liked it there with the other children, my friends Zachariah and Emily. And Gustaf and Wilhelm, until they both went to new families. Last year, lots more children arrived, but hardly anyone went to new families. Before you knew it, the bunk beds were full! The nuns were pretty nice and tried really hard to look after us all. We had lessons with Sister Marta every day, except Sundays. We played in the gardens and learned how to grow vegetables to eat, and how to take care of the goats.

On Sundays, we all walked into the town to go to Mass at the big church. Twice -once for morning Mass, and again in the evening. We were like penguins, all huddled together to keep warm and look after each other. One fuzzy, fluffy colony keeping the little ones inside for protection. Plus, I sometimes liked to imagine the nuns as giant penguins in their black and while costumes, shuffling around in search of sardines.

 As everyone lined up before leaving the convent, Mother Superior reminded us, "You must be good Catholics now," as if we weren't always. Sometimes, the newer orphans would be confused during the service. The nuns would whisper to them to keep their heads down, be quiet and do what the rest of us do.

I quite liked the singing and the pictures on the walls, even if I didn't understand what was being said half the time. The smoke from the incense got in my throat sometimes and made me cough – usually at the worst time! I coughed and spluttered and everyone would look at me as if I was doing something terrible, even though I couldn't help it.

I knew I was the lucky one, though. My Mama lived with me at the convent. Almost all the other children had to leave their parents. Not, I think, because they wanted to. Some people's parents died and they had to live with us. Having never had a Papa, I don't miss having one. It's always been me and Mama, a tiny family within a bigger family of nuns and the orphans. Perhaps we were the largest family in our small town.

Mama wasn't a nun, because the nuns can't have babies. She did all the sewing and some cleaning, gardening and cooking. By the courtyard window in our bedroom was her sewing machine, with the big pedal underneath to make the needle whirr and chomp through the fabric. Sewing was probably the only time she sat down, altering clothes so they fitted everyone with a little smile on her face. Sometimes, she was given whole strips of material to sew new dresses, and that made her happiest. I suppose, because of her work, that's why she and I had our own room. All the other children slept in the bunk beds, which seemed more fun. When I asked if I could sleep with the other boys too, Mama said, "And leave me all on my own?" She looked so sad.

"Of course not," I said. "I never want to leave you." And I thought of all the other children who cried because they missed their families. "I'll never leave you."

She smiled then. "When you grow bigger than me, you might think differently. But for now, I'd like to share your childhood." Then she looked down at her clenched hands and I remembered how her parents died when she was little and she had to grow up with another family, who didn't really want her.

"I'll never grow up," I replied. "I'm Peter Pan."

Mama laughed. "I hope not. How awful to never grow up."

At the time, I didn't think anything of it, but now I wonder if she knew what was going to happen.

My favourite nun was Sister Luisa. She didn't try and make me remember bits from the Bible, like Sister Marta and Mother Superior did. When Mama gave me my camera, a Zeiss Ikon Box-Baldur, she looked at the photographs I took and said, "You've got a really good eye, Freddie."

"I have two eyes," I replied and blinked, because who doesn't have two eyes? "Which is the good one?"

She laughed at that. When I took the camera apart to clean it, she helped me figure out how to put it back together again. I learned about how to size up the picture you wanted to take by looking through the lens. Each time you snapped a photograph, you had to twist the wind-on knob until it clicked, then the film was ready to take another. When the film ran out, the button would twist and twist until the film negative was safely inside the roll, ready to be processed. Putting it back together was tricky, but Sister Luisa lent me a screwdriver which was better than the knife I used to unscrew it, and a soft cloth to clean the lens with.

I'll never forget her. She told me to hide, and that kept me alive. Hers was also the first dead body I ever saw. You don't forget a thing like that.

We were taking pictures in the chapel when it happened.

Over breakfast, Sister Luisa asked if I would help her with some paintings, given to us for safekeeping. They had been piling up next to the confessional booths for months and needed cataloguing. "Bring your camera. Look on the bright side - you can miss lessons this morning."

I nodded then nearly choked on my porridge when she handed me a new roll of film!

It was a lovely morning, just Sister Luisa and I, in the quiet chapel. I helped her bring out the paintings in their heavy frames and she told me I was a strong boy. We wiped off the dust then propped each one against the plain stonewalls, in a shaft of sunlight so I could take a clear picture of it.

Then, we both heard strange, muffled pops from the courtyard. She pushed back her wimple and told me, "Hide in the pulpit Freddie while I find out what's happening."

Only the priest was supposed to go in the stone pulpit. "I'm not allowed," I said, still wondering what the pops outside meant.

"It's the safest place," Sister Luisa said, then she glared at me. She didn't usually frown. "Take your camera."

"Well if you say so," I replied, and grabbed it.

"Hurry child."

I ran across the tiles and crouched inside. It smelt musty and a little bit like stale socks.

Then I heard Mama's voice. "Freddie?"

I stood up and called back to her.

"Get down," she hissed. I thought she must be angry because I was somewhere I wasn't supposed to be. I was about to tell her that Sister Luisa told me to, but she pushed me against the pulpit wall. "Stay silent until it's all over."

It was her eyes which shut me up more than what she said. They were wide and her face was white. She and I huddled against the cold walls and her arms shook. My camera rattled and she clamped her hands on it just as I heard a man's voice.

It sounded deep and sharp, all at the same time, talking about the paintings. I didn't really understand what he said, as if there was a layer behind what he said, in that way grown ups do when they say one thing but really mean another.

Mama craned her neck to see out of the entrance gap in the pulpit, but her hand kept my head in her shoulder so I couldn't move.

The man talked about taking the paintings for an exhibition, for Hitler. Sister Luisa said, "They belong to us."

Mother Superior was there too, and tried to argue with him as well.

But the man's voice turned hard as he disagreed. His footsteps grew closer to the pulpit, and Mama's arms tightened around me.

A loud bang made me flinch.

*****

'Boy, Resisting' and **'Sewing Resistance'** launched on Kickstarter with the generous support of our backers. You can view the project here: https://www.kickstarter.com/projects/janfoster/exciting-uplifting-ww2-french-resistance-duology

ORDER YOUR COPY OF THIS SHARED STORY, SUITABLE FOR 9-12 YEAR OLDS, AT www.books2read.com/boyresisting